Y0-DVC-942

Sun
Warm You

Gene Baumgaertner

Mason:

May the sun warm you in
all your endeavors...

Gene Baumgaert

© Copyright 1992, 2003 & 2007 Gene Baumgaertner

All rights reserved. No part of this publication may be reproduced, stored in a retrieval system, or transmitted, in any form or by any means, electronic, mechanical, photocopying, recording, or otherwise, without the written prior permission of the author.

Note for Librarians: A cataloguing record for this book is available from Library and Archives Canada at www.collectionscanada.ca/amicus/index-e.html

ISBN 1-4251-1254-4

Printed in Victoria, BC, Canada. Printed on paper with minimum 30% recycled fibre. Trafford's print shop runs on "green energy" from solar, wind and other environmentally-friendly power sources.

Offices in Canada, USA, Ireland and UK

Book sales for North America and international:
Trafford Publishing, 6E–2333 Government St.,
Victoria, BC V8T 4P4 CANADA
phone 250 383 6864 (toll-free 1 888 232 4444)
fax 250 383 6804; email to orders@trafford.com

Book sales in Europe:
Trafford Publishing (UK) Limited, 9 Park End Street, 2nd Floor
Oxford, UK OX1 1HH UNITED KINGDOM
phone +44 (0)1865 722 113 (local rate 0845 230 9601)
facsimile +44 (0)1865 722 868; info.uk@trafford.com

Order online at:
trafford.com/06-3013

10 9 8 7 6 5 4 3 2

DEDICATION

I WOULD LIKE TO DEDICATE this book to my loving wife, Kathy. Without her encouragement, both direct and tacit, I probably would never have started writing. Without her interest, I might never have known the excitement that writing gives to me. Without her help, I might have laid this story aside, unfinished. Thank you, my love.

I would also like to dedicate this book to my little Chow-Chow, who lay at my feet, or in my lap, or on a blanket in a nearby chair, and who stayed with me and helped me write this story. I regret that she was not able to stay with me much beyond that. Thun varm du, little one.

SUN
WARM YOU

(ORIGINALLY TITLED "THUN VARM DU")

THE ANCIENT CHRONICLES OF THE RED DAWN TRIBE

ACKNOWLEDGEMENTS

I WOULD LIKE TO THANK *a number of people who have had a significant impact upon this story, some directly, others indirectly. I would first like to thank all the paleontologists that have worked so hard, many investing a lifetime, so that we might know more about the past. I would especially like to thank Dr. John R. Horner, Dr. Philip J. Currie, Dr. Robert T. Bakker, and Mr. Gregory S. Paul. Although I have had an interest in dinosaurs since I was five years old, when I re-discovered dinosaurs in my early forties, these gentlemen had a profound impact upon the way I viewed them.*

Doctor Horner's findings, and his hypotheses, fired my imagination. Suddenly dinosaurs became real to me. They were no longer just an interesting intellectual pursuit – they became flesh and blood. I could see them crossing the plains in vast herds. I could see them mating, and nesting, and raising young. Dr. Horner's beliefs, and the stirring of my own imagination that his beliefs inspired, planted the seeds that were later to become this story.

I could say pretty much the same for Dr. Currie. With Dr. Horner, I saw for the first time, herds of thousands of hadrosaurs traveling across the open plain, much like the bison did only a century ago. With Dr. Currie, I discovered that the Maiasaurs were not unique, and that large herds of Monoclonius, and perhaps many other kinds of dinosaurs, did the same. He also made it obvious to me that the great herds had to share their environment with predators of all sizes. He gave me more seeds, helping give depth to the story.

Later I saw Dr. Bakker on television. With his frayed straw hat, he looked to me as unlikely a doctor of vertebrate paleontology as I had ever seen. But when he spoke, he said marvelous things. Then I had the delight of discovering his book, "The Dinosaur Heresies". Dr. Bakker's theories, that I read with a passion, and believed with the fervor of a new convert, were the soil and the water that made the seeds grow.

When I had almost finished this story, I came across Mr. Paul's authoritative work, "Predatory Dinosaurs of the World". In many ways it helped confirm many of the "feelings" I had about the way predatory dinosaurs should behave.

Thank you, gentlemen, for the wonderful things that you have done for vertebrate paleontology. Thank you for bringing those remarkable, ancient creatures to life.

Next, I would like to thank my first editor and father, Louis R. Baumgaertner. It was you who buried deep inside me the desire and the will to write stories. Well, dad, it took over three decades, but here is the first one. I'm glad you liked it.

Finally, I would like to thank Daniel Downs. It was you, Dannyboy, who helped me remember the true magic of dinosaurs. For who can see the wonder of these magnificent creatures better than a five year old boy. Thanks Daniel.

... Oh, and lest I forget, I would like to thank that little muse, that little stuffed ridgebrow, that sat upon the top of my computer throughout all the long months that I worked on this story. Thanks Maia.

Table of Contents

LIST OF FIGURES

Map 1. The Range of the Great Eastern Herd

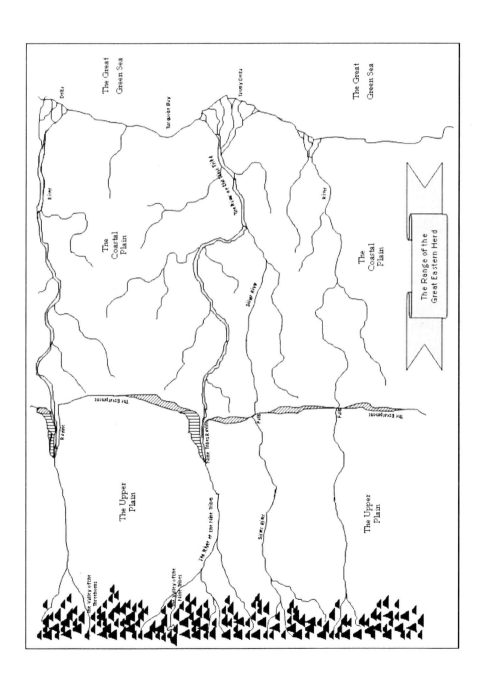

Map 2. The Home Ranges of the Nine Tribes

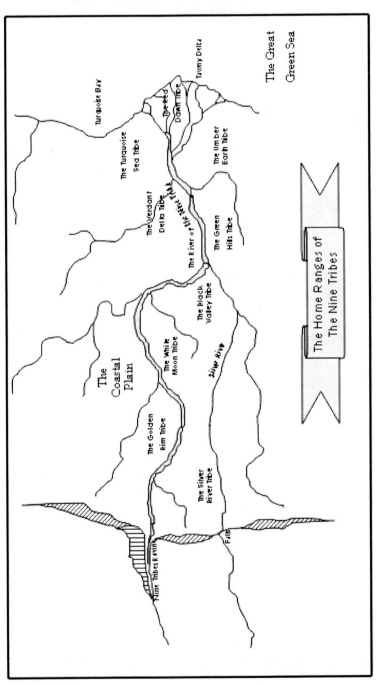

The Great Green Sea

Turquoise Bay

The Delta

Doam Tribe

Tawny Delta

The Umber Earth Tribe

The Turquoise Sea Tribe

The Verdant Delta Tribe

The River of the Nine Trails

The Green Hills Tribe

The Coastal Plain

The White Moon Tribe

The Black Valley Tribe

Silver River

The Golden Rim Tribe

The Silver River Tribe

Nine Tribes Ravine

Falls

The Home Ranges of The Nine Tribes

Map 3. The Roams of the Red Dawn Tribe

The Great Green Sea

The Coastal Plain

The Sturdy Tree Roam

The Black Sand Roam

The Green Water Roam

The Many Rivers Roam

The Wide Waters Roam

The Two Rivers Roam

The Yellow Mud Roam

The Dragonfly Roam

The Winding River Roam

The Crescent Beach Roam

The River of the Nine Tribes

The Rushing Water Roam

The Two Trees Roam

The Gray Rock Roam

The Land Below Water Roam

The Falling Waters Roam

The Crooked Tree Roam

The Tawny Delta Roam

The Three Pebbles Roam

The Horn Rock Roam

The White Fern Roam

The Roams of the Red Dawn Tribe

FOREWORD

THIS STORY TOOK PLACE a long time ago. The world was different, then, from the way it is now.[1] The land and the vegetation were not so very different. If we were plunked down in the middle of it all, we would recognize most of it. Not all of it, but most of it. But the people that roamed the land were different. Very different.

And yet, perhaps, the people were not so very different from us today. For they lived, and loved, and died. They grew up with hopes and aspirations, and spent a lifetime trying to achieve them. They found mates, raised their young, and fought off those that would do them harm. In some ways they were a people very different from us. But in other ways, perhaps not so different.

Today we refer to them as *Cerasphoros*.[2] *Cerasphoros* means "horn bearer". They often referred to themselves as **hornbrows**.[3] Yet this is not how they really thought of themselves. When they considered themselves collectively, when they thought of how they interacted with each other, they thought of themselves as separate and apart from all the other denizens of their world. Then, more universally, they thought of themselves as The People.

---

1   For more information, see Appendix One – The Setting: Late Cretaceous North America

2   For more information, see Appendix Two – Late Cretaceous Inhabitants of Western North America.

3   For more information, see Appendix Three – Glossary of Terms. As new words are first introduced, they are shown in **bold** to alert the reader that he or she may wish to refer to the Glossary.

CHAPTER ONE
THE PEOPLE

THE PREDATOR HUNG AT the edge of the forest, hidden by the thick overlapping branches and dense undergrowth. He stood motionless, concentrating on distant sounds. He sniffed the air quietly, seeking tell-tale fragrances. Then he again directed his attention to the spoor that lay upon either side of the slow, meandering river that flowed past his hiding place. The river was wide here, and difficult to swim, but he had no intentions of crossing it. Even from this distance, it was obvious that thousands of the prey had passed this way, trampling a path on both sides of the river that even a blind hatchling could follow.

He extended his jaws, exposing a series of sharp, serrated, not-quite uniform teeth. The teeth were two and three inches long, well-adapted for the slashing and tearing of flesh. His moist tongue seemed to taste the air, in anticipation of things to come. He took a slow, tentative step forward, partially penetrating the edge of the woods. In the shadows cast by the late afternoon sun, he was still difficult for all but the most observant to detect. His striped skin and earthy coloring blended well with the broken shadows and flickering sunlight of the jungle's edge.

He looked cautiously downstream. As he had expected, there was nothing to be seen, at least nothing worth his attention – no prey, and no other predator. With cool grace he swung his fierce, long head slowly around to the left, and gazed up river. His cold forward-looking eyes seemed to calculate quickly, as they stared from between little hornlets that protruded from his brow. The prey that had traveled upstream was long gone. But they had left a wide path of trammeled earth and stripped vegetation that pointed like an arrow to the route they had taken. He listened carefully once more, and again tested the scents in the air.

Satisfied that nothing was about, he walked on two powerful hind legs towards the river. Although almost two tons in weight, he moved with the practiced skill of a natural sprinter. But he was in no hurry now, and only ran when he had to – to catch and kill, or to avoid being killed himself. He was twenty-four feet long, but not nearly as tall. He walked bent slightly forward, head bobbing somewhat with each step, stiffened tail extending straight back behind him.

Halfway to the river, he stooped to examine the spoor before him. Many thousands of prey had left their mark upon the earth. He sniffed carefully. **Hornbrows**, he thought to himself, or maybe **ridgebrows**. Possibly even **longsnouts**. The trail was old, perhaps two days since the herd had been here. But he would move faster than such a large herd, and he would catch up with it.

He continued to the river, waded into the shallows, and drank. He gulped copious amounts of the cool liquid. Suddenly he stopped, and became very still. He glanced suspiciously downstream. No competitors were in sight. He looked speculatively upstream. About a half mile away, the river entered a ravine, and began to climb up a mild gradient. The ravine had been cut out of a tall escarpment, one of the few barriers in the predator's world. But the ravine breached the barrier. And the herd of prey had climbed the ravine to the top of the escarpment, to the plain above.

The predator left the river. He walked along, among and over the footsteps of the unsuspecting quarry. He moved at an easy gait, loping along at a pace that would rapidly close the distance between him and his prey. It would take awhile, for they had a sizable head-start. But he was in no real hurry. He wasn't yet hungry, and it was inevitable that he would catch the herd. He would find them: if not in the ravine itself, than in the open plain above.

Occasionally he glanced behind him. There was little he had to fear in this world, and almost all creatures feared him. But there were predators larger than he, much larger. He thought about that, and if he could have smiled to himself, he would have. He was too smart, too fast, and too careful to ever fall victim to a predator larger than himself.

He reached the gradient, and paused. He searched the ground carefully, not to be sure that the prey had climbed the ravine, that was all too evident. He was looking for indications that other predators had passed this way. He saw no sign that any had. He was the first, at least on this side of the river. He searched behind him yet again. Still nothing to worry about. He licked his chops in keen anticipation, and strode up the ravine.

*   *   *   *   *

Grendaar leaned forward and browsed the succulent berries from the shrubs along the ridge of a knoll. Occasionally he would use his forepaws to investigate the suitability of a food-substance, or to push off of the ground to help his massive tail counterbalance his great bulk. He was large for his species, weighing some four tons, and stretching 39 feet from the tip of the soft snout that covered his hard beak, to the end of his broad tail.

He walked a little further, his head bobbing gracefully back and forth, and then stooped to investigate some small shrubs on the edge of the knoll. Grendaar's people had evolved so that they could walk equally comfortably either on all fours, or just on their hind legs. They had long, massive hind legs that could propel their owner forward at a brisk rate by long, even strides.

The forelegs of his people were much thinner than were their hind legs, and were barely half their length. Thus they were more comfortably bipedal, and only used their forelegs for locomotion when it was expedient to do so. Each hand had four fingers with which to manipulate the greens on a tree, or to grasp berries from bushes, or to flip over rocks to search for possible delicacies.

When Grendaar walked, he walked on his two hind feet, holding his body almost horizontal, his massive tail held straight out behind him for balance. His head was supported on a gracefully curved neck, and would bob back and forth, redistributing his body weight as he seesawed on his two hind legs. When he ran, it was a different matter. Sometimes he ran on all fours, especially if he wanted to keep a low profile. Then he would move at something like a gallop. Sometimes, if startled into quick flight, he would stand straight up, spread his forearms out to the sides for balance, and sprint on his hind legs. Then sometimes his tail would drag on the ground, but sometimes that just didn't matter.

Grendaar's people had also evolved a horn that protruded from the forehead. This horn was relatively small, and was used more for display than for defense. **Nestlings** and **fledges** and **yearlings** didn't even have horns, although **hatchlings** did have a temporary eggtooth to help them break free of the shell. Although not strictly a weapon, the horn of an adult male was something to avoid in a fight, for it ranged from a foot to sixteen inches long. An adult female had a more feminine horn, generally in the range of five to eleven inches in length.

Another feature common to the People was a narrow frill along the backbone. This frill extended from just behind the neck, all the way down the back, to finally blend into the upper tail. The horn and frill were both larger on males than on females. And the frill, like the horn, was a display feature used primarily as a device to attract a mate.

When on all fours, Grendaar stood fifteen feet high at the hips. When he reared upright, his head and shoulders were well over 20 feet above the ground. His horn extended a proud sixteen inches from his forehead. His frill, normally a golden brown most of the year, was already darkening dramatically as the breeding season neared. His broad tail swept backward almost twenty feet from his body. He was a proud representative of his race – still strong, alert and commanding.

Grendaar was old, having lived through 31 springs. That was very old for the People. He was perhaps the oldest of all the People: oldest throughout all the vast plains, and oldest among all the members of all the great herds. But he still remained strong, strong enough to maintain his dominant position as the leader of his own **roam**. Sometimes he was referred to, although not in his presence, as the Ancient One. He was aware of this sobriquet, but even so he preferred his hard-won and long-held epithet, Groundshaker.

Although Grendaar was strong, he was well past his prime, well past the time when most of his people would have ceased to be able to elude the predators. Yes, he was still strong, but he knew that he wouldn't be strong forever. And he couldn't be a dominant male forever. He was aware of this, and the thought sometimes troubled him. Fortunately, long ago he had realized that while he was losing some of his strength and agility, he was gaining in wisdom and cunning. Perhaps, he thought, this wisdom and cunning would serve him as well as his strength and agility had.

Still munching, he raised himself up on his hind feet and stared towards the southeast. A while ago he thought that he had seen movement far off within the ravine. He examined the ravine that the herd had finished ascending only yesterday. Then his mind slipped into reverie, and saw what his eyes could not. In the hazy distance beyond the edge of the plateau, although not really visible, he imagined that he could almost see the coastal plain and the Great Green Sea beyond. They had left the sea weeks ago, and had traveled along the River of the Nine Tribes, across the coastal plain to the ravine.

The ravine was a little over five miles long. It rose from the fecund coastal plain, rising a bit over 400 feet, to meet the sweeping, dusty upper plain. The River of the Nine Tribes, which eons ago had carved the ravine out of the plateau, now ran down its middle. The river was only three hundred feet wide for most of its turbulent journey down the ravine, but then it slowed and widened perceptibly at the bottom, before broadening even more on its trip to the sea.

The floor of the ravine was wide near the foot of the escarpment, and gradually narrowed as it approached the top of the plateau. It was over seven hundred feet wide, on each side of the river, at the bottom. It narrowed to only a few hundred feet wide on each side of the river as it reached the upper plain. And during that long climb from the coastal plain below to the upper plain above, it held itself to a gently sloping rise.

The floor of the ravine was scattered with rock outcroppings and weather-worn boulders. Here and there clusters of trees had found a foothold, and occasionally a small forest covered the floor of the ravine from the river's edge to the craggy wall. The walls of the ravine were nearly precipitous, and were virtually unscalable. Only along the floor of the ravine could a way be found from the coastal plain to the plateau. It had taken the herd three hard days to work their way up the ravine, following the river, to the top.

For more than half of the year Grendaar and his kind spent their days on the coastal plain, living off the lush vegetation growing along the edge of the Great Green Sea, or up the many fertile deltas that fed into the sea. But once each year, just before breeding season, vast migrations were made from the lower plain up to the plateau, and then across the upper plain to the western foothills. These migrations preceded the rituals of mating, nesting, and raising hatchlings.

Normally Grendaar might be thinking of such things as dominance fights and mating. But his thoughts were not on these matters now. For the tenth time in the last hour, he studied the ravine where he had first seen movement. Were his old eyes playing tricks on him, or had he really seen something? Was a group of stragglers hurrying to catch up to the camaraderie and safety of the herd? Or was a ravager hoping to find an easy meal? If it was a roam of the People, it wouldn't try to hide its presence from the herd. If it was a predator, it would do everything possible to mask its approach until it was ready to attack and kill.

Grendaar shifted his attention to the plateau. His position on the knoll offered him a good vantage point from which to observe much of the herd. He looked about him. He gazed fondly at the roam-members grazing near his knoll. Just to his south and west were the other 74 members of the Green Water Roam, the clan that he had led and helped protect for half a lifetime.

The Green Water Roam was one of 20 roams that made up the Red Dawn Tribe. Now, as part of the annual trek, his roam happened to be located near the eastern edge of the Red Dawn Tribe. The tribe stretched for miles to the west. To the north and south and west of the Red Dawn Tribe, but mainly to the west, were the eight other tribes that made up the Great Eastern Herd. From where he stood, he could still see portions of the Golden Orb Tribe, the White Moon Tribe, and the Black Valley Tribe.

The Red Dawn Tribe had been the last of The Nine Tribes to climb the ravine to the top of the plateau. Many of the other tribes, having finished the climb days earlier, had already moved off towards the west on the trek to the foothills.

The Nine Tribes came together once each year, just before the breeding season, to journey together to the ancient breeding grounds. Together they formed one of the four great herds. The great herds, along with perhaps a dozen minor herds, and numerous micro-herds, were all doing the same thing. If one could but fly like the furry pterosaurs, or the little, feathered birds, one would see that for hundreds of miles north and south of the Great Eastern Herd, there was a grand migration of staggering proportions. Hundreds of thousands of **hadrosaurs** were moving westward into the long range of foothills to continue the cycle of life.

As Grendaar watched the Great Eastern Herd move slowly upon the plateau, grazing off of what was left of the vegetation, he sensed that its numbers must be a wonder to behold. If one could only find a viewing place high enough to see the entire herd, one would see some 17,500 individuals – so many that most of them were lost to Grendaar's view in the moisture-laden haze and the gently rolling terrain of the plateau.

Grendaar returned his attention to the ravine. He still could see nothing, but he felt uncomfortable. He had seen the sudden charge of ravagers too often in his 31 springs to be caught unready now. He signaled to Rohraar on the adjacent knoll to the south. Between him and Rohraar, in the dale between the two knolls, grazed the Green Water Roam. Three other roams of the Red Dawn Tribe lay between the Green Water Roam and the edge of the herd. In addition, perhaps a dozen packs formed a perimeter guard between the roams and the mouth of the ravine. Even so, he knew that the roam was in an exposed position.

Rohraar signaled back to Grendaar. He was less than half Grendaar's age, and consequently considerably more agile. He also could see much further than the old male. At ten springs of age, he was not quite as long as Grendaar. In fact he was only 33 feet long, and he was a sleeker 3.7 tons in weight. His horn was a little over 13 inches long. Rohraar was Second Male of the Green Water Roam. He, along with Trugahr, the Third Male, and the other two adult males of the roam, shared responsibility with Grendaar for the safety of the females and young.

"Younger brother," Grendaar called to Rohraar, "Can you see anything yet?" The People had a limited vocal vocabulary, but through a series of words, sounds, hand-signals, and facial and body language, they managed to communicate a considerable amount of information. It was thusly that Grendaar really posed his question to Rohraar, through both hand signals and words.

In response, Rohraar came sauntering down from his knoll, across the dale, and up to his roamleader. He nodded in respect, and offered Grendaar a succulent twig he had brought with him. Grendaar took it, and chewed on it appreciatively.

"May the sun warm you, elder brother," said Rohraar deferentially.

"And may the sun smile on you, younger brother," replied the older male. They nodded, and wagged tails. They scratched the earth, and continued to exchange pleasantries for awhile, re-affirming their bonding, and their relative positions in the social hierarchy of the roam. Then Grendaar got to the matter at hand.

"What have you seen in the ravine, younger brother?"

"Occasionally I see blurs of movement, elder brother, but not enough to identify the source", said Rohraar. "I cannot tell if I see one creature or many, nor can I tell whether I am looking at a hornbrow, or another green-eater, or a ravager. It worries me greatly. Do you think ravagers are following our trail up to the plateau?"

"Yes I do, younger brother. I have a feeling here, deep in my head, that I cannot explain. It tells me that ravagers are coming up the ravine. They may be here soon. We cannot delay much longer."

"I agree, elder brother. We are in an exposed position here. And the only place to run is right up the backs of the other roams and the other tribes."

"These are my thoughts too, younger brother. And the longer we delay, the more certain I am that we will have no place at all to run. That leaves only unpleasant alternatives."

They both stared at the southeast for awhile. Finally, Rohraar asked, "What are your wishes, elder brother?"

"Send my respects to my brother, Renthot, roamleader of the Yellow Mud Roam. Ask him if he or any of his brothers have seen ravagers. Tell him that if the predators attack, I think that it is wisdom that we bring our roams together, so that more males will be available to fight the killers. See if he can agree to this."

Rohraar nodded, saying, "Yes, elder brother," and turned to carry out his instructions.

Grendaar watched as Rohraar trotted back down the knoll towards the southeast, and towards the roam next closest to possible danger. He then switched his gaze to where Trugahr grazed and guarded along the western flank of the roam. He honked to get Trugahr's attention, and then with hand signals he directed Trugahr to take position on the southern knoll until Rohraar returned.

Sleek and handsome, Trugahr made his way swiftly towards the knoll. He was young for Third Male. He was only eight springs old, but he was already 31 feet long, and a scrappy 3.4 tons in weight. His horn was a little over a foot in length.

Trugahr was an eager young male who had come out of the packs three years ago to attach himself to the Green Water Roam. He had never challenged either Grendaar or Rohraar in a dominance fight, but he had successfully asserted his dominance over the other two males of the roam. He had always shown great deference to Grendaar, and respect for Rohraar. And he always kept the interests of the roam foremost in his mind.

As Trugahr made his way to the southern knoll, Grendaar called to the two **adolescent** males of his roam. He had a task for each of them. He could not afford to send any adult males off with danger so close, but he believed he could do without the adolescents for awhile.

Both were ever aware of the exact location of their roamleader, and responded immediately to his signal. Each often watched him, hoping to learn the ways of leadership. Now they came loping anxiously at his call. They were already aware of the possibility of imminent danger. It hung in the air like a heavy mist. They knew the signs, and had been watching the five dominant males of the roam for the last hour. Panthrar, the older of the two, approached first, as was his right. Dandraar hung back a few paces.

Panthrar nodded several times in respect, and asked, "Yes, my father, how may I be of service to you?"

He offered Grendaar a branch of juicy leaves and a few ripe berries. Grendaar munched on them with relish. Panthrar was five years old and already 2.8 tons in weight and 27 feet long. He had a ten inch horn. He was on the verge of adulthood, and couldn't wait to prove himself. There was even the possibility that in the breeding grounds to the west, he might, this very spring, wage his first dominance fights. If he won enough of those fights, and especially if he won the right ones, he might even breed this season.

Grendaar nodded approvingly of the lad. "Panthrar, my son, I wish you to undertake an important mission for me. It may be fraught with danger, and I do not want you to take any unnecessary risks. Do you understand me, my son?"

"Yes, my father," Panthrar said without hesitation. Yet he wondered what mission might be fraught with danger.

"This is good, my son. Now attend me well. I want you to go to the packs near the ravine, to the pack of my brother, Draggot, once of the Two Trees Roam. Give Draggot my respects. Tell him that we have seen something coming up the ravine. I fear that ravagers may be ascending the ravine at this very moment, stalking us, following our only too obvious trail. Ask him to be ever vigilant."

Panthrar nodded in understanding.

Grendaar continued, "Also ask him if he will send a scouting party a short distance down the ravine to see if it is a lost roam that we have detected, or indeed the killers coming to prey upon the People."

Panthrar began to quiver with excitement. At last, a mission to show his courage. A mission worthy of an adult. He basked in his roamleader's trust.

He also thought of the packs – those free-wheeling, fast-moving alternatives to roamlife that helped form the outer defenses of the herd. Each pack was composed of several adult males, and several dozen adolescent males. Packs contained few females, and no young. They did not form for the rearing and protection of the young. They formed because some adult males, and most adolescent males, and even a few adolescent females, needed to break away from the confines of the roam, at least for awhile, and become independent. The adolescents were still too young to break entirely away, as many adult males did. So they joined packs.

The entire herd was surrounded by such packs, many dozens of them. Independent and unreliable most of the time; amorphous, dynamic, ever-changing all of the time; in times of predator attack they rose to the occasion. For they would fight courageously, and if necessary, risk death to protect the herd.

Grendaar, who had been silent through most of Panthrar's reverie, spoke again. "But Panthrar, do not take any chances," he repeated. "Do not fall victim to the teeth of one of the killers. Do you understand me, my son?"

"Yes, my father."

"Then be off with you."

As Panthrar descended the knoll towards the southeast, Dandraar approached the roamleader. He nodded several times, and offered Grendaar a large juicy beetle, one that he had been carrying for hours, hoping for just such a chance to offer to his roamleader.

"How may I be of service to you, my father?"

Grendaar smiled in anticipation of the tasty morsel.

"Dandraar, my son," he said, as he took the proffered beetle and popped it into his mouth, "I have an important mission for you, too." He paused to relish the juicy crunchiness of the beetle, smacking his lips in unfeigned delight. When he finished, he said, "Thank you, my son, that was a tasty, big springbug."

"You're very welcome, my father," smiled Dandraar. He was a young adolescent of four springs of age, 2.4 tons in weight, and 25 feet in length. He rubbed the tip of his eight inch horn with his left hand.

"Dandraar, I want you to find the elders of the Red Dawn Tribe, and deliver a message for me. You must do it very quickly, for I will need you back here if the ravagers attack."

Dandraar nodded in understanding.

"Find the elders, and give them my respects. Advise them that I believe that ravagers are ascending the ravine. Tell them that I believe that there is wisdom in beginning the trek anew, rather than waiting another day. Tell them that I believe that it would be wise to begin the journey now. Do you understand me, my son?"

"Yes I do, my father." Dandraar paused for a moment while he thought through his assignment. He pawed at the ground first with his left hand, then with his right. He was clearly troubled with something. "May I ask a question?"

"Yes, my son."

"What if the ravagers attack before I find the elders? Do I continue to search for them, or do I hasten back to the roam?"

"A very perceptive question, my son," mused the old male. He thought a moment, and then said, "If the ravagers attack, then make haste to rejoin your roam. If they attack before you deliver my message, the elders will have the message none-the-less."

Dandraar thought about this for a moment. Finally, he said, "I understand, my father."

"Good, then, young son. Be off with you, and be quick, but be careful."

Dandraar scampered down the western slope of the knoll and dashed around and between the many roams as he proceeded towards the middle of the gathered tribe, looking for the elders.

Grendaar watched him until he was lost in the milling masses of the great herd, then he again looked to the ravine. After awhile, he could see the scouting party forming up and heading down into the ravine. He wasn't sure, since his old eyes sometimes played tricks on him, but he thought that he could see Panthrar with the other adolescents of the scouting party.

That young rascal, he thought to himself.

CHAPTER TWO
ROAMMERS AND TRIBESMEN

GRENDAAR TURNED AND LOOKED over his roam. Unconsciously, he counted adults and adolescents, youngsters and yearlings, making sure that all were accounted for. At the moment, four adult males (himself included), thirteen adult females, and eight adolescent females. The younger ones were harder to count: there were so many of them, and they scampered about so much. Especially the yearlings. There were twenty-six youngsters and twenty-one yearlings. There must be. There were supposed to be, in any event. He made a more conscious effort to count them. Tessah caught his eye while he was counting, and he motioned for her to approach him.

Tessah was the First Female of the roam. She too was old, but only 19 springs. She was also a little small for an adult female. Her compact frame was only 3.1 tons in weight and 33 feet in length. Her brow horn was a more feminine ten inches in length, and was a pale ivory in color. She was small and old, yet she was wise and strong, a good breeder that produced a large clutch of eggs every year, and she was fiercely protective of the roam.

She nodded deferentially, and asked, "How may I serve you, my brother."

He looked upon her with undisguised fondness. They had been consorts for a long time. He had been the first to mate with her when she had come of age. Then, she was a sassy six, and he was eighteen and still in his prime. Since then, during the many intervening breeding seasons, they had produced many hatchlings together. He would mate with her again, when the time came, at the end of the trek. Once she had been one of the most desirable young females of the tribe. He had had to fight fiercely and often to keep her. Now she was too old for the tastes of many of the younger males. Grendaar didn't mind this. To him she was ever-young, and ever-beautiful.

"May the sun warm your face," he said to her.

She basked in his affection, and moved closer, almost touching him. "And may you live forever, my brother."

They stood in the silence of mutual affection for a time. Each was lost in thoughts of their younger years together. He nuzzled her around the back of her head and along her neck. Finally, Tessah reminded Grendaar with a subtle signal that they had more pressing matters now.

Grendaar snorted, and asked, "My sister, you know of my concern about the ravagers?"

"Yes, my brother. I would be an ignorant hatchling indeed if I had not noticed your concern over an hour ago."

"We may need to move quickly, and soon, my sister." The possibility of a stampede worried them both. "Or we may have to stand and fight." That was possibly even worse than a stampede, because none of the People, not even a large and strong male like Grendaar, was equipped to fight on an even footing with a ravager. "Gather your sisters and young about you, good mother, and be ready for either eventuality."

"Yes, my brother." They browsed some of the last remaining berry bushes on the knoll together. After a while, she ambled down the slope towards the roam. No one needed to tell her or any of the other roam-members what to do in the event of a predator attack. Those old enough had lived through literally hundreds of such attacks. Now she went to tell her sisters to gather the young in preparation for either flight, or a fight.

* * * * *

Meanwhile, Dandraar made his way amongst the many roams of the tribe, seeking the elders. Most of the tribesmen towards the interior of the herd seemed totally oblivious to the danger that Grendaar was preparing for. But Dandraar never doubted either the wisdom or the ability of his roamleader. He had traveled perhaps a mile when he heard his name called.

"Dandraar, you young pup, is that you?"

Dandraar bristled. He stopped and looked about him for the source of what he considered an insult. He had never been a **pup**, and he hadn't been a fledge for a long time. He saw Kinput, a solitary old male, lumbering in his direction. Kinput was at least 13 springs old, and was 3.8 tons in weight and over 35 feet in length. His umber-tipped brow horn was 14 inches long. Dandraar liked Kinput, and loved to tag along with him on those rare occasions when Kinput would let him, down on the coastal plain, through the dense forests. So he decided to forget the insult. Knowing Kinput, it was probably a joke anyway.

"May the sun warm you, elder brother. How are you this fine day?" asked Dandraar.

"And may it warm you, younger brother," returned Kinput. "As good as can be expected when one is forced to go on one of these annual treks, younger brother. And how are things with you?" replied Kinput.

Kinput was one of the many solitary males that joined the herd on its annual pilgrimage to the mating grounds to the west. Fully forty percent of the adult males in the annual trek were solitary – they belonged to neither roam nor pack. They preferred to live most of their lives alone, browsing the lush shrubs along the river banks with no one's company but their own. Sometimes they traveled with one or two other solitaries, but mostly they traveled alone. It was only at mating season that they joined up with their tribe, to help protect it on its journey to the west, and to fight for the right to mate at the journey's end.

"I am fine, elder brother, but I am on a most urgent mission for my roamleader at the moment, and I cannot dally."

"An urgent mission, you say? What has the Ancient One got you doing, if I may be so impudent as to ask?"

34

Dandraar thought for a moment, and then volunteered, "I am to find the tribe elders and ask them to take up the trek at once."

Kinput pondered this. It was an incredible request, considering that the herd had just spent the last three days laboring up the ravine to the top of the plateau. Normally it would rest a day or two to allow the young to regain their strength. But he didn't think that Grendaar had yet lost his senses, even if he was an old bag of leather and dry bones.

"What is amiss, younger brother?"

"My roamleader believes that ravagers are ascending the ravine right behind the herd, and may attack soon."

"This is a serious matter, younger brother. You be off and fulfill the mission of your roamleader. I will gather some lazy young solitaries that I happen to have an acquaintance of. We will meet you at you roamleader's side."

"Yes, elder brother, and may the good sun warm you."

With that, Dandraar sped on his way towards the center of the tribe, looking for the elders.

*   *   *   *   *

Panthrar edged down the ravine cautiously. To his right was the river that meandered down the middle of the ravine. The river neatly bisected the ravine here, before curving away to the left. The ravine angled slightly downward, and was strewn with large boulders and outcroppings of jagged, granite-like rock. The walls of the ravine sloped steeply upward. Shoulders of rock jutted out from the walls, affording many hiding places for ravagers. And the ground before him, with its many large boulders, some three or four times as high as a ravager is tall, offered many more places where a creature as cunning and as devious as a ravager could hide in ambush. Panthrar was keenly aware of this, and did not want to be trapped by one of the killers.

Panthrar was part of the scouting party that fanned out from the left bank of the river. A second scouting party was similarly spread out to the right of the river. There was one packer to Panthrar's right, between him and the river, and three more spaced at intervals to his left.

Panthrar turned and looked behind him. At the top of the ravine a dozen packs, representing some 200 members of the perimeter defense, had gathered. They waited for the scouting parties to either confirm that it was only stragglers hurrying to catch up to the herd, or that it was something worse. If it was a ravager, the scouting party would either spot it ascending the ravine, or else flush it out of hiding as bait.

Panthrar had been proud and excited when his roamleader had sent him on this mission. He had been even more excited when Draggot had allowed him to join the scouting party, even though he was sure that Grendaar had not anticipated that this was how he would carry out his instructions. But now he was beginning to suffer from second thoughts. He knew that he and the other adolescents in the scouting party were in a very exposed and vulnerable position.

This was not like running swiftly on the open plains, away from the danger, dashing and veering, revelling in the energy and exuberance of youth, where only the weak or the slow fell prey to the ravagers. There, speed and endurance could best even the most rapacious of predators. Nor was this like fighting in circles, where every roam-member fought together for the common good, and strength and cooperation could turn back a ravager. And if you died, you did so protecting your roam. A nobler death no one could imagine. But this was not like that. Now he could taste a sourness in his mouth. He did not want to die. Not like this, as bait.

He continued onward with the rest of the scouting party. He noticed that the scouts to his far left were getting too close to the edge of the ravine wall. If there was a killer there, a scout would fall too easily to an ambush. He signaled to them to be careful. The scout furthest to the left signaled back that he knew what he was doing. Panthrar shrugged. These packers were a little bit reckless. But that was probably why they left the roams and joined packs in the first place.

Panthrar climbed a small rise and stopped to examine the terrain ahead of him. He glanced up at the sun. It was already well past mid-day. He inspected the ground before him. The river began to narrow and turn to the left here. He would have to start veering to the left himself to avoid it, and to keep equispaced with the rest of the party members. Three large boulders stood almost directly in his path. They stood like gray-black fingers pointing towards the sky. The middle one was the tallest. It stood over sixty feet high. The one on the right was slightly bent, like a crooked finger, broken and swollen at the joint.

He would have to skirt the three rocks. They were too obviously a place where a ravager would hide in ambush. Should he pass to the right, in the narrowing space between them and the river? If he did, there would be little space for maneuvering if a predator suddenly charged from behind one of them. There was only a hundred feet between the boulders and the river bank.

The river itself was swollen and threatening to overflow its banks due to the spring rains and the melting of the snow on the peaks to the west of the hills. The river might offer some safety from a predator, if he didn't drown in it in the process.

Should he pass to the left of the boulders, and cluster with the scouts near the wall of the ravine? Then he'd be between the boulders and the wall, between two possible ambushes, with almost nowhere to run.

He signaled to the scout to his right. He would confer before deciding. His decision affected the other scout anyway.

The packer jogged over towards Panthrar. While he waited for the scout to join him on the rise, Panthrar turned again to look back up the ravine. Now some 300 pack-members had gathered near the top. That many defenders would intimidate even the largest of predators, and might block the exit from the ravine long enough for the herd to get safely away.

Far beyond the packers, he could just see two distant knolls. On each knoll he could see the lone figure of an adult male. It was too far to be sure, but he was certain that the one on the right was Grendaar. How could the Ancient One have seen so far down the ravine to have first noticed movement so many hours ago? Either his eyesight was far better than he let on, or he had a sixth sense about these kinds of things.

Pippit, the scout from Panthrar's right, joined him on the rise. Panthrar tried to act normal while they talked, but he would stare at his companion covertly whenever he could get the opportunity, while still trying not to be rude. He had rarely met a female packer before, and wondered what could have motivated her to leave her roam. She was a comely female about Panthrar's age, about 2.2 tons in weight, and a little over 20 feet in length. Her pale brow horn was only four inches long, barely a horn at all.

They discussed the relative merits of proceeding to the right or to the left of the group of boulders, and finally decided that the route around the right was the better one. They also decided to go together, and proceeded cautiously. They gave the boulders as wide a berth as possible, hugging close to the river bank. Even so, they moved as slowly and silently as they could. Both were ready to turn and bolt at the first sign of an ambush. Being young and confident, they both believed that they might out-run a predator, given enough of a head-start.

Panthrar's heart pumped vigorously. His eyes were wide open and were as dilated as he could get them. Every little sound that he heard was processed as a possible threat. He could tell that Pippit was as jumpy as he was. Fortunately, the scouts to their left and right had proceeded further than they, and were making a lot more noise. Unless a predator was well-hidden behind the boulders, and had its heart set on one of them, they were probably safe. Either the other scouts would have seen a predator hidden behind the boulders by now, or they would have distracted it by all the noise.

Finally Panthrar and Pippit edged far enough forward to see clearly around the boulders. A few small lizards scurried away at the sight of them, but there was no predator hidden there. Panthrar snorted like a predator. Pippit laughed. Suddenly both were light-hearted, the immediate threat of a predator charge having passed.

They noticed that they had fallen well behind the advance of the other scouts. They hurried to catch up, passing another large boulder a little less cautiously.

Soon all the scouts had passed around the bend in the river. They were temporarily out of sight of the plateau, at least until the river curved back again towards the right. They could no longer see, nor be seen by the packs at the top of the ravine.

* * * * *

Grendaar watched the progress of the scouting parties until they were temporarily blocked from view by the curve of the river. Then he automatically examined his roam, checking the defenses and the positions of all of the adult males, noting the locations of all the adult females. He even tried counting the young once more, to be certain that all were accounted for.

He glanced to the west. He now wished that he hadn't sent Dandraar on his mission. It would be difficult to find the elders in time, and even more difficult for such a young male to convince the elders that the tribe must move now. Even with the message coming from Grendaar, who's opinion held great weight in the councils of the tribe, even that might not be enough to get the tribe moving in time. Besides, if it came to a defensive battle, he might need the young male to help complete the circle.

Grendaar turned and walked over to a better vantage point on the knoll. He fretted about Panthrar. He should have known that at his age, with the transition from adolescence to adulthood, that he would be tempted to take more risks than were good for him. Plus, he thought, he also might be necessary to complete the circle.

Grendaar observed that Trugahr still stood sentry on the knoll to the south. The attention of the Third Male never wavered. Constantly he turned: first checking the location of roam-members; then observing all who wandered near the roam, checking to be sure that they held no hostile intent; and then peering off to the southeast, the most likely direction from which danger would come.

Rohraar still stood with the Yellow Mud Roam. Earlier he had signaled Grendaar that Renthot had not seen any ravagers, but that he was agreeable to joining roams in the event of a ravager attack. Now he was conferring with Renthot and his brothers about contingency plans if ravagers broke through the packs at the top of the ravine. The attention of all of them was directed toward the southeast.

Grendaar heard a footfall behind him. He turned quickly, angry with himself for becoming so preoccupied that he had allowed someone to get this close without him being aware of it. He must be getting old, he conceded to himself.

It was Kinput and three other males. All of them had the look of solitaries. Grendaar's eyes blazed. He leaned forward, and stuck his tail straight back, in the stance of a male preparing for a fight. His tail began to slowly swing back and forth, arcing gently. It wasn't quite an explicit challenge. This was not a good time for a dominance fight, he thought to himself.

Kinput saw Grendaar's anger, and recognized the implicit challenge. He spoke quickly, lest Grendaar get the wrong idea and attack them first, asking questions later.

"May the sun warm you, elder brother," he said politely.

"And you too, younger brother," responded Grendaar. "And your brothers also. What are your wishes?" The tip of Grendaar's tail started flicking involuntarily. Unconsciously he began to maneuver for a better fighting position, away from the edge of the knoll.

"We have come to offer our services, elder brother. I just ran into your young roamsman, Dandraar, and he indicated that you feared a ravager attack."

Grendaar noticed for the first time that Kinput held a small branch from a berry bush. All of the solitaries carried berry bush branches. Grendaar grew quiet. His tail stopped flicking.

"That is indeed kind of you, Kinput, my younger brother. And of your brothers. Might you introduce them?"

"Forgive me, elder brother, my rudeness." Kinput inwardly breathed a sigh of relief. The threat had come and gone so quickly. He did not want to have to fight Grendaar, especially by accident.

"I was so pleased to see your venerable old face again, Groundshaker, that I forgot my manners." He turned to the three males with him and gestured to each in turn. "This is Gaffstar, once of the Three Pebbles Roam."

Gaffstar nodded, and said, "May the sun warm you, elder brother."

"And this is Tanmont, once of the Crooked Tree Roam," continued Kinput.

Nodding, Tanmont added, "May your days be many, Groundshaker."

"And this is Sevren, once of the Black Sand Roam."

Sevren nodded. "And may your hatchlings make the earth tremble, mighty Groundshaker," he said with a flourish.

"And me, elder brother, you know me quite well. For I am Kinput, once of the Green Water Roam. We are here to help you defend the children."

Grendaar looked deeply into Kinput's eyes for a moment. He nodded to each of the four. He was clearly touched. He coughed, and said, "May you never know the Cold. May you never feel the Loneliness. You are all welcome. Stand with me here for awhile, until we determine the shape of things."

They gathered together, and all turned toward the southeast. Kinput looked sidelong at Grendaar. The tip of the old male's tail was flicking from side-to-side again. Just the last foot or two, but it was enough. Kinput knew that the Ancient One was worried. Kinput turned to face the southeast. Why worry, he thought to himself, until there was something definite to worry about.

As he watched, another of the roam's adult males, Wubbar, joined Trugahr on the southern knoll. Rohraar finally left the Yellow Mud Roam, and was coming back to report to Grendaar. Halfway up the knoll, he stopped short and turned toward the southeast. Grendaar thought he heard something also. So had many of the other People spread out along the southeastern flank of the Red Dawn Tribe. Apparently the packers, much closer to the source, had heard it, for they began to move about in agitation.

After awhile, they heard thumping. Still later, they heard a repetition of the sound that had first alerted them. From far off, perhaps a mile or two away, came the plaintive hooting of a hadrosaur in distress.

CHAPTER THREE
FRIENDS AND ENEMIES

PANTHRAR AND PIPPIT CONTINUED to scout together. As they progressed, the ravine widened noticeably. They passed through a marshy area, and then through a small forest of tall evergreens. They continued to move cautiously. Panthrar saw another rise, and automatically moved towards it.

During the last fifteen minutes or so, they had managed to get ahead of their companions to their left. The scouts to their right, however, those across the river, were slightly ahead of them. None-the-less, they decided to wait on the rise until their own party got back in line with them.

As they settled down on the top of the rise to wait, a commotion broke out on the right side of the river. The scout near the sandy right bank of the river was honking excitedly, and pointing down-river and towards the ravine wall. Panthrar followed his direction, and squinted. At this angle, it was hard to see what was being pointed at.

"Can you see what he's pointing at, my sister?" asked Panthrar.

"No, my brother, but that's a very inappropriate way for a scout to act," commented Pippit. "Can you imagine if there is a predator sneaking up the ravine right now? It certainly knows that we are here, and probably knows exactly where Duffnott is. But Duffnott never was too smart."

They continued to look in the direction indicated. At first they couldn't see what the scout was pointing to. Then Pippit saw. "There. Look there near the ravine wall," she instructed Panthrar.

A quarter of a mile down, just filing out from behind a shoulder of the ravine wall, was a male hadrosaur. It was a ridgebrow, a very close cousin to the People. Behind him came another male, and then another. Soon an entire roam was seen marching up the ravine – adult females and adolescents, with youngsters and yearlings scampering about.

The scouts on the right side of the river were all honking now. They charged in a mad rush towards the stragglers. The lost roam saw them, and honked gleefully back. Soon they were all mingling together, rubbing against each other, bowing and stooping, swinging their massive tails back and forth in a display of excitement.

In was not unusual to mingle with ridgebrows on the upper plain, but rarely did the two species trek together. For one thing, the ridgebrows tended to stay up on the upper plain. They migrated along a north-south axis on the dry plain, while the People tended to migrate on an east-west axis. Occasionally ridgebrows would descend to the coastal plain, but not often. The cousins might indeed be lost. Why were they following the Great Eastern Herd on its trek? The scouting party and the ridgebrows began swopping stories about the harrowing and tiring climb up the ravine.

Panthrar was to learn later that the ridgebrows hadn't descended to the coastal plain by choice. They were forced to do so. While grazing by a ravine near the top of the plateau, they had been surprised and chased by a ravager. They followed the ravine down to the coastal plain as they made their escape. Blocked from ascending that ravine by the pursuing ravager, they had hidden in the forests of the coastal plain for a time. Later, when it was safe to move onward, the ridgebrows had traveled along the escarpment wall looking for another path back up to the plateau. They had happily found the ravine of the Great Eastern Herd, and had been ascending it for the last three days.

The scouts on Panthrar's left, attracted by the honking coming from the right side of the river, had joined Panthrar and Pippit on the rise. They also became excited by the appearance of the ridgebrows, and wanted to find a way across the river and greet them.

Panthrar wasn't sure this was the correct thing to do. He wasn't sure why he felt this way, but he thought that a little more reconnaissance was in order. Perhaps he was overly influenced by Grendaar, who was always excessively cautious, but something told him that this was not what had worried the old roamleader. There was always something uncanny about the way Grendaar sensed danger. And you didn't get to be twice the age of the average hadrosaur by being wrong too often.

Panthrar looked at Pippit, wondering what she thought was best. She was in an animated discussion with the scout-leader, a male of five springs named Trimellon. Trimellon wanted to cross the river at a ford that they had recently passed, and join in the merriment going on with the ridgebrows. Pippit seemed to think that their assignment was not yet completed, and apparently she shared Panthrar's opinion that a little additional scouting should be done.

Panthrar was reluctant to interfere with pack decisions, and therefore reluctant to get involved in this discussion. He was an outsider, being a roammer, and somewhat suspect from a packer's perspective. Too conservative. Too unwilling to take chances. So he decided to wait and see what the scouting party would decide.

He looked across the river at the ridgebrows. They and the other scouting party had turned and were proceeding back up the ravine. He contemplated ridgebrows for a moment. They were very much like the People. They were perhaps just a little smaller, reaching maximum lengths and weights of 30 feet and three tons respectively. The most distinguishable difference between them and the People was a short, bony ridge or crest on the ridgebrows, extending forward between their eyes. This was why they were called ridgebrows. Instead of a ridge, the People had a small, pointed horn.

Panthrar was pulled from his reverie by a question from Trimellon. "Well, Panthrar, are you coming with us, or are you going to scout forward with Pippit?" Trimellon was clearly put out with Pippit, and wanted nothing more to do with her.

"I think it would be best if we all scouted a little further down the ravine before we turn back," offered Panthrar. "If you disagree, then Pippit and I will go on a little farther ourselves." Pippit appeared pleased with his decision. Trimellon was not.

"Suit yourself", Trimellon said in a hooty manner. "I'm surprised that you are willing to take such an unnecessary risk. It seems so out of character for a roammer." Not only were the words insulting to a hornbrow, but the way he emphasized the word "roammer" left little doubt that he held most roam-members with some contempt.

A low rumble escaped from Panthrar's throat. He leaned forward and his tail lashed right and left in an almost uncontrollable fashion. He surprised even himself, since usually he was a very agreeable sort, even when insulted. Now he had a strong urge to trounce Trimellon. The other young males backed away, expecting that Panthrar might attack their leader on the spot. Instead, he suddenly quieted, and said, "Perhaps, younger brother, you are right. Or perhaps I feel a greater sense of responsibility to the herd than you."

Trimellon caught the term "younger brother", which implied that Trimellon was Panthrar's junior. He was not, neither in age, both were five, nor in his present assignment as scout-leader. He knew that Panthrar hadn't used it casually, or by mistake.

They stood glaring at each other for a moment. Then Trimellon signaled his charges and turned back up the ravine towards the ford. Panthrar turned and looked at Pippit. She had a glow in her eyes.

"I hope you don't think that I'm unreasonably ill-mannered, my sister," he offered in way of an apology. "I really wasn't going to pounce on that rude mud-wallower. Even if he did deserve it."

She coughed and looked away. Was there a trace of a smile on her face? She turned back and said, "I'm not sure what I expected, my brother. He was rude, that was plain for all of us to see. And it did look like you were a breath away from teaching him some manners."

She stroked the ground with her right hand, drawing lines in the dirt. Then she continued, "Perhaps it is just as well that he didn't accept your challenge. This is not the time nor the place for such a lesson. I think he's afraid of you, though. You better be careful of him in the future."

She mused a bit longer, and finally said, "And I wouldn't be surprised if he tried to take it out on me when we get back to the pack."

Panthrar, who had been leaning down close to Pippit, heads less than a foot apart, straightened himself up, and gazed after Trimellon and the scouting party. They were slowly working their way across a ford of flat rocks. Impulsively, he said, "Rest assured, Pippit, that if he makes it difficult for you in any way, he will have to answer to me."

Panthrar surprised himself for saying it. Plus he had used her name – something that was rarely done. With a title, like "my sister", it was done on formal occasions. Without a title, it was only used by intimates, consorts. What changes were taking place in him? Was it because she was such a lovely female? He had hardly noticed the differences between males and females in the past. What could be happening?

Pippit looked down at the ground a moment longer. Then she straightened up and looked across the river at the group of packers and ridgebrows that were proceeding up the ravine. Finally she mumbled a barely audible, "But, Panthrar, I wouldn't want someone as important as you to waste his time worrying about me."

They both leaned back down, heads almost touching. Pippit drew some more lines in the dirt. Panthrar tried to speak, but found it difficult. He pushed some pebbles around with his left hand, not really conscious of the action. He looked long and hard at Pippit. Her form was so pleasing to him. And she smelled wonderful, like the star-burst flowers on the mountain laurel. He felt something stirring inside him that he had never felt before. He couldn't explain what it was, but he suddenly felt very protective of her. He looked at the pile of pebbles that he had assembled, but he didn't really see it. He decided that he would take on the whole pack, if need be, to protect her against the slightest insult. He was about to tell her this very decision, when the sound of kicked gravel from across the river attracted the attention of both of them.

They both saw it at the same time, directly opposite from where they stood. A ravager was sprinting at full speed towards the last stragglers in the group of scouts and ridgebrows. He had been following the spoor of the Great Eastern Herd all the way up the ravine. More recently, having discovered the lost roam of ridgebrows, he had been hiding behind some tall rocks waiting for the right moment – when the prey was looking in the opposite direction. Now he moved with terrifying speed straight at the unsuspecting quarry.

The ravager propelled himself on two strong hind legs, holding himself almost horizontal, with his stiff tail held straight back for balance. Panthrar saw that he was a **dreadrunner**. He looked to be 24 feet long, and almost two tons in weight. He had a large reddish patch on the back of his neck. More importantly, he held his massive jaws agape, exposing his many rows of serrated, blade-like teeth. Each tooth was sharp on both sides – ideal for killing, and ideal for tearing apart flesh.

Instinctively, Panthrar and Pippit immediately hooted a warning to the intended victims across the river. The two adolescent females that were trailing behind the rest of the roam turned towards Panthrar and Pippit, as did Trimellon's scouts and many ridgebrows near the rear of the roam. Panthrar pointed to the dreadrunner, and he and Pippit continued to hoot the danger signal.

The young females turned the rest of the way, saw the dreadrunner, and squealed in panic. One took off in the direction of the river and didn't stop until she was shoulder high in the cold water. Unfortunately, the other female stood frozen in shock and fright.

The dreadrunner bore down upon the motionless female at a frightful rate. He ran silently, low and almost horizontal, straight at her. Suddenly, at the last moment, the female ridgebrow turned and bolted in the direction of the roam. Too late. With one great leap, the dreadrunner covered the last 50 feet and landed full upon her back. She honked a loud and powerful distress call just as the dreadrunner buried his fangs into the back of her neck. She squirmed and fought to break free from the dreadrunner's hold, but he hung on and forced her to the ground.

Panthrar roared the challenge of a dominant male, the first of his life, but he felt helpless. There was nothing he could do to save the female. Pippit shuddered, and began backing down the rise, away from the ravager. Fearful, she crouched low as she backed away. Panthrar's tail made one mighty crash onto the ground. Then his head darted to the left and right, looking for other possible sources of danger.

Panic reigned in the roam. The youngsters and yearlings tore up the ravine as fast as their legs could carry them. They tripped and stumbled in their haste to get away from certain death. Adolescent females followed at only a slightly more restrained pace, keeping themselves between the ravager and the young. Adult females followed, keeping some semblance of a moving barrier between the ravager and the others. Their broad tails swung back and forth in a defensive display.

Meanwhile, the adult and adolescent males, including the packers from the scouting party, arranged themselves in a line between the ravager and the roam. They bellowed their frustration and rage. The more dominant males made charging gestures at the ravager, and gradually drew closer to the scene of the tragedy. They honked loudly, and beat the earth with their broad tails. Eventually, in sufficient numbers, they might have worked up enough rage and courage to actually attack the ravager. But nothing they could do would be in time to save the life of the young female.

Panthrar watched as the life slowly drained from the victim. Her struggles to escape from the jaws of the ravager gradually lessened. The dreadrunner never loosened his vise-like grip. Finally, from shock, loss of blood, and partial suffocation, she gave up and died. The dreadrunner shook her hard, but she showed no signs of life. He released her, and roared his defiance at the approaching males. He then grabbed the female by the neck again, and tried to drag her back towards the rocks.

Pippit moaned. She turned and fled for the relative cover offered by the small forest of tall evergreens that they had so recently passed. Panthrar waited to cover her retreat, and then slowly backed down the rise in her direction.

Suddenly, two more dreadrunners broke from behind the rocks and charged the roam. They were both smaller than the first ravager. Dreadrunners don't normally hunt in packs, so the appearance of two more of them surprised the male ridgebrows considerably. In fact, these two hadn't been hunting with the first dreadrunner. They had been ascending the ravine together, when they had noticed Red-patch lurking behind a large boulder. And when he charged from behind it and ran up the ravine, they naturally became curious.

One of the two new dreadrunners, a young male about 23 feet long and 1.7 tons in weight, with a gnarled right paw, leapt at Red-patch. His intent was to try to intimidate Red-patch sufficiently that he would give up his prey. Red-patch dropped the prey, and snapped and hissed at Gnarled-paw. They slowly circled each other, around the body of the poor lifeless female, hissing and snapping, heads jerking forward with each snap.

Meanwhile, the third dreadrunner, a young female with a very long tail, charged towards the male ridgebrows and hornbrows. Gnarled-paw decided to give up worrying Red-patch, and followed Long-tail.

Except for the two most dominant male ridgebrows, all the other males immediately turned around, and displayed their broad tails to the approaching dreadrunners. The two dominant males honked loud challenges at the ravagers. Meanwhile the remaining males began to strike the ground loudly and repeatedly with their tails. Thunk... thunk... thunk, thunk, thunk, thunk... thunk, thunk.

The dreadrunners, who were still several hundred feet from the ridgebrows and hornbrows, paused at the thundering display. They hesitated at the ferocity of the drumming. Long-tail hissed and snapped her large jaws repeatedly at the line of defenders, but she balked at approaching any closer.

Gnarled-paw was suddenly distracted at the sight of the female ridgebrow splashing in the river. She was slowly working her way back towards the shore and a sound footing, dog-paddling with all fours. Like a dart, Gnarled-paw threw himself towards her. Low and horizontal, he raced towards the river. With one heroic leap from its edge, he landed upon her back. They both sank below the surface.

Panthrar, who had been hurrying towards the forest to rejoin Pippit, was startled by the loud splash. He feared that a dreadrunner had seen him, and was crossing the river to pursue him. He turned to see hunter and quarry rise to the surface of the water.

The dreadrunner had wrapped himself around the back of the female. His jaws had a death-grip upon the back of her neck. The female tried to shake the ravager loose, but she was in too deep to find firm footing. The killer hung on with teeth and claws. Water splashed and cascaded in the unequal struggle, as the pair repeatedly sank below the water, and then struggled back up for air again. Blood spread around the struggling pair, and the foaming water raised by their thrashing turned pink.

Panthrar knew what the inevitable conclusion to the battle was, so he turned and raced for the cover of the conifer forest. When he reached its edge, he glanced back at the river. The dreadrunner was splashing his way towards the shore, the carcass of the now quiescent female held tightly in his jaws.

The defensive line of male hadrosaurs began to slowly move up the ravine. They continued to pound the ground and honk loud challenges, but they knew that they were supporting a losing proposition. The two females had been lost, and now members of the line were themselves threatened. Long-tail followed them at a discrete distance, hissing and snapping most of the way, but she was sufficiently intimidated by the thunderous display to keep her distance.

Pippit and Panthrar, watching from the relative safety of the forest, witnessed the slow withdrawal of the roam. Its retreat was tediously slow, but effective. The two dominant males, walking backwards, directed the retreat. The rest of the line tirelessly pounded the earth in a steady, but monotonous staccato. Eventually they rounded the curve in the river, and were lost to view. The female dreadrunner, kept at bay, followed them up the ravine, hoping for an opportunity to find a weakness in the defense.

Red-patch had consumed almost a quarter of the carcass. He did it by tearing off large mouthfuls of flesh, chopping each up with a few shearing chews, and then swallowing them, still virtually whole. Finally he was full. So he grabbed a hind leg in his jaws, and pulled the carcass into a defile between two large boulders. There he lay down next to his kill, and dozed.

50

Occasionally he would stir, look over at Gnarled-paw to ascertain that no threat came from that quarter, and then he would doze again.

Gnarled-paw hastily gobbled up chunks of his kill. He frequently glanced first at the dozing male, and then up the ravine where the female had disappeared. It seemed that he half expected one or the other to come and challenge him for the remainder of the carcass.

Panthrar and Pippit moved as quietly as they could deeper into the forest to avoid alerting the two dreadrunners to their presence. They confided in whispers and gestures as to what to do next. They could not follow the scouts and roam up the ravine without risking being attacked by the female. They could only hope to get past her if she had already made a kill. And that was a terrible thought.

They could possibly stay hidden in the forest, and hope that the dreadrunners, after they had consumed their kills, would continue up the ravine after the herd. They knew that was the direction that the dreadrunners would go, in the direction of food, not back down to the lower coastal plain. Pippit and Panthrar weren't likely to starve while waiting, as there were still some berry bushes about, even though the Great Eastern Herd had stripped much of the vegetation from the ravine in the past several weeks of trekking.

Unfortunately, this plan would mean that they would have the dreadrunners between them and the herd for most of the trip across the plateau to the western foothills. Separated from the herd, they would be particularly vulnerable to ravagers, smaller ones as well as the larger ones.

They could wait until the dreadrunners left, and then work their way down the ravine to the coastal plain. There would be plenty of food on the coastal plain, and fewer of the larger predators than at other times of the year. But they would be separated from their fellows. Pack or roam, they would both miss the camaraderie of their own kind. Besides, both were beginning to feel a biological urge that neither had ever experienced before. Both felt a compulsion to continue the westward trek to the ancient breeding grounds in the foothills.

So it was decided. They would leave the forest from the side furthest from the river. Then, using the terrain and the large outcroppings of rock as cover, they would work their way to the ravine wall. They would then hug the wall all the way up the ravine. If they went slowly and carefully, they could probably avoid detection by the dreadrunners on the other side of the river. Once on the plateau, they would just have to trust to their luck and skill to try to reach the herd safely.

Having decided, they determined to move expeditiously. If they got to the top of the ravine quickly enough, the pack defenders might still be there, blocking the exit. With all the noise that three hundred hadrosaurs made shaking the earth, the dreadrunner might be sufficiently distracted for the two of them to make a break for the line.

As if on cue, they heard a rumbling roar coming from the direction of the plateau. Apparently the retreating roam had come into view of the packers, and they had started the pounding in an attempt to frighten the female dreadrunner away. Panthrar smiled. One young female dreadrunner was no match for three hundred packers, and in time they would work up enough courage to attack her. If they got her surrounded, they would stab her with their horns, and club her to death with their broad tails. Then it would be easier for Panthrar and Pippit to get safely out of the ravine.

He shared this thought with Pippit. She did not seem as convinced as he that their troubles might soon be over. Thus engrossed, they made their way through the forest. At the edge, they looked in all directions to see if the way was clear. Panthrar looked up the ravine in anticipation of escaping their predicament. Pippit looked down the ravine. She moaned, elbowed Panthrar in the ribs, and then dropped silently to the ground.

CHAPTER FOUR
MIXED SIGNALS

DANDRAAR HAD JUST FOUND the tribal elders when all the commotion started. The grand chief, Eldooran, Herdmaster and Protector of the Vast Plains, both of which being completely ceremonial titles, sat on a mound by a watering hole with his two subchiefs, Zurgott and Adeldraar. Eldooran, a heavy old male, four tons at least, and 25 springs old, was also roamleader of the White Fern Roam. He was 38.5 feet long, and had a long and unusually thick horn. The horn was as long as Grendaar's, a good 16 inches long, but because it was so thick, it actually looked shorter.

Zurgott, roamleader of the Dragonfly Roam, was rather young and trim in comparison, being only 19 springs old, and 3.7 tons in weight. He was over 37 feet long, with a 15 inch horn.

Adeldraar, roamleader of the Winding River Roam, seemed the most dignified of the trio, or at least might have except for his broken horn. He was the oldest, 27 springs old. Although he was younger than Grendaar, he looked older. He was thin, only 3.3 tons, while being 38 feet long. His horn should have been an impressive 15 inches long, but it had been broken many years ago in a dominance fight with Grendaar. What was left was ten inches long, and looked thin and brittle.

To Dandraar, they all looked old, very old. They sat on the mound in the midst of the largest combined roam that Dandraar had ever seen – almost four hundred adults, adolescents, youngsters, and yearlings. A dozen adult males sat with them, while dozens more ringed the roam. The elders sat placidly while their females engaged in their favorite pastime of exchanging the latest information, and their young frolicked before them. Some of the adolescents and the young drank at, or waded in, the watering hole.

All three chiefs carried badges of their high position. Eldooran had a large and beautifully colored shell. It lay before him, on the ground. It was unlike any that anyone had ever seen before. Legend had it that it was from the shore of the Desolate Isles themselves. It was very old, and rather fragile. That it was still whole was a tribute to the value that the tribe placed upon it. When Eldooran traveled, one or another of his adolescent males would walk along beside him, carrying it for him. It was a task accompanied by considerable honor.

Zurgott carried a beautiful bluish stone that some river current had worn a hole through the middle of. The stone lay before him, on the ground at his feet. He always carried it personally, not entrusting it to anyone.

Adeldraar carried a staff of wood. It was of a very special, very hard wood – eight feet long, and six inches thick. Designs had been carved into the wood. No one knew what the designs meant, but they were wonderful to behold none-the-less.

The shell, the stone, and the staff were ancient and valued treasures of the tribe. They had been handed down to chiefs and subchiefs for many generations, and were three of the most sacred symbols of the Red Dawn Tribe.

But Dandraar wasn't thinking of any of this at the moment. The eastern edge of the tribe was beginning to stir in agitation. Hooting and honking of warnings and challenges were coming from the packs at the top of the ravine, and already some of the young were beginning to worry.

Dandraar stood at the edge of the Chiefs Roam, debating whether or not he should turn around and return to his own roam as quickly as possible. While he debated with himself, Eldooran, his subchiefs, and all the males around them had sprung to their feet and were staring off in the direction of the ravine. "What is amiss?" cried Eldooran. "What is happening in the ravine?"

Dandraar decided that having come this far, he must complete his mission. To the adult male closest to him he yelled, "Make way for a message from Grendaar. Make way for a message from Grendaar."

This rewarded him with the immediate attention of all those around him, and an quick escort to the presence of the elders. An adult male lead him to an open space before the elders. As they watched him being lead before them, they and the lesser elders again sat down. All had quieted now. The females had stopped their conversations, and the young had stopped their frolicking.

Dandraar nodded deferentially several times. "May the sun warm you, Great Eldooran," Dandraar said to the herdmaster. "And may the sun warm you Great Zurgott, and you Great Adeldraar."

Suddenly he remembered that he had brought no offerings of food, as custom and politeness demanded. He was very embarrassed, but decided that circumstances were such that he might be excused for his blunder. He looked up at Eldooran on the mound, wondering how the great chief would react to his breach of etiquette.

"And may it warm you, my son," said Eldooran, in no way indicating that anything untoward had occurred. "What news do you bring from Grendaar, my brother, roamleader of the Green Water Roam? Does it have anything to do with the noise and worry that I see along the eastern flank of the tribe?"

"I am Dandraar, of the Green Water Roam," began the young male. "I bring to the tribe elders a message from Grendaar, roamleader. Grendaar sends his respects to you, Herdmaster, and to you, Stonekeeper, and to you, Staffholder."

"And you must return our respects to my brother, Grendaar," said Eldooran affably. There was not a hint of worry in his voice, even though the noise from the eastern flank of the tribe was increasing in volume.

Dandraar bowed in acknowledgement, and continued with his message. "Grendaar says that he believes that ravagers are ascending the ravine, following the trail of the Great Eastern Herd. He says that he believes that it is wisdom to begin the trek immediately, rather than wait one more day. He respectfully requests that you begin the trek at once."

Consternation met Dandraar's news. While Eldooran's attention never wavered, Zurgott and many of the lesser elders were no longer looking at Dandraar. Even before he had finished his message, they had risen and turned to stare off in the direction of the ravine. They were trying to assess the seriousness of the threat, but it was too far away for them to see anything of import.

When Dandraar was finished, Zurgott said to no one in particular, "If ravagers are close at hand, it would indeed be wise to move westerly."

"Grendaar is old and half blind," commented Adeldraar.

"Grendaar is stationed close to the ravine," noted a lesser elder. "He would be in an excellent position to know."

"Grendaar is notorious for seeing ravagers in his own shadows," added Adeldraar.

Dandraar bristled at the insults that the Staffholder was directing at his roamleader, insults he knew would never have been spoken if Grendaar were here himself. But Dandraar kept his own council, knowing that to speak out while the elders debated would be an utter breach of good manners. It would be especially bad to argue with one of the elders, since he was only an adolescent, and had no real standing yet. Only an adult had the right to do that. Instead he watched in silence.

Zurgott turned and faced Adeldraar. "Something obviously is causing a stir along our eastern flank. What do you propose Adeldraar, my brother? Waiting until a ravager is snapping at your illustrious tail?" This got a few honks of approval.

Adeldraar fumed, and grasping his staff tightly in his left hand, shook it at Zurgott. "You puffed up young sky-gazer, uhhh," he stammered. Several of the lesser elders grumbled and glared at Zurgott. Tails switched aggressively.

Dandraar had never seen such overt impoliteness except on such occasions, when council-members spoke to one another. Eldooran finally intervened, saying, "Now, now, my brothers, this is no time to bicker." He surveyed all the council-members with a stern face and a deep frown, making sure they knew he was serious. Then he turned to Adeldraar, and asked, "Adeldraar, my brother, do you have an alternate proposal?"

"Ummm, my brother," mused the Staffholder, "We could send someone to the ravine to confirm that there is indeed a ravager there...."

The debate began anew. The majority seemed to be in favor of moving west, while a minority seemed to want to use this as an opportunity practice politics. Adeldraar, no friend of Grendaar's, was using this as yet one more chance to undermine his rival. Dandraar was astounded that the debate was taking place at all, since the apparent proof of Grendaar's premonitions seemed to be reflected in the rising volumes of hooting and honking coming from the eastern side of the tribe.

Suddenly the packers at the top of the ravine began to pound the ground with their tails. This was an ominous sign. There was a pause in the deliberations. Dandraar stepped forward, bowed low, and said, "Excuse me Great Ones, but my roamleader has commanded me to return to the roam at once, if the ravagers attacked in my absence. It sounds to me like something momentous is happening, and I must return to my roam. May I be excused?"

A roamleader's commands were law, and no one would think of asking a subordinate to disobey them. Such an issue could only be taken up directly with the roamleader, himself. Since he wasn't here, no one could argue with his dictates to his own subordinate.

Eldooran signaled for silence. "Does anyone have any further questions of this adolescent?" Virtually everyone had seemed to have forgotten that Dandraar was even there until he had spoken up. Now no one seemed to have anything further to say to him. Eldooran looked down upon him in an almost fatherly fashion. "Thank you, my son, for bringing us this useful, but disturbing information. You are excused, and may return to your roam. Give Grendaar, my brother, my respects."

Dandraar did not wait to hear more. He bowed, and then turned and sped away in the direction of his roam.

As he moved eastward, he saw increasing agitation amongst the People. Many were standing on knolls, or ridges, or mounds, or any other high ground that they could find, and were staring off towards the east. Some roams were already moving slowly westward, not needing any greater excuse than the mere hint of a ravager on their flank. Others were indecisive, and Dandraar could see dominant males arguing with each other about the best course of action to take. He did not catch much of it though, he was in too much of a hurry to get back to his roam.

*   *   *   *   *

With the mounting volume of noise coming from the packs at the top of the ravine, Grendaar decided that he must not wait any longer to move. He signaled to Renthot, and the Yellow Mud Roam began to form up and move toward the Green Water Roam. At another sign from Grendaar, Tessah, and Monah, and Koowoo, the First, Second, and Third Females of the Green Water Roam, circled up their charges. Yearlings and youngsters took the center. Adult and adolescent females formed a ring around the young. Thus they began to move towards the west.

The adult males of the Green Water Roam, much fewer in number than the females, stayed on the knolls, waiting for the Yellow Mud Roam to merge with the Green Water Roam. The adult and adolescent males of the Yellow Mud Roam would join with the adult males of the Green Water Roam, and try to form a defensive line.

The Green Water Roam moved at a leisurely pace towards the west. The Yellow Mud Roam moved somewhat more briskly, so as to catch up to the other roam. Grendaar stood on the northern knoll, along with Kinput and the three other solitaries. He had sent Rohraar and Hew, the Fifth Male of the roam, to join Wubbar, the Fourth Male, on the southern knoll. Meanwhile, Trugahr, as Third Male, by custom took over leadership of the retrcating roam. Custom demanded that Trugahr stay with the roam no matter what happened, until relieved by his roamleader. Death was the only legitimate excuse that a Third Male had for leaving a roam leaderless.

The Green Water Roam, with the Yellow Mud Roam trailing it, began to weave around some of the other roams. As Trugahr passed less decisive males, he advised them to take up the trek at once. Some heeded his advice, some didn't.

*   *   *   *   *

Panthrar looked down at Pippit, squatting behind some flowering dogwoods that grew at the edge of the small conifer forest. She was doing her best to blend into her hiding place. She looked up at him and signaled danger with the muscles around her eyes, then she turned and stared through the dogwoods down the ravine.

Panthrar followed her stare. About a half of a mile away, just clearing a large outcropping of granitic rock on their side of the river, was an adult female dreadrunner. This one looked to be larger than the others. She was 26 or 27 feet long, and over two tons in weight. She was trotting at a slow pace near the edge of the river. Her attention seemed to be directed towards Gnarled-paw, feeding on the other side.

Panthrar slowly and quietly sank to his knees beside Pippit. If the dreadrunner noticed them, it was very likely that one of them would be dead within a matter of minutes. A shudder, unbeckoned, went through him. Pippit was shaking almost uncontrollably. He had to save her. He had to save them both. He considered his options.

If they made a break for it, there was an outside chance that they might be able to stay ahead of the dreadrunner until they got to the top of the ravine. Then they would be in the relative safety of an army of packers. If they could get started unseen, which seemed likely, their chances would be better. But dreadrunners were fast under any circumstances, and very fast for short distances. It was more likely that she would catch the slower of the two before they could get to the top. Panthrar gazed upon Pippit. He could not bear the thought of those cruel, hot fangs burying themselves into her soft neck. He would have to trail behind her to make sure she escaped.

He considered another possibility. Perhaps they could wait quietly here, and hope that the dreadrunner wouldn't discover them. Once she had passed, perhaps they could then make good an escape. This was risky, since dreadrunners have excellent eyesight, keen senses of smell, and very acute hearing. Their only hope was that the spoor of thousands of hornbrows was still so overwhelming in the ravine, that she wouldn't be able to pick up their individual scents. The plan to ascend the ravine, however, even if this dreadrunner passed them by, would never work if the ravager stayed on this side of the river.

Panthrar wasn't sure what to do. He leaned closer to Pippit. The contact of his huge body against hers seemed to give her some comfort. Her shivering grew less violent.

They watched the dreadrunner make her way up the ravine. This one's stripes seemed to be more intense than usual. She was staring fixedly at the young male dreadrunner across the river. The young male was still happily consuming his prey, unaware that Stripes was so close. Suddenly the large female stopped. Her head darted back and forth several times, and then she remained perfectly still. The breathing of the two hidden hornbrows stopped also, but their hearts raced on.

Gnarled-paw rose from his kill, and stared up the ravine for a moment. It was as if he half expected to see the young female dreadrunner, Long-tail, coming back to challenge him for his kill. He then glanced back at Red-patch, the dozing male, near the boulders below him. Red-patch seemed dead to the world. Gnarled-paw looked down at the carcass at his feet for a long time. He then leaned down and grabbed it between his jaws, and tried to haul it towards the ravine wall. It was still too large for him to handle easily, and the going was slow.

The large female dreadrunner flared her nostrils. She sniffed tentatively. Her head darted back and forth several more times. Then slowly, and with exceptional care and patience, she began a slow, stalking walk up the ravine towards the ford. When Gnarled-paw was struggling more than usual with the carcass, she quickened her pace. Whenever he stopped to check up and down the ravine, Stripes would freeze. For whatever reason, Gnarled-paw never gave much of his attention to the other side of the river.

Meanwhile, the larger ravager passed from the view of Panthrar and Pippit as she moved between the forest and the river. Pippit began to shake uncontrollably again. Panthrar felt very uncomfortable himself. It was one thing to watch the predator stalking something else. But now they couldn't see her at all. What if the stalking had been a charade, and she was really after them the whole time? Dreadrunners could be pretty tricky. What if Stripes was sneaking through the forest right now? Panthrar had to fight down an almost overwhelming urge to make a break for the top of the ravine. To do so now would be tantamount to suicide. Pippit stirred. He felt certain that she was about to bolt. He nuzzled his head against hers, placing his lips close to her ear.

"Stay quiet, my sister," he said very gently. "It is our only hope. Have no fear. If the ravager finds us, I will fight her."

She closed her eyes, and lay her head on the ground. She did not move again, except for an occasional shudder.

"Stay here, I'll be back shortly," he added.

A low moan escaped her lips, but she did not open her eyes.

He arose as quietly as he could, and turned toward the river. Making his way through the evergreen forest, his head still darted in every direction, alert for a possible ambush. He stepped carefully, trying to avoid fallen twigs, and trying to step on patches of needles. For the most part, the forest was carpeted with moss, ferns, and thick layers of pine-straw. He used this soft flooring to move cautiously to the side of the forest facing the river.

It seemed like an eternity, but he finally came to a place where he could see the female dreadrunner through the dogwoods and berry bushes growing along the edge of the woods. She was about halfway across the ford. The well-fed, unalert Gnarled-paw still was not aware of her presence. Panthrar wondered how close she would get before Gnarled-paw finally discovered her. He did not have to wonder much longer.

From down the ravine, came a soft but clear, high-pitched roar. The sound of it was horripilating, and sent waves of shudders rippling up and down Panthrar's back. Almost in unison he and Gnarled-paw turned to see what had made the noise. Stripes did not turn. Instead she roared a challenge calculated to unnerve the young male, and charged.

Panthrar, who had looked downriver along with Gnarled-paw, had difficulty catching everything that happened next. The roar of the female made him jump almost a foot off the ground, so unexpected, so close, and so terrifying was it. Down the ravine, he saw that a small, yearling dreadrunner had appeared from behind the same outcropping that the adult female had. Panthrar realized that Stripes wasn't surprised by the high-pitched roar, because she knew that her impatient offspring had made it. But she used the distraction, and her own deep-throated roar, in the hopes that it would confuse Gnarled-paw long enough to decide the issue in her favor.

As it was, she hopped from one flat rock to another, the rest of the way across the river, and then ran at a frightful rate towards Gnarled-paw. Red-patch, dozing by the defile with his own unfinished kill, leapt to his feet without knowing the exact cause for alarm, and began snapping and hissing in all directions.

Gnarled-paw, who before the interruption had still been struggling with the carcass, was caught in the opening with his only-partially devoured kill. He saw the large female bearing down on him. Standing over the kill, he opened his large, gaping mouth, bared his numerous saber-like teeth, and roared back a threat.

The female never slackened her charge. She ran straight for Gnarled-paw, leapt over the kill, and smashed into his chest with the force of a tidal wave. The impact bowled him over, and he and the female tumbled over each other, snapping and hissing. They bit and raked each other with tooth and claw as they tumbled. Jaws snapped like steel springs, powerful hind legs lashed and kicked viciously, and even the tiny forepaws clawed and scratched. It is difficult to imagine anything more ferocious and deadly than two dreadrunners fighting each other.

They rolled to a stop, and hastily disentangled themselves. They both scrambled to their feet as quickly as they could, and began circling each other. Stripes let lose another horrific roar. Gnarled-paw roared back an equally impressive response.

Stripes darted forward, striking at Gnarled-paw's right shoulder. Gnarled-paw sprang backwards, just barely avoiding the female's jaws. The young male circled rapidly around to the right, hoping to place himself between the carcass and the female. She anticipated him, and moved more quickly. Now she stood between Gnarled-paw and his kill. In frustration, he charged directly at her. She snapped her huge jaws at him, hissing with each backward step he forced her to take. He charged again, and this time she met him full on. Their jaws snapped and darted at each other, as each hoped to find an opening and sink their fangs into their opponent.

Hisss-snap, a massive pair of jaws sought to close upon its adversary. Hisss-snap. Hisss-snap. The sounds echoed through the ravine. Red-patch watched the battle from his position at the defile. Occasionally he would nudge his kill deeper into the defile with one of his muscular hind legs, but he never took his eyes away from the conflict.

The yearling dreadrunner raced up the ravine to the ford that he had watched his mother cross. He ran right past Panthrar's hiding place in the process. He slowed as he passed the spot where Panthrar hid, and glanced in Panthrar's direction. Panthrar thought that he was well hidden, and didn't move a muscle. He hoped that it was only chance that had caused the dreadrunner to look in his direction. The young dreadrunner then picked up his pace, until he stopped at the ford. There he waited, jumping about excitedly, roaring and hissing all the while, watching while his mother fought Gnarled-paw.

Panthrar realized that he and Pippit would never get a better chance to make their escape than now. All the ravagers in sight were watching the struggle over the remains of the poor female ridgebrow. Panthrar hurried back through the forest, being careful not to attract the attention of the yearling ravager. He found Pippit huddled where he had left her.

"Come, my sister, this is our chance for escape. The ravagers are fighting each other over who will possess the ridgebrow. Let us race to the ravine wall while we have this opportunity."

At first Pippit wouldn't move. With some urging, he got her to her feet. He pushed her towards the wall. Once up and moving, she veritably flew to the wall, Panthrar only a few steps behind her. Near the wall, they ducked behind some rock outcropping. They both looked back and inspected the ravine behind them to see if they had made it this far undetected. With the forest blocking their view of the dreadrunners, not a ravager was in sight.

Meanwhile, Gnarled-paw feinted to the left, then feinted to the right, and then leapt straight at the female. She took several steps backward, then leapt to the left, avoiding the lashing teeth of the young male, as still in mid-air, he swung his outstretched jaws in her direction. Snap-snap. Stripes stayed just out of the reach of Gnarled-paw's deadly jaws, then she launched herself at his flank and buried her teeth into his right shoulder. Gnarled-paw screamed in rage and pain. His roar was so load that the packs at the top of the ravine heard it over their own thumping, and many shuddered.

Panthrar also heard the cries of pain and rage, and although the roars made his knees feel like jelly, he used them as his cue to move. He and Pippit rushed up the ravine to the next shoulder of rock that offered cover. The conifer forest still obstructed the view of the ravagers, so he decided to make a rush for the next hiding place, a group of tumbled boulders lying near the ravine wall. As quickly and as quietly as possible for creatures weighing more than two tons each, they sprinted for the boulders.

While the two hornbrows tried to make their escape up the ravine, the two ravagers were clenched in combat. Gnarled-paw rolled to his left, dragging the female off balance. She loosened her grip on him as she fought to stay upright, allowing Gnarled-paw to pull himself loose. He stumbled, but kept his footing. Blood spurted from his wound. He ignored the blood and the pain. They circled again. This time Gnarled-paw was more cautious.

At the fallen boulders, Panthrar looked back, while Pippit huddled to catch her breath. Now the conifer forest was no longer between them and the ravagers. Panthrar could see the fight still being waged in the distance. He looked back up the ravine. One more dash and they would be around the curve in the ravine, and out of a direct line of sight of the ravagers. He and Pippit raced for the next cover.

Stripes charged Gnarled-paw. Gnarled-paw rolled to the left, lashing at her with the talons of his left hind foot. He gashed her across her right knee. She screamed and jumped back. Gnarled-paw scrambled to his feet. The female charged again, snapping center, left, right, center, left, right –

forcing Gnarled-paw backwards, further and further from his kill. Stripes nipped Gnarled-paw's right fore-paw by chance, and Gnarled-paw yelped and retreated several paces. He looked down at his gnarled and now bleeding paw, and then up at the female. He roared horribly, and backed up a few more paces. Stripes seemed content to hold her ground. Gnarled-paw examined his paw again. He snapped and hissed at the female a few more times. Then he began to slowly back away from the scene of combat.

Stripes watched until he was several hundred yards away, then she turned and walked back to the kill, her back to Gnarled-paw. She stooped and took a mouthful from the carcass. As she gulped down the meat, she looked back over her shoulder at Gnarled-paw. He stood watching her, occasionally licking his right fore-paw. After a while he turned silently, and made his way up the ravine, never again looking back.

Stripes now completely ignored Gnarled-paw, or at least seemed to. Periodically she would glance over at Red-patch. Each time she did, Red-patch would open his gaping mouth, showing her how well-armed he was. Once or twice they exchanged hisses. Otherwise, she ignored Red-patch also.

Gnarled-paw, working his way up the ravine, did not notice Panthrar and Pippit on the other side of the river. They were well ahead of him by now, and doing their best to stay out of his line of sight.

It wasn't until Gnarled-paw was completely out of her sight, and around the curve in the ravine, that Stripes signaled to her cub to cross the river. Then she stopped eating, stood up to her full height, and stared at Red-patch as if daring him to make even one overt move towards her cub.

Red-patch was content to protect his own kill. The yearling crossed the river, and joined his mother. They devoured the carcass with obvious relish. Red-patch again lay down beside his kill, watching the two satisfy themselves with remains of the female ridgebrow.

CHAPTER FIVE
RETREAT

A LEISURELY PACE HAD BEEN set to help keep the youngsters and yearlings from panicking unnecessarily. Trugahr lead the procession around roams still preparing to withdraw. Tessah walked beside him. Monah had originally taken a position in the rear of the roam, as was her responsibility as Second Female. But now that the Green Water Roam and the Yellow Mud Roam had mingled together, she realized that she would have ended up in the middle of the latter roam. So she took a flanking position to the left of both roams instead. Jedraar, Third Male of the Yellow Mud Roam, took a rear-guard position behind both roams. Jedraar was nine springs old and a little larger than Trugahr. He was 32 feet long, three and a half tons in weight, and had a thirteen inch horn.

The noise and tumult arising from the packers at the top of the ravine seemed to be reaching a crescendo. Trugahr had noticed before leading the two roams to the west that over three hundred packers had gathered at the ravine. That many hornbrows could make quite a din if they wanted to. Apparently they wanted to.

Something very disturbing must be happening back there, thought Trugahr, otherwise the packers would have tended to take a watch-and-wait attitude rather than making all that racket. What he didn't know at the time was that the young and the females of the roam of ridgebrows had come charging around the curve in the ravine. The younger ones were exhausted from their headlong flight, and from the abject fear that such a close encounter with a ravager often brings. Many were stumbling repeatedly, and some did not want to go any further, regardless of the consequences.

The surprised packers were honking their encouragement. Almost a hundred of them hurried down the ravine to escort the ridgebrows back up. Fortunately for the young, who were still panic-stricken, they thought they were being rescued by a herd of protecting ridgebrows, not the less familiar hornbrows, so they didn't scatter and make things worse.

Some time later, the retreating male ridgebrows and hornbrows came up the ravine. Again the packers set up a din of encouragement, and again almost a hundred of them rushed down to reinforce the retreat.

Trugahr wondered if the packers had spotted a ravager. It sounded like it. It must have been premonition that made him think that, or maybe it was just the packers' predictable behavior. Whatever it was that made Trugahr wonder about the appearance of a ravager, was answered by the distant, but unmistakable roar of one. Judging from the volume and direction of the roar, it came from near the top of the ravine. What Trugahr heard, was Long-tail pursuing, somewhat cautiously, the retreating male ridgebrows and hornbrows. Her roar was in surprise and frustration to learn that an army of hornbrows awaited her at the top of the ravine.

Trugahr turned to check his charges. He could see panic on the faces of the yearlings, and only slightly less distress on those of the more tender youngsters. The roar of a ravager often did that, even to adult hornbrows. If the young hadn't been surrounded by adult and adolescent females, they might have bolted.

He noticed that Tessah was carefully watching him. "Tessah, my elder sister," he said to her, "circle the roams around to the north. Keep them going in that direction until I return."

He gestured towards a nearby rise. "I am going to that rise over there to see if I can find out what is going on. If a stampede starts, it will be safer towards the north... more room to run."

She looked towards the north, and then glanced at the rise that he had indicated. She seemed unhappy that he was not staying closer to the roam. "Yes, younger brother."

As the two roams moved off towards the north, carefully working their way around other roams still heading towards the west, Trugahr trotted over to the rise. He advised Jedraar of his intent, placing him in temporary charge, as he passed him on his way to the rise.

Even before Trugahr got to the rise, he could see that things were changing in the herd. There was little hesitation or debate about whether or not the tribe should be moving towards the foothills. If there was any disagreement at all, it was about how fast it should be done. In fact, while some groups were still moving sedately, many more were hurrying away.

Trugahr ascended the low rise, but could not get a clear picture of what was happening near the ravine. He heard the ravager roar horribly again and again. Many answering hoots came from the packers.

There were still a number of adult males clustered on ridges and knolls and other high points – all observing the goings-on at the top of the ravine. Trugahr could see both Grendaar and his solitaries, along with Renthot and some of his males, standing on Grendaar's knoll. Rohraar and the rest of both roam's other males, were standing on Rohraar's knoll. They, like many others, were keeping a close watch on the packers. Periodically, the packers would signal reports to the males on the nearby high spots. From these, and from what they could see, they could assess the level of danger to the herd.

Grendaar was waiting on his knoll with his rear-guard, waiting for the roams to get further away from the ravine, and further away from the threat of the danger contained therein. He saw the ridgebrows arrive at the top of the ravine: first the young and females, and then the males and hornbrow scouts. He also watched as the ridgebrows, mourning the loss of their two females, hastened westward with the retreating herd of hornbrows.

While Grendaar watched, the packers began a renewed round of hooting and honking. The ravager that Grendaar knew to be at the top of the ravine, although he could not see it because of the hundreds of packers blocking his view, began to roar in response. Suddenly a lot of agitation became apparent among the packers. Those on the right side of the river, where the majority had congregated to block the ravager, suddenly began a hasty crossing of the river to the left side. Some crossed at fords, while many others splashed into the cool water and swam rapidly towards the other side. Grendaar was certain that the ravager was crossing the river downstream, and in full sight of the packers. He was also certain that the packers were responding to again block its forward progress.

Grendaar turned and looked in Trugahr's general direction, checking on the status of the roams' retreat. Trugahr waved to Grendaar, attracting his attention. Grendaar waved back. Grendaar then said something to Renthot, and he and several other males also turned to observe Trugahr.

Trugahr communicated with Grendaar through a series of guttural hoots and honks. He used a deep, low-frequency honk to avoid confusion with the other hooting and honking going on all over the plain. He added to these a combination of hand signals and body positions, as well as simple pointing. In this manner, Trugahr advised Grendaar not only that the roams had turned north, but of their exact position and precise direction of travel.

Grendaar acknowledged the message, and passed along information that he had received from the packers at the ravine. He did this using the same low-frequency honk that the other had used. Grendaar also told Trugahr to keep the roams traveling north for the time being. Then Grendaar returned his attention to the ravine, the place that had occupied his attention for most of the day.

Trugahr looked back at the slowly retreating roams. Tessah and Jedraar, both walking at the rear of the group, were looking over their shoulders at him. He signaled to them that all was well, and that they were to continue north. He would give them the details later. They acknowledged. Tessah then trotted to the head of the roams, encouraging the young with a gentle, "Come my children, let us not dawdle", as she went.

As Trugahr prepared to follow after the roams, he heard his name called. He turned towards the west to see an excited Dandraar running towards him.

"Trugahr, elder brother, may the sun warm you," cried Dandraar happily.

"And may the sun warm you, younger brother. I am happy to see that you have returned safely," responded Trugahr.

"Where is the roam?" asked Dandraar. "Where is the Groundshaker? I must report to him."

"The roam is there," said Trugahr, pointing to the north. "And the Groundshaker is there," he continued, pointing to the east.

"Oh," said Dandraar. He had not expected this complication.

"Stay with me, younger brother. We will go to the roam. Help me protect it. You can report to the Groundshaker later."

"Okay," agreed Dandraar, clearly disappointed. He was excited after his adventure. He didn't get a chance to speak directly to the herdmaster very often. He had wanted to report to Grendaar all that had transpired, all that he had seen and heard, since he had been sent on his mission.

Trugahr glanced back at Grendaar one more time. He watched as Grendaar, apparently as an after-thought, signaled to Rohraar to take his company and follow after the roams. Rohraar and the half dozen males with him sauntered down the knoll and headed towards Trugahr.

Trugahr felt considerably relieved that reinforcements would soon be with him to help protect the roams. He always disliked this kind of an assignment, being the only adult male left to protect the roam. Having Jedraar draw the same assignment hadn't been much consolation. Ravagers weren't the only things he would have had to have protected the roam from, especially during the breeding season. Not with so many eligible females. Not wishing to leave anything to chance, he turned to Dandraar and said, "Stay here, younger brother, and wait for Rohraar. When he joins you, direct him to the roams. I will go back and rejoin the roams now."

"Yes, elder brother," responded Dandraar as he stared first at Rohraar's approaching group, then at the roams retreating northward, and then back towards Grendaar.

"Elder brother, may I ask you a favor?" he asked Trugahr.

"What is it, younger brother?" Trugahr answered impatiently.

"May I wait here on the rise until Grendaar comes to join the roam?"

Trugahr smiled inwardly. It was evident to everyone in the roam that Dandraar adored Grendaar.

"It is an agreeable request, younger brother. But make sure that Rohraar approves of it."

"Thank you, elder brother."

"You are welcome, younger brother."

With that, Trugahr scampered down the rise, and after the roams.

*   *   *   *   *

Panthrar and Pippit knew that the young female, Long-tail, was somewhere ahead of them. Hopefully she was on the other side of the river. They also knew that at least four other ravagers were behind them: Red-patch, Gnarled-paw, Stripes, and Stripes' cub. Again they hoped that all four of the ravagers were on the other side of the river.

Panthrar recollected that Stripes' cub had looked directly at him when he was hiding in the forest. Had the cub seen him? If so, it was possible that one or more of the ravagers behind them could be pursuing them at this very moment. Perhaps Stripes' cub hadn't seen him hiding in the forest. Even if he had, perhaps he wouldn't bother to tell his mother that more prey was nearby. Perhaps they both were no longer hungry, and it wouldn't matter anyway.

Panthrar was still pondering this as they negotiated the curve in the ravine. Before they had even reached the curve, and before they could see the packers at the top of the ravine, the thumping had stopped. Panthrar hoped that it meant that the packers had killed Long-tail.

He and Pippit still hung close to the ravine wall, using every bit of cover they could find. As they reached the curve, they rounded it very carefully. The top of the ravine was still a considerable distance away, and it was difficult to see clearly what was going on up there. It looked like hundreds of packers were either on their side of the river, or were wading or swimming in the water, crossing to their side. Maybe this was why the pounding had stopped. The packers were changing sides of the river. Panthrar expected them to be on the other side, the side that the ridgebrows had ascended, and the side that Long-tail climbed up in pursuit of them. There seemed to be only about fifty or so packers on that side of the river.

Since this wasn't what Panthrar expected, he and Pippit decided to continue to climb the ravine cautiously. They moved from cover to cover, and inspected the terrain before each mad dash to the next group of boulders or columns of outcroppings. They also kept scouting the terrain behind them, and across the river, to reduce the possibility of being surprised by a ravager.

After they had come about a third of the way up the ravine past the curve, they stopped to rest. Panthrar used the opportunity to get a better look at the ravine floor ahead of them. This had not always been possible, as they were moving up the ravine, since the floor was scattered with boulders and outcroppings, as well as clumps of tall vegetation. At each stopping point, they got a slightly different perspective on what lay ahead of them.

Panthrar stretched up on his hind legs, and peered over the top of a large rock. He finally saw Long-tail. She was on their side of the river. She apparently had crossed it at some point during her ascent, or after she had arrived at the top. This explained why most of the packers were now on this side of the river. They had moved to block Long-tail.

Long-tail was strutting back and forth along the line of the defenders, hissing and snapping, and periodically making aggressive, charging motions. But she still refused to actually come to grips with the line of defenders. As fearsome as a ravager is to the People, and as inconsequential as a sole hornbrow is to a ravager, several hundred determined young packers make a mighty intimidating obstacle. The packers were all facing the ravager, hooting threats and challenges, and daring her to be so foolish as to come within range of their horns and their tails.

Panthrar told Pippit what he had seen. They both knew that they were in a very bad situation at the moment. They could not continue up the ravine much further without risking being discovered by Long-tail. On the other hand, if they did not find a good hiding place, and soon, they might be spotted by one of the other ravagers ascending the ravine behind them.

They decided that they should immediately seek a better place to hide. Panthrar examined the ravine wall from where they presently sheltered. He saw that a little way up the ravine, some large boulders had tumbled off the wall, and were lying close to it. From where they hid, it looked like the boulders formed a large inverted "U", with a bit of open area behind the boulders. It looked like enough space for them to move about in. From this distance, it seemed to Panthrar like a little grove, almost surrounded by rocks, some weather-worn, some still sharp-edged. It was a natural place in which they could hide. It looked like it offered screening from both up and down the ravine, and could only be distinguished from the actual wall of the ravine if you stood close to it. Pippit agreed that it would make an ideal hiding place.

They waited until Long-tail was strutting in the opposite direction, then they made a dash for the little grove. Some of the packers saw them make the dash, but Long-tail did not. Word began to spread among the packers that Panthrar and Pippit, whom most feared had been killed by the same ravagers that had gotten the adolescent ridgebrows, were safe. The packers watched as the two adolescent hornbrows raced up the ravine. Some of the packers honked even louder and longer than usual, and even made overt charges at the ravager, to help keep her distracted. They were rewarded to see Panthrar and Pippit disappear behind a cluster of boulders.

Pippit and Panthrar didn't know this at the time. They scurried into their hiding place, and caught their breath. Very cautiously they peeked from behind the screen of boulders to see if they had been spotted. Long-tail's attention was still directed at the packers blocking her way. Panthrar and Pippit looked at each other and smiled. It seemed that they were safe for the time being.

Panthrar turned his attention in the other direction. He surveyed the curve down the ravine. He had heard the ravagers roaring earlier, but quiet had reigned for a while. He wondered if Stripes had defeated Gnarled-paw, or if Gnarled-paw had successfully defended his kill. Even as he speculated on the results of the recent combat, Gnarled-paw came into view, trotting up the ravine.

CHAPTER SIX
ATTACK

As ROHRAAR AND HIS companions approached the rise upon which Dandraar sat, the adolescent sprang to his feet and hurried forward to meet them. They greeted each other in the fashion of the People. Then Dandraar gave information to Rohraar, the ranking male of the group, on the present whereabouts of the two roams. Dandraar also asked if he could wait on the rise for Grendaar, and accompany the roamleader back to the roam. Rohraar, knowing the adolescent's affection for the Ancient One, gave his permission. Then Rohraar and his group headed towards the roams, while Dandraar went back to the top of the rise to await Grendaar.

Grendaar, meanwhile, waited on his knoll. He now believed that a rearguard action would no longer be necessary, and that it would be best if the males returned to their roams. He shared this thought with Renthot, who agreed with him, and ordered all the remaining males back to the roams.

Grendaar took this opportunity to thank Kinput and the other solitaries for their help, and released them from their offer of assistance. He shared with Kinput that it still would be appreciated if they continued to travel in the vicinity of the roams. He offered that Kinput and the other solitaries might also find that pleasant. Grendaar couldn't actually offer that they travel with the roams, he could only suggest that they travel in the vicinity of them, as that would otherwise create hierarchal problems. It was also generally something that solitary males preferred not to do. Living with roams was just too constraining for them. This notwithstanding, Kinput and Sevren agreed to travel near the roams. Gaffstar and Tanmont declined the offer, and instead decided to head directly west after the retreating Great Eastern Herd, and rejoin the Red Dawn Tribe.

Now, Grendaar thought, all the males of the two roams, with the exception of the two roamleaders themselves, and the two missing adolescent males from the Green Water Roam, would soon be back protecting the roams. This gave him comfort. In addition, two male solitaries would also be traveling in the vicinity of the roams, offering additional help. Grendaar reasoned that this provided agreeable protection for the two roams.

Meanwhile, although he would not express it to anyone, he still worried about the two missing adolescents. He still hadn't heard that Panthrar had been seen and was safe, hidden in the ravine. And he still wasn't aware that Dandraar was sitting on a hillock only a half of a mile behind him.

Renthot demurred at Grendaar's suggestion that he too return to the roams. Renthot had decided to stay with Grendaar. And Grendaar had decided to keep an eye on the activities at the mouth of the ravine for a while longer, to assure that no belated threat faced the roam, or the herd. He also hoped that Panthrar would yet show up, safe from the dangers of the ravager in the ravine.

Even as he stood there, thinking of Panthrar, a packer at the ravine signaled a message to him. The message was a happy one. Panthrar and Pippit, an adolescent female packer traveling with Panthrar, had been seen safe and in hiding down the ravine. Grendaar pawed the ground with his left hand, smiling to himself. The roam would be safe for the time being, under the guidance of Rohraar. Grendaar would wait a while longer, and greet Panthrar when he escaped from the ravine.

* * * * *

Gnarled-paw hurried his pace when he saw that Long-tail was blocked on the other side of the river by a small herd of soldier hornbrows. He and Long-tail had traveled and hunted together ever since they had formed a lasting bond in the nest of their mother. They had great affection for each other. They always shared their kill.

For some reason, this time, Long-tail had become too excited by the chase itself, and hadn't bothered to stay with Gnarled-paw. Harassing ridgebrows all the way up the ravine had become a game, an end in itself. Now, as he hugged the wall of the ravine, his occasional glimpses of the mass of hornbrows at the top of the ravine told him that she might not get a meal at all. If she wasn't careful, the hornbrows might accomplish something that almost never happened – the trapping and killing of a ravager. There were certainly enough of them, and if she got herself cornered, she might live just long enough to regret it. He decided that his reckless sister needed help.

He darted from boulder to boulder, working his way up the ravine without being discovered by the packers. Panthrar and Pippit had seen him almost immediately, but they couldn't advise the packers without the possibility of giving away their position, a potentially disastrous act. Gnarled-paw got most of the way up the ravine before he had to make his presence known. When the packers finally saw him, he let out a blood-curdling roar. Long-tail roared back, and then quickly ran to the river to cross and join him.

The packers were not happy to see another ravager, especially on the other side of the river. As soon as he was discovered, about a hundred packers started to cross back over to the other side of the river in an attempt to block him. Then, when Long-tail started crossing the river to join Gnarled-paw, yet another hundred started across to help those already trying to re-group on the right side. There just weren't enough places to easily ford the river. And swimming was a slow process in the swollen, turbulent current. Yet many others were swimming, in addition to those wading across at the fords, trying to get across as fast as possible. It was going to be difficult for the packers to get a sufficient number in place in time to block two ravagers.

Gnarled-paw broke into a run as he neared the top of the ravine. He passed Long-tail as she worked her way across the river. He sprinted for some daylight where the packers' defensive line was the weakest, and broke into the ranks of the packers before they could close them up. Some of the packers fled as Gnarled-paw, roaring and hissing, ran amuck amongst them. Others tried to re-group and head him off. Still others did their best to cross the river before Long-tail got across. If she beat them across, matters would deteriorate beyond their ability to repair.

Gnarled-paw avoided attacking any one packer – it would have consumed too much time. He also avoided charging any group of packers greater than a dozen or so – they might actually stand and try to fight him. Instead, he limited himself to rushing about at groups of three or four, forcing them to scatter. He seemed intent on keeping the packers from forming a group large enough to actually threaten either him or Long-tail, at least until Long-tail could join up with him.

From a distance, this tactic was not readily apparent. Instead, the running hornbrows, with an occasional glimpse of a ravager, looked more like some wild melee, without any discernable pattern. This is what Grendaar and Renthot saw, as did dozens of other dominant males watching from the nearby high points. It was clear that the situation at the top of the ravine was turning sour, but the extent of the problem was not yet visible. If it had been, the adult males would have joined the packers to try and repulse the ravagers.

Even so, Grendaar was becoming certain that the ravagers would eventually break out of the ravine. He noted this to Renthot. Renthot stared toward the ravine and the melee for a considerable time. There was no defensive line on the right side of the river, and the packers for the most part seemed to be in constant, agitated motion. Long-tail was far enough down the ravine at the moment, that both Renthot and Grendaar could see her crossing the river to Gnarled-paw's side. From their position on the knoll, it was also clear that Long-tail would cross the river well ahead of the majority of the packers. Renthot was certain that Grendaar was correct, but he suggested that they wait a while longer to see if the packers could salvage the situation. Grendaar would have preferred to act now, but he was patient enough that he could wait a while longer.

Meanwhile, the race across the river between Long-tail and the hundred packers hoping to cut her off, was going against the packers. Long-tail had reached the right bank, and began her run to the top of the ravine to join with Gnarled-paw. There were barely a hundred packers in total to meet them. Only one group of packers was larger than ten, and it seemed that both ravagers avoided any group larger than five.

Yet it was not fear or an inability to cope with such a group of hornbrows that discouraged the ravagers. It was expediency. Taking on a group of five or ten hornbrows was both risky and time-consuming. The hornbrows might stand and fight, they might even try to wound the ravager, a potentially dangerous consequence. Yet a determined ravager would take that chance if necessary. On the other hand, why risk being wounded by a resolute hornbrow soldier, when there were so many panicky ones running around in fear of their lives, without any defensive organization whatever?

It probably would have taken a group of packers in the order of fifteen to twenty to successfully intimidate a hungry ravager. In the melee caused by Gnarled-paw, none that large had been able to form. And Long-tail was hungry. There were no organized groups large enough to oppose her. There seemed to be only wildly running packers, scampering this way and that, each packer trying to avoid the lethal fangs and claws of first the one, and now both ravagers.

As Long-tail charged into the packers, Gnarled-paw changed his tactics. Before he had been trying to chase, without actually making contact. Now he began attacking packers indiscriminately. He was not trying to kill, but he was trying to intimidate and discourage. Several packers were left bloodied but still mobile before the packers realized what was happening. Casualties started to limp away from the field of battle.

Long-tail managed to trip a young male, and got her massive jaws in a death grip on the back of his neck. He cried in pain and distress, and several groups of packers rushed to his aid. Gnarled-paw rushed to the defense of his sister.

The male packer shook and struggled, trying to break away from Long-tail. She wrestled and snorted, but she would not loosen her grip. Instead she kept tightening her hold, sinking her blade-like fangs deeper and deeper into her victim, while the packer slowly weakened.

Gnarled-paw joined the melee to help his sister. Hornbrow tails rained down on both Long-tail and Gnarled-paw. Long-tail was stabbed once or twice by eight or ten inch horns. She still refused to release the hornbrow. Gnarled-paw's teeth and claws raked right and left, trying to give Long-tail enough time to kill her victim. Long-tail also kicked out, and punched with her little fists, trying to ward off her attackers, but she would not release her prey. The hornbrows wavered before the unflinching aggressiveness of the ravagers, wanting to save the packer, but not wanting to end up like him.

Finally it was apparent that the male packer was dead. Long-tail shook him hard, released him, and roared triumphantly. She and Gnarled-paw then took the offensive, and began raking and biting every packer that got too close. Dejected and defeated, the packers backed away.

Some of the younger or less disciplined of the packers turned and fled in the direction of the Great Eastern Herd. The others withdraw a safe distance from the ravagers to re-group. They formed into packs, units of twenty-five or so.

Those packers still on the left side of the river, seeing the shambles that the defensive line on the right side was now in, also withdrew a short distance. They formed into a large fighting circle, double ringed, with leaders and reserves stationed in the middle. Their leaders waited to see if the packers on the right side of the river would stay and fight, or retreat. Whatever was decided, they would support.

Meanwhile, the packers on the right side of the river tried to move far enough away from the two ravagers so that they could safely catch their breath, tend to the wounded, and decide what next course of action was best to take.

There was much discussion about whether to stage an offensive and try to drive the ravagers back into the ravine, where it would be easier to hold them, or to admit defeat and withdraw back to the herd. It was apparent that both ravagers were now out of the ravine, and that it would be much more difficult to contain them. It was also apparent to the more experienced packers that there were now fewer packers than would be necessary to successfully drive the ravagers back into the ravine. Casualties were likely to be high.

A tactical withdrawal was ultimately decided upon. With this decision, the packers formed into larger, tighter, more disciplined fighting circles, with double rings, and leaders, reserves and the wounded in the centers. They formed up much like those across the river had done. Thus they began a cautious retreat.

Grendaar looked at Renthot, a question in his facial expression. Renthot nodded agreement. Grendaar trotted with slow dignity over to the western side of the knoll. He stretched upward to his full height, raised his mouth towards the heavens, and gave forth a long, sorrowful, low-frequency honk.

"Hoonnnoonnnoonnn."

Twice more he gave the same signal: a long, deep, wavering, almost wailing honk.

"Hooonnnooonnnooonnn. Hoooonnnoooonnnoooonnn."

All the adult males on all the ridges and hilltops were looking towards Grendaar and Renthot. Many of the packers not running for their lives also took time to glance their way. Renthot had joined Grendaar on the western edge of the knoll. They exchanged glances. Together, in perfect synchronization, they pounded their tails on the ground three times.

THUMMMP! THUMMP! THUMMP!

They paused, and then repeated the three loud blows. This time many of the adult males on the high points pounded with them, in a perfectly coordinated display that could only have come from a lifetime of repetition, or from genetic coding itself.

THUMMMP! THUMMP! THUMMP!

They all paused, and then all the adult males repeated the three blows once again.

THUMMMP! THUMMP! THUMMP!

After another brief pause, Grendaar and all the other adult males honked mournfully three more times. Then they repeated the three blows, times three, in a slow but certain ritual. They were warning all the tribes and all the hornbrows within hearing or feeling, that tangible danger again threatened the herd.

Grendaar stared toward the west. Far off across the gently undulating plain he thought he could see the stragglers of the herd quickening their pace. It was difficult to be sure, since the retreating herd was raising so much dust. There was nothing more he could do for the herd now. Now his major responsibility was to his roam.

He was pleased to see Dandraar sitting patiently on a rise to the northwest. It was the same rise that Trugahr had been sitting upon earlier. He waved to Dandraar, who waved back. Dandraar then signaled a request to join Grendaar. Grendaar told him to wait on the hillock in case he needed to get a message to the roam.

Many of the other adult males were vacating the high places where they had kept their vigil, and were joining with the packers in their retreat back to the herd.

Renthot, who still stood beside Grendaar, said, "I don't think there is anything more we can do here, my brother. Let us make haste back to our roams and the comfort of the females." Without waiting for a reply, he began trotting down the western slope of the knoll, in the direction of Dandraar.

"You go, my brother. I will stay awhile longer, to see what the ravagers will do next."

Renthot stopped short. He was clearly surprised. Looking over his shoulder, he said, "Grendaar, my brother, why must you tempt your fate so much? It is no longer safe for any of the People to be anywhere near the vicinity of the ravine."

"This very thought is uppermost in my mind, my brother. I must stay. Rohraar will lead the Green Water Roam quite well in my absence. May the sun warm you, my brother." Grendaar thought for a moment, and then added, "May your hatchlings make the earth tremble."

Renthot grumbled something under his breath. He turned back towards Grendaar, and slowly climbed back up to the top of the knoll. Grendaar had also turned and was walking over to the southeastern side of the knoll, to better observe the ravagers at the top of the ravine. Renthot followed him, still mumbling under his breath.

Long-tail was squatting beside her kill. She was leisurely tearing off chunks of flesh, chewing briefly, and then swallowing them virtually whole. Gnarled-paw stood beside her, like a sentinel. He was gazing down the ravine to see if any other predators were ascending to challenge him or his sister. None were visible. Then he turned, and while she ate, he licked at her wounds, trying to clean them.

Grendaar and Renthot watched the two ravagers. Renthot could not bring himself to leave the Ancient One, although he did not think that staying had any merit whatever. They were the only two of the People that had decided to do so. He felt that he must at least find out why Grendaar wished to put himself at such risk. He said, "Tell me, Groundshaker, why are you risking your life like this? Your roam needs you. Mine needs me, for that matter. Why are we staying?"

Grendaar turned and looked at his friend for a long moment. Perhaps he was trying to decide whether he should say or not. Finally, he said one word. "Panthrar."

Renthot realized the depth of feeling this old bag of leather must have for his roam-members. There was no use discussing the matter further. Renthot stood silently beside his friend and waited.

Gnarled-paw next turned his attention towards the retreating phalanxes of packers. They were moving off at an unhurried pace. Gnarled-paw knew that they were unafraid, and that they were as yet unbeaten. Given the chance, they would still risk their lives to try and kill him or his sister. He was content to let them go. He knew that he and his sister would find the herd of hornbrows when next they wished to. A blind sea turtle could follow the trail that a herd this large would leave.

Suddenly Gnarled-paw became aware of the two hornbrows that had remained behind. Two adult males were standing on a knoll off to the northwest. They were watching him and his sister. He moved a few paces in their direction, expecting them to hurry away. They did not. He wasn't hungry, but maybe he should investigate. He continued walking in their direction.

CHAPTER SEVEN
WITHDRAWAL

Renthot turned to Grendaar and said, "I don't think we can resist the ravager for long, my brother." He paused just long enough to glance at the approaching dreadrunner. "I believe that it is wisdom that we leave. Now, and quickly."

Grendaar hesitated, not wanting to leave without knowing the fate of Panthrar, but he knew that Renthot was right. It was unlikely that he and Renthot could best the ravager. And even if they might actually be able to, it wasn't worth the risk. Little of real value could be gained, and much might be lost. There was little more he could gain by staying here any longer. He would have to trust that Panthrar could get out of the ravine using his own wits, and that he would safely make his way across the upper plain to the foothills on his own. Grendaar was saddened by the prospect, for he knew that alone, without the protection of the roam, it was very unlikely that he would ever see Panthrar again.

"You are right, my brother," Grendaar said. Renthot noticed that the voice of his friend was rather flat. He thought that he knew the reason why.

Without further delay, they turned and proceeded toward the northwest at a lively, but dignified pace. They were roamleaders, after all, and were too proud to scurry away like frightened fledges. They headed straight for

Dandraar. About halfway between the knoll and the rise upon which Dandraar sat, Gnarled-paw appeared on the knoll they had recently vacated.

Dandraar signaled that danger threatened from behind them. They stopped and turned. If the ravager wished it, then here was where they would fight to the death.

The ravager stood on the commanding knoll, studying them, but he did not follow. Gnarled-paw was not hungry, and he did not want to leave his sister again. He was not particularly concerned about two adult male hornbrows. He was content to watch them retreat.

Dandraar's heart skipped a beat when he first saw the dreadrunner. He watched it surveying the plain, wondering if it would follow and attack the two roamleaders. All kinds of horrible thoughts crossed his mind as first he imagined it attacking his roamleader, or if not that, then instead following them all the way back to the roams. But it didn't. It just stood there on the knoll, watching Grendaar and Renthot.

Grendaar and Renthot, seeing that the ravager did not intend to pursue and fight them, turned and continued toward Dandraar. Finally Dandraar could resist it no longer. He hurried down the rise towards his roamleader.

"May the sun keep you warm, my father," said the adolescent, as he got into step beside the two adults. He glanced fearfully back at the ravager. Then he turned back, and said to Renthot, "And may the sun warm you also, elder brother."

"May the sun warm you too, younger brother," smiled Renthot.

"And may it keep you warm also, my son," responded Grendaar. "I am happy to see that you have returned from your trip to the elders. How did you fare?"

"I think, my father, that they did not believe that a ravager was going to attack us."

"I see, my son. Well, perhaps they have changed their minds by now."

"May you forgive me, my father, but I think that the great Adeldraar may still not be sure."

"I'll forgive such disrespect this time, my son."

"Thank you, my father."

Together the three males trotted along the path of the two roams. The trail was clear and easy to follow. First it showed a leisurely pace, with the roam-members traveling north, and browsing as they walked. Later it was apparent that the two roams had clustered tighter together, and moved at a much more rapid rate. For a while they continued north, and then they turned toward the west. After about three miles on this westerly path, the pace of the roams again slowed. It continued west for most of the afternoon, and then slowly began to veer towards the southwest, and the general direction of the Red Dawn Tribe, and the Great Eastern Herd.

The three males moved at a much more rapid rate, and relentlessly closed the distance between themselves and the roams. Dandraar used the opportunity to tell Grendaar all of the details of his meeting with the elders of the tribe. Grendaar kept his thoughts to himself, but that didn't stop him from contemplating his next meeting with Adeldraar.

Only occasionally did they slow or stop to browse. Twice they drank, once at a shallow lake that was slowly refilling from small seasonal streams, and once at a small stream. The lake's water was very alkaline, not sweet like the streams in the western foothills. The smaller streams of the upper plain, though, were not much better.

Occasionally Dandraar would turn to reassure himself that the dreadrunner wasn't stealthily following them. Once, while his roamleader and Renthot crossed a small stream that ran across their path, Dandraar sat upon a ridge for a long while, examining the direction from which they had come. Eventually he was convinced that the dreadrunner was not tracking them. He scurried down the ridge, scampered across the stream, splashing cascades of water into the air in his haste, and dashed after the two adults.

Towards sundown they caught up with their roams. They found the others settled for the night in the curve of a shallow, narrow stream. The stream encircled three sides of the gathering of hornbrows, and a small hillock dominated the fourth side. A small cluster of tall pines stood at the foot of the hillock. Minor scatterings of dogwoods spotted the river's edge on either side. At the place of the curve, a broad sandy bank, more like a small beach, facilitated drinking and wading.

Adult males formed a tight perimeter at strategic points around the gathering, and adolescent males were stationed at a few key approaches further out. There was plenty of food for the taking, as this far north, the landscape had not been so effectively denuded as had the primary path of the great herd further to the south. Berry bushes were in great abundance.

An adolescent male of the Yellow Mud Roam saw the rear-guard approaching, and signaled this news to the roams. By the time Grendaar, Renthot, and Dandraar had joined the gathering, great excitement had welled up in anticipation of their arrival. There was no honking or hooting, as with the sun about to fall, the hornbrows did not want to advertise their location to any predators. But there was a lot of bowing and nodding and stooping. Tails wagged in delight, and virtually the entire gathering, minus the adolescent male out-sentries, rushed to meet and greet them.

First the adult males approached the three, to be absolutely certain that no threat was being presented to the roams. The males from both sides, Grendaar and his party, and Rohraar and his, approached each other carefully, sniffing as they closed upon each other. With the light failing, as the red sun edged below the distant western mountains, one couldn't be too careful. Heads bobbed, and then they came closer still.

When they got almost within touching distance, they sniffed again, and looked each other over carefully. With heads bobbing, Grendaar and Rohraar got within a foot of each other. So did Renthot and Gathraar, his second male. The other males stayed further back, awaiting the outcome of this encounter. The females and young stayed even further back, until the males signaled that all was clear.

Grendaar and Rohraar extended their heads. They were so close that Grendaar's head passed to the right of Rohraar's, left eyeball staring at left eyeball. They sniffed. Grendaar said, "It is good to see you again, younger brother."

Rohraar pulled his head back, passed his head to the other side of Grendaar's, right eyeball to right eyeball, sniffed, nodded his head, and said, "May the moon guard you well, elder brother."

Grendaar then nuzzled Rohraar. Rohraar nuzzled him back. By now Renthot and Gathraar had also formally recognized each other. The other adult males came closer, and exchanged greetings. There was much wagging of tails, bowing and nodding, and nuzzling and rubbing of bodies. After the male bonding was enacted, the adult females went through a similar ritual of recognition, obeisance, and affection. Rohraar went through a similar but briefer ceremony in greeting Dandraar, but the roles of dominance and subservience were reversed. Then all three of the returning males were greeted more freely, and less formally, and with a less inhibited show of real affection, by the adolescent females and the young of the roams.

Eventually, with the greetings over, a calm returned to the roams. Many went off for a final feeding or a drink, before all settled down for a night's sleep. With light almost completely gone as the sun slid behind the umber mountains, there was little for the People to do but to sleep. Or to guard those that slept.

As tired as Grendaar was, he walked the entire outer perimeter, conversing with each of the adolescent males of the Yellow Mud Roam, and with Dandraar, who also formed part of the outer defense, before he returned to the center of the roams. Here he took a prominent position along with Renthot, ready to direct his roam in case of a night attack.

Youngsters and yearlings clustered in close to the two roamleaders. Except for Tessah and Fordah, all of the adult and adolescent females formed a pretty complete ring around the roams, encircling the young. The two first females sat with each other. They occupied a place of honor, close to where the two roamleaders sat. The other adult males dozed at strategic spots along the periphery. Many snuggled close to their favorite females.

The adolescent males remained wide awake and vigilant at their out-sentry posts. Their own preservation, as well as the protection of the roams, depended upon them staying awake and alert enough to detect a predator before it detected them.

The moon made its way across the heavens while the roams slept. The night was, for the most part, uneventful. Very early in the morning however, while darkness still covered the roams, a pack of about six **razorteeth** penetrated the perimeter of adolescent males and approached close to the sleeping hornbrows. Razorteeth were like miniature ravagers. They were small bipedal meat-eaters, with slim jaws bristling with pointed, saw-edged teeth. They had long arms with grasping fingers tipped with large claws. They could run very swiftly on slender, bird-like legs and feet, while they held their stiffened tails straight back behind them for balance. Each foot, in addition to normally large claws, was equipped with an extra-large, sickle-shaped toe claw that through special musculature, swung back and forth like a switch-blade knife. It was a dangerous weapon that was used both for hunting and for defense.

For a creature of this era, the razorteeth had unusually large brains. They were fast-moving, quick-witted creatures that had evolved an efficient pack-hunting technique. They also had large, prominent eyes with overlapping fields of vision. Thus they had excellent depth-perception. Their eyesight was also particularly well adapted for night hunting. Although they only grew to be about six or seven feet long, they could be a formidable opponent, especially in packs. If they caught a lone hornbrow away from the roam, especially a yearling or a youngster, they were deadly. Even an adolescent male would have difficulty surviving the onslaught of an entire pack.

This pack of razorteeth was not so desperate, though, to attack an adolescent male guarding a roam. Assistance would have arrived long before they could have killed their prey, let alone get away with the carcass. So they had slipped past the guards to get a closer look at the main body.

The razorteeth watched the roams for over an hour. Occasionally one of the hornbrows would awaken and walk over to the stream for a drink, and then return to the warmth of the clustered bodies of its companions. Whenever a yearling did so, the razorteeth would get excited, and let themselves imagine, if only for a moment, that they could safely attack and kill the young one, and get away with the body. Frequently, on one or another of the predators, a sickle-shaped toe-claw would jerk in anticipation of the kill. Once or twice a razortooth impulsively chattered its teeth, mimicking the dead bite. But they knew that they could not make a successful kill against a roam. Not without heavy casualties. And death was too high a price for a meal.

About an hour before dawn, the wind shifted. One of the perimeter guards was able to pick up the scent of the razorteeth. He hooted a quiet warning to the roams. Most of the adults were immediately on their feet. Adult females began checking the whereabouts of all their charges. The adult and adolescent males began a series of communications and maneuvers, the goal of which was to isolate the location of the predators.

Adult males moved outward from the ring of females, inspecting possible hiding places. They were careful, but they knew that they didn't have to fight in a circle. They knew they were looking for razorteeth, possibly a pack of them. The scent of the razorteeth was as unique and identifiable as was that of any other predator. If a male discovered the hiding razorteeth, he would call for assistance before attacking, and the males would try to surround and kill as many of the razorteeth as they could before the rest got away.

The razorteeth, knowing that now even the advantage of surprise was lost to them, slipped quietly away and into the night.

After awhile it became evident that danger had passed. The adult males returned to their strategic places, and the adolescent males to their sentry posts. The roams calmed down, and soon most were back to sleep again. The adult males themselves were all soon dozing, and the adolescent males wished that they too could be getting some sleep.

Grendaar awoke as the sun began to push its edge over the escarpment to the east. He, like all the other roam-members, was awakened by the first sentry to see daylight slipping up over the escarpment. The young male honked a loud and prolonged greeting to the new day. He was answered by the other adolescent males, all honking and hooting the arrival of a new day. Soon all the members of both roams were honking their own greetings. It was an impulsive ritual that hornbrows and all their relations had been doing for a millennium of millennia.

In the distance a large ravager roared his own greeting to the sun. The roammers quieted, but only for a moment. Then they honked and chirped more greetings to the new day.

As the rest of the roammers prepared for a new day, the adolescent males were called in. Most of the roam-members browsed a breakfast in anticipation of beginning the trek anew, but the adolescent males napped while they could. Soon both roams would be heading west. Or southwest, to be more precise.

Before long, Grendaar and Renthot lead the combined roams onward again. Rohraar and Gathraar took positions in the rear. Trugahr took the left flank, while Jedraar took the right flank. The rest of the adult males, Wubbar and Hew of the Green Water Roam, and the other three adult males of the Yellow Mud Roam, spread themselves out loosely around the roams. Sometimes the males walked alone, sometimes they joined in groups of two or more, as their whimsy dictated. Kinput and Sevren, who had actually slept with the roams, tagged along with the roamleaders. Since the roamleaders sometimes traveled as far as a half mile ahead of the rest of the roam, traveling with the roamleaders didn't quite seem like being in a roam.

The roams marched most of the day. Three times they stopped, to eat and drink, and allow for a short rest. Each time, the adolescent males napped, looking forward to the time when they rejoined the Nine Tribes. Then the packs would provide sentry duty, and the adolescent males could sleep at night like the rest of the roam.

For the first half of the morning the roams followed the stream southwestward. About mid-morning, as Grendaar and Renthot and Kinput and Sevren rounded a curve in the stream gully, they came upon a small herd of robrunners drinking from the stream. There must have been almost two hundred of the eight foot long, bipedal omnivores congregated along the stream. Robrunners have small heads, large eyes, and strong jaws. They have short arms with claw-tipped, five-fingered hands. They also have long, agile shins and feet, and a tendon stiffened tail for balance. They were sprinters that could outrun almost anything that they couldn't eat. They didn't usually travel in herds, and rarely one this large, but it was spring, and many of the non-carnivores joined together at breeding time.

Hornbrows didn't particularly like robrunners. Among other things, they were eggsnatchers and hatchling-nappers. These very robrunners would likely be causing the herd daily problems in the not too distant future. Normally Grendaar might have detoured around a gathering of non-carnivores, not from fear, but from politeness. But not this time. He had had too much trouble with robrunners in the past.

When he saw the robrunners, he hooted the challenge of a dominant male hornbrow and charged at the small herd. His three immediate companions followed suit. The robrunners looked up as one, bleated a startled response, and scattered in panic. Grendaar rushed in among the tardy, swinging his tail to the right and left, giving the slower ones an added incentive to run. He and Kinput chased a bunch up the right side of the gully, while Renthot and Sevren chased another group up the left side. When they reached the top of the gully, they paused to watch in amusement as the robrunners ran for their lives. The two roams trailing behind the leaders came upon the scene in time to witness the last of the robrunners scurrying up over the gully wall and dashing across the plain. The robrunners protestations of alarm could be heard until they faded into the distance.

The roams decided to take their first rest break at this same watering place. The hornbrows had been amused to see so many robrunners running for their lives. The incident occupied much of the conversation of the group for well over an hour, long past when the roams had resumed their journey again. Among the younger males, there was a lot of recounting of the event, and with each re-telling, the size of the herd of robrunners and the casualties that they sustained, grew. Among the females, there was much conjecture, and perhaps hope, that a number of the slower robrunners had had their hips or legs broken by the swinging tails of the pursuing males. The more that were thus immobilized, the fewer there would be to try to steal eggs from the nests in the west.

During the rest period, Grendaar and Kinput stayed on the ridge at the top of the gully. They had detected a herd of **trumpeters** far to the north, and decided to keep an eye on it. Trumpeters were distantly related to hornbrows. Sometimes the two species even traveled together for short distances. They even spoke a similar language, but there were so many different words, and different pronunciations of the same words, that in reality they had a hard time understanding each other.

Grendaar and Kinput stared into the distance. It was a good sized herd of several thousand at least, but the precise size of the herd was difficult to determine from this distance. They were trumpeters though, that was unmistakable. Clear evidence of how they got their name could be heard quite distinctly here at the top of the gully. And the five-foot-plus crests arcing from the back of the heads of the males, and the colorful frills that spread out like sails from the crests, were visible even at this distance. The females and young also had crests and frills, but theirs were smaller and less colorful.

The structure of the crests of the trumpeters were ossified, bony devices with extended nasal passages attached to the trumpeters vocal gear. They curved gracefully back from the top of the head in a gentle arc. The long passages within the crests allowed the trumpeters to create extremely low-frequency sounds that could easily be heard for miles. Even now, when no danger threatened them, they kept up an almost steady cacophony of tooting and trumpeting that announced their passage.

The trumpeters were also bipedal/quadrupedal herbivores. From a distance, except for the crests and the elaborate frills, they looked very much like hornbrows minus the horn. They were the same size and body shape, the same length and weight, and had many of the same behavioral characteristics.

Other members of the roams joined Grendaar and Kinput on the ridge to observe the other herd. They watched the trumpeters moving slowly towards the north and west for the entire rest break. From this distance the dust rising up behind the herd looked strikingly like a prairie fire, only lighter in color.

It was possible that the trumpeters didn't even notice the hornbrows, since they were relatively few in number. Even if they did though, they probably wouldn't have come over to investigate. Even the sudden appearance of some one hundred robrunners, dashing madly across the plain, didn't arouse sufficient interest to cause any of the trumpeters to divert from their course. It was safer staying with the herd. This was something that every hornbrow also knew. And this reminded them that it was time to continue onward to rendezvous with their own herd.

Shortly thereafter, the roams left the stream gully, which had switched back towards the northwest. Instead, the roams continued out onto the open plain, in a southwesterly direction. They continued across an almost featureless terrain, stopping in the early afternoon by a small, alkaline pond for their second rest break of the day.

About mid-afternoon, they noticed a herd of about one hundred onehorns to their south, traveling in a northwesterly direction. The onehorns were traveling rapidly, and must have passed to the east of the rear elements of the Great Eastern Herd. At some point, today or tomorrow, the paths of the roams and the herd of onehorns would cross.

All afternoon Grendaar and Renthot kept an eye on the onehorns. They were quadrupedal herbivores, therefore they didn't offer a threat to the roams in the traditional sense that a carnivore would. But they could be pretty cantankerous. And they weren't too bright, sometimes having difficulty telling the difference between a friend and a foe. The males were prone to displays of charging. The fact that they tended to be near-sighted seemed to make them more likely, rather than less likely, to charge anything that got too close. Grendaar did not intend to get too close.

At twenty feet long, and two and a half tons in weight, they were nothing to trifle with. They were equipped with a large, sharp nose horn, considerably more intimidating than the horn that hornbrows were equipped with. They also had two short brow horns and a short, bone-hard frill that ringed their necks. Bony knobs and spikes stuck out from the top of the frill.

Grendaar knew that the colorful frill was mainly a display device, used to attract mates. He also knew that the horns were used more for besting rivals at mating time than anything else. On the other hand, he had seen more than one onehorn use its horn as a very lethal defensive weapon. And if predisposed to charge, as they seemed abnormally so in the spring, they could be deadly to a hornbrow.

All afternoon the paths of the two slowly converged. By nightfall they were less than a mile apart. The roams settled down to an uneasy night. They slept in a small copse of pines, watered by a small, seasonal brook that was barely moist at the moment. They had to dig into the bed to get at drinking water. They placed sentries as usual, but one adult male or another frequently awoke and peered into the darkness towards the south, hoping that the onehorns were peacefully asleep.

Late into the night, the pack of razorteeth again slipped past the sentries, and moved in close to observe the hornbrows. After almost an hour they concluded that there was less chance of a successful kill than on the previous night. Killing a hadrosaur or anything else that size was really wishful thinking on the part of the razorteeth anyway. But that didn't stop them from looking for opportunities. So they moved off into the night to find something smaller and less well protected. They hoped to find a robrunner, perhaps, or its cousin a **redrunner**, or maybe a **swiftstealer**, or its cousin an eggsnatcher, or maybe even a hive of little mammals or a nest of lizards.

Morning came without incident, and the Green Water and Yellow Mud Roams again began their journey westward. They expected to rendezvous with the Red Dawn Tribe today, once they got successfully around the onehorns. The onehorns were moving faster than the hornbrows, so Grendaar and Renthot decided to let them pass ahead of the roams. The roams would then cross behind them and be on their way without incident.

All morning the two groups pulled steadily closer to each other. At about a quarter of a mile apart, the onehorns became aware of the hornbrows. It was a wind shift that allowed them to scent the roams, otherwise they still might not have noticed them. Suddenly alert, the onehorns pulled into a tight circle, with the young on the inside, and the adults on the outside. Several of the adult males placed themselves between the group and the hornbrows. Meanwhile, the roams closed up ranks, and Grendaar and Renthot, along with Rohraar and Gathraar and Kinput, placed themselves between the onehorns and the roams. The roams also slowed to allow the onehorns to get ahead and pass.

The dominant male of the onehorns kept himself directly between his herd and the roams. He frequently stopped to eye the roams carefully. He would stand completely still and rigid for a moment, sniffing the air. Then he would snort noisily, bow his head, and paw the ground. Then he would take a few tentative steps towards them, threatening to charge.

Each time the dominant male onehorn did this, Grendaar and his group of males would stop and remain perfectly still. They had tried to never get closer than about five hundred feet to the dominant male onehorn. The roams had been instructed to stay a good five hundred feet behind the protective males, and to keep moving at a slow but steady, unthreatening pace past the rear of the onehorns.

It wasn't until the two groups were at their closest, that the dominant male decided to charge. If he had waited a few more moments, the gap between them would have started to enlarge again. But he didn't feel like waiting. Without provocation he trotted to within three hundred feet of the hornbrows, while his own group moved steadily away.

In reaction to his approach, the roams veered more to the south to give themselves a greater clearance. Meanwhile, the male hornbrows again stopped and stood perfectly still. The onehorn sniffed in their direction, his beaked nose pointing slightly upward. He was so pungent that the hornbrows could easily smell him. His sense of smell might not be as acute as theirs, still he couldn't help but detect that they weren't carnivores. By now he could also see them fairly clearly.

He snorted resonantly, lowered his head, and pawed the ground. Each time he pawed, great clods of earth were thrown back, and dust rose behind him. He advanced a few paces, shook his head, and snorted again. The five male hornbrows remained motionless, staring fixedly at the onehorn. He pawed the ground, and made thrusting motions with his head, as if stabbing upward with his large nose horn. Suddenly he charged forward about fifty feet, and then stopped just as suddenly. A cloud of dust rose around his hind quarters, and slowly drifted in the direction of the hornbrows, slightly obscuring the onehorn.

He snorted. He sniffed the air, nose pointing upward, and then snorted yet again. He pawed the ground, and charged another fifty feet closer to the hornbrows. The male hornbrows began to spread out, slowly but surely, with Grendaar in the middle, two males to his left, and two to his right. They spread out about a hundred feet apart. Then the males closest to Grendaar slowly advanced about twenty-five feet, while the ones on the wings advanced about fifty feet. They formed an inverted "U" facing the onehorn. If the onehorn advanced more, they would spread out more, and advance around his flanks.

The onehorn eyed the hornbrows suspiciously. He swung his great head and frill around to gaze at each one of them. At each he snorted, and pawed the ground. He advanced a few more paces, pawed the ground, and made stabbing motions with his long, sharp horn. The hornbrows slowly continued the encircling maneuver. The onehorn stopped pawing, spread out all-fours in a rigid stance, and bellowed a squeal-like roar at them. Then he turned around, and trotted back in the direction of his herd. He never glanced back at them. They watched as the dust rose behind him. When they were sure that he was really leaving, they turned and hastened in the direction of the roams.

Early in the afternoon, the two roams topped a gentle rise, and beheld the rear elements of the Great Eastern Herd, about two miles to the southwest of them. The packs, having taken a more direct route, had already re-joined the herd, and had re-deployed as a perimeter guard. The two roams hurried over the rise and in the direction of the herd. The packs signaled happily to them, and they returned a joyful response.

CHAPTER EIGHT
DETAINED

Panthrar and Pippit spent the day in hiding. From behind the boulders that masked their little grove, they had watched as Gnarled-paw raced up the other side of the ravine to the aid of Long-tail. They had witnessed the battle at the top of the ravine, the killing of the packer, and the eventual withdrawal of the packs.

Pippit had refused to watch Long-tail eat the packer, so she had slumped down behind the boulders. Eventually she had consoled herself by nibbling at the vegetation that grew in the grove and sprouted between the cracks in the wall of the ravine. Her own feeding kept her mind off of the gruesome event occurring at the top of the ravine.

Panthrar decided that it was better to keep an eye on the ravagers, so he had continued to observe them. Thus he saw Gnarled-paw keeping watch while Long-tail fed upon her kill. After awhile, he saw Gnarled-paw head off onto the plain, but from where he hid, Panthrar couldn't see what motivated the ravager, or where he had gone.

Before Long-tail had finished her meal, Gnarled-paw returned. He lay down near her and dozed. When she had finished eating, she and Gnarled-paw each took hold of the carcass, and dragged it towards the ravine wall on the other side of the river. The wall was very low where the ravagers hid their kill, hardly more than tumbled boulders breaking up a small elevation change between the plain and the slope of the ravine. The ravagers disappeared into the boulders along with their kill.

Panthrar turned his attention in the other direction, down the ravine. No other ravagers were in sight. None were visible anywhere between the top of the ravine to the right, and the curve in the river down the ravine to the left. So Panthrar turned and gave his attention to Pippit. He told her what he had seen, leaving out the details about the feeding. They decided to rest until nightfall, and then decide whether or not they should try to sneak out of the ravine under the cover of darkness.

All afternoon, Pippit and Panthrar either browsed or slept. For awhile, the excitement of their near encounter with the ravagers, and their subsequent dash up the ravine, kept them wide awake. But after eating, and after their adrenaline had drained back out of them, they became drowsy. First they dozed. Then they napped. Finally they fell into a sound sleep.

Near sunset, the cooling of the evening air roused them. They browsed on what was left of the berry bushes in their hiding place, but they had no water. After eating, Panthrar stood up to his full height, and looked over the top of a boulder. Pippit, somewhat shorter, looked around the edge of a boulder and through a gap that didn't afford her the wide panorama that Panthrar had, but still gave her a pretty good view.

There were no ravagers in sight. There was no hint of danger anywhere within their range of vision. Yet they were not fooled into an unconsidered move. They were convinced that Gnarled-paw and Long-tail were still holed up with the remains of their kill. The ravagers were not likely to travel too far away from readily available food while it lasted. And Panthrar and Pippit did not propose to allow themselves to be their next kill. So the two hornbrows knew that they would have to stay hidden until the kill had been totally eaten, and hunger drove the ravagers away after another kill.

Meanwhile Panthrar and Pippit had more immediate concerns to take care of. Food in the hiding place was running out, and there was no water. They would have to sneak out of the hiding place for both.

Fortunately, each was near at hand. Berry bushes, and young green, newly formed leaves from small hardwoods, grew all about the ravine floor in the vicinity of their sanctuary. And water, gushing from the ravine wall only a hundred yards from where they hid, trickled down the wall, and ran in a tiny stream towards the river. All they had to do was to wait until the dead of night. Then, if they were extremely careful, they could leave the safety of the boulders and satisfy their thirst and their hunger. With this plan, they again allowed themselves to fall back into a less than peaceful sleep.

Thus, near the middle of the night, they awakened themselves. Still, they waited until their faculties were no longer dimmed by sleep before they would risk venturing from their hiding place. For over an hour, they observed the ravine from their little grove to see if any carnivores were about.

Cold moonlight splashed off of the clusters of rock outcroppings, and danced in the needles and the leaves at the tops of the trees. Murmurs arose from the river as it made its eternal trip to the sea. A light breeze rippled through the needles of the evergreens, and kissed the foliage of the hardwoods. Nothing else stirred in the ravine. All was quiet near the top, where Gnarled-paw and Long-tail probably slept near their kill. All was quiet down near the curve in the river, beyond which Red-patch and Stripes and her cub still remained. All was still, even the insects had hours ago stopped their chirping and buzzing.

Panthrar slowly, very slowly, eased from behind the cover of the boulders, and ever so quietly inched towards the miniature waterfall near their hiding place. Fifty feet behind him stalked Pippit, like an extended shadow. Panthrar reached the waterfall, and quenched his thirst. Then Pippit did the same. Panthrar took another drink, and then began browsing the berry bushes and the tender new shoots of the hardwoods. He nibbled the new growth and young cones of the spruces and pines, yet he never stopped scrutinizing the ravine. Not just the top and the curve, but he kept sweeping the entire section before him, looking for anything that might hint of danger. Pippit did the same. They used all of their faculties, visual, olfactory, and auditory. There was never a moment when one or both of them weren't searching for trouble.

They ate for almost an hour, periodically returning to the waterfall for another drink. When they were so full that they could not eat another bite, they pulled berry branches from the bushes, and carried them back to their hiding place. They did this very carefully, because they feared that if they snapped too large of a branch, the sound might carry to a ravager, and all would be lost. So they took only the most tender, and therefore the most desirous of the branches, and carried them back for a later meal. They tried to include as many ripe berries as possible, for this would give them needed moisture during tomorrow's long, hot day.

By two-thirty, they were back in their little grove. They kept watch for awhile, but the fullness of their stomachs induced a soporific effect that they couldn't resist. Soon they were fast asleep.

The cry of a passing **skygiant** awakened Pippit. It was just past dawn, another new day had begun. Pippit resisted the urge to greet the rising sun with a call of her own. She watched the winged giant as it circled over the spot near the top of the ravine where the ravagers were hiding with their kill. Almost as an after-thought, she noted that this one was not the largest skygiant she had ever seen. Its wingspan seemed to be only about forty feet wide. She had seen much larger. It circled three or four times, and then lazily glided down the ravine, looking for a safer carcass to scavenge.

Pippit roused Panthrar. He yawned and stretched, smiling to himself, listening to the morning insects chirping and clicking. He jumped with a start when he suddenly realized where he was, and why he was here. He looked at Pippit, hoping she hadn't noticed. If she did, she didn't let on. She seemed busy checking out the extra provisions that they had gathered during the night.

He whispered to her, "Good morning, my sister. May the red dawn give you comfort."

"Good morning to you, my brother," she responded cheerfully. "And may this day bring you many rewards."

They nuzzled for a moment, and Panthrar noticed that it didn't feel anything like the formal greetings he had given others so many times before. In fact, this time it felt almost wonderful. It embarrassed him, and he aborted it a little earlier than usual. He noticed that Pippit was affected by it in some peculiar way also. As she turned to look away, he was certain that he saw a glow in her eyes.

Panthrar noticed that his heart was beating exceptionally fast, as if from fear, or excitement. What could it be? Why was he having these feelings? He hadn't yet realized that he was becoming an adult, no longer an adolescent. And it was spring. Things would never be the same for him again.

Pippit also was embarrassed. The overwhelming feelings that surged within her for Panthrar were so new, that she couldn't make any sense of them.

She was a tom-boy, she knew it. That was partially why she had joined a pack. Adult males were someone to respect and obey, but to otherwise avoid. Adolescent males were comrades, someone to play chase-and-catch with, someone to go exploring with. That's all. Nothing more. So what was this that she felt for Panthrar? And why? She also hadn't yet realized that she was growing up. And it was spring. Things would never again be the same for her, either.

Time passed, and they both regained their composure. To distract Pippit, and to help give himself more time to collect his thoughts, Panthrar said, "My sister, have you seen or heard any ravagers this morning?"

She immediately smiled, and responded, "No, my brother, but let us take a careful look, and see what we can see."

They chose a boulder to hide behind, from which they both could view the ravine. At first they saw nothing of import. But with nothing better to do, they stood behind the boulder for long periods of time, surveying the ravine. Their observations were broken at points with a snack upon the berry branches that they had stored up.

During one of these early morning observation sessions, they saw Long-tail appear from behind the rocks where she had hidden her kill. Long-tail ambled over to the river, and quenched her thirst. While she was drinking, Gnarled-paw also climbed from behind the rocks, and he also went to the river to drink.

After Long-tail had finished drinking, she watched her brother drink. He finished, and turned back towards the place where the carcass was hidden. Long-tail crouched, and stared at Gnarled-paw fixedly. He had proceeded only about half way back to their den, when Long-tail gave a muffled roar, and charged him. Just as she was about to collide with him, he sprang almost fifteen feet into the air, and to the left. Long-tail rushed right through the spot where Gnarled-paw had been only a second before. She immediately stopped, and crouched down. Gnarled-paw hit the ground, and sprinted away to the left. Long-tail charged after him again, and leapt upon his back. They rolled over, hissing and growling. Then she lost her grip. Gnarled-paw sprang to his feet, and bolted to the left again. Long-tail dashed around to the right in a big circle. They both stopped, facing each other, about two hundred feet apart.

Panthrar and Pippit looked at each other in amazement. They had never seen or heard of anything like this before in their entire lives. They watched in fascination as the two ravagers continued their antics.

Long-tail began to preen herself. Gnarled-paw crouched low, and began a stealthy approach. She acted as if she didn't even know he existed. Slowly he crept closer and closer to her. When he was only a hundred feet from her, he charged her at a ferocious speed. She continued to preen a moment longer, as if he wasn't there. As he was about to make his final leap at her, she jumped straight up into the air, hind-claws and fore-claws extended towards him, tail arced back for balance. Instead of jumping at her, he immediately countered by jumping straight up in front of her, hind-claws and fore-claws also extended. They struck each other, fore-claws to fore-claws, and hind-claws to hind-claws. When they hit the earth, Gnarled-paw immediately tackled Long-tail, and they rolled over and over.

Panthrar and Pippit were spell-bound. They couldn't believe what they were witnessing. These two ravagers had been so friendly with each other before. Now it looked like they were going to tear each other apart.

The ravagers rolled to a stop, and both sprang to their feet. Miraculously, neither seemed the least bit cut or hurt. Gnarled-paw roared, and Long-tail bolted to the right about a hundred feet. She began preening herself again. Gnarled-paw crouched down for a moment, then he stood up and began preening himself.

The hornbrows finally understood. The ravagers were playing. It was a mighty ferocious type of playing from a hornbrow's perspective, but it was playing none-the-less.

Gnarled-paw finished preening himself, and walked over to the place where the kill was hidden. He disappeared behind the boulders. After awhile,

Long-tail also finished preening, and she too went behind the boulders for a meal and a nap.

Thus it went all day. Periodically, either Gnarled-paw or Long-tail, or both, would come out into the open and stretch and romp, or just get a drink of water. Most of the time, though, they stayed hidden with their kill. No other ravagers appeared from down the ravine. All must be feeding on their individual kills. Sooner or later, though, their food would run out, and they'd have to go in search of more.

When darkness finally fell, the berry branches had long since run out. Panthrar and Pippit anxiously awaited the time when they could safely sneak out for food and water, especially water. They forced themselves to sleep, and around midnight, they again woke. Panthrar observed the ravine for about fifteen minutes, before deciding that it was safe to seek food and water.

Slowly, and softly, they crept to the tiny waterfall. Long shadows were cast by a three-quarters moon. All was quiet in the ravine. After slaking their thirst, they fell upon the berry bushes and young branches of the surrounding trees with a passion. As the night before, when they had satisfied their appetites, they collected food for the following day. They were almost finished, when they heard a noise from the vicinity of the river. It was just a little noise, some gravel kicked against a rock. But in the ubiquitous stillness of the night, it carried far. And the message it carried with it was profound. They were not alone.

Suddenly alert and frightened, they dropped silently to the ground. They strained to see what it was that had made the noise. There it was again, only a little further down the river this time. They tried to pierce the darkness with their wills. Then they saw movement. It was a thin, quick figure running along an open space beside the river. Then they saw another, and another. There were seven of them in all. A pack of razorteeth. They were headed down the river, in search of quarry. Apparently the razorteeth had not yet detected them.

Pippit began to shake uncontrollably. Panthrar fought down a sudden and strong urge to do the same. They lay still for over twenty minutes, but they heard nothing more. The razorteeth did not return. They gathered what branches they had with them, and hurried back to the grove. They collapsed together in a heap, clinging to each other. They were safe again, they hoped.

At least for the time being. Panthrar comforted Pippit, and after awhile she let her fears pass, and fell asleep, snuggled up against him. Holding her, his heart swelled.

At first he couldn't go to sleep. All he could think about was what would have happened if the razorteeth had found them. It would have been terrible. Even if they had been able to fight off the razorteeth, they probably would have ended up sorely wounded. Worse, the dreadrunners would have been alerted to their presence. They would never have gotten away from the two dreadrunners.

They had been lucky. They didn't really have enough food to get themselves comfortably through tomorrow. They would be hungry by the next nightfall, but you had to be alive to be hungry. Panthrar decided hunger wasn't all that bad. He also decided that it wasn't safe for both of them to sleep at the same time. He decided to try to stay awake for a time and then to wake Pippit and ask her to keep guard.

He looked down at her, snuggled against him. He thought of how lovely she was. Of how beautiful were the trim curves of her body. He thought of how lucky they were that the razorteeth were running so close to the river that they didn't hear him and Pippit. And he thought about how they were going to get very hungry by evening tomorrow. Still thinking about food, he fell asleep.

Pippit was again the first one to awaken in the morning. Panthrar was lying upright, his rear legs tucked up under him, his forelegs folded under his chest. His chin was laying upon his chest. He was still sound asleep. Pippit had still been snuggled up against him for warmth and protection when she awoke. She looked at him. He was an extremely handsome young male, she decided.

She got up without disturbing him. She climbed onto a small boulder so that she could look over a larger one, and scrutinized the ravine. The dreadrunners weren't about yet. She wondered what had become of the razorteeth. Had they returned to the upper plain, were they still descending toward the coastal plain, or were they somewhere nearby?

She looked about the grove. She and Panthrar had stripped the place of everything edible. The only provisions that they still had available were those that they had managed to collect before the razorteeth had shown up. It wasn't much, but it would have to do.

A skygiant appeared in the skies to the west, alternately flapping and gliding, flapping and gliding, heading towards the ravine. It slowed as it reached the top of the ravine, and lazily circled the spot where the two dreadrunners and their kill resided. Slowly it descended in ever tightening circles towards the ravagers' lair. Perhaps it could only see the carcass, and didn't know that the ravagers were near by. It was only a few hundred feet above the ravagers, when it suddenly cried out in alarm, and dove away across the ravine. It flapped hard to regain altitude, crying out its protest the whole way across the ravine. As it soared above the secret grove, Panthrar opened his eyes.

They greeted each other in the formal ways of their people. Pippit told Panthrar of all that she had seen, or hadn't seen, since she had awakened. Then they settled down for a short, light breakfast. After that they took up their vigil again. Sometimes both, sometimes only one, would keep the ravine under observation. There was really nothing else to do, and they needed to know when the ravagers finally left. The day dragged on much like the day before. Until early afternoon. Then Pippit, whose turn it had been to keep watch, called to Panthrar that she could see Stripes ascending the ravine.

Panthrar joined Pippit to watch the approach of the ravager. She made her way fearlessly but carefully up the ravine, avoiding places of obvious ambush potential. She was unusually careful because of her cub, who trailed several hundred feet behind her. She did not stop to drink, and she clearly wasn't hunting. She seemed determined to get out of the ravine and onto the open plain as quickly as possible.

As she neared the top of the ravine, Gnarled-paw climbed out of his lair. He stood on a small boulder, and stretched. Then he hopped down, and casually walked on a course that would intercept Stripes and her cub. Stripes rumbled a warning at him. As if in response, Long-tail climbed out of her resting place, and glared at Stripes.

Stripes stopped and turned. She growled some communication to her cub. The young male immediately ran to the river, followed it until he came to a likely place to ford, and promptly began crossing it. Stripes watched until the cub was in the water, heading towards the other side. Then she trotted up the ravine towards the other two ravagers. Long-tail had by now joined Gnarled-paw, and they both stood blocking Stripes.

Stripes slowed as she approached the other two. Finally she stopped. She was waiting for her cub to successfully cross the river, and to move directly opposite her on the other bank. When he had reached the desired location, she continued upward again. Now she moved forward with some confidence, unhindered by the fetters of motherhood. She roared a loud and blood-curdling challenge at the two ravagers awaiting her at the top of the ravine.

Long-tail returned her roar. Gnarled-paw hissed like a broken steam pipe. Stripes' walk turned into a stiff-legged, lurching movement. She hissed and grumbled as she went. Gnarled-paw roared. He too began walking stiff-legged, with his body turned slightly sideways, towards Stripes. The tip of his tail flicked back and forth.

Long-tail began to cautiously circle around to the right. Stripes' moved faster, her stiff legs see-sawing towards Gnarled-paw. Gnarled-paw also moved more quickly towards her. Long-tail moved even more quickly to the right. Stripes gave one more horrible roar, and then she charged towards Gnarled-paw. She held herself low, and moved with alarming speed. Gnarled-paw opened his mouth wide, displaying a frightening array of saber-like, serrated teeth. He hissed forcefully, and then he charged, low and horizontal, at full speed towards Stripes. Long-tail crouched low, and continued to maneuver forward and to the right for position.

The two ravagers sprang into the air about eighty feet apart. Each held forelegs and hindlegs extended, claws outstretched, mouths opened widely, and fangs exposed. They struck each other with a loud thud. Still in mid-air, Stripes and Gnarled-paw battled fiercely, clawed hands and feet swinging wildly, jaws snapping like steel traps. They crashed to the ground in a heap, still thrashing and snapping. They tumbled and wrestled for perhaps thirty seconds, dust rising all about them as they struggled for dominance. Then they broke apart, and tried to catch their breath. It had been a short, but extremely fierce fight. Both were bleeding from dozens of minor tooth punctures and claw cuts.

Gnarled-paw took a step backwards, limping slightly. Long-tail sprang forward like lightning, moving in a blur. Stripes turned to look in her direction just as Long-tail struck her hard in the side. Long-tail bowled Stripes over with the fury of her attack. She had the larger female by the shoulder, blade-like teeth buried in soft flesh. Stripes cried out in pain, and rolled over and over trying to dislodge Long-tail.

Long-tail lost her grip, and both females scrambled to their feet. Stripes lunged at Long-tail, jaws snapping. Long-tail feinted away, and then lunged back at Stripes. They hissed frightfully at each other. Feinting, lunging, parrying. Great clods of earth were torn up as they lunged and parried. Dust swirled around them. They moved with lightening speed, lunging and snapping, parrying and charging. They clenched again, clawing and biting in a fierce, frenzied contest.

Both looked exhausted. Long-tail took several steps backward to regain her breath. So did Stripes. As she did so, Gnarled-paw threw himself at her. She took the charge full on, and was pushed backwards twenty or thirty feet by the implacable, unrelenting Gnarled-paw. Stripes began a fighting retreat. She worked herself around so that her back was to the open plain. As she snapped and hissed, lunged and parried, she backed out onto the plain. Gnarled-paw followed her remorselessly, threatening her at every step. They scratched and clawed, kicked and bit each other at every step.

Stripes' cub followed his mother's retreat on the other side of the river. He screamed in protest, and snapped his jaws in a convincing mimic of his mother. He hissed and roared. He jumped up and down. He clawed furrows into the ground. He charged this way and that. His sympathies were with the losing side.

Finally, Stripes broke off the engagement. She began to back steadily away, hissing and roaring. Gnarled-paw and Long-tail followed her, returning her challenges. They harried her unmercifully for awhile, forcing her back hundreds of yards. Finally they stopped pursuing her.

Stripes continued to back away, periodically hissing her displeasure. The other two ravagers hissed back at her for a time, and then stopped and silently watched her go. Apparently they were satisfied to have punished her, and did not intend to try and kill her. Still, occasionally one or the other would open its mouth wide, displaying fearsome dental weaponry.

Stripes stopped hissing. She looked for her cub across the river. He roared encouragement to his mother. She crossed the river to join him, swimming with powerful kicks of her hind legs in the strong current. She was badly mauled, but she would survive. The cold water invigorated her. And she had saved her son from serious jeopardy. When she reached the other side, her cub licked at her wounds, as did she. After she had cleaned as many as she could reach, and her cub had attended the rest, they moved off towards the west.

Long-tail and Gnarled-paw stood and observed Stripes and her cub for a long while. They sat on their side of the river, and attended each others wounds. Each had received many, although neither had received the kind of punishment that they had dealt Stripes. After Stripes and her cub had disappeared behind a rise in the plain, they strutted about near the top of the ravine, quite proud of each other. Then they retired to the safety and comfort of their lair, and ate what was left of their kill.

After the fight between the ravagers, Panthrar and Pippit mostly stayed hidden in their grove. From time to time, they would peak out to keep tabs on what the ravagers were doing, but they had seen enough violence for a lifetime. They had seen things about ravagers that few hornbrows had witnessed and survived to tell about. If they ever got back to the roam, they would have many exciting stories to tell the others.

The day ended without further incident. Around ten that evening they sneaked out to get food and water. They hoped that this would be a time when dreadrunners had finished hunting, and before razorteeth started hunting. They weren't correct, but they successfully avoided detection anyway. They returned to their little grove full, refreshed, and with a decent supply of food for the next day. This night, unlike the others, they took turns keeping guard. Now that they knew that razorteeth were about, they deemed it unsafe to sleep at the same time.

Panthrar had the last sentry duty of the night, so he witnessed the rising of the sun the next morning. Pippit awoke shortly thereafter. They munched on a light breakfast, and took turns watching the ravine. Shortly after the hornbrows had eaten, Long-tail and Gnarled-paw stirred. They climbed out of the rocks, and stretched and yawned. Gnarled-paw scampered about, mimicking the hunt. Long-tail sat and preened herself for awhile. They strolled over to the river, and drank their fill. Then they both preened a bit longer. Finally they turned and followed the river west. They had quit their interim den for the last time.

Panthrar and Pippit were delighted. They watched the two ravagers following the trail of the Great Eastern Herd until they disappeared into the gently rolling terrain. Panthrar and Pippit discussed how long they should wait before quitting the little grove forever. Two hours at least, they decided. Maybe even a half day. They would make a final decision by mid-morning.

Around mid-morning, while they were discussing when to leave, Red-patch came sauntering up the ravine. They congratulated themselves for not having vacated their hiding place too early. Otherwise they would have been caught between Red-patch and the others. They decided to wait until mid-afternoon before leaving. This would give the ravagers plenty of time to get far ahead of them. They also decided not to directly follow the trail of the herd. All the ravagers would be on that same trail. Since they were on the north side of the river, they would circle around, taking a more northerly route to the ancient breeding grounds in the foothills to the west.

Meanwhile, they watched the ravine to see if any other ravagers would appear. They were fairly certain that none would. They believed that they knew of all the kills that had been made near the top of the ravine. All the killers were accounted for. Hunger would have driven any other predators onward before now. The only thing they had to fear was a ravager who was just now climbing up the ravine from the coastal plain. That could happen at any time. There would never be a time when they were absolutely certain that no ravagers were about. They would just have to trust that none would appear once they were out in the open. They both knew that they would never be really safe again until they were back with the Green Water Roam, and the Red Dawn Tribe.

Towards the middle of the afternoon, they left the little grove, got a final drink at the miniature waterfall, and walked out of the ravine. Turning in a northwesterly direction, they set out to face the uncertain challenges of the fifty mile wide upper plain. It would take them four or five days to reach the western foothills, if all went reasonably well.

CHAPTER NINE
THE GATHERING

IN THE MIDDLE OF the fifth day after the retreat from the ravine, the Green Water and Yellow Mud Roams approached the ancient breeding grounds. Traveling at the rear of the Great Eastern Herd, they had been following the river valley for days. It was the same river that descended the ravine onto the coastal plain. It was the same river that, on the coastal plain, provided a habitat for many of the tribes of the People. To the People, it was known as the River of the Nine Tribes.

When living on the coastal plain, the Red Dawn Tribe was the eastern-most of the Nine Tribes. Most of the tribe lived in the broad delta that spilled into the Great Green Sea. It was a rich habitat that the tribe shared with the Tawny Delta Tribe and the Umber Earth Tribe. The Red Dawn Tribe was located right on the edge of the delta, along the wide white beaches and in the dense tropical forests that thrived in that climate. They had the furthest to go when migrating to the ancient breeding grounds. Therefore the tribe was always the last to arrive at the top of the plateau, and generally always last to arrive in the western foothills. The two roams were the last elements of the Great Eastern Herd to arrive at the Gathering Place this season. Except, of course, for the rear-guard of packers.

The river valley was very wide here, perhaps a mile wide. The wide river flowed quietly, the waters only partially tinged by mud flushed by the spring rains. The ground on either side of the river valley had been rising for the last ten miles. Thus the valley occupied a lower elevation than the surrounding land, and near the end of their long journey, the valley was more like a wide canyon.

At the end of the river valley, the roams entered into the ancient Gathering Place of the Nine Tribes. It was a vast topographical bowl, that provided more than enough room to comfortably fit the entire Great Eastern Herd. It was slightly elliptical, with hills bordering more than three sides: the northern, western, southern, and part of the eastern sides of the bowl. Only on the eastern side was there a break in the hills, and that opening, out of which the River of the Nine Tribes flowed, formed a large gateway into the Gathering Place.

Perhaps the bowl had been formed by the impact of a meteorite ages ago. Or perhaps it had been scooped out during the last ice-age, some fifty thousand years ago. No one could say for sure, certainly none of the People. But the Gathering Place had been used by the People since beyond memory. Many hundreds of generations had been coming here, and its location was virtually genetically implanted in the memory of all the members of the Great Eastern Herd.

Nine large streams flowed out of the foothills into the Gathering Place. They helped create a small lake in the center of bowl. The lake overflowed, and the overage flowed eastward, forming the source for the River of the Nine Tribes.

A small, craggy island sat in the middle of the lake. Sharp-toothed, gull-like birds lived on the island, and fished in the lake. The People called them **feathered flyers**. They too had been migrating to the Gathering Place to breed since before memory.

The island that rose sharp and angular out of the center of the lake was a sacred island. Indeed, all here was sacred to the Great Eastern Herd. The lake, the nine streams that flowed into the lake, the topographical bowl that captured the lake, the river course that flowed from the lake and across the plateau, the ravine where the river gained speed and turbulence, and the mighty, ambling water course of the coastal plain that slowly made its way to the sea. They all formed a fundamental part of the daily and annual lives of the herd. The People could not imagine their lives without this essential geography. If they worshipped anything, if anything came close to taking the form of a deity for them, it was this river, and all its accessories.

Grendaar and Renthot lead their roams into the ellipse and down to the lake. They passed remnants of the Black Valley Tribe and the Tawny Delta Tribe, the Turquoise Sea Tribe and the Umber Earth Tribe. The tribes were spread out throughout the elliptical bowl, grazing and resting, cavorting and dominance dueling.

As the two roams approached the lake, they mingled with the Golden Rim Tribe for awhile, greeting old friends. Finally they came to the shores of the lake. Here they drank from its waters, refreshing themselves in the special waters of this special place. Featheredflyers, inured to sharing their habitat with the rambling giants, refused to take flight. Instead, they fluttered here and there around the bulky hornbrows, poking beaks into the shallows, looking for tidbits to consume.

After the roams had dallied awhile by the lake, they set out for their tribe. They traveled around the lake, and found the stream, one of the nine, beside which the Red Dawn Tribe camped. There was much rejoicing amongst the Red Dawn Tribe when the two tardy roams arrived. The tribe had scattered at the top of the ravine, and for days roams had been rejoining it. These two were the last to appear, and there was collective relief when it was determined that they were intact. Only Panthrar was still missing. And it was reported that an adolescent female, a packer by the name of Pippit, was possibly with him. If they were both still alive.

Grendaar had noticed as they traveled through the ellipse that dominance fighting had already begun. It was not unusual. Some tribes had been here for days already, and the breeding season stirred one's blood to get things going. In a day or so the adult females of the Red Dawn Tribe would begin to ascend this specific stream valley. They would ascend the valley, and chose a small side-valley, or combe, in which to make their nests prior to laying their eggs. Meanwhile the adult males would fight for the privilege of mating with the females.

Neither he nor any of the males of the two roams, including the sojourners Kinput and Sevren, were rested enough for such combat. Not that this made a difference to anyone else. So by common consent, the thirteen adult males gathered together for the remainder of the day to discourage any interlopers.

They put up a united front throughout the day, which was not only unusual, but quite effective in redirecting the attention of most of the other males elsewhere.

Tomorrow it would be back to the normal rules of combat. This benefitted Kinput and Sevren perhaps more than the roamers, but all were thankful for it none-the-less. In this way they were able to get some rest after their long journey. It had been a journey that had taken twelve days across the wooded coastal plain; three days up the ravine; a brief rest period, such as it was, at the top of the ravine; and then five days across the upper plain.

The next day the adult females of the tribe went up the stream valley to select a combe or glen in which to make their nests. The best sites were well-known, as this was the Valley of the Red Dawn Tribe, and many of the females had their favorite spots. Groups of females filtered into various glens as they climbed up the main valley, until all had disappeared into one or another of the combes. The females of the Green Water Roam chose the same little dale as those of the Yellow Mud Roam, the Black Sand Roam, and the Horn Rock Roam. The fifty-nine females of these four roams got along well enough, and there were plenty of good locations for all, so there was no problem with this.

The nesting sites from last year had been washed out by the winter storms, so each female began to select a new site. These things had to be done with great care. The choice of a poor site could spell tragedy for the potential offspring. The eggs might not hatch at all. Or if they hatched, the young might not survive the forty days required in the nest for the rapid growth to gain the strength necessary to survive outside the nest.

Each adult female walked around with keen attention to details. Each inspected the ground, the conditions of the soil, the proximity of neighboring nests, the distance from potential cover that could hide predators, the route to food and water for the adults, and a host of other things.

The soil had to be dry, and it had to drain well, because wet soil would rot the eggs. It had to be fairly hard, so that one could form the nest, but not so hard that it was difficult to dig. Each nest had to be about thirty feet apart from the other nests, because the adults needed room to move about without disturbing the nests. The nests couldn't be any further apart than that, because they had to be close enough to discourage the many small predators that would try to steal eggs and nestlings. Rearing young was a community project, and neighbors would keep a watchful eye on one another's nests while the parents were away gathering food. So neighbors had to be relatively close to each other. The nests also had to be close to the stream that ran down the middle of the valley, and close to the berry bushes that thrived in this environment. For the adults had to eat and drink throughout the nesting period, and they had to gather food for the young for the same extended time.

Each female chose a site that she felt best met the necessary requirements. Then she began to scoop dirt with her forepaws, pushing it towards the chosen spot, or dig soil with her hindlegs, shoving it towards the incipient nest. She would frequently stop to check her progress, and to make sure that the nest was developing just so. She continued this until she had the right amount of soil. Then she slowly and carefully shaped the mound with her forepaws. She meticulously circled the mound, forming a conical hill some four feet high and six or seven feet in diameter. Finally she excavated the top, flattening it out somewhat, to form a three foot wide hollow in the middle of the nest. This was the place, after she had selected a mate, in which she would deposit her eggs. Now the nest was virtually, but not quite totally, finished. Each female would put the finishing touches on her nest, with the help of her mate, as part of the courting ritual.

All day long the females toiled constructing their nests. There was a lot of visiting of friend's nests, and a lot of discussion about the locations, and the sizes and shapes and heights and widths of the nests. There was always helpful criticism about how to make the nests better, whether one wanted it or not. Older females were always happy to give such advice to the younger ones, if they were asked for it, and sometimes even if they weren't. With a lot of scooping, and patting, and molding throughout the morning and afternoon, the adult females were finished near sundown.

As the sun inched toward the western horizon, the adult females returned to lake-side in the Gathering Place, to check on the status of the younger members of the roam, who had been left under the nominal care of the adult males all day. But more importantly, now it was essential for the adult females to be with the adult males of their roams, and to see what other selections were available from which to chose a suitable mate.

The adult males spent their day somewhat differently. Dominance fighting had begun in earnest. The ellipse was full of strutting champions and dejected losers of hundreds of such contests. Most of the competition of this day was waged by solitaries and adult male packers. Some forty percent of the males in the herd were solitaries, and another twenty percent were adult packers. These males had little or no hierarchal status like roammers did, so they had to fight for position.

The adult male packers at least had some hierarchal status, for such was necessary to control packs. Thus their challenge was not as great as was that of the solitaries. For the male solitaries held no status whatever. Thus, each year, they had to start from scratch to re-establish their status.

Only among the roams was hierarchal status firmly fixed. Thus, on this day, there was little fighting between roam-members. Their position in the hierarchy had been pretty well established throughout the year. An adult male roammer could fight to change his position just about any time he wanted. He didn't have to wait for the mating season to establish his order in the roam.

Some adult male roammers were content with their positions, and if not successfully challenged from below, might remain in their positions their entire lives. They were unlikely to challenge someone above themselves. Other males were far more aggressive, and wished for a more dominant position.

Generally this latter type of male roammer bided his time, growing older, stronger, and heavier, and perhaps more cunning, before he challenged the next male up in the hierarchal ladder from himself. When there came the time that he thought he could beat the more dominant male in a hierarchy fight, he would challenge the male to battle. If the dominant male declined to fight, the challenger won that male's position in the roam without bloodshed and bruises. However it was rare that a dominant male gave up his position without a vigorous and determined effort to beat the challenger.

If the challenger won, the two males exchanged positions in the roam. There are some dominance fights that turn particularly vicious. Although not common, if a fight turned vicious, the winner might expel the loser from the roam. If the dominant male won, he had the choice of letting the defeated challenger remain, or else he could expel him. In the case of the latter, only a roamleader could intercede, and prevent a loser from being cast from the roam. If the winner didn't like the decision, he was free to fight the roamleader for his position.

If a challenger lost to the same dominant male twice, he frequently left the roam of his own accord. It just as often became a matter of pride that forced the loser to go. Sometimes, after a period of self-imposed exile, he would join another roam. Sometimes he became a solitary for the rest of his life.

Dominance fights occurred in roams, although not with great frequency, at least often enough that they almost never occurred at mating season. At that time of the year, even more was at stake for the roam than usual. Only the addle-brained, or the supremely confident, or the woefully desperate, would precipitate a dominance fight in his own roam during mating season.

So this day passed with contests among the solitaries and the packers. Some males, defeated more times than their ego could take, quit fighting and forewent the privilege of mating this year. These included those too old to win a dominance fight anymore, and those too young and inexperienced. It also included the weaker members of the herd, and those maimed at hatching, or in an accident, or from predator attack, but only if that malady prevented them from fighting and winning. The winners, however, expected more fights on the next day. And in a day or two, the winners of these fights would start to challenge roammers directly. They would challenge them, and fight them, for the privilege of mating with the females under their protection.

Even then, roamleaders were almost never challenged over a mate. For one thing, they were the strongest, largest, heaviest, most cunning, and most experienced fighters of the herd. They had won their position by being the best fighters, and they kept their positions by daily placing themselves between danger, in any form, and their roam. They were the first to fight at the first sign of any threat to their roam, and they were the last to leave a place of danger. To challenge a roamleader over a mate, was to also challenge his position as roamleader. Before someone did that, he had to be very strong, very confident, or very desperate. If nothing else, he had to be highly motivated.

Even so, sometimes roamleaders were challenged over a female, Grendaar reminded himself. If a roamleader aspired to the very best that the herd had to offer, sometimes he had to defend that aspiration. Thus it was that at eighteen springs of age, Grendaar, a roamleader, had had to fight four other roamleaders, five roammers, including one from his own roam, four solitaries, and two packers, all over a period of three days, to keep Tessah for himself. Those memories were laced with both pride and nostalgia. He remembered those days as if they were only a few days ago.

Tessah the beautiful, whose beauty had lasted a lifetime. Tessah the gentle, whose mystique had captured the hearts and imaginations of a whole generation of males. Tessah the wise, who had so subtly helped guide him, and who had kept him from making some of the worst decisions of his life. Yes, Tessah was an exceptional female, and Grendaar would have died before he would have let another male have her.

That spring, thirteen years ago, he felt like he had come close to dying. He couldn't have successfully held off too many more males. Maybe not even one more male. But the others didn't know that. Each knew that if you couldn't beat the unsuccessful challenger, how could you beat the champion? So no more tried. By the end of those dominance fights, Grendaar had become a folk hero. He could have commanded the entire Red Dawn Tribe, if he had wanted. Two other tribes asked him to command them. If he wanted to. But he didn't want to. He only wanted Tessah.

The next year, twelve years ago, there were new challenges. If anything, Tessah had become even more beautiful. She carried with her a mystique that beguiled all but the hardest of hearts. Apparently, in one year's time, the memories of some of the unsuccessful challengers had faded. They thought that now they could best Grendaar. The preceding year they had been over-tired, or over-confident, or had slipped, or had been tricked.

That following year, twelve years ago, they were more rested, or were stronger, or had grown more cunning. And then there were new young males, who hadn't fought Grendaar the year before, and who thought that they were stronger than the old male. Grendaar had to fight his first dominance fight of that season even before the roam had gotten to the Gathering Place. He had had to fight eight dominance fights, the last two with roamleaders, before the challenges stopped.

Eleven years ago, no one had challenged Grendaar. And perhaps because of that, or perhaps due to the heady euphoria of his unassailable reputation as unbeatable, he had acted with reckless abandon that year. Perhaps even he believed the stories they told about him: indomitable, no matter how many males came at him, no matter how large they were, no matter how strong and agile. Whatever the reason, something inside him had compelled him to mate with seven different females that year, from four different roams. He had never mated with seven females in one spring before in his life, or since.

Ten years ago, he again went unchallenged, but he restricted himself to only four females that year. After that, he would receive one or two challenges a year. There was always someone who wanted Tessah so much that his memory and his judgement clouded. There was always someone who wanted to best him. None had yet. And these days, he was more conservative, and mated with only two, or sometimes three, females.

He put these happy memories aside. Now he was much older, some might think more assailable. Tomorrow new challenges would come, of that he was sure.

CHAPTER TEN
TRAVELING COMPANIONS

Panthrar and Pippit continued in a northwesterly direction the rest of the day. They figured that with each step, they were pulling further and further away from the path that the predators would be taking, which they expected would be due west. They grazed as they traveled, and towards sunset they began to look for a safe place to spend the night. It was not easy. The ravine might have been a dangerous place for a hornbrow because of its confined spaces, but it had plenty of places to hide. The plain had plenty of room in which to run, which was good when you were moving in broad daylight, but it offered few places that provided real security to a sleeping hornbrow. Moving and sleeping in roams, and in tribes, and in the great herds, was the method that the People, and many other green-eaters for that matter, had evolved to protect themselves from predators. It wasn't very safe to move about singly, or in pairs.

In late afternoon they came upon a stream that flowed southeasterly, towards the River of the Nine Tribes. They walked upstream along the streambed, since the stream flowed from the same general direction that they were going. Even when it took erratic turns, they continued to follow it. They reasoned that it probably came from the western foothills, their eventual destination, so it wouldn't lead them too far astray. In addition, walking along the minor depression that served as the streambed meant that they were less visible from the plain proper, which was desirable from their perspective.

Plus, they had immediate access to water, which after their ordeal in the ravine, didn't seem like such a trivial matter.

About an hour before nightfall, they came to a curve in the stream. At some previous time, the stream had run much more heavily, and had carved a cave-like overhang out of a hill. Now the stream came within ninety or a hundred feet of the opening to the cave that the overhang created. There was a sandy beach in front of the overhang, and many small ferns had sprung up along the edge of the stream. They decided to investigate the cavity in the hill and see if it would serve as a safe place to spend the night.

A quick inspection showed a not insignificant amount of room under the overhang, certainly more than enough for the two of them. In addition, a small inner cave had been eroded into the hill in the back of the overhang. The inner cave was large enough to barely fit Pippit, but was too small to hold the bulk of Panthrar, let alone the both of them. Rather than continue onward during the last hour of daylight, and risk having to sleep in the open, they decided to stop here for the night.

They grazed along the stream banks, enjoying the lush ferns, and then retired to the overhang to sit quietly with each other until darkness set in. As they approached the overhang, they heard and saw the hasty scurrying of little figures into the recesses of the cave. Their curiosity aroused, they went to the back wall to investigate. They found that the walls of the cave were riddled with little holes, each about four or five inches in diameter. They sniffed at these holes, and found that they were presently occupied by small opossum-like mammals. They were the **night-scroungers**, the largest of the little mammals that inhabited the region. There were dozens, perhaps scores of nests of the little mammals.

Panthrar poked around the openings to the nests for awhile, but all he succeeded in doing was to scare the creatures deeper into their nests. Pippit kept chiding him about tormenting the little things. After awhile he stopped and shrugged. The little pests wouldn't really bother something so large as a hornbrow, so why not just leave them alone and share with them the accommodations that the overhang provided? As night fell, the two hornbrows snuggled close together in the deepest recesses of those accommodations, and one after the other, lapsed into sleep.

Around ten that night, first Pippit, and then Panthrar, was awakened by the scurrying of little feet as the opossums tried to leave their homes for a night of foraging. The night-scroungers warily worked their way around the substantial bodies of the two erstwhile sleepers, and dashed in short sprints followed by momentary pauses, out onto the beach. The hornbrows watched the creatures disappear into the moon-illuminated darkness outside the cave. Then they tried to ignore any further antics of their hosts, and fell back into a fitful sleep.

Around the middle of the night, they were again awakened by the scurrying of little feet. The opossums were rushing back into the cave, and showed little or no regard for the immense hornbrows. They ran around and over Pippit and Panthrar in their haste to reach the safety of their nests.

Panthrar was about to protest, when it dawned upon him that perhaps something more frightening than a hornbrow had caused them to behave this way. He and Pippit, who was also awake, exchanged glances. They didn't have to wait long to learn the cause of the opossums' fear. Carefully, with prolonged and deliberate footsteps, and with his head jerking this way and that, a razortooth walked along the near bank of the stream, searching for prey. He moved as silently and stealthily as a shadow. He would pause every third or fourth footstep, sniff the air, and cock his head to the left and right. Then he would proceed another several footsteps, and repeat his search tactics. He continued downstream, past the opening of the cave, and out of the range of vision of the two hornbrows.

About ten minutes later, the razortooth came back, on the far side of the stream. He took a few steps into the view of the hornbrows, and then stopped, sniffed, and cocked his head. He lingered overlong there, his keen eyesight searching for movement.

He took another step, and then stopped, frozen in mid-motion. Almost imperceptibly, his head rotated in the direction of the overhang. If they had not been watching him carefully, they might not have noticed that he was there, so immobile was he. He seemed unreal, like a figure cut from wood, or from stone. His head turned with such languorous grace, that it was difficult to see motion. Yet, where once the razortooth had been looking forward up the stream, now he was looking directly at the opening under the overhang.

It was dark inside the cave, and the razortooth could not possibly see them, as quiet and motionless as they were. But still he stared. He did not move for almost five minutes. It was eerie to watch him standing there, like stone, not fidgeting or pawing, like so many green-eaters were wont to do. Unless their lives were in jeopardy. Then they too could remain as still as the Great Horned Rock itself.

The razortooth took a slow, tentative step in their direction. Even in the moonlight, he was a black, wiry figure, with thin, muscular arms and strong, sinewy hindlegs that could propel him forward at incredible speed. But he did not charge, as the situation did not call for that. He took another step. Then he took another. Step by step, he slowly crossed the stream. He moved with such stealth that he barely disturbed the water. He crossed the sandy beach that lay before the overhang, barely disturbing a pebble, and stopped, frozen.

He listened intently. He peered into the impenetrable darkness of the recess. His cold, unblinking eyes glistened in the moonlight. He sniffed ever so quietly. He did not have a keen sense of smell. Razorteeth had sacrificed that sense for other assets. He smelled the spoor of night-scroungers, of that he was certain. But there was something else. Something out of place that he couldn't quite identify, so masked by the smell of night-scroungers was it. He was suspicious. And that made him nervous. But he was also hungry, and in the end, it was that which impelled him forward.

He crouched low, expecting a small quarry, and slowly advanced into the darkness before him. As he had been crossing the stream, Panthrar had quietly risen to his feet, and had advanced a step or two, still invisible in the darkness. The razortooth paused while his eyes adjusted to the greater darkness of the cave. As his large eyes began to see again, his head began to dart left and right, searching for movement. His attention was focused at ground level, where he hoped to catch a night-scrounger dashing for cover.

Panthrar took another cautious step forward. The razortooth immediately caught the movement, and advanced several steps forward, staring intently at Panthrar's left hind foot. Finally he could see it, though not too clearly. He looked at it with his overlapping fields of vision. He pivoted his head, so that he stared at it with just his left eye. Then he pivoted his head again, leaning forward, and stared at it with his right eye. He raised his focus a little, and stared at the ankle. Then he quickly followed the ankle up to the shin and knee. He froze, as realization began to dawn on him. The thing he was examining began to move. He jumped backward just as Panthrar pivoted hard and fast on his left foot, bringing his tail around with a lightning strike.

The razortooth was quick, but not quick enough. He had gotten too close. Panthrar's tail struck him a terrific blow just below the shoulders, throwing him heavily against the wall near the overhang. Half stunned, he tried to rise and scuttle away, but Panthrar was too quick for him. The adolescent rushed up and stepped upon the razortooth, crushing the life from him.

Next, Panthrar cautiously approached the opening of the overhang, and peered out. Pippit came up beside him. Together they tried to determine if other razorteeth were about. Razorteeth frequently hunted in packs, and if a pack was about, it would be a dangerous threat to the two hornbrows.

There were no razorteeth to be seen. Panthrar left Pippit at the entrance to keep a lookout while he returned to the body of the one lying by the wall. Panthrar leaned down cautiously to inspect the body more carefully. He had never had the leisure to investigate a razortooth this close up before.

It was indeed dead. He sniffed the carcass. It had that characteristic smell of a meat-eater. He examined the head, fascinated in a morbid way with the many cruel, sharp teeth that bristled from its slender jaws. It had long arms, and thin grasping fingers, equipped with large, death-dealing claws. The equally equipped feet each had, in addition, one exceptionally large claw that could be extended or retracted. They were the sickle-claws, ideal for ripping the flesh of even a creature as large and as magnificent as a hornbrow. Panthrar was glad that it was dead. He was glad that he had killed it before it had the chance to alert its pack. If he hadn't, before long, he and Pippit would be fighting for their lives. That might soon be happening anyway.

Panthrar returned to the opening. For a long while he and Pippit watched the moonlit landscape. They listened in the stillness of the star-studded night, and sniffed the coolness of the air, trying to detect the presence of other razorteeth. For over an hour they did this, but no razorteeth came. So they quietly retired into the recesses of the cave, and took turns sleeping.

The next morning, they took up their journey once more. They followed the stream-bed until it had turned so far north that it had turned to the northeast. They decided that if this persisted, it would take many extra days to reach the western foothills. So, finally, they had to abandon the stream-bed and turn directly west across the open plain.

Panthrar worried about the potential for trouble that they had been fortunate enough to escape from last night. He knew he couldn't expect to have that same luck every night. Nor did he think that he and Pippit could successfully ward off a determined attack by a pack of razorteeth, not without both of them being seriously hurt. He had conceived of a plan that, if it worked, might offer them better protection. So all day he looked for the necessary missing ingredient to make it work.

He was hoping to run across a roam of hornbrows, or ridgebrows, or **longsnouts**, or even some **cresttops** or trumpeters. Any of these would have made life easier, especially if he could find some of the People, or some Cousins. He could speak with them directly. But even the more distantly related cresttops and trumpeters would probably have been okay. Even though they couldn't speak to each other very well, he could still have made his wants known. He would ask to travel with them to the western foothills. Then, although the others would go off to their own special breeding places, the two hornbrows would be relatively safe.

Most of the large predators, although they would follow the herds all the way across the plain, killing prey as they needed to, wouldn't actually enter the foothills. There were too many of the People there, and too many Cousins, and other hadrosaurs. For in the foothills the landscape favored the hunted rather than the hunters, and their roles reversed. The People (and the other green-eaters) would hunt, trap, and kill a ravager found in the foothills, and do it with a determined vengeance. Individual losses became irrelevant. If they didn't kill every ravager that attempted to hunt in the foothills, their very future would be jeopardized. Not the future of a few individuals, but of the whole race. They couldn't afford for the ravagers to get into the breeding grounds. The foothills were the only really dangerous places for a ravager, and the ravagers seemed to know it. So they stayed away. All Panthrar and Pippit had to do was to get across the plain, and into the foothills.

Panthrar, of course, knew this. His plan was to find a roam of hadrosaurs, any hadrosaurs, and try to talk his way into a temporary alliance. But, by a continuation of the poor luck that seemed to be following them, they saw no hadrosaurs. Shortly after mid-day, they did come upon a small herd of **threehorns** traveling in the same direction as they.

The threehorns were grazing in a little dale, and Panthrar and Pippit came upon them just as they crested a small hillock that enclosed the dale. There were about thirty adult threehorns, and about half that number again in young. The young were one-third-size replicas of their parents.

Threehorns were quadrupeds. The adults were between twenty-five and thirty feet in length, and about six or so feet high at the shoulder. They had small nose horns, that were still pretty impressive when compared with the horns of the People. More impressive still were their two prominent brow horns. On males, the brow horns could exceed three feet in length. They also had solid neck frills that encircled the back of their heads, protecting their necks. They were about nine or more feet high at the top of the frill. They ate with a strong beak-like mouth that could produce a fierce bite. All this was packaged in a bulky body with a short tail. The females weighed over five tons, while the males could reach over six tons in weight.

For all their size and bulk, they were pretty fast and agile. Like onehorns, they had poor eyesight. And like onehorns, their poor eyesight did nothing to inhibit their ingrained desire for a full-speed charge. Sometimes at anything that moved. They were shorter than a hornbrow, but were almost double the weight. They were treated with great respect by all those who encountered them, including the ravagers.

Panthrar was about to show his respect by quietly detouring around them, when by chance they caught the attention of the primary male. The primary male had been on the other side of the herd. As he trotted around the herd in their direction, other adults stopped their grazing and glanced up at them. The young, who were already clustered near the middle of the group, packed in even closer together. The adults quickly encircled the young. All except the primary male that is, and one or two other dominant males. The other dominant males stationed themselves between the herd and the two interlopers, while the primary male trotted up the rise toward the hornbrows to investigate.

"Pippit, my sister," Panthrar whispered breathlessly, "Turn around and walk away. Walk, don't run."

There was a time, not so long ago, when Pippit's first inclination would have been to do that very thing – retreat with all due speed. Not so this time. She felt a stronger desire to stay and help Panthrar than to protect herself. It was a curious thing. Something that surprised her greatly. Instead, she just stood there.

"What, my brother," she replied, "And leave you here to reason with our brutish friend? Forgive me, but I cannot."

The threehorn stopped about a hundred feet from the two, and pawed the ground. He snorted, shaking his head at them. Panthrar expected him to charge at any moment. He felt a strong sense of urgency.

"Go, Pippit, and immediately. This is not a request."

Amongst the People, it was difficult for a female to disobey a male. Not impossible, but difficult. It went against a lot of heredity. Pippit began to back down the hillock away from the threehorn. Panthrar felt a little relieved. Now he had only his own life to worry about. He would have to stall for awhile so that Pippit could get clear of this threehorned quadruped.

"Do you not recognize me, my blind brother?" he asked the threehorn in a calm, level voice. The threehorn just stared at him.

"It is I, Panthrar the Swift, of the Green Water Roam of the Red Dawn Tribe. And what is your name?" The threehorn lowered his head and pawed the ground, first with his left front foot, and then with his right.

"I am a hornbrow, you slow-witted boulder-brain, not a ravager," explained Panthrar. "Can you not see that I am not a ravager?" The threehorn snorted, made a squealing-roaring sound, and then charged. Straight at Panthrar he came, picking up speed at an alarming rate. The charging quadruped lowered his head, the sharp tips of three horns pointing straight at Panthrar's abdomen.

Panthrar waited until the last possible moment, and then darted to the left. Even so, the threehorn just missed him. Panthrar tripped in his haste, rolled completely over, and landed back on his feet. He looked back at the threehorn, expecting to see it slowing and turning towards him.

The threehorn began to slacken his speed and turn to his right, towards Panthrar, when suddenly he changed direction and spurted forward again. He stumbled as he changed speeds and direction, churning dust and soil, kicking up great clods of dirt as he went. His new momentum took him over the rise in the hillock, and two hundred feet beyond Panthrar, before he came to a complete stop. Panthrar could clearly see why.

Pippit had been standing about seventy-five feet behind Panthrar. After the threehorn had missed Panthrar, she stood there waiting for him to charge her. Rather than stopping and turning to pursue Panthrar, the threehorn elected to charge the new target standing so invitingly in front of him. Just like Panthrar, she waited until the last possible moment, and then darted to the right, away from Panthrar. The threehorn could not make up his mind whether to turn right towards Panthrar, or left towards Pippit, so he just went straight, instead. Finally he stopped, turned back towards the interlopers, and pawed the ground. He shook his head, trying to see just what kind of creature, or creatures were confronting him.

Keeping an eye on the threehorn, Panthrar hastened in Pippit's direction. As he ran, he took a second to look back at the herd to see if the disappearance of the primary male over the hillock had aroused the curiosity of either of the other two dominant males. It hadn't, at least not yet. Panthrar stopped as Pippit started moving towards him. He faced the threehorn.

"So," said Panthrar to the threehorn, "I see that you are called Thundermaker."

Pippit jogged up to Panthrar, and said, "Forgive me, my brother, but I was unclear about how far away you wanted me to go. Did I do right?"

"No, you did not do right, my foolish and courageous sister. Now let us keep our wits about us so that we do not end up on the horns of this cloddish brute." He paused, and then added as an afterthought, "Or on the horns of one of his fellows."

Further discussion was cut short by the threehorn. He squeal-roared again, and galloped into a full speed charge at the two hornbrows. They stood there, side-by-side, until they risked imminent impalement, and then Panthrar darted to the right, while Pippit bolted for the left. The threehorn skidded to a stop, and turned in the direction of Pippit. He charged after her. Panthrar looked over his shoulder, and saw what was happening. He stopped short, and ran after the threehorn, calling to alert Pippit.

Pippit scampered in a tight circle to her right, managing to stay just ahead of the horns of the quadruped. Panthrar calculated Pippit's course, and positioned himself accordingly. As Pippit and the threehorn ran past him, he darted between the two, on a course perpendicular to that of the threehorn. It was a bold and reckless move, but it was all that he could think of to distract the threehorn.

All the threehorn saw was a blur that ran dangerously close to his horns, between him and his intended victim. It then disappeared out of the range of vision to his left. He braked to a halt on four stiffened legs. The dust from his pounding feet reared up behind him, drifted over his now immobile body, and was carried along on the breeze. For a few moments, neither Panthrar nor Pippit could see the threehorn. Nor could he see them. He was completely immersed in dust. The two hornbrows used the opportunity to put more distance between themselves and the threehorn, and to catch their breath.

The threehorn walked out of the dust cloud, and looked around. He saw the two hornbrows, again standing side-by-side, about three hundred feet away. He was no longer certain that they were ravagers. They didn't smell like ravagers, he was certain of that. He had gotten a really good whiff of their scent – he had been within feet of their heat-soaked bodies. No, they didn't smell like meat-eaters. And they sure didn't act like any ravagers he had ever seen.

He snorted, and walked carefully towards them. He stopped at about a hundred feet and stared at them fixedly. He swung his head from side to side, trying to see them better. He snorted again, and pawed the ground just once. He turned sideways. He swung his head back towards them, and again examined them carefully. They didn't move. Ravagers would have tried to take advantage of his more vulnerable stance. He turned away from them, and walked a few paces. Then he suddenly turned back towards them, ready for any treachery. They still had not moved. They must not be ravagers, after all. He turned back towards his herd, trotted over the hillock, and disappeared from their view.

Panthrar beckoned to Pippit, and followed the threehorn. He stopped when he could see over the hillock. The threehorn stood just beyond the crest, as if he was waiting for them. They froze. The threehorn watched them for a few minutes, and then trotted back to his herd. The herd had again taken up the trek, led away from possible danger by the other two dominant males. One of the other dominant males preceded the herd, while the second trailed along behind it. This latter frequently stopped and turned, apparently concerned about the primary male. He wasn't happy until the primary male had re-joined him, and together they trotted back to the slower-moving herd.

The herd of threehorns was going in a direction somewhat north of west. It wasn't a bad direction. Panthrar and Pippit climbed to the top of the hillock, and watched them depart. When the herd was about a quarter of a mile away, Panthrar led Pippit after them.

They followed the herd, at a safe distance, all afternoon. The primary male occasionally took the lead of the herd, but more frequently, he trailed behind it, keeping an eye on the two hornbrows. As the day wore on, the primary male trailed further and further behind his herd, and closer and closer to Panthrar and Pippit. Two hours before sundown, he finally stopped and waited for them. They bravely continued on until they were about three hundred feet from the threehorn, and then they stopped and waited. There was no sense getting any closer, since they had no idea what was on his mind. He made his intentions known fairly quickly.

The threehorn pawed at the ground, snorting and shaking his head. He bellowed several times at them, then began trotting in their direction. The two hornbrows spread out a little, so he would have to choose one or the other to charge at. He picked Panthrar, and began to gallop. When he was within a hundred feet, he charged at full speed. Pippit bolted to the right, honking and flapping her arms. Panthrar stood his ground, and at the proper moment, jumped to the right, and sprinted after Pippit. The threehorn turned predictably to the his left, after Panthrar, so Panthrar cut to the right again, away from Pippit. The threehorn followed him.

Pippit, seeing this, turned around, and ran at the threehorn, again honking and flapping her arms. The threehorn became distracted by Pippit, so he stopped pursuing Panthrar, and turned and looked at the crazy antics of this female hornbrow. Pippit halted her headlong flight toward the threehorn. The primary male pawed the ground, squeal-roared at Pippit, and charged at her. She immediately darted to the left. As she did so, the threehorn continued to arc in her direction. Suddenly Panthrar ran past his horns, with only a few feet to spare, on a course perpendicular to that of the threehorn. He swung his head and horns after the retreating Panthrar, but missed him. The threehorn stopped short again, and bellowed his frustration.

He stood there pawing the ground for several minutes. He took out his frustration by pawing up chunks of the soil, and hurling them behind him. First he would do this with his front feet, then with his rear feet. All the while, he grumbled and snorted. And all the while, he kept his eyes on either Panthrar or Pippit. They were slowly circling him at a distance, and finally joined up on the side furthest from the herd.

He began to trot towards them again. They again spread out, and he again chose Panthrar. At one hundred feet he broke into a full charge. Pippit sprang to the left this time, again trying to distract the threehorn by honking and flapping her arms. When it was almost too late, Panthrar tried repeating the previous strategy by first cutting towards Pippit, and then cutting away. The threehorn followed both maneuvers, as before. Pippit turned back towards the threehorn, running and honking with all her might. This time he wouldn't be distracted. He continued to charge after Panthrar.

The male hornbrow cut left and right, and then left again. The threehorn followed every move. Panthrar tried an all-out sprint, but still the threehorn followed. All the while, Pippit ran behind the threehorn, honking loudly. She even picked up rocks, and hurled them at the creature, several bouncing off his thick hide. But the threehorn was not to be distracted. He chased Panthrar for a half-mile, before he finally stopped. Panthrar didn't stop until he had put over five hundred feet between himself and the three sharp horns of his pursuer.

Meanwhile, Pippit made a wide detour around the threehorn. He watched her, and snorted and pawed the ground. He made a few short charges in her direction, but they were more threats than actual attacks. Each time he did, she would turn directly away from him, and put even more distance between herself and the threehorn.

Pippit finally re-joined Panthrar. They stood there together, breathing heavily, watching the threehorn. He bellowed at them one more time, shook his head forcefully, and turned and trotted back towards his herd.

Pippit, still trying to catch her breath, asked Panthrar, "Well, my brother, now what do we do?"

Panthrar, also breathing heavily, shrugged his shoulders, and said, "I'm not sure, my sister. Let me think while we catch our breath."

About an hour before sundown, Thundermaker, the primary male of the small herd of threehorns, turned to look back at the trail that his herd had been following. To his surprise he saw the two hornbrows traveling about a quarter of a mile behind. He stood there, watching them approach, as his herd proceeded westward.

Panthrar and Pippit moved to within five hundred feet, but wouldn't come any closer. They had already decided that if he approached them again, they were going to turn around, and run flat-out as fast as they could go. There was no wisdom in trying to frustrate the male threehorn. Sooner or later he was going to get lucky, or perhaps more likely, their luck would run out. So they stood there and watched and waited, ready to turn and run at the slightest provocation.

The threehorn did the same. It was beyond the ken of a hornbrow to know what might be in the mind of a threehorn. They weren't going to take any chances. If he could wait, so could they. So they did. And so did Thundermaker, the threehorn. So they waited longer. And so did Thundermaker.

Panthrar knew that time might be on the side of the threehorn, even if the threehorn didn't know that. If they didn't find a safe place to spend the night, it could have disastrous consequences. He began to believe that this idea of his wasn't going to work out after all. If they had only run across a group of

The People, or of Cousins, sometime during the day. Things would be a lot better now.

Thundermaker gave up his vigil, and trotted back to his herd. He knew for sure that these pests weren't ravagers. But they were the most persistent pair of hornbrows he had ever seen. What could they possibly want, that they kept annoying him so much?

Just before sundown, the herd of threehorns found a nice little glen to settle down in for the night. The young were allowed to graze a little, and then they were rounded up, and clustered in the middle of the herd for the night. The adults circled around them, and formed a living barrier between the young and the outside world. Periodically, one or another of the three most dominant males would get up and patrol around the outskirts of the herd.

During one of these patrols, shortly after darkness, Thundermaker came upon the two hornbrows huddled together, over the crest of a low ridge. They were about a thousand feet from the herd. He saw them from the top of the ridge. Or at least he thought he did. He couldn't be sure, for his eyesight wasn't all that good. He stared at them for a long while, sniffing to make certain that it was them, and not predators. Then he walked back to the herd.

As he settled down into a comfortable position to sleep for awhile, he saw the two hornbrows come over the ridge. The herd was suddenly alert. The second male of the herd, Hidepiercer, sprang to his feet and snorted indignantly. He began to trot towards the two hornbrows. He stopped when Thundermaker rumbled something to him.

Hidepiercer couldn't believe it. The primary male had told him to leave the two crazy hornbrows alone, that they would not harm the herd. The second male stood there a minute or two, watching the hornbrows. They just huddled there together, near the top of the ridge. He was indecisive. He looked over at Thundermaker, who had closed his eyes. Hidepiercer approached the two hornbrows tentatively, and at a hundred feet, sniffed noisily. They were just hornbrows, very frightened hornbrows. He patrolled the outskirts of the herd, giving them a wide berth, lest he alarm them. It was never good to go up against Thundermaker without a very good reason. Then he too re-joined the herd and went to sleep.

A few hours later, Thundermaker awoke, and made another circuit of the dale. He found that the two crazy hornbrows had moved even closer to the herd, and lay only about a hundred and fifty feet from it. He stood there watching them in the moonlight. The young male hornbrow was staring back at him. After awhile, the primary male went back to his favorite female, snuggled up against her, and fell into a peaceful sleep.

CHAPTER ELEVEN
MUTUAL INTERESTS

Panthrar lay quietly. He watched while the primary male of the herd of threehorn's stood observing him and Pippit from the darkness. He wasn't sure what to do. Experience told him that Thundermaker, the threehorn, would likely charge them. On the other hand, it was Thundermaker who had intervened on their behalf earlier in the evening. Thundermaker had permitted them to get close to the security of the herd. So, experience aside, it didn't seem likely that Thundermaker would charge now. So what should Panthrar do?

The threehorn stood a short distance away, calmly staring at them. He did not seem very threatening now. Panthrar was reluctant to awaken Pippit unnecessarily, but they might have to retreat hastily at any moment. She needed sleep every bit as much as he needed it. But to be safe, he decided to awaken her. Even as he made the decision, the big threehorn turned away, and ambled back to his herd.

Panthrar reflected upon the decisions that he and Pippit had made, that got them to approach this closely the herd. He knew they had taken a big chance coming this close. But it was really a matter of choosing between several almost equally undesirable alternatives. Either they could wait by themselves somewhere out there on the plain, knowing that sooner or later a pack of razorteeth, or a full-sized ravager, would come upon them. Or they could hope for the unpredictable mercies of the unfathomable mind of a horned quadruped, one that they could barely communicate with. And worse, one that had been trying to impale them all that day. Panthrar had convinced Pippit that they had to choose this latter option. After all, they had a lot in common with the threehorn, and perhaps he had belatedly realized that. Perhaps that was why Thundermaker hadn't objected to them getting so close to the herd as night fell.

Panthrar let Pippit sleep longer. After the moon had moved some distance in the heavens, he woke her. It was her turn to keep watch. And very likely she, like Panthrar, would spend more time observing the sleeping herd of threehorns than watching out for other possible dangers.

During the night, a pack of razorteeth came close to the herd. Pippit could smell their distinctive odor. So, apparently, could the threehorns. The herd began to stir, and Hidepiercer sprang to his feet and headed over a ridge in the direction of the pack. The scent of the razorteeth grew fainter. Later, Hidepiercer came back to the top of the ridge. He stood for a long time, silhouetted in the moonlight, staring into the darkness toward the south.

Pippit had dozed on and off while Hidepiercer was away. After Hidepiercer had returned to the herd, she felt even safer. She closed her eyes. When next she realized it, Hidepiercer was standing about twenty feet away from her and Panthrar. It startled her to find him so close, and it made her jump. That in turn awoke Panthrar. Hidepiercer snorted, pawed the ground, and turned around and trotted back to the comfort of his present consort.

Pippit and Panthrar exchanged glances. Somehow they must have broken through to these threehorns. They were not dangerous. They were not a threat. They might even be friendly. They both breathed a sigh of relief.

Dawn was near at hand. Together, they watched the sun break the horizon. They stood up and stretched, and climbed up the ridge into the growing sunlight to catch some warmth. They both raised their mouths to the heavens, and hooted a greeting to the rising sun. It was the first time they had been able to safely do that in days.

Behind them the herd of threehorns was also stirring. Soon they had company on the ridge, as threehorns also sought the warmth of the early morning sun. The threehorns bellowed their own greetings to the new day. They grazed for a while, watching the bottom of the sun break free from the arms of the earth. The sun fled from its night's companion, and began another day's journey across the sky.

The herd also began its journey again. The two hornbrows followed close behind it. The herd traveled about an hour toward the northwest before coming to a small lake. The lake was not yet very large, and was more like an oversized pond. When the spring rains began in earnest, the pond would rapidly swell into a lake. The pond was shallow and alkaline, and about five hundred feet in diameter. It lay in the middle of a wide, dry hard-pan, that was slowly re-filling from the early rains. Even the youngest of the threehorns could walk all the way across the pond without having to swim.

The herd headed straight for the lake. The threehorns almost completely surrounded it, drinking their fill. Panthrar and Pippit waited patiently off to the side, until most of the threehorns had finished. Then, while the threehorns grazed, the two hornbrows walked down to the water's edge, waded into about two feet of water, and drank. The few threehorns still drinking, looked up at their approach, watched them enter the water, and then resumed drinking. When Panthrar and Pippit began to splash each other, jumping and giggling, some of the younger threehorns, more skittish than the adults, hurried over to the far side of the pond. They wanted to put more distance between themselves and these strange creatures that kept following the herd.

None of the adult threehorns had offered any threats to either Panthrar or Pippit, either now or during the preceding early morning journey. When they started romping in the water, Thundermaker did come over to investigate. After he got a good look, and smelled their scent carefully, he snorted and went back to patrolling the perimeter of the herd.

The herd grazed for about a half an hour off of the succulent new growth feeding off of the new lake. As the herd was preparing to move on, Panthrar caught the scent of a dreadrunner coming down on a breeze from the north. He became suddenly alert. Pippit had caught the scent also. None of the threehorns seemed to be aware of it yet. Panthrar honked at Thundermaker. The primary male, and most of the rest of the herd, all looked at Panthrar. He honked a warning, clearly understandable to a hornbrow. The threehorns just stared at him. Worse, some of the adults went back to grabbing a few last bites to eat before the trek began again.

Panthrar waved his arms and tooted at Thundermaker. Then he ran toward a shallow rise north of where the threehorns grazed. Pippit followed more slowly. Panthrar surveyed the ground before him all the way to the horizon. No dreadrunner. But that didn't mean anything. There were a lot of rises and falls to the terrain. The dreadrunner could be hiding anywhere.

Panthrar turned back and looked for Thundermaker. He was still in his position on a nearby rise, about a thousand feet away. Even so, he kept his eyes on Panthrar. Panthrar honked the warning again. Thundermaker pawed the ground. Panthrar jumped up and down, pointing toward the north. Thundermaker honked, and trotted over to the mad two-leggers to see what all the commotion was about.

Pippit watched Thundermaker carefully, lest he charge them when they weren't paying attention. Meanwhile Panthrar inspected the terrain to the north. Thundermaker came up almost beside them, causing Pippit no end of alarm. He was not as tall as they, but much more massive. Nor could Pippit forget his three-foot long horns. Their primary purpose might be to wrestle with other dominant male threehorns, but their secondary use as defensive weapons didn't mitigate their lethality one bit.

Yet Thundermaker did not make any threatening moves, as he had done so often the day before. He looked at Panthrar and Pippit curiously. Panthrar pointed to the north. He exaggerated sniffing. Thundermaker sniffed also, he didn't have to try to exaggerate. Panthrar then made leaping moves like a dreadrunner, and pointed again to the north. Thundermaker looked at him suspiciously. Then he looked to the north. He sniffed.

The scent of the dreadrunner was getting stronger. The threehorn might not see the dreadrunner until he was almost on top of him, but surely he could smell him. Panthrar began to worry about his own and Pippit's safety. If the threehorn didn't understand soon, or detect the dreadrunner himself, the two hornbrows would have to make a run for it on their own.

The threehorn suddenly stiffened. He raised his head high, his neck arched back, and his short nose horn pointing directly upward. He sniffed noisily. Then he reared up on his hind legs, his eyes almost even with Panthrar's, and sniffed again. He came down on all fours with a heavy thunk. "Huuooooonnnnn," he screamed at the north. Startled, Pippit scooted away. Panthrar took three or four steps back. Thundermaker turned in the direction of his herd. "Huuoooooonnnn."

All heads were up. All were staring either at Thundermaker, or further toward the north. Thundermaker turned toward Panthrar and Pippit and made a few deep, rumbling grunts. He nodded his head, and swung it this way and that. He seemed to be saying that he understood.

Pippit approached Thundermaker cautiously. She got very close, obviously very nervous, but also very determined. She came within five feet of his great horned and frilled head, and held up her hand before his right eye. She displayed two fingers to him, and then pointed northward. She was now so vulnerable to his horns, that all he had to do was to jump forward, and he could have impaled her before she could have gotten away. But Thundermaker was not so inclined. He felt something towards the two hornbrows that he still couldn't quite explain, but it was neither fear nor dislike. Pippit repeated the action. He stared at her, first her hand, and then her face. He shook his head, and snorted.

"Panthrar, my brother," she said, "Jump like a ravager again."

Without questioning her, Panthrar sprang about like a ravager, growling like one to add to the image. Pippit did likewise. Thundermaker backed away. He grumbled at them suspiciously, and pawed the ground.

They immediately stopped prancing. Pippit, looking at Thundermaker, touched Panthrar's shoulder, and said, "One ravager." She touched her own chest, and said, "Two ravagers." She then pointed to the north.

Thundermaker looked first at Pippit, then at Panthrar, then to the north. He rose up on his hind feet again, and sniffed, testing the scents in the breeze. He came back down with a thud. He looked at Pippit, swinging his head. He repeated the few deep, rumbling grunts that he had made before. Then he trotted down towards his herd. They had already formed up in a tight circle, and were moving towards the northwest.

"I think he understands, my sister. Come now, let us make haste to get on the other side of the herd of threehorns."

The two hornbrows circled the herd at a fast trot. They, like many of the threehorns, kept looking to the north. But they also kept scanning in all directions. With their superior sense of smell, they would detect anything upwind long before the threehorns. And with their better sense of sight, they would see a ravager long before a threehorn could.

As they moved to the southwest side of the herd, Panthrar offered Pippit some advice. "My sister, if the ravagers get close enough to stampede the herd, we must do everything we can to keep up. Threehorns can race faster than we can run, but only for short distances. Over the long run, we could probably outrun them. We'll just have to keep our wits about us."

Pippit nodded her understanding. Panthrar continued, "If the herd stampedes, we cannot be in front of it. In their panic, they'll be very likely to run right over us, friends or not."

Pippit frowned. The prospects of being trampled by threehorns, whether they did it by mistake or not, wasn't very pleasant. She looked at Panthrar. He went on, "All that considered, we would be best to keep the herd between us and the ravagers, and to stay somewhere near the front of the herd so that it won't outrun us."

The herd moved toward the northwest at a brisk, but wary walk. Thundermaker stayed along the northeastern flank of the herd, while Hidepiercer took the northwest. Quickcharger, the third dominant male, took the lead, and kept the herd moving at a steady pace. Panthrar and Pippit were on the southwestern point. The attack came directly from behind the herd, from the southeast.

The ravagers had been traveling on a converging path with the herd, and as they got close to it, they had swung around behind it. They then approached it, partially masked by the herd's own dust cloud. The dust not only helped obscure them visually, but also affected the ability of the prey to hear or smell them.

The first that the herd knew of their proximity was when both ravagers made a dash at a younger male threehorn trailing a bit too far behind the rest of the herd. Pippit, who had exceptionally good eyesight, and who happened to be looking towards the rear of the herd at precisely the right moment, saw the swiftly moving dreadrunners materialize out of the dust. Pointing, she honked a loud hornbrow warning. Fate was apparently still protecting the laggard, because something caused him to quickly and clearly understand just exactly what Pippit was doing. He turned and looked behind him to see the ravagers come rushing out of the dust cloud. He squealed in panic, and bolted forward towards the herd. Two hugh streaks of flesh and muscle closed in on him. The herd itself, attracted first by the honk, then by the squeal, and seeing two charging ravagers and a squealing, panic-stricken threehorn rushing towards it, also surged forward.

It wasn't quite a stampede. Quickcharger tried to keep the herd under control. Panthrar and Pippit tried to keep up with it without getting run over by it. The herd was moving at a full gallop, and the two hornbrows were running on their hind feet, arms flung out to the side. Panthrar looked behind him as he ran. He thought that he recognized Gnarled-paw and Long-tail.

The young male threehorn knew that the ravagers were too close for him to escape by running away, so he turned and faced his attackers. Until then the ravagers had been running full out, holding themselves low and horizontal to the ground. Since they had failed in their initial charge to reach and kill their prey in one surprising burst of speed, a different set of tactics was now in order. They slowed their charge, and rose up more vertically on their hind legs. They began to spread out so that they could attack the threehorn from two sides. One of them would have to risk the intended victim's horns, so that the other could get a quick, clean kill. They had to try to kill him quickly before assistance arrived from the dominant males of the herd.

Thundermaker looked up towards Pippit and Panthrar when he heard the honk of warning. As soon as he heard the first squeal, he immediately wheeled in his tracks, and headed towards the rear of his herd. Hidepiercer did likewise. As they closed upon the young male, Thundermaker squeal-roared a deep challenge, as much to distract the ravagers as to alert the male that help was coming.

The young male backpedaled as rapidly as he could, trying not to be outflanked before succor arrived. He would swing his horns first in the direction of Long-tail, and then in the direction of Gnarled-paw, and then back towards Long-tail. He kept trying to threaten each with his horns, holding them off, all the while briskly walking, almost running, backwards.

The ravagers closed upon the young male. First one would lunge, then the other. Neither would get too close to the two foot horns of the young male. A moment longer, though, and they would be in position so that one of them would be able to lunge at an exposed flank when the male tried to defend himself from the other.

Thundermaker rushed upon Long-tail, the closer ravager, at a full charge. Hidepiercer was perhaps five hundred feet behind him, also charging to the rescue at thirty miles per hour. The ravagers, keenly aware of what the three-foot long horns of an adult male threehorn could do, never lost track via their peripheral vision of where the dominant males were. As Thundermaker lowered his head for the final charge upon Long-tail, the female dreadrunner sprang up and to the side to avoid the horns. She must have cleared twenty feet off the ground, and landed about fifty feet to the right.

Thundermaker stabbed at air as he ran past the front of the embattled young male. He braked hard, and swung his head towards Gnarled-paw, on the other side of the male. Gnarled-paw faced Thundermaker, and hissed loudly. The young male threehorn, suddenly in an even more exposed position between the two ravagers due to Long-tail's leap, turned quickly to put horns and an armored frill between himself and Gnarled-paw. Long-tail lashed out with her right leg as the young male turned, inflicting a serious wound upon the rear quarters of the young threehorn. She might have done him more lethal damage had not Hidepiercer arrived at that moment.

Hidepiercer snorted, lowered his head without breaking stride, and attempted to spear Long-tail with his two brow horns. The alert female again leapt out of the way of impending death. She struck out at Hidepiercer as he went by, tearing him in the shoulder. Blood started to gush from the foot long wound. Hidepiercer stiffened all four legs, and slid to a stop. He turned angrily toward Long-tail before she could follow up her attack, and made short charging motions towards her. She backed away, hissing frightfully, snapping at Hidepiercer in frustration.

Gnarled-paw also backed away. The attack had failed. The opportunity had been lost. To persist in the attack now was to invite serious consequences. He and Long-tail continued to back away from the threehorns, alternately hissing in warning, grumbling in frustration, or roaring in challenge. The threehorns tightened into a defensive circle, backing their tails into each other, horns and frills facing outward. They would not unnecessarily risk exposing themselves to further attack by pursuing the ravagers. After the ravagers had backed about two hundred feet away, Gnarled-paw and Long-tail turned around and walked jauntily towards the south. Occasionally one or the other would look back at the threehorns and hiss.

Once the dreadrunners were far enough away so that they could not try another quick charge and a leap, the threehorns all lined up facing the retreating ravagers. The two dominant males slowly and cautiously followed the ravagers – while the younger male lingered behind them. When the ravagers were about a thousand feet away, the young male broke ranks with the two dominant males, and ran to join the retreating herd. When the ravagers were almost a half of a mile away, Thundermaker and Hidepiercer felt that they were no longer a threat – it was safe enough to head back to the herd.

By the time that they caught up to the herd, it had calmed down considerably. All the herd-members were still in a heightened state of alertness and excitability, but now they only walked. None-the-less, they were all ready to sprint off again at a second's notice. And still, adult males and females kept looking about them, checking to make sure that nothing else threatened them. The youngsters were particularly skittish.

Thundermaker and Hidepiercer had shared a thought on the way back to the herd. They joined Panthrar and Pippit, and walked quietly near them for awhile. Finally Thundermaker approached Panthrar. As they walked and casually grazed, he spoke at great length to the hornbrows. He spoke to both of them, Pippit as well as Panthrar. The discussion was frequently interspersed with pauses to munch on an appetizing plant, chew it, and then swallow.

The hornbrows chewed their food much longer than almost any of the other creatures of their world. They had good grinding teeth, and cheeks to help them manipulate the food better, so they could process a great variety of food. The threehorns had good clipping beaks, and could shear just about anything. They also had good cutting teeth. They were developed differently from a hadrosaur's. While hornbrows could grind up a considerable variety of plants, threehorns didn't grind, they sliced. Hadrosaurs could process just about any plant material available, not only leaves and tender shoots, but twigs and small branches and pine cones, and the like. This saved a lot of wear and tear on their stomachs. Of course, they liked berries, and berry bushes. And there were plenty of those around. Threehorns also had cheeks, and used them in combination with their slicing teeth to also pretty efficiently process food. They just didn't do it as well as a hornbrow. So their stomachs had to work a lot harder to digest their food.

Thundermaker had a serious proposition to pose to Panthrar and Pippit, and Hidepiercer helped him put it to the hornbrows. But understanding did not come quickly, and the delay was not really caused by the casual, but consistent feeding. The primary difficulty in the discussion was that neither the hornbrows nor the threehorns could understand the other's language. They often had difficulty understanding the other's way of thinking, so language was only a part of the problem. Further, the hornbrows were still a little intimidated by the deadliness of the weapons that the threehorns were equipped with.

Eventually Panthrar and Pippit pieced together that each of the threehorns wanted one of the hornbrows to accompany him. Panthrar and Pippit decided to risk separation, since they could still see and communicate with each other, but they could not figure out why the threehorns wanted to separate them.

Panthrar went with Thundermaker. They traveled along the southern flank of the herd all day. Pippit went with Hidepiercer, and they patrolled along the northern flank. Meanwhile, Quickcharger kept the lead.

Thundermaker kept trying to tell Panthrar something. He would grunt and rumble, and turn his head in all directions, watching Panthrar as he did so. After he had completed such an exercise, he would get particularly insistent with Panthrar. But Panthrar was perplexed. Once or twice, Thundermaker, while patrolling along a ridgeline with Panthrar, rose up on his hind feet, and pawed the air in the direction away from the herd. Something about what he was doing was beginning to strike a chord with Panthrar. But it was Pippit who figured it out first. She tooted to Panthrar, and then with some words, but mainly with arm signals, she said, "They want us to be their lookouts."

Of course, thought Panthrar. The threehorns could hardly see at all, at least from the perspective of a hornbrow. And their senses of hearing and smell weren't a lot better. Panthrar suspected that their language wasn't as rich as was that of the People, either. But did they ever have a formidable defense! Threehorns didn't have to run for their lives every time they saw a ravager, nor band into groups of hundreds or thousands for mutual defense. A threehorn could tangle with a ravager almost on a one-to-one basis.

Panthrar smiled to himself. What would the world be like if hornbrows and threehorns always traveled together. The hornbrows could be the early warning system when predators were around, and the threehorns could be the soldiers to protect the less well-defended. Oh well, it was quite a dream. Hornbrows and threehorns didn't usually talk to each other, let along help each other. But on this particular trip across the great upper plain, they had mutual interests to protect.

CHAPTER TWELVE

THE ELIMINATION BOUTS

By THE END OF the day, Kinput had fought three dominance fights. The first one had come early. It had been with a younger solitary male named Heddar, once of the Falling Water Roam. Heddar was about nine springs old. He was 32 feet long and 3.6 tons in weight. Although younger and smaller than Kinput, he was very energetic, and a rather scrappy fighter.

About mid-morning, Heddar approached the vicinity of the Green Water Roam. Kinput had been lingering in the vicinity of both this roam, and the Yellow Mud Roam. Two young females, one from each roam, had attracted his attention. He was hoping to mate with one, and if really successful this spring, with both of them. He had made his intentions known to each, and neither had done anything to discourage him. After all, at thirteen years of age, and 3.8 tons and 35.5 feet in length, he cut quite a figure. His 14 inch horn was not unimpressive, and his frill showed a beautiful reddish sienna brown in the bright sunlight.

Kinput, who had been successful in the previous day's contests, was swaggering back and forth in front of both roams. His intentions were quite clear to all members of the roams, and the younger adult males of the two roams knew that within a day or two, they could be fighting Kinput themselves to preserve their right to mate.

Heddar had also been successful in the previous day's contests. He was virtually assured of being able to mate, so long as he maintained his current position in the emerging rankings. That is, as long as he didn't desire a female that was also desired by a male he couldn't best. And as long as the female he selected approved of him.

Heddar had his eye on Gumboo. Gumboo was the fifth female of the Green Water Roam. She was eight years old, about 25 feet long, and had a sexy seven inch horn. She was a good looking female, and Heddar decided that she was going to be his. Unfortunately for Heddar, Gumboo was the female from the Green Water Roam that had attracted Kinput's fancy.

Heddar of course knew this. He wasn't stupid, just a little ambitious. So, as the sun climbed halfway up from the horizon towards its meeting with the top of the sky, Heddar came to the place where Kinput was. He began to strut before Gumboo, letting her see his deep sienna frill, and the attractiveness of his thirteen inch horn. Gumboo was flattered that two such handsome males would want to mate with her. She was careful not to discourage either of them, lest she end up with neither.

Kinput, who had been pacing in the same vicinity, back and forth, for over an hour, changed his tack so that his path would cross Heddar's. Heddar saw him coming, and sat down and pretended to be inspecting some curious goings-on down near the lake. When Kinput was about fifty feet from where Heddar sat, he too sat down to watch the same imaginary goings-on. There were a lot of younger hornbrows frolicking in the water, so it wasn't totally imaginary.

After a few moments, Kinput said to Heddar, "May the sun warm you this beautiful bright day, younger brother."

Heddar responded in kind, "And may the sun warm you to, elder brother."

They sat for a while longer, watching the other males strutting before the roams, and the youngsters splashing in the water down by the lake. Finally Kinput ventured, "Heddar, younger brother, you seem to be a long way from home."

Heddar casually scratched the left side of his head before responding. After a while he said, "Kinput, elder brother, home is where one makes it."

Kinput leaned forward, and for a time pushed a pebble around with the left-middle finger of his right hand. Then he said, "This is so true, younger brother. But one must often be careful how and where one chooses, mustn't one?"

Heddar rocked a little, and then waved to a traveling companion of his. Eventually he turned to Kinput and said, "One should always be careful, elder brother. But sometimes one must do what another may think is imprudent."

"Younger brother, it would be considered rash by some if you were to select a home where another has flattened the bushes." Kinput paused, and then added, "But there can be homes enough for many. I know there can be a home for both you and for me. Even here." Kinput looked directly at Heddar, so that the other would not take too lightly his meaning. "Choose another, and we may both be brothers with the Green Water Roam."

Heddar paused to reflect upon this for quite some time. Eventually, he said, "You are more than generous, elder brother, but I'm afraid that I can not accept your offer."

Kinput flicked the pebble that he had been playing with away and said, "Then it would seem that we both desire the same thing, younger brother. And both of us cannot have it."

"I suppose you are right, elder brother," said Heddar. He sat for a long while staring down at the lake where most of the youngsters and yearlings were wading and splashing. Occasionally flocks of featheredflyers flew overhead, disturbed by the playful youngsters.

Finally Heddar rose to his feet. Slowly he turned and faced Kinput. He gathered himself to his full height. "I am Heddar," he said, "once of the Falling Water Roam of the Red Dawn Tribe. Make way for me, or feel my wrath."

Kinput slowly rose to his feet and faced Heddar. Now that the ritual words had been spoken, there was no going back. He looked Heddar directly in the eyes and said, "I am Kinput, once of the Green Water Roam of the Red Dawn Tribe. Make way for me, or feel my wrath."

With that the two males began to circle each other. Virtually all of the adult males and females of both the Green Water and Yellow Mud Roams, for they both sat together, leaned forward in anticipation. Many had been watching the two covertly, not wanting to be rude. Many had some stake or other in the outcome of this battle.

Although most had pretended to be concerned with other things, most knew that a dominance fight would be the most likely outcome of the seemingly polite discourse that the two where having. Dominance fights could be great entertainment, for those not directly engaged in them. The adult males began to discuss in an undertone who would most likely win, and what strategy he might employ to best his opponent. The females were likewise involved. They glanced frequently at Gumboo, whom the fight was over, to see how she was reacting to it. On the outside she remained cool and calm, but on the inside she was concerned lest either one of these two handsome champions get unduly harmed.

Kinput and Heddar leaned low and forward. They slowly circled each other, stepping sideways, moving cautiously. They swung their stiff tails back and forth behind them, in ever expanding arcs.

Each was trying to get the measure of the other, assessing whether the other would charge first, or whether he should be the one who made the first move. They had had an opportunity to watch each other fight in the previous day's battles, knowing that they might soon be fighting each other. So they had a fair idea of how the other fought.

Kinput watched Heddar carefully. He was determined to let the younger male charge first. Heddar was a bit impetuous, so Kinput half expected him to make the first move without provocation. He examined Heddar's eyes, and measured the swing of his tail. With each arc, Kinput calculated just how Heddar must strike, if he moved on that swing.

Heddar, the younger and less experienced, charged first. He ran straight at Kinput, and at the moment before actual contact, he stopped, pivoted on his left foot, and swung his tail in a mighty counterclockwise stroke predicted to knock Kinput completely off his feet.

Kinput jumped forward and to the right of Heddar, causing Heddar's mighty blow to completely miss its target. Heddar almost lost his footing, since the blow did not connect as expected. Kinput kept going, and as he brushed past Heddar's side, he bumped him hard. Heddar lost what balance he had still managed to retain, and fell. Kinput ran to a position about fifty feet behind Heddar, and waited for his opponent to get to his feet.

Heddar rose, embarrassed and indignant. Had he heard snickering from the nearby roams? He glared at some of the younger adult males. Still, he circled Kinput more warily. Now he was even more determined than ever to best him. Heddar charged again. This time they grappled, wrestling with their arms, locking their horns. Neither tried deliberately to impale the other with his horn, but even unintentionally, accidents like that occurred.

They pushed and pulled each other, trying to trip the other, or to push the other so far backwards that he would have to release his grip to avoid losing more face. Here, Kinput had the advantage. He was larger, heavier, stronger, and more cunning. He and Heddar wrestled this way and that for three or four minutes, and then Kinput managed to trip Heddar. Heddar fell to the ground with a noisy thud.

The contest continued to wage for more than thirty minutes. It was long, if not overly exciting. Five more times Heddar charged Kinput. All but one of those times, Kinput was able to bring Heddar to the ground. In the one struggle that Kinput couldn't trip up Heddar, neither could get an advantage, and ultimately they had both been forced to break the hold to try to get a better grip on the other.

Both males were getting tired, but Heddar refused to give up the unequal struggle. He also refused to charge again. Kinput wondered if all the elaborate maneuvering that they were now going through was accomplishing nothing more than providing time for Heddar to catch his breath.

Kinput decided that he would not let that happen. He sprang forward, feinting first to the left, then to the right, then straight at Heddar. Heddar backed up at each feint, allowing Kinput to gain momentum. Kinput struck Heddar so hard that Heddar had to give way. They grappled with their arms, trying to lock horns, all the while Kinput was steadily pushing Heddar backwards.

Dirt churned as Heddar scrambled to regain his balance and stop Kinput's momentum. Yet, trying not to get into a disadvantageous position again, Heddar continued to back up faster and faster. Suddenly Kinput let Heddar go. Kinput slowed to a halt, while Heddar kept retreating backwards. After back-pedaling about a hundred feet, Heddar made a graceful pivot, and trotted away. He looked over his shoulder once. Kinput was standing where he had left him. The victor was looking to the right and left – more interested in who had witnessed his defeat of his rival, than in the retreating rival.

Heddar decelerated into a walk. He left the scene of the contest with as much dignity as he could muster. He would go rest for awhile. He would lick his wounds, more to his ego than to his person. This afternoon he would fight again. He knew of a cute little six year old belonging to the Flat Rock Roam of the White Moon Tribe. He shouldn't have wasted his time over here anyway. The six year old was a lot better looking.

Kinput liked Heddar too much to embarrass him further by honking a victory call. Besides, everyone that he might have wanted to notice his skill in subduing the younger challenger had watched the entire fight. Kinput strutted back over to the two roams. He looked directly at Wubbar and Hew of the Green Water Roam, and at the three lesser adult males of the Yellow Mud Roam. He wanted them to think about what was in store for them if they did not make way for him. Then he began his pacing again.

The next challenge came a little after mid-day. This time it came from Fanfahron, a solitary male of fifteen springs. Fanfahron was somewhat larger than Kinput, being 37 feet long and weighing 3.9 tons. His horn was an impressive 15 inches. Kinput knew that this would be his toughest challenge yet. Fanfahron was interested in Panehh of the Yellow Mud Roam, a comely female of nine springs. Panehh was slightly longer and heavier than Gumboo, as would be expected, since she was older than the other female. But she was also very desirous, from Kinput's perspective, and he intended to fight for her.

Fanfahron sought him out directly. He had none of the finesse of Heddar, and his abruptness bordered on impolite. Fanfahron was not known for his mental prowess, and he was not much of a conversationalist. He walked up to Kinput and said, "May the sun warm you, younger brother."

"And may the sun warm you too, elder brother," replied Kinput.

While Kinput was deliberating a possible line of discourse with Fanfahron, so that they could each understand the other's intentions without having to be bluntly indelicate, Fanfahron said to him, "I am Fanfahron, once of the Sparkling Water Roam of the Green Hills Tribe. Make way, or feel my wrath."

"Come now, elder brother," responded Kinput. "You appear to be in such an unseemly hurry. Perhaps you might wish to discuss the weather, or some other subject of more interest, first?"

Fanfahron looked at him blankly, took a threatening step forward, and said, "I am Fanfahron, once of the Sparkling Water Roam of the Green Hills Tribe. Make way, or feel my wrath."

"Well, elder brother, I believe that you already said that," retorted Kinput. After a short pause, he tried, "There are many clouds in the sky. We do not all have to sit under the same one ...."

"I am Fanfahron, once of the Sparkling Water Roam of the Green Hills Tribe," said the other. "Make way, or feel my wrath." With that, he lunged at Kinput.

Kinput was not taken completely by surprise. He knew Fanfahron, and in fact had fought him last year. Fanfahron had bested Kinput in that contest, but that fact did not daunt Kinput now. Due to the experience, he was better prepared to deal with Fanfahron this year. Fanfahron had been this blunt last year, and in fact, last year he had charged Kinput after only two challenges. And like this year, he had done it without waiting for the formal response.

Kinput dodged out of Fanfahron's way as the larger male charged by. All he received was a slight bump as the other tried to compensate midway through the charge to grapple with Kinput. Kinput immediately pivoted, and prepared for an intense confrontation.

Murmurs of disapproval arose from those witnessing the contest. It was uncalled for to be impolite, even in dominance fights. Further, Fanfahron had not even waited to see if Kinput would accept the challenge. Plus, Kinput was a local favorite. Not only had he once belonged to the Green Water Roam, but he had made a lot of friends in the Yellow Mud Roam when he had accompanied the two roams across the upper plain.

As Fanfahron collected himself for another charge, Kinput repeated the ritual acceptance, "I am Kinput, once of the Green Water Roam of the Red Dawn Tribe. Make way for me, or feel my wrath." He then began to circle to the left. Fanfahron did likewise.

Kinput would have liked to have charged Fanfahron first, and to have knocked some manners into the older male, but he was uncertain whether he could best Fanfahron in a direct test of strength. So he decided to wear the other down. Fanfahron was not known for his patience. Also, since he had won last year's duel, he probably expected to win this year's without too much effort. The combination of these two made it seem like it was only a matter of time before Fanfahron charged again, perhaps hoping to finish this new battle all the more quickly.

Halfway through the fourth time that they circled each other, Fanfahron charged. Kinput back-pedaled three slow steps, allowing Fanfahron to get closer. Then he bolted forward and to the right, just past Fanfahron. He jumped to miss the larger male's tail as he went by, for Fanfahron had tried to stop, pivot, and strike Kinput with it as Kinput dodged past him. Kinput jumped completely over Fanfahron's tail. Then he slapped Fanfahron a light blow with his own for good measure, before scooting away to get a better position for the next charge.

For the next fifteen or twenty minutes, Fanfahron worked hard at trying to come to grips with Kinput, and Kinput worked even harder to keep that from happening. They were both beginning to become exerted after all the activity, even if they hadn't actually made any real contact yet. Fanfahron had made all the charges, and Kinput had done all the dodging. It was difficult to tell who was the more winded.

On the tenth charge, Fanfahron was able to trip Kinput as he tried to again jump over the latter's tail. Kinput fell heavily to the ground.

Fanfahron turned, and rushed for Kinput. He tried to jump on Kinput, his right foot landing on Kinput's extended leg. Kinput barked in pain. Kinput wiggled free and tried to pull far enough away from Fanfahron so that he could get to his feet unmolested.

Fanfahron followed too closely. He kicked at Kinput, striking the younger male in the chest. Kinput again coughed in pain. As Fanfahron tried to kick him again, Kinput grabbed his leg, partially cushioning the blow. Fanfahron was obviously not interested in either a fair or a dignified fight. He was solely interested in winning. By this point in time, Kinput had also decided to dispense with the niceties of civilized combat. All he wanted to do now was to beat Fanfahron.

Kinput managed to scramble to his feet, while Fanfahron rained down blows upon his exposed back with clenched fists. Still hunched over, Kinput rapidly fired a series of quick punches into the pit of Fanfahron's stomach. Fanfahron jumped back in surprise, rubbing his abdomen.

Kinput didn't want to give up the initiative, so he charged Fanfahron. As he closed with his adversary, he launched himself at Fanfahron, striking him in the chest. Fanfahron was bowled over, with Kinput groping for a good hold upon the other's neck. Fanfahron warded off the attempt, and they both rolled and struggled in the dust, each trying to get an effective hold upon the other. They punched and scratched. They threw dirt into one another's face. They twisted and turned, grasping and grabbing, but neither could get a good hold upon the other. All-in-all, they fought in a most undignified manner.

Fanfahron managed to get to his feet. He kicked at Kinput, but Kinput rolled out of his reach. He rushed after Kinput, and tried to kick him again. Kinput rolled away from Fanfahron, but the latter quickly closed the gap. Just as Fanfahron leapt for Kinput, Kinput reversed his roll, moving towards the spot that the other had just vacated. Kinput rolled under the in-flight Fanfahron, and jumped to his feet. Fanfahron hit the ground in a crash of dust and scattered debris. Kinput pivoted hard and fast, striking Fanfahron with his tail. Fanfahron lumbered away, trying to regain his balance. Kinput rushed after him, grabbing him around the waist. Fanfahron swung back and forth, trying to hurl Kinput away. It wasn't working. So he then fell to the ground, and tried to roll on top of Kinput.

Kinput released Fanfahron, and regained his feet first. He struck Fanfahron with another blow of his mighty tail. Fanfahron scrambled to his feet, and lunged for Kinput. Kinput dodged back and forth, while the exhausted larger male still lurched for him. Kinput was finally able to sidestep Fanfahron. He rotated around, and grabbing Fanfahron by the shoulders, Kinput threw Fanfahron over his outstretched leg. Fanfahron tumbled in a heap. Kinput saw his opportunity. Before Fanfahron could rise again, Kinput rushed over to him, pounced upon him, poised his horn at Fanfahron's throat, and said simply, "Yield."

Fanfahron tried to squirm away, but Kinput held him tightly, pushing his horn deeper into Fanfahron's neck. "Yield," he repeated.

Fanfahron ceased to struggle. Kinput's horn was crushing his windpipe, and was threatening to puncture it. He coughed out something indecipherable. Kinput relaxed his hold a little, and eased his horn away from Fanfahron's throat. Fanfahron croaked out a barely understandable, "I yield."

Kinput sprang to his feet. He walked about seventy-five feet away from Fanfahron. He turned and stood watching as the larger male slowly pulled himself to his feet, and waddled away. As he departed, Kinput, still trying to catch his breath, none-the-less found the energy and the wind to honk the victory cry of a successful fighter. Fanfahron waddled away even faster, not wishing to have insult added to injury.

Kinput stood catching his breath for over ten minutes. Then he resumed his pacing before the Green Water Roam and the Yellow Mud Roam. He moved a little more slowly than before, but he still moved with dignity. Both Gumboo and Panehh were thrilled with admiration for the indomitable Kinput. After awhile, Grendaar left his perch in the midst of his roam, and ambled over to Kinput.

"May the sun keep you warm, younger brother," Grendaar said.

"And may the sun keep you warm too, mighty Groundshaker," returned Kinput.

"May I walk with you awhile, younger brother?" asked the older male.

"As you wish, elder brother."

They walked together, and talked together, engaged in who knew what weighty subject. Shortly after Grendaar had approached Kinput, Renthot joined them. For the next hour, Grendaar and Renthot walked beside the solitary. Other males also paced before one or the other of the two roams. There were other successful males, who had interests in other females, and who were asserting their claims. They posed no challenge to Kinput. There did appear to be other challengers in the vicinity, that might have wanted to challenge Kinput, but none would dare to interrupt the three males in serious conversation. Especially when two of them were roamleaders.

Shortly more than an hour after the end of his second challenge of the day, and within minutes after Grendaar and Renthot had re-joined their roams, Kinput was challenged again. It was over Panehh again, and by a packer of twelve springs of age, by the name of Draggot. The challenge was a cordial one, and the challenger fought fairly and with dignity. Kinput bested him after a twenty minute struggle. The packer remained in the vicinity. But he had changed the target of his aspirations to a female of the Green Water Roam. Now he fancied Binboh, fourth female of the roam. Later that day, or perhaps on the morrow, Draggot would challenge another male for the privilege of asking her to mate with him.

CHAPTER THIRTEEN
WHILING AWAY THE TIME

Dandraar had been spending his days with the packers. Watching dominance fights can be great entertainment, but what the packers were doing was even more exciting.

He spent a lot of time with Davgot. Davgot was an adolescent packer of four springs of age. He was formally of the Green Water Roam, and in fact had been one of Dandraar's nestmates. A year ago Davgot had gotten the urge to leave the roam, and become a packer. Dandraar missed Davgot a lot, but still he was convinced that his decision to stay with the roam was the right one for him. At the last annual gathering they had bid their sorrowful farewells. When Dandraar left with the Green Water Roam, Davgot had gone off with one of the packs. Now, a year later, the annual gathering gave them an opportunity to catch up on lost time.

Their first day together, Dandraar and Davgot went into the foothills to the east. They joined with Davgot's pack, which was patrolling against ravagers. The foothills to the east of the Gathering Place were full of packers. Their task was to locate any ravagers trying to penetrate the foothills. No ravagers had made such an attempt in their patrol area, but they heard packers to the south of them signaling that a ravager had been spotted there. Leaving a few packers behind to keep watch, the remainder of the pack had hurried south to help repel the ravager. Several other packs had also joined in the chase.

The remainder of the day was spent in playing a potentially deadly game of hunt-and-chase with the ravager. It was a dreadcharger, a closely-related, stockier, larger and even-more-deadly version of a dreadrunner. Dreadchargers were bipedal meat-eaters like their smaller relatives. They had huge heads, more fully formed than a dreadrunner. They also had vast jaws which held many serrated, saber-like teeth. The teeth were sharp on both sides, and ideal for both killing and tearing apart flesh. The head of a dreadcharger had semi-forward facing eyes, thus they possessed binocular vision. They were also equipped with a thick, short, muscular neck, and a short, deep, broad-chested and narrow hipped body. They possessed a relatively short and slim tail. The great legs bore three forward-pointing toes with relatively short, rounded claws. The fore-arms were strong but tiny, although larger than in a dreadrunner, and the fore-arms ended in two-fingered hands. Dreadchargers were fast runners, and frequently broke into a succession of rapid hops. At full speed, the body was held nearly horizontal, with the stiff tail held straight back, helping to keep balance. This particular dreadcharger was young and still fairly small. Yet even so, it was still 28 feet long, and three or more tons in weight.

From the simplest perspective, a dreadcharger could be viewed as the perfect killing machine – it was all jaws and hindlegs. The powerful hindlegs were used for catching the prey, and few could escape it. The jaws and teeth were used for killing and eating the prey. Anything that didn't serve these primary objectives – catching and killing prey – was allowed to wither away. Thus the tiny fore-arms and the relatively short tail. Dreadchargers were large enough to tackle any living thing that came their way, and they had the look of deadly and efficient killing machines. They lived up to expectation, and were held in awe by all who encountered them. The one possible exception to this were packers, in the spring, in the foothills.

The packers teased the ravager, but never let him get too close. They were not unafraid of him, but they were seriously determined. They let him chase them, but only when they knew they could get to a place of safety fast. They threw rocks at him, and handfuls of pebbles, and pieces of wood. Mainly they did this when they were in the rocks above his head, pelting him with whatever came to hand. They lead him this way and that, but never towards the herd, always away from it. After many hours of what was sport to a packer, and probably torment to a ravager, the dreadcharger turned back toward the east and into the great upper plain.

The second day, Dandraar and Davgot went into the foothills to the west. Many packers were here also. They roamed the foothills and the dales in close proximity to the nesting areas, searching for robrunners, and redrunners, and the occasional pack of razorteeth. Their sport was more deadly near the nesting areas. They killed every small predator that they could catch. It was even more fun than tormenting ravagers.

Late in the morning, Dandraar and Davgot, with three other adolescent packers, came upon a flock of robrunners. There were perhaps a dozen of the yellow-green creatures, feeding in a small glen. At sight of the hornbrows, the robrunners scattered in headlong flight. The packers pursued a group of three, which became a group of two when one of the robrunners jumped over a large rock, clambered up an embankment, and got away. The packers chased the other two. One of the robrunners tried to climb a tree, while the other continued in precipitous flight. Three of the packers surrounded the tree, while the other two continued pursuit of the second robrunner.

Dandraar, Davgot, and another packer waited under the tree, while the robrunner, very awkwardly, attempted to pull itself out of their reach. Robrunners did not make good tree climbers, only desperation drove this one upward. It was hilarious to watch. It stopped climbing, not because it considered itself safe, but because it could not pull itself up any further. It looked down at its tormenters, large eyes dilated in panic. Davgot searched around on the ground for a suitably sized rock. He found one, and hurled it at the robrunner.

The rock struck the robrunner on the rump, and it bleated in protest. The rock provided the motivation for the robrunner to try to climb higher. All three of the hornbrows began searching for rocks to throw at the robrunner. They couldn't dislodge him from his tree, but they did force him ever higher and higher.

About a half hour later, the other two packers returned. They were flushed with both the exertion of the chase, and with the success of the hunt. They had trapped their robrunner when it had tried to duck into a shallow grotto, in which there was no other way out. They caught it when it tried to come back out the way it had gone in. They broke both of its legs, and left it as a warning to other robrunners.

The five adolescents spent most of the rest of the day trying to dislodge the robrunner from his tree. They tried shaking the tree, but it was too large for them to have much effect. By late afternoon, the robrunner was as high up in the tree as could bear his weight, and the hornbrows were tired of throwing rocks and pushing against the trunk. Finally they left the robrunner, wondering to themselves if he would ever get back down without breaking his neck. They hoped he wouldn't.

The third day after the roam had reached the Gathering Place, Dandraar and Davgot went back into the foothills around the nesting areas to hunt eggsnatchers. The fourth day, they went into the foothills to the east, to again bait ravagers. On the fifth day, Dandraar decided to stay near the roam. The dominance fights were nearing an end, and soon all of the selections for mates would be confirmed.

Dandraar was interested in seeing who each of the adult females of his roam selected for a mate. The politics of such selections were very intriguing. He was particularly interested in the two eldest adolescent females, Mungu and Tuojah. He had noticed recently that they were changing, transitioning from playmates into adults. He missed the fact that they would no longer be available to play hunt-and-chase, but he was intrigued by the changes they had gone through. Lessu and Kammah, the same age as Mungu and Tuojah, hadn't yet gone through such changes.

By now, most of the preferences of the adult females were fairly well-known, although few were formally announced. Tessah, the first female of the roam, would select Grendaar, the roamleader. This didn't surprise anyone.

Monah, the second female of the roam, would choose a large solitary, once of the Verdant Delta Tribe. A female of her ranking would normally have been expected to select a dominant male of either her own, or a closely allied roam. But Monah always had been a bit independent.

Koowoo, the third female, would choose Rohraar, the second male. Koowoo and Rohraar had mated for a number of years now, so this selection also didn't surprise anyone.

Binboo, the fourth female, had let it be known that she had a preference for Draggot, the packleader. Draggot had seemed to have found time to be with Binboo on an amazing number of occasions for a packleader. He had even spent some time with her on the climb up the ravine.

Gumboo, the fifth female, had disclosed rather early this morning that she wanted Kinput, the solitary. Panehh, of the Yellow Mud Roam, would also select Kinput at the appropriate time. So it seemed that Kinput would spend time with both of his choices.

Tandah, the sixth female, would select a solitary, once of the Umber Earth Tribe. No one had actually met this solitary, but they had all seen him strutting up and down before the roam. He would pay his ritual respects to Grendaar, and ask Grendaar's permission for Tandah, once Tandah had officially selected him.

Sungu, the seventh female, would also select Rohraar, becoming his second mate. Sungu found Rohraar devastatingly handsome, and he found her rather attractive also.

Zannah, the eighth female, would select Trugahr, the third male. Trugahr, young himself, had a strong preference for young females.

Eaceh, the ninth female, would select Wubbar, the fourth male. Eaceh and Wubbar always did seem to spend a lot of time together, not just on the treks or at mating time, but all year long.

Ghirarah, the tenth female, had spoken of a preference for Trugahr, becoming his second mate.

Treah, the eleventh female, had been proud to have been approached by Grendaar. She would become his second mate. Rumpoo, the twelfth female, would also select Grendaar, becoming his third mate.

Ahbrell, the thirteenth female, had been approached by Renthot, the leader of the Yellow Mud Roam, and she would agree to be his third mate.

Mungu, the new fourteenth female, would choose a male from the Yellow Mud Roam. Dandraar was not too surprised after he thought about this, for Mungu had mentioned this handsome young male several times to Dandraar during the trek across the plain.

Tuojah, the fifteenth female, had been approached by Zurgott, the Stonekeeper, roamleader of the Dragonfly Roam. It was a noteworthy honor for one so young to have been asked, and it was expected that she would accept becoming his fourth mate.

In addition, Rohraar had been attracted by a comely female from the Yellow Mud Roam, and it was expected that she would agree to become his third mate.

Trugahr had also been smitten by a young female packer, who was just now transitioning into adulthood. She would select him, becoming his third mate. Her name was Jasmaan, once of the Crescent Beach Roam, and she would join the Green Water Roam in the process, becoming the sixteenth female.

Hew, the fifth male of the Green Water Roam, had not been successful in attracting a female from his own roam. He had also not met with success with any of the females of the Yellow Mud Roam. But Hew was, if nothing else, persistent. Late yesterday evening, he had won the attentions of a young female of the Black Sand Roam. She was expected to select him later today.

Dandraar knew most of these things already. He just wanted to see them confirmed. Since that wouldn't happen until later in the day, he rambled from roam to roam, and from tribe to tribe, meeting other adolescents, making small talk and exchanging information as he went. It was while thus occupied, that he heard an unsettling rumor. An adolescent of five springs of age told him that Ograar, a solitary male once of the Silver River Tribe, an unusually large male of fourteen springs, was going to challenge Grendaar for Tessah. Dandraar had never seen Ograar, so he hastened to the stream valley where the Silver River Tribe resided, to search him out.

Within the hour, he not only had come to the Silver River Tribe, but he had discovered something else that worried him. He was mingling with the various roams of that tribe, obliquely asking the whereabouts of Ograar. He was told that when he came upon Ograar, he would recognize him, for Ograar had no left eye, and had a deep scar running down the left side of his face. Rumor had it that Ograar had received those scars, and many more, defending his former roam from a ravager attack. According to the rumor, he had killed the ravager, something almost unheard of, and never boasted about casually.

As Dandraar was searching for this visage, he saw Adeldraar in the distance, speaking with a large male. Dandraar was immediately suspicious, and hence very cautious. Old Broken Horn did not have his staff with him, which in itself was unusual. But the male he was conversing with aroused further suspicions.

Dandraar approached the two in a most roundabout way, always careful not to let either of the two, but especially Adeldraar, see him. Soon he was close enough to confirm his suspicions. Adeldraar was deep in conversation with a male exceptionally large for his age – if it was Ograar, and fourteen springs of age. The male was a good four tons in weight, and thirty-eight feet in length. His horn was a slender, but very sharp fifteen inches long. Dandraar maneuvered to get a closer look at the male, and saw that he had a deep scar down the left side of his face. Much of the left side of his body was also heavily scared.

As Dandraar watched them, they ended their conversation. Ograar headed almost directly towards Dandraar, while Adeldraar headed off in the opposite direction. Dandraar walked over to a group of female youngsters, and struck up an immediate, but superficial conversation with them. Ograar passed by without even noticing him. Dandraar looked after Adeldraar. He was hurrying away towards the stream of the Turquoise Sea Tribe.

Dandraar decided to follow Adeldraar, and see what mischief he was up to. He stayed far behind, so that Old Broken Horn wouldn't detect him. Adeldraar got to the place of the Turquoise Sea Tribe, and slowly filtered through groups and roams. Occasionally he would stop to chat with one adult or another. None of it seemed particularly suspicious. He talked to a roamleader, who did a lot of nodding and said very little in response. He conversed with several older females, but his demeanor was one of distracted interest. He even talked to some youngsters for awhile, and patted one of them on the head as he left. Dandraar didn't know what to make of it. Eventually, though, Adeldraar stopped to talk to a large male whose physique was reminiscent of Ograar's.

Dandraar tried to get close enough to overhear what they were saying. The two conspirators were careful enough to keep some distance between themselves and those around them. Dandraar couldn't get too close without giving himself away. But he could tell from the hand signals of the two, and from the facial expressions of the strange male, who faced in Dandraar's direction, what some of the content of their conversation was. Dandraar caught words like "challenge", and "over-tired", and phrases like "put an end to it", and "tired old tyrant". Then he caught the other male acknowledge that "Tessah was indeed still beautiful".

Dandraar needed to see no more. He made his way directly back to the stream of the Red Dawn Tribe, and the locale of the Green Water Roam. He sought out The Ancient One, but could not find him.

He saw Rohraar, so he approached the second male. Nodding, he said, "May your days be full of berries, elder brother." He handed Rohraar a branch from a berry bush that he had picked on his way back to the roam.

"And may your days never know want, younger brother," replied Rohraar as he accepted the branch, and began to munch the berries.

"Do you know the whereabouts of the Groundshaker, elder brother?" asked the adolescent.

Rohraar chewed contemplatively. Then he said, "I believe that he received an invitation to visit the Black Valley Tribe." With that, Rohraar gestured vaguely in the direction of the Black Valley Tribe. It was the same general direction in which the Silver River Tribe and the Turquoise Sea Tribe resided.

Dandraar began to fidget. Rohraar looked carefully at the adolescent, and asked, "Is there something amiss, younger brother?"

"When did my father go to the stream of the Black Valley Tribe?" asked Dandraar.

"Oh, perhaps a half hour, or an hour ago."

"And who invited him, elder brother?" pressed Dandraar.

"I'm not sure, younger brother. I don't think it was someone from the Black Valley Tribe, now that I think about it. I think it was someone from the Chiefs Roam. The Chiefs Roam of the Red Dawn Tribe, that is."

"Then elder brother, I believe that there is something amiss." With this he told Rohraar all that he had seen or heard, and all that he believed to be true. He told of the rumor that Ograar of the Silver River Tribe was going to challenge Grendaar for Tessah. Ograar, who was overly large, and yet half Grendaar's age. Ograar, who was reputed to have killed a ravager. He told of seeing Adeldraar conversing with Ograar. Adeldraar, of the Chiefs Roam of the Red Dawn Tribe. He also told of Adeldraar's discussion with another large male, this one of the Turquoise Sea Tribe. Finally, he conjectured that it was an unfortunate coincidence that Grendaar had been lured away from his roam at the same time that all these other things were going on.

Rohraar stood up to his full height, and stared in the direction of the Black Valley Tribe. He could just discern a large group of hornbrows congregated around some activity. He stood immobile for two or three minutes. He couldn't make out what the center of attention was. Then he called to Trugahr. Trugahr jaunted over, lost in thoughts of his three new mates. He was especially entranced with Jasmaan. He nodded to Rohraar, smiled at Dandraar, and then said to the older male, "How may I serve you, elder brother?"

Rohraar looked sternly at Trugahr. He said, "May the sun keep you warm, younger brother."

Trugahr began to get a sense that there was trouble brewing. He quickly dismissed his thoughts of pleasant times lolling with his females. "And may it always keep you, elder brother," he responded without really thinking.

Without further preamble, Rohraar had Dandraar tell Trugahr all that he had discovered. As he neared the end of the information, Trugahr also turned to stare in the direction of the Black Valley Tribe.

When Dandraar was finished, Trugahr said, "Hew is off dallying with his new mate. We do not have time to locate him. Wubbar is here now. Let us leave him here in charge of the roam. I shall go get Kinput and any other males I can find, and meet you at the stream of the Black Valley Tribe as quickly as we can get there."

"I concur," said Rohraar. "Dandraar, go to Renthot, and tell him all that you have told me. Ask him to send as many males as he can spare to rendezvous with me at the stream of the Black Valley Tribe. Do you understand, younger brother."

"Yes I do, elder brother."

"Good, younger brother. Now go, hurry. And you, Trugahr, younger brother, you go. I will see you soon."

Dandraar sprang in the direction of the Yellow Mud Roam. Trugahr hastened toward the Green Water Roam, to direct Wubbar, and to collect Kinput. Rohraar did not watch them go. He had already departed. He moved at a fast trot directly toward the stream of the Black Valley Tribe.

CHAPTER FOURTEEN
THE DOMINANCE FIGHTS

GRENDAAR HAD NO CAUSE to worry. For the first time in many years, he had not even had to fight a dominance fight. He had expected that maybe someone might challenge him for one of the younger females. But none yet had. It was beginning to look like no one would.

When he had received an invitation to visit with the roamleaders of the Black Valley Tribe, his suspicions had not been aroused. He had spent probably half his time since reaching the Gathering Place doing just this with all of the tribes. Meeting with the leaders and the other older males, catching up on the newest events, reliving past adventures, re-kindling old friendships: a lot of congenial time had already been spent doing these. Even the fact that the messenger was not from the Black Valley Tribe, but was rather someone he had never met before from the Chiefs Roam, even that was not a cause for his suspicion. So he went to visit with the roamleaders.

He was a little perplexed when he met with the first roamleader, and the fellow didn't seem to know anything about the invitation. His name was Rattan, of the Purple Sand Roam of the Black Valley Tribe. They still had a pleasant enough conversation none-the-less. They reminisced an adventure with a onehorn that they had shared in their younger days. It was the fact that he never quite made it to the second roamleader that caused Grendaar to re-think the previous events, and to see cause for suspicion. But that came later, when he had the leisure time to think. For the following events were to command his complete attention.

A large male approached Grendaar as he made his way to the neighboring roam. Grendaar would have ignored him, but he stopped in the middle of Grendaar's path, and said, "May the sun warm you, elder brother."

Grendaar stopped and examined him. He was considerably younger and looked more agile than Grendaar, but he was virtually as large. He was missing his left eye. He had a deep furrow of a scar running from below his left nostril, up along his cheek, across where his left eye would have been, over the eye ridge, past the left side of his horn, and back along the top of his skull, where it ended. It was a ferocious scar, and must have been painfully acquired. There were numerous other deep scars running down his left side. They also looked like they were painfully gained.

"And may the sun warm you also, younger brother," returned Grendaar.

"I have heard much about you, elder brother," said the scarred one.

"That is good, younger brother. But I must apologize to you, for I do not know who you are," replied Grendaar. This was not strictly true, for although Grendaar had never actually met this male, he thought that he knew of him by reputation. Surely this must be Ograar, he thought to himself. Certainly the scarred body fit Ograar's description. It was hard not to have heard of Ograar.

"Forgive me my rudeness, elder brother," responded the other. "I am Ograar, once of the Quiet Tributary Roam of the Silver River Tribe. And you are Grendaar, of the Green Water Roam of the Red Dawn Tribe."

"Yes, I am, younger brother. And you are the great Killer of Killers. Greetings. Is there some service I can provide you?" asked Grendaar.

"All in good time, elder brother, all in good time," said Ograar.

Grendaar stood patiently waiting for the other one to get to the point. He had given Ograar an opening, but Ograar had declined to take it. To rush him would be impolite. So Grendaar waited.

Ograar sat quietly on the path, and did not come to the point. He also refused to move. Grendaar might have detoured around Ograar, but decided not to do so. There was something ominous about Ograar, and Grendaar thought that it was best that he yield to him as little as possible.

"I know many things about you, Groundshaker," Ograar finally said. "They say that you can't be bested in battle. They say that you can fight many males, one after another, and never tire. They say that, even now, in your old age, that only a fool would challenge you. What do you say to that?"

Grendaar contemplated the younger male. It was obvious that he was not here by chance. He had a purpose about him. Grendaar wondered how he fit into that purpose. Grendaar thought of many possible responses to Ograar. He decided upon one. "All things have a beginning, younger brother. And all things have an end," answered Grendaar, which was no real answer at all. "And who am I to say who is a fool?"

Some of the youngsters from the roam that Grendaar had just quit finally noticed these two large males, apparently blocking each other's path. Some started to congregate at a safe distance, to see what would come of it. Others ran to the adult females of their roam to report that a dominance fight between two great males was about to commence. Over whom, was the immediate thought on each female's mind, for great males did not fight each other except for notable females.

"Well said, Grendaar," offered Ograar. "You also have a way with words. But I say to you that the end has come. I say that you can be bested. What do you say to that, oh Ancient One?"

"Many have tried, and many have failed," returned Grendaar. "There may yet come one who can succeed. Do you know such a one, younger brother?"

Grendaar realized where this conversation was going. Without changing his bantering style, and without giving his adversary any indication that he was preparing for a contest, he began to casually inspect the terrain around him. If a fight did start, he wanted to know where the most advantageous ground was.

A circle, actually more like an ellipse, of interested bystanders continued to form around the pair. It ranged itself about a hundred feet from the two males, who sat about seventy-five feet apart.

"I say that you are old, elder brother. I say that your time has past. I say that you can no longer live on an old reputation. I say that it is time that you quit flaunting your past prowess, and accept a lesser role. What do you say to that?" Ograar seemed amazingly sure of himself, thought Grendaar. He wondered if Ograar knew something that he didn't.

Rattan, the roamleader who Grendaar had so recently visited, was attracted by the growing crowd near his roam, so he came to investigate. Along with him came his dominant males, and some of his females. The crowd was many hundreds in strength by now, and still growing. Rattan heard Ograar's last pronouncements, and perplexed, scratched his head. He was not sure that he could believe that anyone would say such things to the Groundshaker. He looked speculatively at Ograar.

"I say that you do a lot of talking, younger brother. Is that all you plan to do?" queried Grendaar.

Ograar visibly tensed. Grendaar was no less ready for combat. Outwardly he remained calm, he seemed almost disinterested. Inside he marshalled his forces. He realized that Ograar might be stronger than he, and he certainly must be quicker. Grendaar hoped he knew a few tricks that Ograar didn't.

"I thought you would enjoy talking, elder brother. It certainly is less exerting than fighting. I wouldn't want to tire an old hornbrow such as you too quickly," rejoined Ograar.

"It is tiring talking to you, younger brother. But one must be tolerant of the young. At times they can be so brash, on the one hand, and so misdirected on the other. Don't you think so?" asked Grendaar.

"Not being young, I wouldn't know. And not being old, I don't tire as easily," responded Ograar.

Grendaar decided to take a different approach. Perhaps if he were more blunt, Ograar would get about the business at hand. "I am old, younger brother, but perhaps not as old as you may think. If you are trying to talk me to death, I don't think it will work."

Amidst some chuckles from the still growing audience, Ograar finally stirred. He stood to his full height, and said, "No, elder brother, I have come for more than talk. I wish something of yours, and I mean to have it."

"Well then, younger brother, ask, and we will see if I can accommodate you," said Grendaar deprecatingly.

"You have a female. I want her."

"I have many females. But why would I give one up to you."

"This one I will take from you," boasted Ograar.

"That remains to be seen. But assuming that I can't stop you, suppose she refuses?"

"I will take her anyway," insisted the scarred one.

"I can not let that happen," Grendaar said firmly.

"You won't be able to stop me," retorted Ograar.

"That remains to be seen," said Grendaar.

"Aren't you curious to know who I want."

"Something tells me that I already know," said Grendaar calmly.

"Tessah," blurted Ograar, obviously waiting for a strong reaction.

"Tessah?" queried Grendaar in mock disbelief.

"Tessah," repeated Ograar.

Grendaar chuckled.

"What do you find so amusing?" asked the confused Ograar. Apparently this was not the response he had expected.

"Come now, younger brother, stop wasting my time," said Grendaar condescendingly. "I am beginning to believe that you truly intend to talk me into submission. Challenge me, or remove yourself from my path."

Ograar shrugged. "Have it your way, old one. I am Ograar, Killer of Killers, once of the Quiet Tributary Roam of the Silver River Tribe. Make way for me, or feel my wrath."

The response came rather quietly. "I am Grendaar, Groundshaker, of the Green Water Roam of the Red Dawn Tribe. Make way for me, or feel my wrath."

Ograar began to circle to the right. Grendaar had to fight down an overwhelming desire to immediately charge Ograar and give him a good thrashing. But he was certain that all that bantering was calculated to provoke Grendaar into doing just that. He would not play into the hands of his opponent, no matter how badly he wanted to. So he too circled to the right.

Slowly the two immense males closed the gap between them. Their tails began to lash behind them. In ever greater arcs the tails swung, as the males inched towards each other. The circling continued until they had made one complete circuit. They were now almost within touching distance. Suddenly Ograar pivoted hard on his left foot, swinging his whole body around in a counterclockwise direction, moving his broad, heavy tail in a club-like fashion against Grendaar. Grendaar pivoted at almost the same instant, but on his right foot, swinging his body in a clockwise direction, arcing his tail around towards Ograar. The two tails struck each other with a loud, resounding thud. The shock of the impact shuddered up both males. Now standing almost side-by-side, they reeled away to prepare for the next attack.

Ograar began to circle Grendaar, Grendaar slowly rotated around the center of the circle, careful to keep his feet spread apart and close to the ground. The tails of the two males continued their arcing back and forth, building momentum. They were so close now that they could almost reach out and grab each other. Grendaar watched Ograar carefully. He timed the swinging of the younger male's tail, careful to keep the correct foot on the ground, waiting for Ograar to swing first.

Ograar again pivoted hard, on his right foot, swinging his body in a clockwise movement, tail racing towards Grendaar. As if on cue, Grendaar also pivoted hard, also on his right foot, body moving in a clockwise direction, willing his tail around at a faster rate than Ograar's. The tails struck like a clap of thunder, hitting the opponent high on the left thigh. The force of the blows bulldozed both males several feet to the right. Again the shock of the impact ran through the entire body of each male. Murmurs arose from the throng of bystanders. Now facing in opposite directions, Grendaar wobbled off to his right to prepare for the next attack, while Ograar tottered off to his right.

Ograar circled Grendaar again, but at a slower, more cautious rate. He also stood ten feet further back than before. Grendaar held the middle ground, stepping carefully, watching the swing of his opponent's tail, coordinating his foot position and tail swing accordingly, gradually closing the distance between them. He again waited for Ograar to swing first. Ograar accommodated, but this time pivoting on his left foot, body swinging in a counterclockwise direction, tail arcing. A fraction of a second later, Grendaar also pivoted hard, on his left foot, body racing in a counterclockwise direction, tail rushing for its target. Another crack of thunder. Each struck the other a hard, brutal blow against the upper right thigh, staggering him to the left. Ograar stumbled, but quickly regained his footing, and lurched off to his left. The crowd hummed with excitement. Grendaar kept his footing, moving off slowly to his left, weaving ever so slightly. Grendaar was now breathing heavily, heat rising off of his body in waves.

Three more times over the next ten minutes, the two great males exchanged fearsome blows. Each of these blows might have crippled a smaller, younger male. But these were massive males, capable of dealing and receiving much punishment. None-the-less, each time, they recovered more slowly. They were each breathing very heavily, and neither could hide a definite wobble as they circled.

Grendaar ached mightily, but he thought that he could discern that Ograar was having a difficult time standing at all. He decided to risk it all with a quick charge. He sprang at the scarred one.

Ograar tried to back-pedal, to keep out of Grendaar's grasp. But he moved too slowly, and stumbled just as Grendaar crashed into his chest. Grendaar pushed him back, and over, and down. Grendaar hugged him tightly, and quickly pushed his horn into Ograar's throat, and demanded, "Yield to me."

Ograar fumed inside for allowing himself to fall into such a vulnerable position so easily. He struggled mightily, trying to shake loose from Grendaar's hold. Grendaar would not loosen his grip. Ograar bucked and shook, but Grendaar held him in an iron-like grip. All that Ograar succeeded in doing was to force Grendaar's horn deeper into his neck.

Blood began to trickle down Ograar's neck. Grendaar repeated, "Yield to me."

Ograar made one last mighty effort, using all the brute strength he could muster, to throw Grendaar off. Grendaar held on tightly, he could not be budged. Ograar sighed. Then, through heavy breaths, he reluctantly blurted out, "I yield."

Grendaar staggered to his feet. Still breathing heavily, he looked down at the vanquished challenger, glad it was over. Ograar seemed disinclined to get immediately to his feet. He looked up at Grendaar, and said, "You are a mighty warrior, elder brother, to that I can attest." There were murmurs of agreement from the throng.

Grendaar extended the scarred one a hand, and helping him to his feet, said, "And you, brother, are a credit to your race. Go now, and prosper."

"May you never know want, elder brother," returned Ograar.

As Ograar reeled in the direction of his tribe, there were pronouncements of approval from the crowd. Some of the younger adult males began to chant, "Groundshaker. Groundshaker."

Grendaar looked around him. There were many smiling faces in the multitude. As Grendaar surveyed them, a large adult male broke from the assembly, and approached him. Rattan also separated himself from the crowd, and walked towards Grendaar from the opposite direction. Grendaar looked at the first male. Behind the new male, almost lost in the mob, Grendaar thought that he detected Adeldraar.

The large male walked to within thirty feet of Grendaar. He was a handsome male, with a deep set of piercing eyes. Without any ceremony whatever, he said, "I am Vectur, once of the Pinnacle Island Roam of the Turquoise Sea Tribe. Make way for me, or feel my wrath." He was a mature male of about seventeen springs, 3.9 tons in weight, and thirty-seven feet long. His horn was fifteen inches in length.

Rattan quickly came up beside Grendaar. "What is this? What did I hear you say?" he asked of the challenger.

"I have just challenged this old male to battle," responded Vectur. "What business is it of yours?"

"None, I suppose, younger brother," answered Rattan, " but do you not know that this male has just fought a mighty battle?"

"What of it, elder brother? This has nothing to do with me," retorted Vectur sardonically.

"This may be so, younger brother," agreed Rattan. But then he urged, "Do you not think that it is indecorous to not allow him a reasonable time to rest between bouts?"

"I am well within my rights, elder brother. I have placed a legitimate challenge. He must either fight, or yield," insisted Vectur.

"But surely ..." began Rattan.

"Leave us," interjected Vectur rudely.

Rattan was clearly agitated. "Know you this then, Vectur the Insolent," he said forcefully to the other. "Whatever the outcome of this contest, next you face me. And I will give you the same amount of time to rest that you have given the Groundshaker."

Vectur stared unblinkingly at Rattan. Finally he said, "As you wish, elder brother."

Vectur then turned to Grendaar. He said, "I am Vectur, once of the Pinnacle Island Roam of the Turquoise Sea Tribe. Make way for me, or feel my wrath."

Grendaar, now breathing less heavily after the delay that the dialogue had caused, turned to Rattan, and said, "Thank you, my brother. I appreciate your concern. But I will fight this battle."

He then turned to Vectur. He crashed his tail into the ground with a mighty blow. The ground actually shook. He said, "I am Grendaar, Groundshaker, of the Green Water Roam of the Red Dawn Tribe. Make way for me, or feel my wrath."

Without a second's hesitation after replying to the challenge, Grendaar rushed at Vectur, striking him in the chest. Grendaar brought Vectur to the ground, and they rolled over and over, grappling with each other. Rattan hastily backed away from the two combatants.

Vectur punched at Grendaar, scratching and clawing, before they finally broke apart, and jumped to their feet. Vectur circled Grendaar, tail lashing back and forth. Grendaar slowly rotated, tail also lashing. As before, Grendaar carefully watched his opponent, measuring the swing of his tail, timing his own responses accordingly. Vectur pivoted on his right foot, body and tail swinging clockwise. Grendaar also pivoted on his right foot. Their tails struck their opponent's body a heavy blow. They both staggered, although it seemed that Grendaar staggered more.

Vectur moved to a new position to deliver the next attack. Grendaar, moving more slowly, likewise prepared for the next assault. Three more times they exchanged heavy blows. Each strike took its toll. Vectur, the fresher of the two, seemed to be gaining the advantage. Grendaar tried to hold his own, conserving his strength as best as he could under the circumstances.

Vectur charged Grendaar. Grendaar sprang forward to meet the attack. They collided with terrific force, punching and jabbing, kicking and shoving. One tripped the other, and they both fell in a heap. Vectur tried to gouge Grendaar in the eye. Grendaar warded off the attempt, and struck Vectur a heavy blow in the abdomen with his clenched fist. Vectur gasped. Then Vectur bit Grendaar in the arm. Grendaar grunted in pain and rage. He pummeled Vectur with the fist of his free hand. Vectur released his bite.

They both pushed away from each other, struggling to get to their feet. Vectur got to his feet first. Grendaar, afraid of losing any advantage, lunged at Vectur from his knees, grabbing the other around the waist. Grendaar pulled Vectur back to the ground, and they rolled in the dirt, throwing up great clouds of dust, as they strained to get advantage over the other.

They fought for what seemed a long time, rolling about on the ground. Several times they rolled into the masses of bystanders, forcing the observers to scramble out of the way lest they be wounded as a byproduct of the more serious intent of the two desperate males. Both were bleeding from a dozen minor puncture wounds delivered from their adversary's horn. They also had dozens of scratches and bruises, and cuts and bumps.

Both were on their feet again, warily circling each other. Both seemed to have forgotten any science or strategy in their efforts to best each other. The bout had been reduced to an effort of brute strength and endurance. Grendaar pivoted hard on his left foot, hoping to knock Vectur down with one more mighty blow of his massive, stiff tail. Vectur had other ideas. He sprang at Grendaar half way through his turn, avoided the tail more by luck than skill, and crashed into the side of Grendaar's still rotating body.

Grendaar was knocked off of his feet, with Vectur sprawling on top of him. Grendaar, the wind knocked out of him, still managed to flip himself upward just enough to dislodge Vectur. Both scrambled around in the dirt, dust partially obscuring them from the on-lookers. Each was trying desperately to grapple with the other. Vectur grabbed hold of Grendaar's foot, and tried to wrench it around, twisting the ankle. Grendaar kicked back with both feet, sending Vectur sliding into some sharp rocks. Vectur groaned in pain, pulled himself to his knees, picked up one of the rocks, and through it at Grendaar. Grendaar, also on his knees by that time, turned his head away from the oncoming missile. It struck him in the shoulder.

Vectur stood, and rushed at Grendaar. He tried to kick Grendaar again, but Grendaar managed to dodge the blow. Grendaar, still on his knees, lunged at Vectur's other leg. He grabbed it, tripping Vectur. He pushed himself forward, grabbing Vectur around the waist. He yanked himself forward again, reaching for the other's neck. They both kicked and pushed the other with their hind legs, pulling themselves almost face-to-face on the ground. Grendaar had never been in such a dirty and undignified fight before in all his many bouts. He was more determined than ever to best this curmudgeon.

With the last bit of strength that he could muster, Grendaar, with his arms wrapped around Vectur, and with Vectur's arms wrapped around him, forced his horn closer and closer to the soft throat of his adversary. Vectur strained mightily to prevent this from happening, tucking his chin down to block Grendaar's horn. Inch by inch, the horn approached its goal. Vectur squirmed and jerked, trying to push away from the approaching horn. As tired as Grendaar was, his strength and endurance seemed to exceed that of Vectur's. Finally his horn just barely touched Vectur's throat.

"Yield to me," Grendaar demanded.

"No," responded Vectur. He kicked at Grendaar, and pounded him on the back with both fists.

Grendaar could not be shaken off. He continued to inch his horn forward. It broke skin, and rich red blood began to flow down Vectur's neck.

"Yield to me," Grendaar insisted.

"No," gasped Vectur.

"Yield, you dunghead," said Grendaar as he pushed his horn another half inch forward.

"I yield, I yield," blurted Vectur.

Grendaar immediately withdrew his horn. He and Vectur lay there gasping for breath. Both were too weak to rise. They lay there a long time. Finally Grendaar pulled himself away from Vectur, and sat up. Vectur still lay there in a heap. Grendaar sat a long while. The crowd was strangely silent, staring first at him, then at Vectur. After a few more minutes, Grendaar pulled himself up to his feet. He staggered, and almost fell, but caught himself. He stood there, legs spread, using his tail to help support his weight, gazing at his opponent still lying on the ground.

There was a murmur from the throng. Grendaar looked up at them quizzically. He heard a faint, "Groundshaker. Groundshaker."

It grew in volume. "Groundshaker. Groundshaker."

Suddenly it died. Grendaar looked around to see what the cause was. A large male, separating himself from the bystanders, approached Grendaar. He stopped fifty feet from where Grendaar stood. Grendaar was swaying slightly, and breathing heavily.

With no more ceremony than the last challenger, he said, "I am Trumpaar, once of the Lush Wallow Roam of the Green Hills Tribe. Make way for me, or feel my wrath."

Grendaar could barely believe what he was hearing. He could hardly stand up straight, let alone fight this male. The male seemed to be only of twelve springs, and much lighter and shorter than he, but at the moment that seemed to matter little.

Rattan began to move forward in protest. This was unheard of. This broke all the rules of propriety. It was not civilized behavior. Rattan growled volubly.

Grendaar tried to collect his last remaining strength as quickly as he could. Before Grendaar could think of an appropriate response to the situation, a massive blur rushed past him. The blur honked loudly and shrilly as it went by. "I am Rohraar ...", it cried just before it struck the challenger with the force of a small avalanche, squarely in the chest.

The challenger tumbled backwards, as Rohraar said, "... of the Green Water Roam ...." Still on his feet, Rohraar continued, "... of the Red Dawn Tribe ...." As he lunged at Trumpaar, wrestling with him on the ground, he finished the ritual phrase, or at least most bystanders thought he did. Even as they punched and jabbed, Rohraar was thought to be heard saying, " ... or feel my wrath."

Rohraar threw himself at Trumpaar like a wild primitive, using neither cunning nor science, just blind fury. The two males tumbled and twirled in a ferocious display of the most undignified style of fighting imaginable. Perhaps only Grendaar's fight with Vectur had been less dignified.

Grendaar watched his roam-mate in growing wonder. He knew Rohraar to be courageous and brave, but he didn't know that Rohraar could fight so fiercely. He had never seen him fight like this before. He would never want to himself face Rohraar in such fury. He hoped that Rohraar wouldn't use this style of fighting, if he ever challenged Grendaar for dominance of the roam. It would make for a difficult situation. And it might result in a fight that only one of them would survive.

Within ten minutes, Rohraar had subdued Trumpaar. Grendaar, indeed the whole assemblage, had stood dumbfounded and entranced by the ferocity of Rohraar's onslaught. Rohraar now stood over Trumpaar, bleeding from a score of superficial wounds, glaring first at the still supine Trumpaar, and then around at the spectators, looking to see if there would be any more challenges.

Grendaar looked about, to see if there were any. Stationed quietly behind him was Trugahr, standing tall and erect. With Trugahr was Kinput, Draggot, Sevren, and a few other adult males. Trugahr walked up beside Grendaar. They exchanged smiles.

As he looked further, Grendaar saw Renthot pushing his way through the crowd. Beside him was Dandraar. And behind them came all of the adult and adolescent males of the Yellow Mud Roam. With them were Wubbar and Hew. Someone had apparently found Hew. They all quietly arranged themselves behind Grendaar. Who is with the roams, Grendaar wondered to himself?

Rattan joined them, along with his males. He said quietly but forcefully, "Groundshaker. Groundshaker."

The males around him followed suit. "Groundshaker. Groundshaker."

More males surged forward, joining the group, chanting "Groundshaker. Groundshaker."

Grendaar looked about him at his friends. He looked over at the heavily breathing roam-mate who was just now backing off of Trumpaar. Grendaar chanted. "Rohraar. Rohraar." He ambled over to his second male, and gave him a nuzzle.

Grendaar put his arm around Rohraar and said louder, "Rohraar. Rohraar."

Grendaar relaxed for the first time in over an hour. He looked around at the demonstration, pleased with what he saw. "Groundshaker. Groundshaker. Rohraar. Rohraar. Groundshaker," came the mixed chant in rising crescendos.

Suddenly Grendaar frowned, and moved forward as quickly as his aching body would permit. He ran into the crowd with such haste, that many hornbrows pushed and stumbled to get out of his way. He approached Adeldraar, who was trying to lose himself in the masses. The chanting died down. Grendaar and Adeldraar stood face-to-face, and suddenly there was dead silence.

Grendaar stared into the other's eyes. Adeldraar fidgeted, unable to return the stare. He was again without his staff.

"Adeldraar," said Grendaar, "I detect your hand in this. I won't accuse you, so you won't have to lie. But know this. I will come looking for you this afternoon, when the sun is halfway on its journey from the top of the sky to the mountains in the west. Be prepared for me then, Adeldraar."

Adeldraar swallowed hard. He glanced quickly about him, head jerking to the left and right. Where were his champions? They had all been defeated, or had melted away. Finally he croaked, "I hear you." Then he turned quickly, and pushing the crowds before him, rushed away.

As Adeldraar sped away, his head was filled with the chant, "Groundshaker. Groundshaker."

CHAPTER FIFTEEN
A THING TOO LONG DELAYED

At the appointed hour, Grendaar walked over to the place of the Chiefs Roam of the Red Dawn Tribe. He had spent the time between the last dominance fight and now, resting. The females of his roam had attended to his wounds. They licked them clean, and as well as they could, had tried to rearrange torn flesh back into its original pattern. He had also eaten a light meal, and had replenished much of the water lost in the exertions of battle.

Grendaar was accompanied by all the adult males of his roam. Dandraar, although not invited to participate, had followed along at a discrete distance anyway. Renthot also accompanied Grendaar, and he too had brought with him all of his adult males. Other males had joined the group, among them Kinput and Sevren the solitaries, and Draggot the packleader. There were seventeen other adult solitaries and packers who had joined the faction – all members of the Red Dawn Tribe.

There were also five other roamleaders from the Red Dawn Tribe in attendance, with all their males. They were the Black Sand Roam, the Crescent Beach Roam, the Crooked Tree Roam, the Horn Rock Roam, and the Three Pebbles Roam. These were roamleaders that understood the gravity of the coming confrontation. They were roamleaders and males who would have followed wherever Grendaar lead. For this could turn into something more than just a dominance fight between two males. Depending upon who in the Chiefs Roam supported Adeldraar's position, and depending upon who else Grendaar might have to fight in the Chiefs Roam, and depending upon what the dozens of other adult males of the Chiefs Roam did when the confrontation occurred, this could become a fight for leadership of the tribe.

More than a score of roamleaders from the other eight tribes of the Great Eastern Herd had volunteered to accompany Grendaar. In the hours that intervened between his dominance fights with Ograar and Vectur and now, many had visited his roam to tell him that they would support him in whatever claim he made. Since he did not want to extend the issue beyond the tribe proper, he had graciously declined their offer of assistance. Many of them accompanied him anyway, but stayed in the background so as not to over-complicate the issues.

Grendaar did not aspire to become one of the leaders of the Chiefs Roam. He simply knew that it was time to confront Adeldraar. Perhaps he should have done so years ago. Thirteen years ago, Adeldraar had been one of the roamleaders that Grendaar had to defeat to keep Tessah. Twelve years ago Adeldraar had challenged him unsuccessfully again. That particular dominance fight, and the events leading up to it, were reminiscent of the events that had occurred earlier today.

Since then, Adeldraar had never directly confronted Grendaar again. Yet, throughout the years, Grendaar had to deal with a variety of situations that he suspected were the machinations of Adeldraar. He had dealt with the situations, but had decided to ignore Adeldraar's involvement in them. Perhaps he should have dealt with Adeldraar. But he had Tessah, and Adeldraar didn't, and that seemed to be sufficient.

Meanwhile, Adeldraar had moved up in importance within the tribe. Now he was a subchief. Keeper of one of the sacred artifacts. Advisor of Eldooran the chief. Staffholder of the Red Dawn Tribe. By the time all these things had occurred, it was almost too late to confront Adeldraar directly. Then such a challenge might have looked more like a challenge for the chieftainship. There was just too much politics in it, and Grendaar had been disinclined to get involved in those kinds of matters. In addition, the more powerful Adeldraar got, the less inclined he seemed toward intrigue, at least as it related to Grendaar. There had not been such an episode in years.

Today, though, had shown Grendaar that things were not all that different. Adeldraar was still up to his old tricks. He was in too responsible a position to be allowed to use it so blatantly for personal vendettas. Worse, Grendaar might have been killed today, if the challenges had been allowed to continue outside the normal confines of accepted hornbrow behavior. Or equally as bad from Grendaar's point of view, he might somehow have survived the battles, but lost Tessah. He had to put a stop to these machinations. Adeldraar must be confronted once and for all.

It was quite a following that Grendaar had as he approached the Chiefs Roam. If he had been overly ambitious, he could have precipitated a civil war. But this was not his purpose. Once he dealt with Adeldraar, he would be satisfied.

As Grendaar approached the outskirts of the Chiefs Roam, Eldooran stepped from the midst of a large group of adult males. Zurgott was at his side. Adeldraar was not yet in evidence. The two chiefs walked directly up to Grendaar.

"May the sun grant you its warmth and light, Grendaar, my brother," said Eldooran effusively. He held the shell in his right hand.

Zurgott nodded almost imperceptibly, and said, "May you be granted days without cold or hunger, oh Groundshaker." The sun glinted dully off of the stone that he carried.

Grendaar nodded to Eldooran, and said, "May the sun also warm you, oh Protector of the Vast Plains." He nodded at Zurgott, and added, "And may your days be filled with children and warmth, Keeper of the Blue Stone."

Knowing full well why Grendaar was there, Eldooran none-the-less said, "I am pleased that you have come to visit the Chiefs Roam. You are welcome. All from your roam are welcome." He paused deliberately to gaze upon the large following with Grendaar, and added, "Indeed, all of your friends are also welcome."

Eldooran and Zurgott then went through the tedious ceremony of formally recognizing each of the roamleaders of each of the roams of the Red Dawn Tribe. By extension, they recognized all the adult males with them. They also went on to recognize the roamleaders of the other tribes. It was an hour before the greetings were complete.

"Come," Eldooran finally said as he turned back towards the place where the Chiefs Roam resided. "Join with us while we sit and enjoy the musings that the stream makes as it travels to the Sacred Lake."

Eldooran and Zurgott turned and walked back to the place where their roams had been spending their days during the dominance fights and the preparations for a new generation of hornbrows. The adult males of the Chiefs Roam that had accompanied them to meet Grendaar, turned and followed their chiefs. Grendaar then followed, accompanied by all his entourage.

They came to an open space. The chief and the subchief ascended a shallow rise, turned back to face their guests, and sat down. The adult males of the Chiefs Roam positioned themselves behind and to either side of their leaders.

Grendaar came and sat before them. Rohraar sat on his right, Renthot on his left. The other five roamleaders of the Red Dawn Tribe that were with Grendaar sat on either side of them, forming a crescent facing the chiefs. The roams spread out behind their leaders. The roamleaders from the roams not belonging to the Red Dawn Tribe, those that had decided to come with Grendaar even though he didn't wish it, sat as inconspicuously as possible with the adult males behind Grendaar. Both Eldooran and Zurgott couldn't help but notice the swollen ranks of the seven roams.

Grendaar looked over the assemblage both before him, and surrounding his group. He noticed several things. The remaining roamleaders of the other roams of the Red Dawn Tribe – the other thirteen – were also here. So were most of the adult males of those roams. So were many of the roamleaders of the other tribes. It was a vast assembly, spilling onto nearby hills, and across the stream of the Chiefs Roam.

Grendaar should have expected it. Whether this was to be just a dominance fight between a great roamleader and a subchief, or if it were to turn out to be much more, all the leaders of the tribe would want to witness, and perhaps partake in the outcome. The fact that so many other roamleaders, from many of the other tribes of the Great Eastern Herd were here also, attested to the importance of the combatants. Grendaar hoped that the outcome would not be blown out of the proportions that he anticipated. He only wanted to fight Adeldraar.

That was the other thing that Grendaar noticed. The absence of Adeldraar. Old Broken Horn was not yet in evidence. Grendaar wondered why he was staying behind the scenes until the formal challenge was made. His reveries along this line of thinking were cut short by Eldooran, who was clearing his throat.

"My brother," began the Herdmaster, "you have not visited me since your roam arrived at the Gathering Place. I was beginning to worry that you would not come at all."

"Not at all, my brother," responded Grendaar. "One has so many responsibilities when the Nine Tribes gather. But in truth, I have stopped by twice, and both times you and the subchiefs were away visiting other tribes yourselves."

"It is true," said Eldooran looking about him. "My females have reported it thus. I was most disappointed that I was not here to greet you."

"No matter, my brother," said Grendaar. "I am here now."

"Yes, and it is good," replied Eldooran. "For I have longed to talk with you." He continued, nodding in agreement with his own words, "The wisdom of Grendaar is well known among the Red Dawn Tribe."

Some of Eldooran's advisors also nodded in agreement, as did many among the assembled leaders.

"I am here now, my brother," Grendaar repeated. Then he added graciously, although perhaps also allowing some false modesty to show, "And it would please me to offer to you what little of value I have learned in all my years, if only you would ask. You do me great honor by the mere suggestion that I could advise you. How may I be of service?"

"Perhaps you can help me understand this," said the Herdmaster. He frowned and scratched his head. "It is a perplexing thing, and I do not yet know what to make of it."

Grendaar knew that Eldooran would ask him why he had come to the Chiefs Roam with so many adult males. Eldooran already knew that Grendaar had come to fight Adeldraar. Everyone knew that. But he would want to know if Grendaar intended more than that. Eldooran would want to know if he himself was to soon be involved in a dominance fight with Grendaar for leadership of the tribe. But he would never ask such a question directly. Such an approach would be an inexcusable breach of etiquette, and unworthy of the Chief of the Red Dawn Tribe.

So Eldooran began. "I visited the Holy Island in the Sacred Lake yesterday. I swam across the warm, clear waters. I climbed up the hillside, and I sat upon one of the rocks of contemplation. I let the warm sun dry me. While I sat there, I saw a curious drama unfold before me. It occurred off and on throughout the day, and disturbed my contemplations. But it intrigued me, and I became quite interested in it as the day progressed."

He paused for effect. The entire assemblage was completely hushed, taking in the proceedings. Grendaar nodded in understanding of what he had already heard, but couldn't begin to guess where Eldooran was going with his story.

Eldooran continued. "While I sat upon the warm stone, I beheld a family of small lizards. They were red-stripers, I seem to recall. But that is not important. They crawled from under a cleft in the nearby stone wall, and spread out to sun themselves. They didn't seem to notice that I was there. There were many of them, fathers and mothers, brothers and sisters, uncles and aunts. I was particularly interested in one family. There was a father, and he had three sons. The father puffed up his neck sack in a proud display, and his sons did him great honor."

Eldooran looked about him to see if he had everyone's attention. All the participants were curious about where this story was leading, and all listened to it carefully. He continued. "Then the lizards went off to hunt. It was perhaps mid-morning. So I proceeded with my contemplations. An hour later they returned. Each had brought back the spoils of the hunt. One had caught a dragonfly; another brought back a roach; still another carried four berries in his mouth; while the last had a worm. The father and his three sons shared their fortune, and ate from the common wealth. Then they lay in the sun again."

Again Eldooran looked about him. He coughed, made a gesture of dismissal, and said, "But I am telling this story in too much detail. Let me be more brief." No one disagreed with him. On the other hand, no one would have complained either.

He went on. "The father and his sons went away to hunt again. They came back with their spoils in the early afternoon, and again shared them. Toward mid-afternoon, they went away once more. Only this time, when they had all returned, two of the sons brought nothing back with them.

"The father and the third son offered to share what they had with the other two, but they refused to accept the proffered food. The two sons who had brought nothing back then began to argue. They argued with each other, and they argued with their father. I could not understand why. Soon they began to fight. It was a messy fight, biting and clawing. Soon the father and the third son, who were trying to make peace, were dragged into the fight. Sides developed, and the first son, the largest one, and the third son, fought the father and the second son. Soon other families joined in, trying to bring peace to the fighting lizards. But then they became embroiled in the battle too. Next thing I saw, father was fighting son, sister was clawing aunt, and uncle was biting mother. It was both terrible and fascinating at the same time. I thought to intervene, but on who's behalf?"

He paused and leaned back, scratching under his chin. "Before I left my contemplations, the battle had ended. Five of the little lizards had been killed, and were already beginning to swell in the setting sun. Many of the rest had scattered, crawling away with twisted limbs and broken tails, leaving behind much uneaten food. Food that soon the ants would be getting. The father lizard had been one of the casualties. And the brothers were scattered, never to be a whole family again.

"I have thought much about this since it occurred. I thought about it on the swim back from the Holy Island. And much of the night. I've thought about it all day today. What could this mean? Sons fighting their father. Whole families becoming embroiled in a senseless thing. The whole group cast to the wind, with scavengers and predators being the only ones to reap the rewards. Does it have any meaning? Was it a premonition?"

Eldooran put his hands on his knees, and looked at the assembled males. He asked, "Should I be concerned with this? Or was it a freakish and meaningless act of nature? Does anyone know?" He looked directly at Grendaar, and queried, "Do you know, my brother?"

Grendaar coughed to clear his throat. Then he said, "I think, my brother, that it was a marvelous thing to behold. I think that you were privileged to be given the opportunity to witness something that few of us will ever see. And perhaps it can give you much insight as you go about your daily tasks of administering to the needs of the tribe. But I do not think that it was a premonition. I think that it was a curious event of nature."

Eldooran might have taken that as an adequate response, but still he persisted. He wanted no doubt left as to Grendaar's intent. "What of the sons warring upon their father, and brothers fighting each other? What do you make of this?"

Grendaar looked directly at Eldooran, and spoke as conciliatorily as possible. "I am not sure that any of us here can adequately explain that. Perhaps it was just an abhorrent anomaly. Sons should do honor to their fathers. And brothers should respect one another. Everyone here believes that."

Amidst murmurs of general agreement, Eldooran leaned back. He visibly relaxed. If Grendaar had come here to fight him, then Grendaar's interpretation of the events just described would have been very different. Grendaar would have somehow justified the actions of the combatants as a warning and precursor to his challenge to Eldooran himself.

Grendaar could see that others were also relaxing. Many had anticipated the challenge between Grendaar and Eldooran that might have embroiled many others in a conflict that none of them wanted. Now they knew that challenge would not come. At least not today.

Grendaar looked at Zurgott. He remained inscrutable. It was difficult to tell what he felt, even knowing that if the challenge had come, Zurgott most certainly would have been involved in the conflict.

"Your story was an interesting one, my brother," said Grendaar. "I think that, as we have more time to digest it, we will all learn something of value from it. It reminds me of an event that I witnessed many years ago."

Grendaar noticed that Eldooran leaned slightly forward, although Zurgott sat impassively. The murmurs and side conversations that had begun to spring up, suddenly subsided. Grendaar would now make his wants known. But like Eldooran, it would at first be through allegory.

"Many years ago, when I was a young packer, I was in the western foothills during the Gathering. I was hunting small predators so that there would be less of them to raid the nesting grounds." There were rumbles of recollection as many of the males remembered doing likewise. Some of the males nodded, others looked off into empty space, conjuring up visions of their own adolescence, when they too stalked robrunners or razorteeth. For this was an occupation that young male and female hornbrows had been employed at for many thousands of generations.

"As I cautiously clambered over a pile of fallen rock, I came upon a small band of redrunners," continued Grendaar. "They were in a small grove, and were nesting. I was still hidden from them, and I was down wind, so they didn't know I was there. Instead of rushing in headlong and ready for smashing every redrunner that I could catch, I lay there quietly and watched them."

Grendaar paused, collecting his thoughts. Many hornbrows had come upon comparable scenes, and many were lost in their own mind's eye, recalling similar events. Grendaar continued. "While I watched, I saw two males arguing over a female. They weren't dominance fighting, since apparently the female had already chosen one of them. This was clear, since she was attending a nest with eight eggs in it. Her mate and the unsuccessful suitor scuffled for awhile. Then the rebuffed suitor left, and the mate returned to the female and the nest.

"As I lay there, observing these things, the male went away to hunt. Then the female went over to a brook to get a drink. While both parents were away, the erstwhile suitor returned. He immediately attracted my interest, since he walked very cautiously, his head darting back and forth, looking all about him. Checking to see that no one was about, he rushed over to the nest. He took one of the eggs from the nest, and darted away into the underbrush, carrying the egg with him. I suspect that he intended to eat the egg."

Grendaar paused as his audience stirred. Ovicide was not uncommon, and it was universally hated. But cannibalistic ovicide was despised and reviled. Many of the listeners were quite outspoken in their aspersions, but soon things quieted down again.

Grendaar waited patiently, and then continued. "The female returned, and stood over her nest. After a moment, she began to squawk loudly. The male returned, and so did the erstwhile suitor. The mate comforted the female. Then he questioned the other male. I could see by the way that they were behaving, that the mate was asking the other about the egg, and the other was denying any knowledge of it. The erstwhile suitor, puffed-up and angry, left.

"Time passed. The female went off to eat, and the male strolled down to the brook to drink. Other redrunners came and went, leaving other nests temporarily unattended, but none was left alone for very long. The erstwhile suitor returned once more. Seeing that there was no one to stop him, nor even anyone to witness his vile act, he ran over to the same nest as before. This time he selected two eggs. He rushed away into the thick bushes to consume another stolen repast.

"As you might expect, the female and her mate returned, and were distraught over the loss of two more eggs. When the erstwhile suitor finally reappeared, the mate was very truculent in his questioning of him. But the erstwhile suitor again denied any knowledge of the event, and ran off into the shrubbery.

"Yet again these events were repeated. This time, the thief took a fourth egg, and again from the same nest. He made a clean escape before either of the parents of the eggs, or indeed any of the other redrunners in the nesting area, returned. This time when the female discovered the loss, she could not be consoled. She ranted and raved, pulled small shrubs up from the ground, and ran around like she was crazy. Eventually she ran off. I could hear her wailing for some time as she ran deeper and deeper into the woods.

"Her mate stood over the nest for awhile, staring at the four remaining eggs. He also seemed disconsolate. Then he too wandered off into the nearby woods. Apparently the thief had been watching all of this. Perhaps he was gloating over the grief he was bringing to his rival and the one who had spurned him. Anyway, no sooner had the male wandered off, when the erstwhile suitor again came to rob the nest. He sprinted up to it, and picked up one of the eggs. As he reached for a second one, the mate, who had been hiding just inside the woods waiting to see if his suspicions would be confirmed, screamed out fiercely, and came charging back towards the thief. Startled, the thief dropped the egg he was grasping, and ran away. The mate pursued him, and I could see that there was murder in his eyes."

Grendaar paused, and looked at his audience. Many seemed mesmerized. He looked at Eldooran. At Zurgott. They were leaning forward, waiting for the outcome of the story. Knowing that he had brought them to where he wanted them to be, Grendaar changed his tact.

"You know," he mused out loud, "I have thought about those events many times in my life. It seems to me that the mate should have followed his instincts about the unsuccessful suitor from the beginning. Only one egg would have been lost then. Or else he should have waited in hiding sooner, and still have reduced the loss to the nest. But he didn't. He didn't see things clearly at the time they were happening. I suppose he mistrusted the other male from the start, but for some reason he wanted proof before he acted.

"We are like that redrunner. Sometimes we don't act when we should. We keep hoping that maybe we were wrong, and that the thing wasn't really as bad as we first thought. Or we think that if we delay, things will work themselves out. Or somehow get better, you know, reverse themselves of their own accord. Or that the one causing all the mischief will come to see the error of his ways.

"But how often does that really happen? Not often, it seems to me. Sometimes things work themselves out; but sometimes they just get worse. Sometimes it would have been better if we had acted immediately. But even when we don't, that shouldn't serve as an excuse for not acting at all. The redrunner showed us that. He finally did understand the situation. And acting even within his own self-imposed limitation of requiring proof positive, he identified and apprehended the perpetrator."

Grendaar hesitated long enough to let what he had just spoken sink in. There were frowns on many faces. But there was the light of understanding on many others.

Zurgott used the lull to say, "The longer a wrong is left unredressed, my brother, the more difficult it gets to repair the harm done."

"This is so, my brother," responded Grendaar, "But we should not be intimidated by the difficulty. I have come before you to redress a thing too long delayed."

Eldooran waved his hand, and all focused their attention on him. "Wrongs should be redressed. I think that we all believe that this is just. And it would be a good thing if a wrong could be righted today. But I think that the fates may have decreed otherwise."

Grendaar felt his anger rising, for suddenly he felt that Eldooran would interfere with his contest with Adeldraar. Why else would he suggest that wrongs wouldn't be righted today?

There was an angry stirring amongst those behind Grendaar as the same conclusion dawned upon others. "No," yelled several, and many sprang to their feet. "Unjust," cried others. But the Herdmaster wasn't finished, and he waved for silence. The disgruntled settled back down, patient but unsatisfied.

"At least the wrong that we expected to see redressed this afternoon won't be," said Eldooran. He paused and looked around for effect. "And I'm sure that Adeldraar would agree with me..." He paused again, and then glanced at Zurgott. Finally he rushed on, "... if only he were here.

"Wrongs should be redressed. But he is not here. Adeldraar is not with us on this auspicious afternoon. He is not with the Chiefs Roam. He is not visiting another tribe. He is not anywhere in the great Gathering Place. He is no where to be found. I have sent searchers looking everywhere for the Staffholder, but it seems that he cannot be found. He has abandoned his staff, and his position of authority."

The Protector of the Vast Plains paused to let this sink into the minds of the assembled masses. There was a sudden stirring as everyone assembled tried to express his thoughts either to his neighbor, or to a larger audience. What could this mean? Was there foul play? Was Adeldraar really gone? Was he gone temporarily, or permanently? Had he truly abandoned his staff? And his position of authority?

Eldooran added, "By best accounts, Adeldraar was reported traveling fast and light into the foothills to the west."

A new wave of questions followed that announcement. Was Adeldraar leaving because of his impending challenge from Grendaar? Was he running away? Was he afraid to fight the Groundshaker? Many would have been. But if so, then he had truly abandoned his position in the face of a challenge.

Zurgott cut further speculation short by noting, "This leaves the Red Dawn Tribe with a dilemma." He reached behind Eldooran, and brought forth the sacred staff. "The tribe is without a Staffholder."

Consternation followed this report. It had already occurred to many. But now, it had been spoken. It was officially and formally recognized. The tribe was without a Staffholder. And the tribe must have a Staffholder. The staff could not be left unattended. It was too valuable an artifact. It must be protected. For no one could make another. No one knew how. Some ancient genius had once carved the intricate designs upon the staff, but who could repeat that feat?

"What the Stonekeeper says is true," said Eldooran. "We have lost our Staffholder. And it is a terrible loss. But we will all get over it. We must go on. For there is no calamity that does not provide some benefit. Even when one of the People falls to a ravager, although it is a sad event, his loss is not in vain. For the rest of the herd escapes, and his death covers their retreat.

"So it is now. That such an event as the loss of the Staffholder should occur during the Gathering is indeed a burst of berries from the branch. For when else can the tribe select a replacement but at the Gathering?"

"All we need is someone worthy enough," added Zurgott. He held out the staff at arm's length before him, and asked, "Can we find someone worthy enough?"

Renthot sprang to his feet. He looked around at the assembled leaders and adult males. Then he turned to Eldooran and Zurgott. He spoke loudly, and gestured expansively, so that all would understand him clearly, even those on the adjoining hillsides. "You do not have to look far, for the one you seek sits before you. He is one who has given much to his roam, and to the tribe, and to the herd, asking little in return. He is a brave and valiant fighter, wise in counsel, true in friendship. He has fathered many offspring, trained many adolescents, guided many adults. He has offered sound advice and the wisdom of many years in the councils of the tribe." He gestured at Grendaar, and said, "I tell you that the Groundshaker is worthy enough. There is none more worthy."

Rohraar and Trugahr sprang to their feet simultaneously, and shouted, "Groundshaker! Groundshaker!"

As if on cue, the roamleaders of the Black Sand Roam and the Crescent Beach Roam jumped to their feet. So did the roamleaders of the Crooked Tree Roam, the Horn Rock Roam, and the Three Pebbles Roam. They all joined in the chant, "Groundshaker! Groundshaker!"

The roamleaders of the other roams of the Red Dawn Tribe were already on their feet. So were their males. So were the roamleaders from the other tribes. They too shouted, "Groundshaker! Groundshaker!"

Zurgott, the Stonekeeper, rose to his feet and shouted, "Groundshaker! Groundshaker!"

Eldooran the Herdmaster, Protector of the Vast Plains, then slowly and deliberately rose to his feet. He took the staff from Zurgott and holding it in the direction of Grendaar, said very quietly, "Groundshaker."

Grendaar at first sat as if in shock. Then he too rose slowly to his feet. He looked about as the acclamation increased in volume. With many mixed feelings, he walked reflectively, deliberately, up to Eldooran. He seemed lost in some vast introspection. He grasped the staff, holding it along with Eldooran, and said, "I accept."

Eldooran released the staff. Grendaar turned to face the assembled males and leaders of his tribe. He held the staff up before him. A hush settled over the throng. "I accept," he repeated.

The assembly went wild with approbation. Stiff, heavy tails began to pound the earth. Soon the blows beat in a coordinated rhythm, shaking the earth, punctuating the chant: "Groundshaker! Groundshaker!"

CHAPTER SIXTEEN
WINNERS AND LOSERS

In the days that followed, the tribes settled down to other matters. Dandraar remembered watching with grave interest as the Chiefs Roam of the Red Dawn Tribe reorganized itself. The Chiefs Roam was actually composed of the three roams of the chief and subchiefs. Thus it formerly was made up of Eldooran's roam, the White Fern Roam; Adeldraar's roam, the Winding River Roam; and Zurgott's roam, the Dragonfly Roam. The Winding River Roam removed itself from the Chiefs Roam, and set up on its own, like the other seventeen roams of the tribe. The Winding River Roam selected a new roamleader to replace the hastily departed Adeldraar. The new roamleader was the second male of the roam, an adult of eighteen springs named Bebann.

Dandraar was rather proud when the Green Water Roam took the place of the Winding River Roam as part of the super-roam collectively called the Chiefs Roam. With that action, he instantly had many new adolescent males and females to meet and make friends with. He set about this task with relish, trying to meet each one as quickly as possible, hoping that the females were pleasant, and that the males were adventuresome.

Dandraar was happy that, while a part of the Chiefs Roam, each individual roam still maintained its own identity. Although the three roams of the Chiefs Roam traveled together, Dandraar felt better that while he was a member of

the Chiefs Roam, he still belonged to the Green Water Roam. It was a roam
to be proud of. It was Grendaar's roam.

Things would be different for awhile. The White Fern, Dragonfly, and
Green Water Roams would stay close to each other throughout the spring and
summer. What little governance of the tribe was necessary would end when
the roams quit the Gathering Place, crossed the upper plain, and descended
the ravine to the coastal plain. This would happen in the coming autumn.
Then the tribe would head for the delta at the mouth of the River of the Nine
Tribes, and each roam would go off and fend for itself.

Since this was his fourth trek, Dandraar had the routine down pat. He
knew that very early next spring, the cycle would repeat itself once more.
The roams and the tribes would begin to collect together again, for the annual
trek to the western foothills, and the Gathering Place. And at the end of that
trek, Dandraar would most likely become an adult. He could hardly wait.

Meanwhile, there were things to do now. The Yellow Mud Roam, closely
allied to the Green Water Roam, also stayed in the vicinity of the Chiefs
Roam. So Dandraar romped with those adolescent males also. They, along
with Davgot and his packer friends, and the other adolescent males from the
Chiefs Roam, went into the foothills to the west more and more frequently.
Now that the adult males and females were in the nesting areas, mating and
laying eggs, it was more important than ever to discourage predators from
haunting the place.

One rainy day, Dandraar, Davgot, and a group of six other adolescents
were in the foothills hunting. It had been raining since the previous evening.
At times during the night, the rain had fallen in torrents. Now it was just a
steady drizzle. Clouds drifted above the hilltops, and occasionally drifted
lower, filling the upper combes and dales.

The group had been hunting close to the nesting area of the Green Water
Roam. This particular day, the group was made up of Dandraar, Davgot, an
adolescent male of the Yellow Mud Roam named Thallaar, an adolescent
male of the Dragonfly Roam named Gemuth, and four fellow packers of
Davgot's. Two of those packers were females, and one was named Rosarah.
Rosarah was once of the Horn Rock Roam.

They had been hunting all morning without success. They had spotted a small herd of eggsnatchers, but the skittish creatures had bolted at the first sight of the hornbrows. They had also seen several small packs of robrunners, but were unable to get close enough to trap any. The little predators were much too canny for that, especially since the packers were in the foothills in force, and the robrunners had to be perpetually on guard if they wanted to survive.

The group of hunters had worked itself close enough to the nesting area of the Green Water Roam that they could see it from an overlook. The overlook was a good place to rest after the morning's exertions, so they settled down on a ledge of rock outcropping. The nesting area was about fifty feet below them. They kept fairly quiet, and did their best to remain inconspicuous, so that the adults wouldn't send them away.

Below them they could see the males and females tending nests. Much of the mating was over, and most of the females had already laid their eggs. In each nest, the female had produced somewhere between twenty and thirty eggs. The first egg had been planted almost directly in the center of the nest. Then the female had carefully planted additional eggs around the first one, spiraling outward from the center. When she had finished the arduous task of laying her eggs, each female then placed soft vegetation over them. The vegetation offered a variety of useful functions. It was laid on very thickly, so that as it rotted, it created warmth. Thus it helped raise the temperature of the incubator nest. It also shaded the eggs from the direct rays of the sun, and helped to hold in the warmth throughout the cooler nights.

The males and females took turns guarding the nests, waiting the twenty-eight to thirty days for the eggs to hatch. Males would go off to eat, while the females made sure that none of the smaller predators got into the nesting areas and stole eggs. Then the males would return to guard the nests, letting the females go off to eat. Males with multiple mates, had double and triple duty. They spent much of their time guarding one nest after another, or traveling between nest sites. Such males tended to loose weight during the mating, hatching and rearing season.

Efficient guard duty was critical. There were multiple dangers to the young during the first weeks and months of their lives. First there were the egg stealers like swiftstealers and eggsnatchers. Swiftstealers and eggsnatchers were small, bipedal omnivores with small heads and very large eyes. They did not have teeth, but instead had a horny cropping beak. They had long, slim, gracefully curved and mobile necks, sitting atop small bodies with long, powerful running legs. The arms were long, especially the forearms, and they had three-fingered hands equipped with large curving claws. The hind legs were long, strong, and capable of high speeds. The feet also had three toes, each with sharp claws. Long tapered tails, accounting for more than half of the creatures' length of ten to fourteen feet, helped keep balance as they darted about.

Swiftstealers and eggsnatchers were quick, agile, and extremely difficult for a hornbrow to catch, but they were only opportunistic egg stealers. They would take eggs when a good chance presented itself, but they didn't habitually raid nesting areas. They were too large, and couldn't successfully weave around the many nests and steal eggs and still be able to escape alive. And what good was it to successfully steal an egg, if you didn't live to eat it.

Then there were the irrepressible robrunners and redrunners. These creatures not only loved to steal and eat the eggs of the hornbrows, but they also had a strong preference for hatchlings. Robrunners and redrunners were smaller than the swiftstealers and eggsnatchers, but they looked a lot like them. They were small, bipedal, eight-foot-long omnivores with small heads and large eyes. They had a horny cropping beak, but also had upper teeth, and self-sharpening cheek teeth that were replaced by new ones as the old ones wore out. They were equipped with cheek pouches, and strong jaws. Their arms were much shorter in relation to their bodies than were the swiftstealers and eggsnatchers, and their hands were five-fingered hands instead of three-fingered. Like the others, they had long, agile shins and feet that allowed them short bursts at very high speed. While the others had three-toed feet, robrunners and redrunners had four-toed feet tipped with claws. And of course they had a long, tendon-stiffened tail for balancing themselves when they sprinted, and when they made sudden maneuvers and quick changes in direction.

Robrunners and redrunners were perhaps the bigger problem to the nesting areas, for they were not just opportunistic thieves. They made frequent and determined raids upon the nesting sites. Sometimes one or two would run through a nesting area, trying to snatch an egg or a hatchling. More often than not, these were unsuccessful. But often they raided in groups, sometimes scores of them. These kinds of raids invariably produced success in the form of stolen eggs and young. Hornbrows hated robrunners and redrunners.

And finally there were the razorteeth. Razorteeth weren't really egg stealers, at least not the adult razorteeth, although given the chance, even they would eat eggs. But they did love to eat a toothsome hornbrow, almost regardless of size. A single adult razortooth would steal a hatchling right out of the shell, or tackle a hornbrow nestling almost as large as the razortooth itself. Even yearlings that were nine to thirteen feet in length and 1200 to 1800 pounds in weight, would have a hard time defending themselves against an ambush from a razortooth, if the razortooth was lucky. What was worse was that razorteeth tended to hunt in packs, so that even an adolescent could fall victim to an attack from a pack. Razorteeth were serious trouble. Even an adult might be unlucky enough to be bested by a pack of them.

Dandraar knew that the threat from razorteeth was even worse than all of that. For razorteeth were very, very clever. Sometimes a gravid female razortooth would sneak into a hornbrow nesting area just after the nests were made, and lay her own eggs. She would lay them in two parallel lines, hidden underneath some thick, low-growing shrub. Razorteeth didn't make nests, and didn't care for their young. They didn't need to. Razorteeth young were very mobile from the moment they cracked the shell. And razorteeth hatchlings were instinctively stealthy hunters from the first moment that their stomachs started to growl. So razorteeth hatchlings, as soon as they broke the shell, might sneak into hornbrow nests, often at night, and steal an egg or a hornbrow hatchling, and make a hearty feast of it.

Hornbrows probably hated razorteeth most of all. They also feared them. Hornbrows would kill a razortooth at every opportunity, whether it was an adult, a juvenile, or still in the egg. If they didn't do everything possible to keep the razortooth population down, then they themselves might be in jeopardy.

Davgot, Dandraar, and Rosarah inspected the nesting ground below them. At the moment, many of the adults were trying to remove puddling from the nests. Most of the nests had been constructed with rain in mind. They tended to drain relatively well. But the torrents of last night had overwhelmed and clogged even the best drainage systems. The occupants of the eggs would drown if the eggs were left under water. So all night the parents had been tending the nests, checking to see that water was not collecting. Parents lapped out puddling water, or splashed it out. In situations where they could not keep ahead of the downfall, they dug little channels in the sides of their nests so that the water would flow out. Later they would remove the channels and repair the nests.

Dandraar pointed out Rohraar to Davgot. Rohraar had mated with Koowoo, the third female of the Green Water Roam, with Sungu, the seventh female, and with a female of the Yellow Mud Roam. It was a good thing for Rohraar that the Yellow Mud Roam also made its nests in this little dale. Mating with three females certainly had its rewards, and did keep the gene-pool well-mixed. But helping three females guard their nests, and feed and rear their young, was a tall order. Only the strongest of the males could do it. And if the nests weren't close to each other, it could be quite a challenge to the male. If they were in different valleys, it could easily convince a male to become monogamous, or at least to select mates closer to home.

Rohraar, the fierce and mighty male that most competitors tended to shy away from... Rohraar, the strict disciplinarian who made adolescents quake for fear of being whacked with his broad tale at the slightest provocation... was seen sloshing hurriedly through the mud with a worried frown on his face. He was heading back from the Yellow Mud Roam to an impatiently waiting Koowoo. When Koowoo saw him coming, she barely acknowledged him before she scurried down to the stream edge for lunch. Many berry bushes grew along the banks of the stream.

Fortunately for Rohraar, Sungu's nest was nearby. Sungu trotted over to Rohraar, careful not to get too close to anyone else's nest. She, like most of the hornbrows, was covered in mud. Rohraar basked in Sungu's adoration for awhile, then Sungu too went over to the stream to get a meal. Rohraar dutifully paced back and forth between the two nests, slipping and sliding in the mud. As he reached each destination, he stared into the nest for a moment, before turning around and heading back to the other. If water was collecting, he would slosh it out, or mash down a clogged channel. Then he would turn around, and head back to the other nest. He seemed a little grumpy, and everyone else stayed out of his way.

Dandraar and his group changed their focus to Grendaar. His was a different story. Grendaar had a tight triangle of three nests almost adjacent to each other. The nests of Tessah, the first female, Treah, the eleventh female, and Rumpoo, the twelfth female, had all been constructed near each other. In deference to Grendaar's many years, and to his status, the females did most of the work. Grendaar just sat equidistant from all three nests, oblivious to the rain running down his hide. His newly acquired staff of office lay before him. He kept careful watch against predators, and periodically he helped with the removal of water collecting in the nests, but the three females did most of the nest-tending.

Trugahr had also been lucky, or smart, or had an agreeable understanding with his females. Zannah, the eighth female, Ghirarah, the tenth female, and Jasmaan, the new member of the roam, all had constructed their nests near each other. Jasmaan had abandoned her earlier nest, which she had constructed in another valley. She had constructed her new nest late, after having accepted Trugahr as a mate. Zannah and Ghirarah had helped her find a good location for the new nest, and advised her on good building techniques. It was obvious that she needed help, since this was her first year at nest building.

Dandraar decided that he wanted to visit the nesting area, and pay his respects to the adults of his roam. So did Thallaar. And Rosarah was curious about nest building. So Dandraar, Rosarah, and Thallaar climbed down a nearby path that wound around to flat ground near the nest sites. Davgot and the others decided to wait for their return on the ledge.

The three young hornbrows climbed down cautiously, careful not to slip on the wet rocks. Dandraar was almost down to flat ground when he heard Davgot honking a warning. Dandraar stopped to listen. Davgot's warning announced that robrunners were in the nesting area, coming from the east, heading west. Dandraar, Rosarah, and Thallaar scrambled down the remaining rocks in their path without care to their personal safety. They charged into the nesting area. Dandraar glanced up at the ledge. It was now empty. It's former occupants were themselves rushing breakneck down the path to the nesting area.

Dandraar looked around, hoping to spot the robrunners. Even without Davgot's warning, he could have told from the commotion on the east side of the nesting area that the robrunners were somewhere in that direction. He and his companions penetrated the nesting area from the southwest, heading east.

Dandraar saw a robrunner coming in his direction. It was dodging left and right, around nests and their defenders. Adult hornbrows lunged at the fellow as he darted by, but none got close enough to him to stop him. The robrunner ran wide-eyed, head jerking this way and that, trying to select a path with daylight in it. He carried a single egg, held before him in both hands. The robrunner's task was more difficult that usual, since Davgot had alerted the entire nesting area to the robrunners before they had even grabbed their first egg.

Normally robrunners could slip into the nesting area undetected, and maybe even get an egg or two before the hornbrows knew they were there. Obviously, the nests near the periphery were in most jeopardy. So this was where the hornbrows watched most carefully. Even so, robrunners often would be able to take an egg undetected, and then make their escape past adult hornbrows that didn't know where the raiders were coming from, or where they were going to. Sometimes the robrunners shot right past a hornbrow still turning in circles trying to find out what all the furor was about.

Thallaar and Rosarah were just behind Dandraar. They too had seen the robrunner. The three of them slanted their path more northerly, hoping to achieve a better interception course. The robrunner had not yet seen them, since he was still dodging around rather determined adults that were trying to trip him up, and the three adolescents weren't yet in the path he had chosen for his escape route.

By now the nesting area was in an uproar. At least six robrunners had staged this raid. One had been tackled and killed. The other five or so were zigzagging through the nesting area on as many different paths, hoping to escape with their prizes. One of them was still unwittingly heading on a collision course with the three determined adolescents.

The other five members of Dandraar's group had gotten down to the flat ground. Gemuth had twisted his ankle in his haste, and was left behind. The other four adolescents were sprinting along the western border of the nesting area, dodging trees and shrubs, hoping to surprise one or more of the robrunners when they left the nesting ground.

Dandraar and his companions still raced toward an interception with the unaware robrunner. They were urgently trying to get between it and the potential freedom at the edge of the nesting area. The robrunner's path crossed Dandraar's, but the robrunner was moving at an astounding rate of speed, considering the muddy conditions. Dandraar mentally calculated his speed and path in relation to the robrunner's. It looked like the robrunner was going to get by him. He made a last desperate leap at the robrunner as it went by. He missed it by inches, but scared the daylights out of it as he seemingly came out of nowhere.

Dandraar crashed into the mud, and slid about thirty feet before crunching into the base of a nest. The nest, an incredibly sturdy mound, was unaffected by the encounter, as was Dandraar. He jumped to his feet, mud dripping from his body. The robrunner had safely bypassed Dandraar, still firmly holding the stolen egg. Dandraar looked after the retreating robrunner. Thallaar and Rosarah had slanted further back, trying to improve upon Dandraar's interception course, but they too had missed the robrunner. Now they were both hauling at full speed after the little predator, hoping to run him down yet.

Dandraar looked back in the other direction, still hoping to catch a robrunner. As he did so, he saw one of the little thieves swerve around three adults trying to block its path. The bulky bodies of the three adults had hidden Dandraar, dripping with and well-camouflaged by the mud he was wearing, from the robrunner's view until the robrunner was midway through its swerve. Then the robrunner saw Dandraar. Dandraar was directly in its path. The robrunner tried to correct his trajectory, but his momentum was too much for the muddy conditions. The robrunner lost its footing, hit the mud face first, and slid on a path that would take it right past Dandraar. It lost the egg it was carrying when it hit the ground. The egg hit the mud, and kept rolling under its own momentum.

Dandraar could hardly believe his good fortune. He dove at the sliding form of the robrunner, and managed to grab it around a thigh. Dandraar rotated in the mud, and sat up. He was still holding the struggling robrunner by the right thigh. The robrunner struggled and squirmed, and almost broke lose, but Dandraar managed to hang onto it. Dandraar grabbed the creature around the neck with his other hand, and turned it around so he could look into its face. He looked the creature in the eye. It looked back at him with very large, very frightened eyes. Dandraar knew that it had a right to be frightened. He decided not to torment the luckless thing, and hastily broke its neck.

Dandraar was quite satisfied with himself. He struggled to his feet. He threw the limp body of the robrunner to the ground, and looked around. His search was immediately rewarded. He spotted the egg lying in the mud about twelve feet away. He stooped over and picked it up. It was still intact. He held it up to his ear and listened. He couldn't hear anything, but that didn't mean anything. He didn't know much about eggs.

Still holding his prize, Dandraar looked toward the west to see how his companions fared. While he searched to see if any of his friends had been equally successful, an anxious male came running up to him from behind. It was Jedraar, third male of the Yellow Mud Roam. Dandraar showed him the egg, still intact. Jedraar whistled a loud sound of relief. He took the egg from Dandraar.

Jedraar's mate came running up next. He showed her the egg. She whimpered in relief. Then she took the egg from her mate, and turned it over and over, examining it scrupulously. Satisfied that it was none the worse for its experience, she gave Dandraar a quick nuzzle, and hastened back to her nest. Jedraar gave Dandraar a breath-stealing hug, then he too hurried back to his nests.

Dandraar watched them go. Then he again looked for his companions. There were several of them in evidence along the western edge of the nesting area. They were standing just inside the woods. He went over to investigate.

Davgot and Rosarah and Thallaar and the others were standing around the body of a dead robrunner. Rosarah and Thallaar had chased the one Dandraar had missed right into the waiting arms of the others. They had managed to trap the agile creature between them, and had made quick work of dispatching the little robber. Unfortunately, the egg had also been a casualty of the confrontation. They had at once been so lifted up by their success in capturing the thief, but were then so quickly downcast when they discovered the fate of the little egg. To help cheer up his friends, Dandraar told them of his success, including the luck of the fumbled egg not getting broken.

Together, they all returned to the nesting area to pay their respects and to learn of the damages. They were met there by their limping friend, Gemuth, who had sprained his ankle on the quick descent down from the overlook. He was alright, but he would be limping for days to come.

Dandraar found Grendaar and Renthot and the other roamleaders in the nesting area. They were assessing the damages themselves. When they saw the adolescents, they gave them hearty congratulations, affectionate nuzzles, and a few strong hugs. It was a moment of many mixed emotions. Three robrunners had been killed, but four had escaped. Two eggs had been recovered, but four were lost. One robrunner had escaped with only his life, he had failed to steal an egg. When the adolescents learned that four robrunners had escaped with three eggs, they went off to hunt again. They were more determined than ever to keep the little predators away from the nesting area.

The nesting area had been lucky this time. If the adolescents hadn't been nearby, all seven robrunners might have escaped. Then it would have been six or seven eggs lost instead of three stolen and one broken. Worse, there would have been three more robrunners alive to raid again tomorrow. If they had their way, there would be even fewer robrunners alive to raid the nesting grounds tomorrow.

CHAPTER SEVENTEEN
NIGHTSTALKERS

THUNDERMAKER KNEW THAT THE dreadrunners were back again, even before Panthrar told him so. He was disappointed that he had not been able to elude them. Their surreptitious re-appearance would mean that trouble lay just ahead.

The dreadrunners had stalked their prey all day. But they had done so downwind, and out of sight of their quarry. Guessing that the herd of threehorns would continue on a northwesterly course, they had skirted the herd by circling around to the south. All day they had moved rapidly, attempting to outstrip the threehorns. Near nightfall, they had been detected by Thundermaker and Panthrar simultaneously. Both dreadrunners had been drinking at an isolated pool. They casually looked up from lapping the water as the herd drew near. Only then, back-lighted by a descending sun, were they easily visible. They were to the southwest of the herd, and relatively close to it.

The herd turned north away from the dreadrunners, looking for a defensible place to spend the night. No natural features in the terrain came to their aid, and Thundermaker was unwilling to travel after nightfall. So Thundermaker selected a flat spot that contained no features that would assist the stealthy approach of a predator. A small pond was nearby, and everyone drank their fill before darkness finally settled. No one but the dominant males would leave the circle of the herd for any reason once darkness fell.

The dreadrunners followed the herd northward. As night descended, the dreadrunners moved in closer. The threehorns formed a tight defensive circle, placing the young in the middle, with the females and smaller males around the outside. Once in this position, they lay down and tried to sleep in that formation. But with the ravagers prowling the perimeter of the herd, sleep came fitfully to many, and probably didn't come at all to some.

The six largest and most dominant males stayed outside the defensive perimeter. They constantly tried to keep themselves between the herd and the ravagers. This prevented the ravagers from coming too close to the herd, but they continued to circle from a distance of anywhere from five to eight hundred feet out, looking for an opportunity to breach the defensive circle, or to attack a dominant male.

As the night deepened, and the dreadrunners refused to leave, the dominant males began to spell each other, sleeping in shifts. There were always at least three males awake, either Thundermaker or Hidepiercer, and two other males. Wherever the ravagers lurked, the males went, forming a buffer between the ravagers and the herd. If the two ravagers split up, looking for a weakness in the defense, the males split up, one male to a ravager, with the most dominant male spacing himself between the other two, ready to come to the point of greater threat. Once, when the two ravagers were on the opposite sides of the herd, Hidepiercer wore himself out just galloping around and around the herd, trying to make sure he would be where he was needed most.

Just after nightfall, the two hornbrows had positioned themselves close to the defensive circle. At first they thought that this would be a good compromise between exposure to the predations of the ravagers, and unnecessarily risking accidental impalement by long, sharp horns. But the first time that the ravagers got too close to the herd, and the six male threehorns went galloping past the little sanctuary where they were curled up together, raising dust and the prospect of getting trampled, the hornbrows finally forced themselves into the circle and mingled with the young threehorns. They got a few curious stares, but little protest. Even the young threehorns were adapting to their unusual scent. None-the-less, the herd was nervous, and both hornbrows did their utmost to avoid getting accidently stuck by a horn.

Panthrar and Pippit didn't get much sleep. The first part of the night was spent jostling with the young threehorns in the middle of the defensive circle. Panthrar and Pippit kept having to step over or around little horned bodies, or get nicked in the shins by diminutive, but none-the-less sharp, little horns.

After midnight, the dreadrunners apparently tired of the game themselves, and disappeared into the darkness towards the south. They went downwind, and just far enough away that they couldn't be seen in the moonlight. There was no way of telling if they were really gone, or were just beyond the limits of sight and smell. The herd, exhausted and edgy, quieted down, and most members went to sleep.

Thundermaker had other plans for the hornbrows. He insisted that one of them stay awake along with the sentries, to add their superior senses of detection to the deterrence of the male threehorns. So Panthrar and Pippit also took turns spelling each other throughout the night.

About an hour before sunrise, one of the dreadrunners returned. It was Gnarled-paw, and surprisingly, he came in from the northwest. The moon had set, and the night was at its darkest. Gnarled-paw advanced stealthily, but Pippit, who was on lookout, sensed his approach. She smelled him first, and indicated to Hidepiercer that a male ravager, most likely Gnarled-paw, was coming. Later, when he was less than a thousand feet away, she thought she saw him. He was just a shadow within the darkness, but she felt certain that she saw the shadow move. Although she could smell him and see him, Gnarled-paw moved so quietly, that she never did catch a footfall.

Pippit pointed Gnarled-paw out to Hidepiercer. He strained to hear or see the dreadrunner, but he couldn't. Nor could Hidepiercer smell the ravager, as the breeze was too light. But still he trusted that Pippit was correct. He was certain that a dreadrunner was approaching.

Gnarled-paw approached the herd very slowly, a few steps at a time. Meanwhile, Hidepiercer and the two other male threehorns stood fanned out in an arc to block his approach. Gnarled-paw advanced to within six hundred feet of the herd before he must have begun to realize that he had been detected. First, he made a sudden dash in their direction, coming to a stop about four hundred feet away. By now, he could see that the three male threehorns, with the one female hornbrow standing behind them, were looking right at him. When he was certain that he had lost the element of surprise, he hissed sharply. Then he again moved boldly towards the group of defenders.

Hidepiercer and his two males, Eager-runner and Groundstomper, decided to meet Gnarled-paw's bold approach with one of their own. They trotted out to meet him. Threehorns tended to be a bit reckless. Pippit thought that this came from all that impulsive charging about that they did.

Pippit was worried over the whereabouts of Long-tail. She sniffed strongly, trying to detect the female dreadrunner. She strained the limits of her eyesight, looking in all directions, hoping to catch movement where it shouldn't be. She could not locate Long-tail. Knowing what she did of the pair, she expected them to work together. She was suspicious. She tried to dissuade Hidepiercer and his two companions from going out to meet Gnarled-paw. They didn't know this particular dreadrunner and his ferocious sister like Pippit and Panthrar did. Pippit expected nothing less than unqualified duplicity from both of them. They were, after all, ravagers.

But the threehorns couldn't understand her, and didn't have the patience to try to figure out what her antics meant. They just trotted off, leaving her in their wake.

Pippit was frantic. Suddenly she was left all by herself, standing alone in the darkness, unprotected, while at least one, and probably two dreadrunners were coming to find themselves a meal. She found herself suddenly faced with three options: go with the three male threehorns, stay out in the open where she presently was, or run back to the defensive circle.

She couldn't stay where she was. If she was right, and Long-tail was somewhere about, she might end up the meal. She quickly looked around yet again, ascertaining that no ravager was sneaking up on her.

She could run back to the safety of the circle. That was probably the smartest thing to do. But that smacked too much of deserting one's friends in the moment of crisis. She looked longingly back towards Panthrar and the defensive circle. She shrugged. Then she hastened after Hidepiercer and his bold, but brash companions.

As she ran after the threehorns, she tooted quietly to Panthrar, to wake him up. He signaled back to her that he was awake. Pippit then told him about Gnarled-paw, the advance of the three dominant male threehorns, and of her concerns about Long-tail. Panthrar tooted back that he would try to alert Thundermaker.

Gnarled-paw roared at the approaching threehorns. He pranced about, hissing and snapping in a noisy display. As the threehorns got closer, he began to back away. Those approaching him probably didn't realize it, but he also slanted more to the north than when he had approached. The three male threehorns and Pippit were now more than five hundred feet from the defensive circle. Pippit trailed behind the slowest of the males, trying to keep up, yet at the same time not really wanting to do so. The other two males, Hidepiercer and a young dominant male named Groundstomper, were in front. Pippit finally caught up with, and walked along beside Eager-runner, the threehorn trailing behind the other two.

Eager-runner glanced at Pippit. She tried to smile at him. He snorted, waved his horns in a bold display, and seemed to prance more proudly than before. Pippit couldn't tell if he was just showing off, or trying to tell her that she was safe with him.

Back at the herd, Panthrar had conveyed enough of the circumstances to Thundermaker so that he understood that the herd was again under attack. He also understood about the possibility of a second ravager. Thundermaker and two other males, along with Panthrar, began circling the herd about three hundred feet out, looking for a sign of Long-tail. Panthrar expected that the female dreadrunner would try a furtive approach from the east, opposite from the direction from which Gnarled-paw had appeared.

Hidepiercer and his males were almost a thousand feet from the herd, and still advancing upon Gnarled-paw. The dreadrunner kept two to three hundred feet in front of them. When the threehorns trotted faster, Gnarled-paw sauntered away at the same pace. When the threehorns slowed their advance, so did Gnarled-paw slow his retreat.

Pippit did her best to position herself in the middle of the three males, not wanting to be caught out in the open. She was wondering what the threehorns would do if Gnarled-paw stopped his tentative and uncharacteristic retreat, and instead just charged them outright. She was also wondering what she would do if the threehorns scattered, if they were sufficiently startled by such a charge. It worried her.

Run and maneuver, she thought to herself, that was her best chance. Run and maneuver in the moon-less darkness. Without knowing where Long-tail might be. That worried her, too. But more than likely, at least one of the threehorns would stay and face the ravager. Maybe all three would. She would just stay behind whoever remained.

Unexpectedly, she was attracted by a noise to her left. She stared, trying to pierce the night. The sky was a jet-black curtain, with a million pin-pricks of light penetrating it. Somewhere in the vast distance, the greater darkness of the foothills defined the horizon. Closer in her field of vision, the lesser darkness of the dry earth stood out in sharp contrast to the sky. The sienna brown of the earth was broken here and there by small, black-green clumps of shrubs, and an occasional grey-green, stunted tree – solitary sentinels in the expansive plain.

As she stared into the night, she saw a figure rising up out of the landscape, dirt and dust falling away from it. She would not have been able to see it in the darkness, had it not been only a few hundred feet away. She quaked in fear. It was a recognizable figure. She could not smell it, all she could sense was the fresh smell of newly dug earth. The figure had been rolling over and over in the dirt to mask its scent. But the dirt could not mask its shape. It was a long, lean bipedal form with a huge head. Instantly upon arising, it leapt at Eager-runner, the closest of the group to it.

Pippit screamed a warning. At almost the same precise moment, Gnarled-paw roared a horripilating challenge. Pippit's warning was lost in Gnarled-paw's deafening roar. Only Eager-runner heard it, and he jerked his head towards Pippit.

Then Gnarled-paw leaned forward and charged. The figure on the left of the group was accelerating frightfully, low and horizontal, toward Eager-runner. Pippit pointed at it, and Eager-runner began to swing his head back in the direction that Pippit was indicating. The figure was closing in upon Eager-runner at an alarming rate. Gnarled-paw, in the front of the group, moved at lightning speed, heading straight for Groundstomper.

For Pippit, time seemed to stand still. Before she could react further, and before Eager-runner had been able to turn to see what Pippit was pointing at, the figure on the left struck Eager-runner like a cannon shot. The figure was Long-tail, and she hit Eager-runner in the neck, just behind the frill. Eager-runner staggered under the force of the impact. He squeal-roared as Long-tail buried her sharp, death-dealing fangs into the unprotected flesh behind his frill.

Hidepiercer and the other male had their own troubles. They stood stiff-legged, waiting for Gnarled-paw to impact. As he ran, Gnarled-paw hissed loudly to keep their attention. The threehorns pointed their three-foot long horns right at Gnarled-paw's chest. But Gnarled-paw stopped short of impact, and roared again, his hot, fetid breath blasting Groundstomper in the face.

Meanwhile, Eager-runner, in the grip of Long-tail's powerful jaws, was thrashing about undetected by his comrades. Pippit screamed another warning, this one not in sync with Gnarled-paw's roars. Hidepiercer turned at her cry, and saw his companion struggling on the ground, Long-tail mounted upon his back, her long fangs buried deeply in his neck. Hidepiercer pivoted, careless of the proximity of Gnarled-paw, and sprang to Eager-runner's aid.

Long-tail saw that time was running out. She shuddered mightily, giving Eager-runner the death bite, partially severing his spinal cord. Long-tail then released Eager-runner, and sprang hastily away from Hidepiercer's advancing horns. She had to spring upward over twenty feet into the air, and fifty feet to the right to avoid Hidepiercer's lethal weapons. Hidepiercer was intent upon piercing Long-tail with them. He roared at her, and continued to charge after her retiring figure. She jerked left and right, trying frantically to avoid Hidepiercer's horns.

Groundstomper jumped at Gnarled-paw. His three long horns stabbed forward, and he jerked his head upward, hoping to lift the dreadrunner upon them. But they struck only air. Gnarled-paw had likewise sprang backwards. He turned and ran away at full speed. There was no sense in facing impalement now. Their ruse had worked. They had killed a threehorn. Now they must avoid the horns of the irate survivors. As he sprinted away, Groundstomper, charged off after him.

Pippit signaled to Panthrar, telling him of the tragedy that had overwhelmed her group. Shortly thereafter, Thundermaker and four other males came charging to the scene. They stared at the fallen body of their comrade. Thundermaker squeal-roared furiously. He and the other males then charged after the hastily retreating ravagers.

Panthrar arrived at a run. He found Pippit leaning over the body of the unfortunate threehorn. He checked to make sure that she was unharmed, sniffing her, and feeling for wounds. As Panthrar examined her, Pippit stroked Eager-runner's deadly horns. She ran her hand along his strong frill. She looked deeply into his unblinking eyes. Her heart ached with the iron grip of grief. Panthrar stood beside her, hoping to comfort her with his presence. He looked into the darkness, assuring himself that no ravagers were close by. He could barely see the rampaging bull threehorns chasing after the dreadrunners, but he could hear them quite clearly.

After awhile, Thundermaker, Hidepiercer, and the other males returned. They came back in two's and three's. The ravagers had made good their escape. The threehorns, with their inferior vision, had lost them in the darkness.

Thundermaker walked up to the inert form of his vassal. He stared into Eager-runner's face. He gently locked horns with him, and tilted his head to the left, and then to the right. He backed away, and looked into Eager-runner's eyes again. Thundermaker rumbled something plaintive to the unresponsive form of his friend. He walked softly around the body, stopping to gaze at it periodically. Two or three times he tried to nudge it into activity. Then he returned to the face, and rumbled again. Eager-runner did not answer.

Hidepiercer tried to nudge the still form with his frill. He did so gently, with no effect. Then he did so again, but more vigorously. Still no response. Hidepiercer lifted his face to the cold, unfeeling stars, and howled painfully into the uncaring night. Thundermaker joined him. Then Thundermaker walked about a hundred feet away, and lay down facing away from his friend, waiting for him to awaken.

All the adult males went through a similar ritual. Many tried to move the still form of their herdmate. Some just stood their sniffing at the body, occasionally howling forth their grief. After an hour, with the early morning sun streaking scarlet red across the heavens, most of the males had moved off to let the females and young get close to the body. The males lay in a ring, circling the body. It looked to Panthrar, who stood off to one side with Pippit, all the world like a defensive circle.

The females pawed at the body, pushing it, trying to get Eager-runner to stand up. Some of the young came close to him. Some whimpered. Others wouldn't go near Eager-runner at all, clearly aware of the rich crimson blood still oozing from the neck wound. One of the very young males crawled up in the folds of Eager-runner's neck, and couldn't be compelled to leave the fallen form of his role-model, until the herd moved off on its journey to the northwest.

By midmorning the herd was ready to take up its trek. Once moving, it moved rapidly away from the scene of the death of one of its own. Panthrar and Pippit went with the herd, continuing their duties as its long range eyes and ears. Panthrar, near the rear of the herd with Quickcharger, often glanced back at the quiescent body of Eager-runner. He didn't tell anyone, not even Pippit, that he saw Gnarled-paw and Long-tail reappear shortly after the herd quit the vicinity of the body. Before the body was out of Panthrar's sight, the two ravagers had settled down to a hearty meal.

CHAPTER EIGHTEEN
THE VALLEY OF THE THREEHORNS

THE HERD TRAVELED ALL day without further incident. It moved rapidly. It stopped three times for food, water, and rest breaks, but each stop was short. The herd seemed to be of one mind to put as much distance between it and the scene of Eager-runner's death as it could. It stopped only when nightfall threatened to impede its further progress.

The night was equally without incident. Several packs of razorteeth passed by during the middle hours, but none came close enough for concern. Near daybreak, Pippit detected a dreadcharger, but its scent was weak. The wind was blowing gently, but steadily from the south. The dreadcharger was miles away, and upwind. Likely, it didn't even know that the herd of threehorns was this close to it. It was stalking something else. Pippit could detect a herd of ridgebrows even farther off.

With daylight, the herd took up its trek once more. The dreadcharger appeared on the horizon, far to the south, late in the morning. It stalked them for most of the day, but the herd was moving too fast for the dreadcharger to close with it.

The herd continued to slant towards the northwest. Panthrar was keenly aware that with each step, this route kept taking him and Pippit further and further away from the Gathering Place. But it was a safe passage across the upper plain, and he couldn't complain about that. To leave the herd now would be to go directly towards the dreadcharger. Panthrar and Pippit were just not going to take that kind of a chance.

The herd of threehorns traveled fast, faster that a herd of hornbrows was wont to travel. They were rapidly approaching the foothills. They'd be there sometime tomorrow. Perhaps tomorrow Panthrar and Pippit would decide to head south towards the Gathering Place.

The next day, as Panthrar and Pippit approached the demarcation point between the edge of the plain and the beginning of the foothills, their resolve to turn south faltered. The dreadcharger had again appeared far to the south, paralleling the herd, but not able to close with it. They had had too many close encounters with ravagers already this crossing, to feel safe if exposed to one now. Their only hope would be to outrun the dreadcharger, and ravagers were pretty tenacious. There wasn't much of a possibility that they could outrun all of the ravagers they happened to meet on their way to the Gathering Place. Certainly not just two hornbrows, traveling by themselves. The odds against them were just too great. They determined that it was safer to stay with the herd of threehorns than to risk meeting this dreadcharger, or any other ravagers between here and the ancient breeding grounds.

Both felt a strong urge to go to the Gathering Place, and to be with their own kind during the mating, nesting, and hatching season. This was especially true since this was their first year as adults, and the first year that they would mate. But they also felt an equally strong urge to stay alive. In the final analysis, they had opted for the latter. Their decision was made even easier when they saw how inviting the Valley of the Threehorns was.

Thundermaker and his herd traveled up the broad, fertile valley that was the ancient breeding grounds of their kind. A wide, slow-moving river flowed down the middle. Equally slow and meandering streams fed the river from the low, gently rolling hills on either side of the valley. The hills were green with vegetation, which would last into the dry season of middle summer, when brown would become the prevailing color.

Other herds of threehorns were here also, many herds. Most of them had traveled up from the south along the upper plain, just like Thundermaker's herd. There were over two thousand threehorns in this one valley, a great gathering which occurred only during the breeding season.

Thundermaker pushed onward up the valley, heading towards the traditional breeding place of his herd. It was near the upper end of the valley, perhaps ten miles away. As he passed other herds, his herd attracted a great deal of attention because of the two hornbrows that traveled with it. It was an unprecedented sight, and many of the threehorns were curious. Thundermaker waved them off without ceremony, continuing unabated towards his final destination. He would not stop until he and his herd were at their favorite breeding site.

Thundermaker had made no complaint about the decision of the hornbrows to stay with his herd. Nor did any other of the herd-members. By now the hornbrows had become a somewhat accepted part of the herd. Even though their talents wouldn't be as crucial in the Valley of the Threehorns, they were now treated more like friends than temporary guests.

It was near evening when the herd arrived at its favorite breeding site. The demeanor and attitude of all the herd-members changed immediately upon arrival. They grazed leisurely, mingled freely with other herds, and dropped most of their defensive traveling habits. They did not form into a circle when they rested for the night. Panthrar and Pippit could see that no sane ravager would knowingly enter the Valley of the Threehorns.

While Panthrar watched the antics of the male threehorns, already starting to participate in dominance displays, Pippit went off to find a secure place for them to sleep. The males showed a lot of aggressive behavior towards each other, none of it immediately harmful, but a lot of it intimidating, as far as Panthrar was concerned. There was a lot of head shaking, accompanied with either swaying of the horns in clear view of a potential competitor, or with actual upward thrusting of the head and horns, in an undisguised stabbing motion. Panthrar sat and watched, intrigued, but happy that he was not a threehorn. He wouldn't want to face those long, sharp, tough horns.

Pippit came back in about an hour, as the sun was touching the mountains to the west. She led Panthrar to a delightful spot close to where Thundermaker's herd was settling down. The spot was on the periphery of the herd, near the top of a low hill. There was a backdrop formed by a small, thick clump of evergreens that crowned the hill. The two hornbrows curled up together beside three dogwoods that grew about a hundred feet from the evergreens. Berry bushes grew all about, from the edge of the small woods all the way down to the stream-edge, and beyond.

The spot that Pippit had chosen for Panthrar lay on a high piece of ground. Besides the three dogwoods, a small grove of oaks and some tall shrubs grew nearby. When they lay down, they were completely masked on three sides, the evergreens behind, the oaks to the left, and the dogwoods to the right. The oaks also provided shade, at least at certain times of the day. The fourth side faced the stream, which lay at the bottom of a gentle slope only about five hundred feet away. A number of the female threehorns had selected spots in which to repose on that same slope, between where the hornbrows lay and the stream. Yet in their selections, the threehorns had chosen spots that lay sufficiently far apart, that a stroll to the stream would seem reasonably unhindered.

Before the hornbrows, as they gazed out the fourth side of their little sanctuary, a vast panorama opened up. Five hundred feet before and below them, lay the stream. It was bordered by low-growing dogwoods, clumps of magnolias, an occasional patch of ficus, and thick shrubs. Beyond that, this side of the valley opened up into a series of broad dales and gently rolling hills, with sluggish, gurgling streams wandering between. Here and there rose isolated clumps of pines and redwoods, small groupings of oaks and hickories and sycamores, and dense patches of thickly-growing shrubs. The view of the valley showed a scattering of hundreds and hundreds of threehorns. And the background to their view, purpling now due to the last rays of the sun, was the young and majestic mountains to the west.

The next several days, Panthrar and Pippit relaxed in the security of the Valley of the Threehorns, leisurely grazing, and watching their hosts at play. By now, it was a foregone conclusion that Panthrar and Pippit would mate with each other. They had bonded strongly during their ordeal in the ravine, and that bond had grown stronger yet during their passage across the upper plain. They were in love. And they wanted to raise hatchlings together. Pippit spent much of her time looking for a suitable site to build a nest.

Panthrar, meanwhile, spent hours enthralled with the dominance displays of the male threehorns. There was much about their aggressive behavior that he was familiar with. There was snorting and pawing up the ground. The snorting was excessive, apparently showing how fierce the male was. The pawing, likewise, was obsessive, perhaps indicating how industrious the male was. Males would tear up great chunks of the turf, first with their front paws, then with their hind feet. Panthrar worried that if these displays lasted too long, the male threehorns would defoliate the entire valley.

The most common type of display, and the most decisive, was horn-locking. First two males would approach each other, and snort and paw. If this didn't discourage one of the competitors, next came waving of the horns, and upward thrusting. Some males were actually discouraged by this alone. But most males went the next step, which was horn-locking. Two males would gradually get closer and closer, snorting and pawing, waving and thrusting. Finally they would get so close, that their horns would touch. They would immediately tilt their heads and thrust forward, so that their horns would lock. Then began a titanic power struggle.

Each male would twist and turn his head, or resist his opponent's twisting and turning. Both would also push forward as hard as they could, front legs churning up sod, rear legs stiffly shoving forward. They would push each other backwards and forwards for ten or twenty minutes at a time, in impressive tests of brute strength. Eventually one or the other would tire.

Escaping from such a contest was perhaps the trickiest part. If a male was careless, he could actually get stabbed by his opponent's horns. It seemed to Panthrar that stabbing and mutilating was not the object of the contest, but accidents did occur. Most of the time, one of the males would suddenly scamper backwards, and then turn and pivot away from the horns of his opponent with as much dignity as he could muster. The possessor of the field was just as happy to let the vanquished retreat, as long as it was in all haste.

While Panthrar was enjoying the dominance contests, Pippit diligently searched for a nesting site. She observed that most of the adult female threehorns were doing the same thing. Pippit had noticed earlier the many mounds of former nests. The nests were roughly the same shape as those of hornbrows, but perhaps a little smaller. They were low, conical mounds ten feet in diameter at the ground, and about three feet high. Unlike hornbrows, who placed their nests about thirty feet apart, which was a comfortable adult body-length of separation, the threehorns apparently built their nests much farther apart. Pippit could detect no nest closer than a hundred feet to another, and some were as far apart as three hundred feet.

With a closer inspection, Pippit saw that the nests had cavities dug out of the top, shaped like a bowl, similar to how hornbrows built their nests. The cavity was about four feet in diameter, and two-and-a-half feet deep. The existing nests were in varying states of disrepair, attesting to differing periods of time since they were last used. Many of the female threehorns chose existing mounds, and spent their time painstakingly repairing them.

Pippit watched the female threehorns carefully as they repaired their nests. They seemed unconcerned with her presence, even when she walked up quite close to see precisely what they were doing. Each female was carefully shaping a nest in the sandy soil. Pippit had never built a nest before, and unfortunately she had no older female hornbrows to give her advice. The female threehorns were full of advice, only she couldn't understand a word they were saying to her. However she learned a lot just by watching them.

After a long fruitless search for an ideal site for her own nest, she gave up and returned to her and Panthrar's sleeping place. While she sat dejectedly gazing out towards the mountains, she noticed an old threehorn mound not fifty feet away. It was in a sad state of repair, which is why she hadn't given it much thought before. But it could be fixed up. It was on ground with good drainage, and was close to this special place of their's. Pippit decided that this would be the place where she would build her first nest. She was so excited with the prospect, that she immediately set about repairing and enlarging the old threehorn nest.

Later that day, when Panthrar tired of watching dominance fights, he went looking for Pippit. He found her meticulously laboring over her nest. He watched her for awhile, sitting quietly in the shade of the oak trees. Pippit had enlarged the nest considerably. It was almost fifteen feet in diameter at the ground level, and almost five feet high. The bowl she scooped out of the top was six feet in diameter, and three or so feet deep. It was an impressive nest. Perhaps a little larger than it needed to be, but Panthrar would never have mentioned that to Pippit.

Later, when Panthrar got hungry, he went and gathered berry bush branches, and brought them to Pippit for them to munch on. By the end of the day, Pippit's nest was shaping up nicely. Tomorrow she would finish it.

The next day, Panthrar helped Pippit work on her nest for awhile. He piled up dirt, and Pippit pushed and formed it into the nest. When the nest was nearly complete, and as Pippit was putting on the finishing touches, Panthrar went to watch the dominance contests again. Meanwhile Pippit finished building her nest.

Over the following three or four days, the contests increased in both the number of participants, and the exuberance with which they fought. Panthrar noticed that dominant males like Thundermaker and Hidepiercer tended to win all of the contests. Panthrar also noticed that the contests tended to be between members of the same herd. There were very few cross-herd contests. Thus Thundermaker, Hidepiercer, and Quickcharger battled all of the other males of their own herd. Over the next several days, Panthrar judged that the three strongest males from the herd would prevail in all their contests.

Six or seven days after Thundermaker's herd had arrived in the valley, the dominance contests were over. As Panthrar had anticipated, Thundermaker, Hidepiercer, and Quickcharger had prevailed against all challengers. They next proceeded to chase all of the other males away, both those of their own herd, and those from other herds who had also lost in the contests.

The unlucky losers, temporarily shunned by their own clans, would slowly gravitate down towards the river, and from there they would migrate down to where the valley opened up onto the upper plain. Within a few days, a vast herd of bachelor males would form. This herd would roam near the valley mouth for the next several months, keeping themselves amused. Yet they would never travel far from the valley, and would never let a large predator enter it. They would wait for the dominant males, the females, and the younger and newer members of their clans to appear. Then the herds would begin their return to the south once more.

With all of the competitors vanquished and chased away, the dominant males like Thundermaker, Hidepiercer, and Quickcharger settled into a more pleasurable activity. They proceeded to attract, entice, and mate with all of the females in their herd. This agreeable task lasted for days.

＊　＊　＊　＊　＊

On the morning of the eighth day after their arrival in the valley, Pippit told Panthrar that her time was near. Panthrar fretted more and more as the day wore on, as Pippit's behavior became more and more unusual. She constantly hovered near the nest, and she refused to eat. She had a worried frown on her face, and occasionally she would just sit over the nest, looking into it, whimpering.

Just before noon, Pippit squatted over the nest, and while honking her uncertain delight to the sun overhead, she produced her first egg. She planted it in the exact center of the nest. Then she turned around and looked thoughtfully at it.

After that, at roughly quarter hour intervals, she continued to produce companions to the first egg. Each egg was accompanied by a soulful honking at the sun. She placed each egg carefully in an ever-widening spiral, around and outward from the first egg. After she dropped each egg, she would turn around and stare into the nest, making sure that everything was just right.

Her honking attracted their neighbors. By the third egg, six or eight of the female threehorns, and even a few males, had assembled to watch her lay her eggs. They stood a respectful distance away, but still Panthrar fretted that they were too close and might disturb her. He tried to shoo them away, but determined threehorns were not likely to be budged by a nervous hornbrow. Pippit, meanwhile, was too occupied to care much one way or the other. That evening she dropped her twenty-fourth, and last egg. She was exhausted, and lay down beside her nest to rest.

Panthrar was extremely proud of her. All day during her labor, he stood by, feeling useless. Frequently though, he would leave for short periods, bringing berry bush branches back to her, or juicy beetles, or some young, green shoots from the evergreen trees. She ate some of these during the day, between eggs. The rest she saved and ate when she was finished laying.

When all had quieted down, and Pippit was contentedly munching on some tender shoots, Panthrar leaned over and looked into the nest. He still couldn't believe what he and Pippit had produced together. There were twenty-four, slightly oblong, eight inch long eggs. They had rough, leather-hard shells, and were mottled in appearance.

He stared at them for a long time, lying there in the soil, standing upright, and in their spiraling configuration. Finally Panthrar placed the soft vegetation that Pippit had collected for just this purpose, on top of the newly laid eggs. He packed it thickly. The vegetation was soft and green. It would soon begin to rot, creating heat as a by-product. The heat would help incubate the eggs, speeding up the maturing process. In roughly twenty-eight to thirty days, the eggs would begin to hatch.

CHAPTER NINETEEN
NESTING

Five days after Pippit had laid her eggs, the female threehorns began to lay theirs. The first female started in mid-morning, and by afternoon, many females were beginning to lay. For three days the ordeal continued before all the females had completed the chore.

Pippit and Panthrar had been dutifully tending their own nest. There really wasn't much to do in these early days. But they still fussed about the nest, tucking in some lose vegetation here, brushing some dirt away there. They did have to frequently check the rotting plant material, to make sure that it was not getting too hot near the eggs. The other important task was to keep predators away. Both hornbrows had kept a vigilant watch for predators, but the Valley of the Threehorns was remarkably free of them. At least at the moment.

When the first female threehorn began to lay her eggs, Panthrar and Pippit were naturally curious. By chance, the first egg-producer occupied the nest closest to theirs, only a little over a hundred and fifty feet away. For some reason, the other threehorns were not curious. Perhaps they had seen threehorn egg-laying too many times before. Perhaps the females were too worried about their own impending session. Whatever the reason, none came to watch.

The youngsters, who might have been inquisitive, had been consigned to a spot down by the main river, that flowed though the valley proper. They played down there in an immense herd of juveniles. The dominant males enforced their ostracism, so it was unlikely that they would return until invited. The bachelor males, who also might have been curious, were gone. They were herding at the mouth of the valley. Only the dominant males and the females remained. The females didn't show much interest beyond their own labors. Even the dominant males didn't seem overly concerned. Occasionally they would trot over and check on a specific female, but for the most part, they stuck to patrolling the periphery of the nesting area.

Even if the others weren't, Pippit and Panthrar were curious. Maybe hornbrows have a greater natural curiosity than threehorns do. Or maybe egg-laying was just too mundane for the adult threehorns. But the young hornbrow parents wanted to see what the others were going through. Finally Pippit could restrain herself no longer. With Panthrar left guarding the nest, she discreetly approached the nest nearest their own. The present occupant of the nest was an old female named Roundfrill, and she was busily producing her fourth egg.

"May the sun warm you, Roundfrill," said Pippit as she neared the other.

Roundfrill gazed in Pippit's direction, but she did not respond until she had finished depositing her fourth egg beside the others. Then she rumbled a greeting to her neighbor.

"Varoom," said a preoccupied Roundfrill.

"I was wondering if I might sit with you for awhile, and keep you company," returned Pippit, making it half a statement and half a question.

Roundfrill said, "Rruuh. Roorrrrah."

Pippit took this as an invitation. She moved as close as she dared to optimize her view, and sat down. Roundfrill got up, turned around and stared into her nest. She gazed at her eggs for a long time, gently moving one or two. Pippit also leaned forward, looking into the nest, mentally comparing threehorn eggs with her own. What an attractive color, she thought to herself.

And they seem so large. Then, apparently satisfied with the placement of the eggs, Roundfrill again squatted over the nest, waiting to lay the fifth egg.

While they waited for the time of the fifth egg, Pippit thought about the threehorn eggs. They were almost the same precise shape as a hornbrow's eggs, oblong, with one end slightly more pointed than the other. The threehorn eggs were about the same size as hornbrow eggs, or perhaps a little smaller, about seven inches long. They just looked larger because of the color.

And what a color? The most eye-catching difference between a threehorn's egg and a hornbrow's egg was the color. Hornbrow eggs were grayish, and mottled with light and dark green patches. Threehorn eggs were a beautiful, soft, very pale, solid plum color. That was quite an unusual color. It was not seen very often, except in flowers. Although, Pippit recollected, she had been told that the Black Valley Tribe had a sandy beach along a tributary of the River of the Nine Tribes that had a dark purple sand. Even if that was true, and she couldn't say since she had never seen the purple sand herself, purple was still an unusual color.

Over the next several hours, as Roundfrill continued to lay, Pippit watched in fascination as she laid more and more pale, plum-colored eggs. They were a beautiful sight to behold, spiraling around the inside of the nest. They looked like precious stones, hidden in a secret cache.

Eventually Pippit remembered her nest, and the patiently enduring Panthrar. Panthrar had also wanted to see the threehorn eggs.

So Pippit scuttled back to her nest, allowing Panthrar to mosey over to Roundfrill's nest as inconspicuously as he could. This was, if you think about, not easy for a 5600 pound, 27 foot long hornbrow to do. Be inconspicuous.

Panthrar felt a little self-conscious. He was a rather virile member of his race, and he wasn't sure if he should be interested in the egg-laying practices of a different species. On the other hand, he had to admit to himself that he was pretty curious. And Pippit had mentioned in passing about pale, plum-colored eggs.

So he went. And he hoped that Roundfrill wouldn't think it odd that he wanted to watch. After all, Thundermaker and crew had watched Pippit lay her eggs. So it must be all right, he assured himself as he neared Roundfrill.

Whatever his own personal reservations, Roundfrill didn't seem to mind his presence as she laid her next to last egg.

"May the sun warm you, Roundfrill," he said to her, as he hovered uncertainly near her nest.

"Ooommmph," said Roundfrill. "Varoom." After a moment, she added, "Zounnn agarr ompett."

"My thoughts, precisely," responded Panthrar politely.

Roundfrill got up, and again turned to look into her nest, as she had done after laying each and every one of her eggs. Panthrar looked in also. There were fifteen strikingly colored eggs, just as Pippit had said. They were certainly easy to see in the nest, easier than it was to see hornbrow eggs in a nest. Hornbrow eggs were more camouflaged. Panthrar wondered if this would create a problem for the threehorns when protecting their eggs against predators.

When Roundfrill finished laying her eggs, she lay down beside her nest to rest, just like Pippit had done. Panthrar decided that it was time for him to leave.

"May your offspring fill the valleys," Panthrar said to Roundfrill as he departed.

"Arrhh, amalgarr," rejoined Roundfrill.

* * * * *

It was three days before all of the female threehorns had finished laying their eggs. On the day following that, the eighth day after Pippit had laid her eggs, Panthrar saw his first small predator in the Valley of the Threehorns.

It was a redrunner. He saw it as he was browsing on a nearby hillside. The red-brown creature was emerging from a dense thicket of shrubbery. It looked cautiously in all directions, but failed to notice Panthrar standing on an adjoining hill. The redrunner, believing that he had not been detected, sauntered down to the stream for a drink of water. Low-growing trees and shrubs near the stream hid the redrunner from Panthrar, just as it hid Panthrar from the redrunner.

Panthrar stealthily crept towards the stream. He softly pushed his way past some shrubbery, and peeked under a tree branch. He could see the redrunner lapping up water.

The redrunner would drink for a moment, and then stand erect, glancing in all directions. It was checking for possible danger. Satisfied that it had not been spotted, it would drink some more. Then it would again search for potential threats. During one of these inspections, it looked straight at Panthrar. It spotted Panthrar, staring back at it. It immediately froze.

Panthrar likewise did not move, hoping that it had not really seen him. But apparently it had. Very slowly, it began to inch its left leg backwards. It planted its left foot behind it, and then froze again. After a short pause, it shifted its weight, and began to move its right foot backwards. Slowly it moved, inch by inch. Panthrar watched with interest as it moved, one clawed foot at a time, towards some thick growth about six feet behind it. It moved excruciatingly slowly, with infinite patience.

Panthrar decided that he didn't have that much patience. With hardly a sound, he burst from the overgrowth he was hiding behind, and charged straight for the redrunner. When Panthrar splashed through the stream, the redrunner turned and bolted past the thick growth that he had originally been inching towards, and instead dashed up the hill towards the dense thicket from which it had emerged earlier. Panthrar charged through the undergrowth beside the stream, and up the hillside after the redrunner. The redrunner leapt into the thicket without a second's hesitation, and disappeared from view.

Panthrar ran up to the thicket, and stopped. He listened. He could hear the redrunner moving in the thicket. The thicket was several hundred feet in diameter, and too dense for him to penetrate. He honked his frustration. The sounds in the thicket stopped. All was quiet.

Panthrar walked around the outskirts of the thicket, looking for a way in. After one complete circuit, he concluded that he was not going to find a better way in. He stared into the thicket, hoping to detect the redrunner. Maybe if he saw it, he would force his way in to get it.

He could see nothing. He could hear nothing. But he could smell a redrunner. He kicked at some shrubs in disappointment. After a while, he gave up, and returned to Pippit's nest.

He told Pippit what he had seen. They decided that they would have to be extremely vigilant, certainly more so than they had been before. The serenity of the Valley of the Threehorns had lulled them into believing that it was safer here than in the Gathering Place. Perhaps it wasn't after all.

It was Pippit's turn to eat, while Panthrar guarded the nest. She decided to visit the thicket that Panthrar had said he had seen the redrunner disappear into. Maybe she would be luckier, and trap and kill the thing.

*   *   *   *   *

Early in the evening of the next day, when the sun had almost set behind the jagged, western mountains, a group of five gray-and-brown eggsnatchers raided the nesting area of Thundermaker's herd. The western sky was a deep shade of red, and long shadows were reaching across the valley, filling the stream beds. Panthrar was observing the descending sun, watching the shadows creep up the hillsides. The nesting area below him was already in shadow, and the edge of darkness was rapidly approaching the nest that he stood beside. Pippit was down by the stream, browsing a late dinner before it was time to sleep.

Panthrar had noticed the eggsnatchers almost an hour earlier. They had been slowly drifting across a distant hillside, foraging as they went. They were primarily consuming greenery, and an occasional dragonfly or beetle. Then they had disappeared behind a clump of cedars. Only five minutes ago, they had abruptly reappeared at the stream-side, below the nesting area.

Panthrar was suddenly alert. He watched as the eggsnatchers began to casually move in amongst the nesting area of Thundermaker's herd. They seemed to be preoccupied with munching at shrubs, or chasing dragonflies. None-the-less, threehorn females began to move nervously. Hidepiercer changed his direction, and slowly trotted toward the eggsnatchers.

Suddenly there was a great commotion in the nesting area. One of the eggsnatchers had grabbed an egg from one of the nests of the threehorns. The female threehorn, who had been momentarily distracted by another of the eggsnatchers, saw him do it, and started squealing vociferously. She charged after the thief, only to have a second eggsnatcher steal another egg from her nest. She twirled towards the second eggsnatcher, and a third tried to take yet another egg. She lunged for her nest, lest she lose any more eggs. Meanwhile, all five eggsnatchers dashed through the nesting area helter-skelter, two with prizes that all hoped to share in.

Thundermaker and Quickcharger galloped through the nesting area, in pursuit of the thieves. Hidepiercer was already in hot pursuit. They raised a lot of dust, but there was not much chance that they would catch any of the eggsnatchers.

Two of the eggsnatchers were coming straight at Panthrar. Panthrar straddled the nest, and hooted a warning to Pippit. Panthrar was rewarded by seeing her burst from the trees near the stream, sprinting as fast as a hornbrow could run, heading in his direction.

Panthrar leaned low to the ground, and began swinging his tail in ever-expanding arcs, waiting for the oncoming eggsnatchers. The two racing towards him saw him standing as if waiting to pounce upon them. They split up, giving him a wide berth. One raced around to the left, the other dashed around to the right. They ran up over the crest, disappearing into the small woods behind Panthrar.

Panthrar turned and watched them go. Pippit came running up beside him, breathing heavily. Then she looked into her nest. None of the covering vegetation had been disturbed. Even so, she uncovered her eggs, and counted them. Then she counted them again. Satisfied, she sighed in relief, and looked up at Panthrar. He gave her an encouraging smile.

* * * * *

The night of the next day, the tenth day after Pippit had laid her eggs, was a night that neither Pippit nor Panthrar was likely to forget for a long time to come. Yet what happened, happened so quickly that there was little in the way of details to remember. It was more the trauma of it that they would never forget.

They had both been asleep. Panthrar lay on the right side of the nest, Pippit on the left. They both were awakened by squealing and roaring from the nesting area just below them. Panthrar could tell by the moon that it was well after midnight. He sprang to his feet, and took a few steps forward, trying to pierce the moonlit darkness to see what was going on. Small bipedal shapes, many of them, were darting about in the nesting area. Larger four-footed hulks were also running about, seemingly chasing the smaller shapes.

As Panthrar turned to tell Pippit what he thought he saw, a small bipedal shape, a redrunner, dashed from behind Pippit, pushed aside the covering vegetation, and grabbed an egg out of the nest. Panthrar honked in rage, and sprang at the form. Pippit also half-turned, and without a sound, she too lunged at the figure. They both missed. The redrunner sprinted away with the pilfered egg. Pippit threw herself over the opening of the nest, while Panthrar charged after the redrunner.

The redrunner raced up the hill, and dashed into the woods. Panthrar sprinted into the woods, but then could not locate the redrunner. He beat about the bushes and shrubs for twenty or thirty minutes, trying to flush out the little predator. Eventually he had to admit to himself that the redrunner had escaped with one of his and Pippit's eggs.

When he returned, Pippit already knew that the egg was not coming back. She had encircled herself around the opening of the nest, so that nothing could get at an egg without stepping on her.

She looked up at Panthrar as he returned. He looked into her face. She appeared stricken. Panthrar sat down beside her, and stroked her back. While he tried to comfort her, Pippit, still encircled around her nest, cried herself to sleep. Panthrar sat there all night, staring into the darkness, swearing to himself that he would never sleep again.

* * * * *

The next night, Panthrar kept his promise to himself. He did not sleep the entire night. But no redrunners came. And the night after that, he tried to stay up all night again. But nature could not be denied, and three quarters of the way through the night, he fell asleep. But still, no redrunners came.

Another two days passed. Then, the night of the fourteenth day after Pippit had laid her eggs, the redrunners came again. Pippit and Panthrar's nest was one of the first attacked this time. Both were asleep, but Pippit now slept encircled around her nest.

The little predator actually had to climb over Pippit to attempt to reach the nest. Pippit immediately awoke, throwing the frightened redrunner from her as she sat upright. Panthrar also awoke. He saw a second redrunner, just out of his reach, push into the nest, and pull out an egg. Panthrar lunged at the thief, but the redrunner was too quick for him. It dashed away, with Panthrar in close pursuit. Behind him, Panthrar heard Pippit signal a warning to the nesting area. Redrunners were darting all about, snatching eggs from other nests as well.

Panthrar chased the redrunner up the hill and into the woods. Panthrar was too close this time for the little predator to hide in the thick bushes. So it kept running at full speed, through the woods, and out the other side. Panthrar kept up the pursuit, but the redrunner was just too fast. It steadily pulled away. Eventually he lost track of it. It either darted into a dense thicket, or slipped down to the stream, where the vegetation would hide it from view, and the gurgling of the water against the rocks would mask any sound that it might make. Disheartened, Panthrar returned to the nest.

By the time Panthrar had rejoined Pippit, the nesting area was beginning to return to some semblance of calm. Meanwhile Thundermaker and Hidepiercer had chased some redrunners into a nearby thicket. Unwilling to let the little robbers get away that easily, they proceeded to tear at the edges of the thicket with their horns. They had uprooted nearly half of the shrubs before the redrunners escaped out the other side.

Not knowing this, the two threehorns continued to pry up all of the other shrubs in that thicket. They stomped the uprooted plants into the ground, one by one, and didn't stop until there was no place left for the redrunners to hide. Then they trampled around for awhile, flattening the ground where the thicket had once stood. Finally they were satisfied, and returned to patrolling the periphery of the nesting area.

All was quiet for the next few days. Even so, during the early afternoon of the sixteenth day, a small varanid lizard furtively crawled into the nest while Panthrar and Pippit kept a lookout for larger predators. The little lizard quietly helped himself to one of their eggs. He cracked it open by punching it with his pointed nose. He then ate the contents of the egg all unbeknownst to the parents. Before nightfall, he slunk back out of the nest, and scurried away without the parents ever knowing that he had been there.

* * * * *

On the nineteenth day, early in the morning, Panthrar walked down to the stream for a drink. The sun had been up for almost an hour, and the two hornbrows and most of the threehorns had just finished grazing. Pippit lay beside her nest, seemingly inert. Her inactivity belied how alert she really was. Only her eyes, which darted unceasingly in all directions, gave evidence of her attentiveness.

As Panthrar leaned forward to lap up some water, he saw over a dozen redrunners lurking in the bushes, several hundred feet downstream. They had been watching his approach, hoping he wouldn't spot them. When they saw that they had been detected, they rushed into the nesting area, trying to steal eggs. Panthrar turned around, and raced for Pippit and their nest. He honked a warning as he ran.

Female threehorns did their best to discourage the redrunners. None would face a threehorn head-on. Nor would any get too close to a foot or a tail. Still, some did get eggs. Quickcharger and Hidepiercer ran through the nesting area, heads shaking, horns stabbing at the little bipedal sprinters, hoping to impale one. Thundermaker ran along the border of the nesting area, hoping to cut some off.

Panthrar, instead of going straight for his nest, instead ran towards the spot where he thought the redrunners would try to exit the nesting area.

Several did try the spot he had anticipated, and he surprised one of them as it dodged between two female threehorns, and jumped entirely over a nest. It held tightly onto a pale plum-colored egg as it gracefully sailed through the air. It alighted on both feet, and then tried to bolt for the cover of some nearby trees.

Panthrar intercepted it, and reached down to grab it. The redrunner sidestepped away from Panthrar, eluding his out-stretched hands. Panthrar stopped short, pivoted on his left foot, swinging his broad tail in a counter-clockwise arc. The redrunner tried to jump over the oncoming tail, but failed to get sufficient height quickly enough. The tail bludgeoned it across the knees. It flew through the air from the force of the impact, twirling somersaults like a propeller, and fell with a sharp whack. Panthrar rushed over to grab the redrunner before it could get away. But this redrunner was not going anywhere. The impact with the ground had broken its neck.

Panthrar found the stolen egg near the crumpled body. It seemed undamaged. He picked it up, and looked around for its owner. The nesting ground was still in chaos. Redrunners were scampering everywhere, and charging threehorns thundered about, miraculously missing nests as they did.

Panthrar heard Pippit signal distress. He dashed off towards her, still clutching the plum-colored egg. While the redrunners were staging their raid, distracting everyone in the nesting ground, a small band of **trailrunners** had decided to use the confusion to their advantage. They had been grazing nearby, at the edge of the woods. Suddenly, all four of them had burst into the nesting area, finding Pippit straddling her nest. Pippit was fending off repeated attempts by the four of them to get past her guard.

Panthrar saw this as he approached. Fearing that he might get there too late to stop a theft, he hooted the loud, deep challenge of a male hornbrow. The startled trailrunners stopped to look, and saw him hurtling in their direction. They decided that a quick departure was called for. One of the trailrunners made one last attempt to grab an egg. As he lunged at the nest, Pippit, hovering over her eggs, lunged back at him. She made contact, and pushed him away, knocking him off his feet. In a panic, he scrambled up on all fours, and lurched away as quickly as he could. Straightening himself up as he ran, he chased after his companions.

By the time Panthrar got to the nest, the trailrunners were disappearing into the woods at the top of the hill. All except one, who, bleating his fool head off, tried to catch up to his friends.

Panthrar and Pippit exchanged glances. Guarding a nest was a full time job, for both of them. It was never really safe to be away from the nest, although the other necessities of life sometimes required that one or the other be away.

Pippit sighed in relief that another attempt to steal one of her eggs had been foiled. While she tried to calm herself down, Panthrar showed her the plum-colored egg. She sniffed it, and held it for awhile, before giving it back to Panthrar. It took him an hour to find the owner of the egg. He never really was sure how the female threehorns knew whether it was their's or not. But although many inspected it, only one claimed it. It belonged to Rollypolly. He was happy to give it to her. And she was happy to get it back.

Early the next day, the twentieth day after Pippit had laid her eggs, the varanid lizard returned. It was hungry when it crawled into the nest. When it left hours later, it was not.

That was the fourth egg that Pippit and Panthrar had lost. Two had fallen prey to the depredations of redrunners, and two had been consumed by the tiny, little lizard. On the night of the twenty-fourth day after Pippit had laid her eggs, a fifth egg was taken from the nest by a very swift, very agile, and very lucky redrunner.

CHAPTER TWENTY
HATCHLINGS

IT WAS MID-MORNING ON the twenty-eighth day after Pippit had laid her eggs. Panthrar and Pippit watched in anticipation as the sun inched upward into the sky. Earlier in the morning, they had removed the rotting vegetation that had covered their eggs for so long. Nineteen eggs still lay intact. They were now much darker than when she had first laid them. Their natural mottled surface had been discolored by the rotting plant-material, as it produced heat to help the eggs mature more quickly.

The rays of the sun were creeping over the edge of the nest. Finally the warming light fell upon an egg. Then another. Soon half the eggs were basking in the glorious warmth of the sun. In a while, they all would be.

Pippit and Panthrar watched the eggs curiously. They leaned over the nest, and lowered their great heads close to the eggs. They could hear sounds. A faint scratching was emanating from many of the eggs. From several, a muffled mewing could also be detected. They looked at each other. Pippit smiled. Panthrar smiled back. Then they straightened back up so that the warmth and light of the sun could signal to the occupants of the eggs that it was now time to come out and experience all the wonders of life.

After awhile, one of the eggs moved. They leaned forward again, and inspected it carefully. They could hear a clear scratching, and tapping, issuing from the egg that had moved. The sounds stopped momentarily when their shadows blocked the sun. Then the sounds began again, this time more frantically. As they watched, a small crack appeared in the egg. They exchanged glances, and moved back just a little to let the sun reach the egg.

The crack lengthened. Then another crack appeared, angling out from the first crack. The tapping grew more insistent. The egg rocked as the occupant pushed and shoved against the interior walls. The crack widened. Suddenly a piece of shell was pushed out from the inside of the egg, and it fell away to one side.

There was a long pause.

Pippit and Panthrar leaned closer, again casting a shadow over the egg. They could see a tiny object through the opening in the egg. A miniature snout pushed out through the hole in the egg. A minuscule eggtooth waved in the air. It was attached to the snout of the occupant of the egg, located not where a horn would eventually grow, but instead on the premaxillary bone in the front of the upper jaw. The snout moved in and out, and circled the edge of the opening. Every move was emphasized by the little white eggtooth. There was a tiny snort. It was as if the occupant of the egg was sniffing the air, exploring the world with the one sense that it had so far exposed to life outside the egg.

The snout retreated into the egg. Another pause ensued. It lasted perhaps only a minute or two, but seemed like an eternity to the watchful parents.

The snout reappeared. It began a mighty effort to widen the hole. It pushed and shoved against the edge. Little bits of eggshell broke away. The hole enlarged. A paw appeared, pushing and punching up against the edge of the hole, breaking larger pieces away.

Then there was another pause, while the occupant rested from its exertions.

Pippit and Panthrar leaned as close as they dared to the egg. Their heads touched, they were so close. Panthrar rubbed the side of his head against Pippit's. She trilled an affectionate response, and rubbed Panthrar back. They could see a tiny eye looking out of the egg at them. It moved, and the other eye inspected them. The occupant bleated a barely audible "Eeeeaaaahhh."

They moved their heads to the edge of the nest, so that they could still watch, while letting more sunlight in. The occupant of the egg looked out frantically. All it could see was the azure sky. It could no longer see the wonderful, large, living things that had been looking back at it. Its head pushed hard against the opening in the egg. More pieces broke away, and the head pushed itself out into the world.

The occupant blinked rapidly. It rotated its head, examining the world before it. Large, darkly mottled eggs occupied most of its view. Partially rotted leaves and twigs stuck up here and there. Clay soil filled the distant horizon. A creeping insect worked its way up the slope of the nest, dislodging some pebbles as it climbed. The pebbles rolled back down the slope into the interior of the nest, splashing into a puddle. Ripples circled outward, crashing into the shore of the puddle.

The occupant of the egg heard breathing. It looked up, and beheld two great heads, staring at it in wonder. "Eeeeaahhhh," it said to Pippit. "Eeee-eeeaahh," it said to Panthrar.

Pippit trilled at it. It trilled back, a tiny, high pitched, little sound.

It began its struggles once more. Panthrar silently cheered it on as it broke more and more of the shell. Bigger and bigger pieces fell away. Soon it had an opening large enough for it to crawl completely out of. It made its way free of the confines of the egg, and pulled itself onto a clear spot between two other eggs. There it lay to rest. It was breathing heavily, looking around at this exciting new world – as much of it as it could see from its prone position.

Pippit leaned in close to examine it. It looked completely normal. She nuzzled it with her nose. It made soft little mewing sounds. She looked up at Panthrar, and said, "I think that it is a male, my husband. First is a son."

She moved back so that Panthrar could get a closer look. He leaned into the nest, his head almost touching the little creature. He said very softly, "Hello First, my son."

First mewed back a greeting.

First was basically a miniature version of his parents. Yet he was only fifteen inches long, less than five percent of the length of his father. He weighed only 1.5 pounds, not even one tenth of one per cent of his father's weight. He had no horn, and wouldn't begin to grow one until his second year of life. His eggtooth, he would lose in just a few days.

His coloration was very similar to that of his parents. As a new hatchling, his basic body color was a deep yellow. It was a dark yellow, like aged lemon. He also had a broad stripe running down his back, not only covering his barely formed frill, but along both sides of it as well. This stripe ran from the upper jaw, across the top of his head, down his back, and all the way to the tip of his tail. The stripe was a mixture somewhere between a brownish orange and burnt sienna. Secondary stripes of this same color ran perpendicular from the back stripe across the flanks of his body, and across the broader base of his tail. These secondary stripes lightened and narrowed as they ran across his body, turning closer to a dark orange. His underside was a very pale yellow, mixed with an off-white. As he grew older, he would lose most of the secondary stripes. In addition, the yellow would darken into a yellow ocher, and the brownish orange into a deep golden brown. As an adult, his frill would darken considerably, especially during the breeding season.

The two adult hornbrows watched as First tried to crawl about the nest. He moved like his bones were made of rubber. And that was figuratively true. First's bones had not yet fully hardened, and wouldn't for weeks to come. They were still primarily cartilage, not hard, ossified bone. First, and his brothers and sisters, would spend their early weeks in the nest with one goal: to grow. They would flop and fall over one another without much ill effect upon themselves. Virtually all of their energies would be devoted to getting larger, so they could cope better in a hostile world. The price their species paid for this rapid growth, was that for the first weeks of their lives, they were virtually immobile. They could not leave the nest. They had to depend upon their parents for sustenance. And for protection.

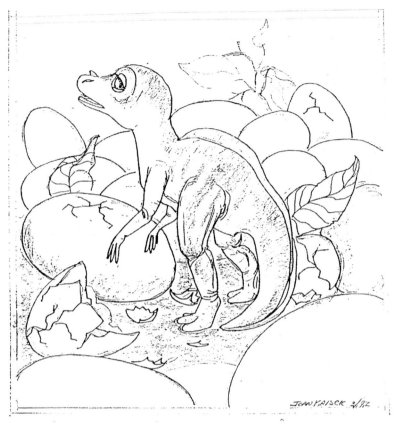

After First had struggled around his nest for close to an hour, the pangs of hunger began to send strong messages to his brain. These urgent new feelings temporarily overcame the sense of wonder and curiosity he felt for his new found world. He bleated long and loud. The intensity of it startled even him. He looked around, as if to find the source of the noise. Then he bleated shrilly again. His parents were just as startled by the tiny ferocity of his demands.

"What is it, Pippit, my wife?" queried Panthrar. "Is he sick? Is there something wrong with him?"

Pippit leaned close to her first-hatched, looking him over carefully. "No, my husband, I think he is hungry."

Panthrar jumped up anxiously. "Stay here, my wife, I will go and get him something to eat."

"No, my husband," countered Pippit, "You stay with First and the eggs, I will find him something to eat."

Panthrar watched after Pippit as she sped away to find suitable food for their hatchling. She returned in short order with a mouthful of partially chewed berries and berry bush leaves. She deposited the mouthful near First. He slithered over to it, sniffed at it tentatively, and then tasted it. He looked up briefly at Pippit, and then plunged into the feast. He made mewing sounds all the while he ate. He didn't stop eating until he had gorged himself. His little belly was swollen from the repast, and he couldn't even crawl away from the remains. Instead, he just put his little head down in the juices, and fell asleep.

Late in the morning, the occupants of two more eggs began to scratch and tap at their confining shells. Shortly after noon, Second crawled, exhausted, from her egg. First woke up, and during his explorations, crawled right over Second. She bleated in protest, and they wrestled each other for a few seconds. Then they each moved off in different directions. A short while later, Third successfully freed herself from her egg, and curled up to rest.

Before long, both Second and Third were hungry. They bleated loudly, at least loudly for such tiny creatures. First, who wasn't really hungry yet, decided to join in. All three hatchlings were soon crying in a chorus, demanding food. Panthrar ran off for food this time. As he returned to the nest, he noticed that he could hear the bleating from quite a distance. In fact, in the hot silence of the early afternoon, besides the buzzing of insects, the bleating was all that he could hear. He rushed to the nest, and deposited a meal for the hatchlings.

While Pippit cooed and trilled at her young, Panthrar surveyed the nesting area. All of the threehorns were looking in his direction. They all had heard the bleating of the newly hatched. Even as he watched them, Thundermaker, Hidepiercer, Quickcharger, and three or four females slowly moved in the direction of the nest to investigate.

Panthrar spoke a word of warning to Pippit. She looked up, and suddenly got very worried. The threehorns were getting closer. She stood up, and straddled her nest.

"Tell them to go away, my husband," she instructed Panthrar.

Panthrar moved into a blocking position, placing himself between the threehorns and the nest. Thundermaker approached him, closely followed by the other threehorns. Panthrar spread his feet, and planted them firmly. He stood fully erect. Thundermaker stopped about fifty feet from Panthrar. Hidepiercer and Quickcharger walked up on either side of the primary male. The females crowded in behind them. Thundermaker rumbled something to Panthrar.

"May the sun warm you, Thundermaker," said Panthrar. "But I must respectfully ask that you and your vassals depart."

Thundermaker took a step closer. "Varoom," he said. Then he asked, "Rammmarrh, garrrumph?"

His fellows also took a few steps closer. Panthrar's tail twitched, and began to swing in lazy arcs, back and forth.

"I have little ones here, my threehorned brother. And my mate is very nervous," explained Panthrar. "I must ask that you do not come any closer."

Thundermaker said, "Zarsarrh himplett zoorooff." He and his group took another step closer.

Panthrar leaned forward, holding himself low and horizontal. His tail began to lash more fiercely.

Thundermaker turned to Hidepiercer and said something to him. He then turned to Quickcharger and spoke likewise to him. The second and third males of the herd backed away, complaining to the females behind them, who were in their way. The females turned and briskly trotted away. Hidepiercer and Quickcharger also turned and walked away. When they were a couple of hundred feet away, they stopped and turned back to face their leader.

Thundermaker now stood alone before Panthrar. He said, "Humpor raff. Rammmarrh, garrrumph?"

Panthrar hesitated, his tail swinging only slightly less energetically than before. From over his shoulder, Pippit said, "Let him approach, my husband. I'm sure that he is curious about hornbrow hatchlings."

Relieved, but still concerned for the safety of his young, Panthrar stepped aside. He gestured towards the nest, and said, "Please, my threehorned brother, come see my beautiful children."

Thundermaker accepted the invitation. Very slowly he approached the nest. Panthrar looked at Pippit. Concern was written all over her face. She said, perhaps as much for her own peace of mind as to reassure Panthrar, "I'm sure that he is just curious. He has probably never seen hornbrow young before in his entire life."

Thundermaker came forward very softly. He did not want to worry the parents any more than he wanted to distress the young. Very gingerly, he inched his head up over the edge of the nest. The three hatchlings were busily stuffing themselves with pre-mashed berries and partially chewed leaves. Thundermaker stood there, as if frozen in place, fascinated by the tiny replicas of the two hornbrows. After almost fifteen minutes of watching, he slowly backed away from the nest.

When he was a safe distance away, he nodded at Pippit and Panthrar in turn. He said, "Jacaab. Meewaotokee." Then he turned and trotted away to continue his duties patrolling the periphery of the nesting ground. Although the other threehorns were likewise curious, none would approach the nest until Thundermaker gave them permission to do so.

First, Second, and Third slept while Fourth endeavored to free himself from his confinement. He had a particularly difficult time, as his shell seemed to be a bit thicker and more resistant than his siblings' shells. Towards evening, he crawled free, but immediately fell asleep.

An hour later, he awoke, starving. Even before he started bleating, his mother nudged him towards some food. He ate heartily, and then fell asleep again. They all slept well that night, with plenty of food immediately available. Only the parents didn't sleep, at least not well. Pippit, still encircled about her nest, kept waking to check on those inside it. And Panthrar, who slept near Pippit, kept waking to prowl around the vicinity of the nest, against possible danger to his young.

The next morning, even before the sun fell upon the eggs, Fifth was busily working her way out of her egg. Throughout the day, Sixth through Fifteenth also broke free of their shells, and joined the crawling, milling mass in the nest. With fifteen little mouths to feed, one or the other of the parents frequently had to run off and get something for the hatchlings to eat.

The parents tried to vary the diet of their young. They mixed the well-loved berries and berry bush leaves with young shoots and newly forming cones from evergreen trees, with leaves and twigs from oaks, hickories, and dogwoods, with tasty mashed roots from a bush that grew along the stream, with soft, succulent fern leaves, with crunchy beetles and grubs that happened to come their way, and with an occasional dragonfly, when they could knock a passing one out of the sky.

The frenzied chorus of fifteen bleating hatchlings, many hungry, some not, pulled like a magnate at the expectant threehorn females. Even so, none came to disturb the hornbrow parents. In the early afternoon, Thundermaker again came to observe the progress in the nest. Panthrar and Pippit were a lot less nervous than they had been the day before. Thundermaker still neared the nest with great care and caution. He looked in for a long while. After a time, he made some soft rumbling sounds at the hatchlings. They were immediately alert, and unnaturally quiet. Thundermaker rumbled softly at them again. Ninth made a tiny rumbling sound. Fourteenth imitated him. Thundermaker looked up at Pippit, and for all the world, it seemed like he smiled at her. She smiled back. Then he backed away from the nest, turned, and cantered down to the stream.

An hour later, Hidepiercer converged upon the nest. He stopped about fifty feet away, and asked, "Rammmarrh, garrrumph?"

Panthrar was alone with the hatchlings, while Pippit was off browsing, as well as getting something for the babies. He stood there, wondering if it would be alright for Hidepiercer to also see the young hornbrows.

While he hesitated, Hidepiercer explained, "Rhommm battamuh, gramm gruffgruff."

Panthrar could think of no reason why Thundermaker could see the hatchlings and Hidepiercer couldn't. So he said, "May the sun keep you warm, Hidepiercer. Would you like to see my children?"

To help convey his words to Hidepiercer, he beckoned to the threehorn to approach. Hidepiercer complied by walking very slowly to the nest. He carefully looked in. After a moment, he rumbled softly at the young ones. All of them stopped bleating, and most of them became very still. Ninth and Fourteenth rumbled back at Hidepiercer. Then First and Third also rumbled. Hidepiercer looked at Panthrar, and rumbled something to him. Then he departed.

That night, a redrunner crept out of the woods that crowned the hilltop, and advanced softly toward the nest of the hornbrows. The night was very still, and the redrunner crept noiselessly down the slope. She stopped, and looked at the two adult hornbrows guarding the nest. It looked to her like both were asleep. One, the female, slept wrapped around the top of the nest. The other, the male, was nearby. He was partially upright, head nodding, caught halfway between sleep and consciousness.

The moon was waning, and the redrunner moved like a shadow in the darkness. She crept closer to the nest. She paused, and examined both hornbrows with great care. Yes, they were both asleep. Although, it seemed that the male might awaken at any time. She came closer. Carefully she stepped over the sprawled legs of the female, first the left leg, then the right. She could just fit between the female hornbrow's right knee and her right elbow without touching her. The redrunner looked over the edge of the nest. What a prize! There were over a dozen hornbrow babies in the nest.

Suddenly the male hornbrow stirred. The redrunner froze. The male hornbrow snorted, grumbled, lifted his head without opening his eyes, and then settled down again. The redrunner breathed a silent sigh of relief. She reached into the nest, and indiscriminately grabbed the first hatchling her hand came to. She lifted Eighth out of the nest. Then the redrunner turned and squeezed between the female hornbrow's knee and elbow. She stepped over the hornbrow's right leg.

Eighth, unused to being held, awoke. He smelled an unfamiliar odor, the scent of a redrunner. He bleated in alarm.

Panthrar's head jerked up. He jumped to his feet. He looked around, looking for the threat. He could distinctly smell a redrunner.

Pippit also awakened. She saw a small figure before her. Her sleepy eyes focused. It was a redrunner, in mid-step over her left leg. It was holding a tiny, squirming object. Pippit honked shrilly. It was one of her hatchlings.

Next, five things happened almost simultaneously. Eighth, hearing his mother, again bleated in panic. Panthrar pivoted around and faced the nest. The redrunner sprang clear of Pippit's leg. Pippit leapt to her feet. And the nest full of hatchlings, awakened by the shrill alarm in their mother's voice, cried out in distress.

Panthrar and Pippit lunged at the redrunner. She bolted left, right, left, in a zig-zagging maneuver trying to avoid the two irate hornbrows. Panthrar chased madly up the hill, after the redrunner. Pippit retreated to her nest, wary that other redrunners might be about.

Through the woods raced the redrunner and the hornbrow. Out the other side of the woods, and down the other side of the hill, ran pursued and pursuer. The redrunner leapt across a narrow brook. A few moments later, Panthrar trudged across it. The redrunner fled up the neighboring hill. Panthrar followed, falling farther and farther behind.

Panthrar got to the top of the hill, breathing heavily. He could not see the redrunner anywhere. He listened carefully, holding his breath so that it would not interfere with his ability to hear the redrunner. He could faintly hear footsteps fading into the night. He could not tell where the sound was coming from. He called to Eighth. He was rewarded only with silence. He pounded the ground with his tail. He pounded it twice more. Then he turned around, wondering how he was going to tell Pippit that they had lost Eighth.

The next day, the second day since First had hatched, Sixteenth through Nineteenth broke through their shells, and joined their brothers and sisters. Panthrar and Pippit soon got over the loss of Eighth. They mourned the loss of their son quietly, but it was not long before they were too preoccupied with feeding the other eighteen. All that the tiny creatures did was eat, sleep, and poop. And they grew. Imperceptibly at first, but surely and steadily none-the-less. They also played for short periods, squirming over each other, wrestling and biting, pushing and bleating, in a frenzy of togetherness.

Pippit told Panthrar that she had never beheld a more wonderful sight in her entire life.

CHAPTER TWENTY-ONE
NESTLINGS

Dᴜʀɪɴɢ ᴛʜᴇ ᴅᴀʏs ᴛʜᴀᴛ followed, Pippit and Panthrar settled into a routine that included ever more frequent trips to gather food for the growing nestlings. They seemed to barely have time to feed themselves, they were so busy feeding their young. The little hornbrows were very demanding, and their parents labored themselves into exhaustion each day, as the appetites of their growing brood kept pace with their growing bodies.

On the fourth day after First had hatched, the varanid lizard returned to the nest. He expected to feast upon another hornbrow egg. He approached the nest quite stealthily, but he was far too small to have been easily noticed by the parents. Still, he was very careful. He scurried from cover to cover, under low growing shrubs, and behind scattered rocks, getting closer and closer to the nest. When Panthrar's and Pippit's attention was momentarily distracted elsewhere, he climbed up the outer slope of the nest, and hid under some discarded berry bush branches. When the adult hornbrows again weren't looking, he scurried over the edge and into the nest.

It was quite an unhappy surprise for him to discover eighteen very curious hornbrow nestlings there instead of unhatched eggs. Before he could safely retreat, First grabbed hold of his left rear leg, and wouldn't let go. He struggled and squirmed, but to no avail. He was forced to stay much longer than he really wanted to, as he was passed from one curious nestling to another. Each nestling in turn wanted to pull him this way and that, trying to understand what he was. His arms and legs were bent in ways that they were never intended to. His tail was pulled and stretched and yanked around so much by one nasty little nestling, probably Seventh, that it broke off. No matter, it would grow back again, but the replacement would never be as beautiful, nor feel quite as right as the original.

When the varanid lizard was finally able to break free, he scurried sorely but quickly out of the nest. His muscles ached, and his limbs refused to work properly. He cursed the day he had ever thought to invade a hornbrow nest, and was determined never again to look for an easy meal among dinosaur eggs.

By the tenth day after First had hatched, the nestlings had grown measurably. Their length had increased to about 18 or 19 inches, and their weight had increased appreciatively. The females were already ten pounds in weight, while the males had increased even more dramatically to fourteen pounds. The young were much more fully formed than when they had broken the shell, and perhaps obviously, they were considerably more round. Yet it seemed that the larger they grew, the hungrier they got.

Tired as the hornbrow parents were collecting food, they never let up on their vigilance against predators. By the tenth day after First had come out of his shell, redrunners had staged three more raids upon the nesting ground. Although a number of threehorn eggs were taken, by some miracle, no more baby hornbrows had fallen into their clutches.

Although the routine of feeding the young was getting more laborious, it was a labor of love for the parent hornbrows. They wouldn't have had it any other way. They were by now quite comfortable with the daily pattern. Besides feeding, a number of other patterns had also developed. One pleasant one was the daily visit by the threehorns. What had started out as an occasional visit by Thundermaker to see how the nestlings were doing, had grown into an early afternoon ritual of visits by all three dominant males, and most of the females. Two or three threehorns would come at a time. More than that couldn't fit around the nest. They would stay for a short visit, and then depart. Then two or three more would arrive. Each group would ogle the tiny hornbrows, rumbling softly at them.

The threehorns received special enjoyment from the fact that most of the hornbrow young would rumble back at them in response. There were rising and falling crescendos of high-pitched hornbrow imitations of threehorn rumbles with each visit of the threehorns. That single factor may have been the greatest attraction for the threehorns – hornbrows speaking like threehorns.

They almost seemed to be communicating with each other, Pippit thought, the hornbrow hatchlings and the threehorn adults. But that wasn't possible, since the baby hornbrows couldn't yet speak their own language, let along this foreign tongue. Pippit spoke to the nestlings at great length, every day, both orally and with facial expressions and sign language. She was determined that they learn to speak as quickly as possible.

Something disrupted the daily visits of the threehorns on this particular day. The first that Panthrar and Pippit were aware that something unusual was happening, was when they heard tiny squeaking coming from the nest of their neighbor, Roundfrill. They looked over toward Roundfrill, to see what might be making the strange little sounds. Roundfrill was kneeling before her nest, chin balanced on the nest's edge, beak only inches from her eggs, staring intently at something inside the nest.

Pippit knew immediately what was going on. She could hardly contain her excitement. It was almost like her own eggs were hatching all over again.

Panthrar could see that Pippit wanted to go visit Roundfrill, but he could also see that she was torn by her desire to stay and guard her own nest. He wished to accommodate her, although he also wanted to see what was happening. He decided that he could wait. He said, "Pippit, my wife, there is something very unusual going on in Roundfrill's nest."

"Oh, my husband, I hadn't noticed," responded Pippit coyly. She had been distracted by the sounds emanating from Roundfrill's nest ever since they had started. Even now, she was actually leaning in the direction of the tiny squeaking, so badly did she want to go see.

Panthrar nodded. Finally he said, "Perhaps you had better go see what it is. Roundfrill may need your assistance. I will watch the nestlings."

Pippit took a step towards Roundfrill's nest, then hesitated. She looked over at Roundfrill, then turned to Panthrar and responded, "Do you think so, my husband? I wouldn't want to burden you with trying to watch these restless little mud-wallowers all by yourself."

Panthrar pretended to consider this for awhile. At length he said, "They're all fed, and half of them are already napping. I'm sure I can manage them, my wife."

Pippit didn't want to appear too anxious, so she too reflected for a moment longer. Finally, she said, "Well, then, perhaps you are right, my husband. I wouldn't want anything ill to come of Roundfrill's eggs."

"Nor I. Now be off with you, my good wife, you'll only be a few feet away if I need you."

"Okay, then, my husband. If you insist."

Pippit hastened over to Roundfrill's nest. "May the sun warm you, Roundfrill," she said in greeting. Roundfrill barely looked up, rumbling acknowledgement as she continued to watch the drama in her nest.

Pippit kneeled down beside Roundfrill, and gazed into the nest. One of the eggs had already hatched, and it looked like three or four more would do so soon. A very dark little form huddled by the broken shell. It was a baby threehorn.

Pippit marveled at it. She had never seen a nestling threehorn, or indeed any other nestlings, except for nestling hornbrows. Oh, and nestling robrunners. The latter, she and her pack had discovered one day while guarding the nesting areas of the Gathering Place. That was just last year. A lifetime ago. They had ferreted out a hidden nest of robrunners while chasing the adults. By chance, the eggs were in the act of hatching just as the packers discovered them.

Robrunner young were very different from either hornbrow or threehorn young. They were mobile not long after they broke the shell. They didn't need much parental care. Not as much as threehorns needed. Certainly not as much as hornbrows needed. But then she decided to block out the other thoughts from that day of the preceding year. This was a day to enjoy the beginnings of life, not the endings of it.

Her mind refocused upon the threehorn nest. The huddled little form stood up on its four tiny legs, shook itself, and looked about. Roundfrill rumbled softly at it. It looked up at its mother, and squeaked at her.

"Hello, little threehorn," Pippit said.

It looked at her in turn, and rumbled a hello.

It was barely recognizable as a threehorn. It had two almost imperceptible little nubs above its brows, where its two long horns would one day grow. There was no evidence whatever of a nub or anything else on its nose, where its third short horn would one day come in. It had a little ridge encircling the back of its head, around its neck, where a frill would eventually be. It had a round little body, and a tail almost too small to see.

Its color was similar to an adult threehorn. Adult threehorns had a dull burnt ocher hide, with undertones of burnt umber, and an underside like light colored sand. On the head and face of an adult threehorn, the colors were brighter. Their three horns tended to range in color from a dull red-brown to a bright carmine red, generally closer to the latter. They also have carmine red accents on the face and frill. These accents were on the upper beak, along the top of the snout, around the base of the horns and around the eyes, and along the ridges and the edge of the frill. In between the ridges of the frill, there were ovals of burnt umber, encircled in rings of red-brown.

The hatchling threehorn was colored much like an adult, only a lot darker. It was a very dark brown, almost a black, over most of its body. Its underside was a lighter, muddy brown. The whole face, however, all the way to the little ridge-frill, was red. A dark, rich, almost stark red – like blood just before it congeals. It was not unattractive, but it was unusual.

Pippit watched several of the hatchling threehorns break out of the shell. Periodically, she would glance over at Panthrar to ascertain that he and the nestlings were doing well. Sometimes he would signal his affection back to her. Most of the time, he seemed completely pre-occupied with his own nestlings. All seemed well. So Pippit felt no urgency to leave.

She realized, as she watched the little threehorns move about the inside of the nest, that they were much more mobile upon hatching than hornbrows were. It looked like they would be out of the nest at a much earlier stage than her own young. She could imagine little herdlets of threehorn young roaming the nesting area in only a few weeks. Would the ten day advantage her own young had had in arriving into the world be enough? Maybe the threehorns would be ready to trek before the young hornbrows were ready. She wondered what this might mean.

Would it affect the timing of when their four-footed friends would want to leave the Valley of the Threehorns? Would she and Panthrar and their young be able to trek together with the threehorns back to the home of her mate, back to the range of the Green Water Roam? She hoped that the young threehorns wouldn't be able to trek too much earlier than her own young.

The squeaking in the nest brought her back to the present. She gazed into those little red-colored faces. They looked so cute. But those crimson faces were even different from juvenile threehorns. They must lose those red faces within the first few months of life, she thought, for she had never seen a fully red face on any threehorns before. Perhaps the bright color helped poor-sighted threehorn females tend to their young more easily.

As Pippit left Roundfrill to return to her own nest, she could hear the squeaking of newly hatched threehorns coming from a number of other nests.

Panthrar didn't bother to examine too closely the threehorn hatchlings that first day. Many were hatching, and would be for the next day or two. So there would be plenty of opportunity to examine them more carefully. He just glanced into Roundfrill's nest long enough to get a good idea of what they looked like.

The next day, he took the opportunity to watch them with greater care. All ten of Roundfrill's surviving eggs had hatched by then. The older hatchlings were already pretty rambunctious. Some of them were already trying to climb out of the nest, and Roundfrill had to keep pushing them back in. If they did get out, for instance when Roundfrill was off collecting food for them, it wasn't likely that they would go far. The nest was still the only secure place for them, and they would probably be terrified to venture too far from it.

* * * * *

By the fifteenth day after First had broken his shell, the hornbrow nestlings were larger, and quite active. They had grown perhaps another inch or more in length, but they had picked up even more weight. The females were now about fifteen pounds, and the males were almost twenty pounds.

Their increased girth didn't seem to inhibit their activity. They waddled all over the nest. They had explored every nook and cranny of the nest so many times that their curiosity for something new sometimes exceeded their natural inhibition against leaving the security of the nest. They had made many trips to the edge of their existence – the rim of the nest. And at least once a day, the ringleaders of the brood, First, Second, Third, or Seventh, would spill over the rim, and tumble down into the outside world.

Each time one of the ringleaders tumbled out, at least one of the other ringleaders would venture out too, so as to not be outdone. Then some of the more timid would follow. Soon five or six little explorers were crawling about the outside slopes or base of the nest, feeling the excitement of discovery and danger.

Before long, though, something would spook the adventurers – a male threehorn passing nearby as he patrolled the perimeter of the nesting ground, a dragonfly buzzing too loudly or too closely to the nest, a **skyglider** screeching overhead, or a returning hornbrow parent. Then all the explorers would crawl as fast as they could back up the slope, over the rim, and into the safety of the nest. They moved especially fast when an adult anything was in the vicinity – for all adults were so much larger than the nestlings, that their sheer bulk could evoke some considerable terror.

Even the bulk of Pippit and Panthrar was intimidating to the young hornbrows. The nestlings had bonded to their parents the very first time that they had seen them, just after the nestlings had hatched from their eggs. Their parents were familiar and loving. They provided a constant supply of food, and comforting sounds, and even an occasional nudge of assistance back into the nest. But to the nestlings they were gargantuan. Even their parents caused little hornbrow hearts to palpitate anxiously if the nestlings were venturing outside of the nest. It didn't take much imagination on the part of the nestlings to understand what the foot of an adult hornbrow would do to one of them, if he or she were accidently stepped upon.

One of the great attractions for the hornbrows was the distant squeaking of the nestling threehorns. From the rim of their nest, they could see the other nest, some one hundred and fifty feet away. It was a considerable distance for a nestling hornbrow. And it was an especially dangerous trip, considering that mammoth threehorns, male and female, cantered between the two nests. But that didn't stop groups of hornbrows from hanging over the rim of their nest, gazing curiously at the distant hive of activity.

And active it was. The little threehorns were already much more mobile than the hornbrows. Small herds of diminutive, four-legged creatures frequently ventured out of their nest. They sprinted and sputtered about, under the watchful eye of Roundfrill. Up and down the slope of their nest they played, or ran round and round its base, in what looked like little races. But every time an adult came by, other than Roundfrill, all would madly scramble back to the safety of the interior of their nest. The nestling hornbrows yearned to visit the squeaking, rambunctious little creatures.

Also, the miniature threehorns weren't oblivious to the existence of the strange creatures in the distant neighboring nest. They couldn't see them very well, but they certainly could hear them. The little threehorns often considered visiting the bleating little hornbrows.

* * * * *

By the twentieth day after First had hatched, all the nestling hornbrows were willingly climbing out of their nest. They were crawling at least as far as the ground at the base of the sloping walls of their nest. Some of the more adventurous might even risk a twenty or thirty foot "dash" out into the real world, before hastening back on all fours, apprehensively glancing over their shoulders. Their joints still seemed to be made of jelly, but they were learning to get around fairly well, considering their handicap.

The return of a foraging parent was no longer a cause for concern at all. They were by now very familiar with the ways of their parents, and knew that their parents would never step on them. But when an adult threehorn came too close to their playground, they would retreat to the safety of the nest.

Yet, even the threehorns did not hold the kind of terror for the nestling hornbrows that one would normally expect. These baby hornbrows saw nothing unusual with living with their ferocious and unpredictable four-legged neighbors.

Part of the incentive of the nestling hornbrows to venture away from the security of their nest was their size. They now ranged in length from 20 to 22.5 inches. The females were about twenty-two pounds in weight, and the males were thirty. Their growth, if anything, seemed to be accelerating. The nest was getting too crowded for its chubby little tenants. They were bumping into each other virtually all the time, now.

Although the People seemed to like this much togetherness, and thus none of the nestlings would think of complaining, lack of elbow and knee room was an incentive for the more audacious among them to see what it was like away from the nest. Even so, they didn't go far.

Although venturing beyond the confines of the nest was one of the more exciting things in their daily routine, getting fed was still the single most important part of the lives of these little creatures. And at twenty days of age, the nestlings were consuming a great volume of food. During all of the intervening hours between sun-up and sun-down, at least one of their parents was away collecting food. And every time the parent with more food returned, the brood set up an excited and noisy chorus of bleating and honking in anticipation of another meal.

The excitement of the hornbrows seemed to be a catalyst for the nestling threehorns to come closer to the nest of their neighbors. The tiny threehorns hadn't yet developed the courage necessary to make the entire trip, but day-by-day, they got closer. Even so, they only ventured thus far accompanied by their mother.

These days, that were full of growing wonder and excitement for the nestlings, indeed, were not without their hazards. Redrunners, and even an occasional night-raid by razorteeth, still took their toll. By the twentieth day, Roundfrill had lost three of her ten nestlings to such predations.

Panthrar and Pippit were not without their own loses. In addition to Eighth, whom they had lost to the redrunner, Pippit and Panthrar lost Third on the sixteenth night, to a razortooth that raided the nesting grounds almost every night. On the eighteenth night, they lost Nineteenth to the same razortooth.

CHAPTER TWENTY-TWO
DAYS OF WONDER, NIGHTS OF TERROR

Bᴜ ᴛʜᴇ ᴛᴡᴇɴᴛʏ-ᴛʜɪʀᴅ ᴅᴀʏ, the nestling hornbrows were often exploring the vicinity around their nest, sometimes as far away as fifty feet from the security of the bowl in which they had hatched. Their cartilaginous bones hadn't completely hardened yet, but their movements were far less feeble than they had once been. Always on these adventures, though, one or the other of their parents was with them, to protect them from what was potentially a harsh world. Many of the inhabitants of their world thought that nestling hornbrows were a tasty and much desired delicacy.

Early on this day, Second was leading a small expedition towards the frequent squeaking that came from the neighboring nest. First was napping next to his father, along with three of his sisters, Fifth, Eleventh, and Eighteenth. They had crawled over to where Panthrar slept, in the shade of the nearby cluster of oaks. Panthrar had taken to staying awake virtually all night, to better protect the nest. This made it more difficult for the redrunners and razorteeth to raid the nest, and actually provided better protection for the whole nesting area, but it put a lot more burden on Pippit during the day. She had to divide her time between gathering food, and watching the nest. Frequently she would rouse Panthrar to watch the nest until she returned from a foraging trip, then allow him to go back to catching up on much needed sleep.

Pippit was guarding the young while Panthrar napped. She was trying to keep track of all sixteen of her nestlings. Only four of them were cooperating by sleeping, and they were with Panthrar. Seven others were in the expedition. Two were investigating the reaction of insects to nest disturbance. Two more were playing rough-and-tumble on the outer slope of the nest. And one was sitting on the tail of a lizard, waiting to see if it could get away.

It wasn't surprising that Second was leading the group of small explorers. Since First was sleeping, the only other nestlings brave enough to consider such a daring enterprise were either Second or Seventh.

But Seventh was elsewhere. He was examining a nest of insects on the other side of the hornbrow's nest along with his sister, Fourteenth. One or the other of these two would poke the hive of insects, retreat to a safe distance, and then watch the excitement while the insects bustled about. The sharp-pincered little things were trying to repair the damage, and find the perpetrators.

Meanwhile, Second lead her little band closer and closer to the familiar squeaking, and farther and farther from their own nest. Periodically, Second would turn and look back at her mother for reassurance. Pippit would smile encouragement, trying to keep an eye on the little explorers, while at the same time keeping track of all the others. With Second was Fourth, Sixth, Tenth, Thirteenth, Fifteenth, and Sixteenth. Fourth was a male with very dark stripes covering much of his body. Sixth was a female with so many very broad, dark stripes on her tail, that the tail looked almost solid in color. Tenth was a very small female. Thirteenth was a plucky little female who, ahead of most of her siblings, could almost walk without stumbling. Fifteenth was a male with a perpetual smile on his face. And Sixteenth was a rambunctious male with an insatiable curiosity.

As Second and her group were approaching the halfway point between the two nests, a little herdlet of seven tiny threehorns, each less than a foot and a half in length, spilled out of Roundfrill's nest. Several of the nestling threehorns saw the approaching party of miniature hornbrows. The herdlet immediately scampered down the slope of their nest, and towards the nestling hornbrows.

Second and Fourth, in the lead of their group, immediately stopped in their tracks to consider the ramifications of this. Tenth and Fifteenth, who were not paying attention, stumbled into their leaders. A scuffle ensued between the members of the small group, and it was not settled until all seven of the nestlings had pushed someone, or had at least bleated their opinion in the matter. By the time they had settled their disagreement, the tiny threehorns were less than ten feet away.

The threehorns had stopped short of actual contact, trying to make sense of the creatures so near to them. They noted that the strange creatures bleated and honked, rather than squeaked and squealed. They kept trying to stand on two legs, but most of them trudged along on four legs. Were they two-legged, or were they four-legged? Neither the threehorns nor the hornbrows had ever been this close to each other before.

The dominant male threehorn nestling reared up on his hind legs to get a better look. He made a tiny snort. He squeaked a warning to the interlopers. His first inclination, even at this tender age, was to charge the strangers. One of his sisters, the dominant female, made small pawing motions in the dirt. One of their brothers was making little charging motions, and stabbing his nose upward into the air.

The mob of hornbrows were quite surprised by the strange creatures before them. The dark, round things were too small for the hornbrows to recognize them as baby threehorns. The nestling hornbrows were too young, and didn't know enough about the world yet, to recognize the concept of babies. To them these were another kind of creature, obviously different from the adult threehorns. They did recognize that these creatures ran about on four legs, like threehorns. Except that one of them suddenly stood up on two legs. Were they four-legged, or were they two-legged? Whatever they were, with all the snorting, and the head-thrusting, they seemed to be a pugnacious lot.

The inclination of the hornbrows, backed by millions of years of genes, was to run at the first sign of danger. Some of the smaller hornbrows, lead by Tenth and Thirteenth, turned and hustled in the direction of safety. Second and Fourth, along with the irrepressible Sixteenth, were also on the verge of flight. Yet they were curious, so they remained steadfast.

After she had retreated a safe distance, tiny Tenth looked over her shoulder. This caused Thirteenth, who was right behind her, to hesitate. Thirteenth stopped and turned to look back at her sister and brothers. Then the other two who were retreating with Tenth and Thirteenth also stopped to look uncertainly upon the boldness of their siblings. Finally curiosity got the better of all four of them, and they returned to face the challenge with their brothers and sister.

Second sniffed tentatively. So did Fourth. Were these creatures friends or enemies? Were they to be ignored as non-threatening, or were they to be run from? Second took a few cautious steps towards the other group. She kept sniffing, her eyes were dilated widely, and her head darted every-which-way. She listened for the slightest threat. After a slight hesitation, Fourth also took a few steps forward. The other hornbrows held back, waiting to see if it was safe to proceed, but ready to turn and run at the merest provocation.

The threehorns also advanced slowly. For the moment they had forgotten their threatening displays, so curious were they about these creatures that were of the same scale as they. Everything else in their world was either smaller than them, or more likely, much, much larger. Here were creatures that were their size. Here were creatures that they might understand.

The two groups closed the distance between them. Each group huddled closer and closer together, the individuals seeking support and comfort from their siblings. Both hornbrows and threehorns were sniffing feverishly. All seemed on the verge of flight.

When they were only four or five feet apart, Second said, "Sun warm you."

One of the male threehorns could restrain his excitement no longer. He squeaked shrilly, and charged forward about a foot.

Second was convinced that the threehorn was coming for her. She bleated in panic and turned to get away. Unfortunately, Sixth was in her way. Second stumbled into Sixth, and both tumbled to the ground. They bleated and honked in their panic to get to their feet and get away.

Fourth also decided that a hasty retreat was the better course of wisdom under the circumstances. He too turned on wobbly legs, and tried to bolt. But not before bleating shrilly. He bleated, turned, and collided with Fifteenth. Fifteenth, with his eyes shut tightly, was certain that he was being attacked by some strange creature. Fifteenth trilled in alarm.

By then, the entire group of hornbrows was panic-stricken, and only wanted to untangle themselves from each other, and get back to the safety of their nest. They bleated and honked so fearfully, that they arose even the concern of their mother, who had been watching the whole relatively harmless episode.

The threehorn nestlings, not sure what had caused the panic, but certain that danger must be present to cause such a stampede by the creatures before them, were also suddenly fearful for their own safety. They squealed their alarm, and started a stampede of their own back to their nest. Seven little threehorns charged back, running right between the legs of their mother, who had been monitoring the whole event from a safe distance in the background.

The other nestling hornbrows, including the four sleeping with their father in the shade of the oak grove, hearing all the commotion and certain that nothing less than a full-force raid by razorteeth was in progress, all skittered back to their nest as fast as their jelly limbs would allow. None stopped to look behind or around, until each was in the safety of the nest. Some wouldn't look even then. These latter remained huddled face down in the damp dirt in the bottom of the nest.

The nestling threehorns thought along similar lines. None of them stopped until they were all safely hugging the bottom of their nest. Only when the friendly face of their mother appeared at the edge of the nest to tell them that all was well, did they stop shaking in fear.

*   *   *   *   *

Later that afternoon, Second lay sprawled near the top of her nest, chin resting on the rim, gazing at the distant nest of little creatures. Lost in deep concentration, she watched the chubby, boisterous things play in the vicinity of their nest, under the watchful eye of Roundfrill. She did this for more than an hour, when a sudden realization dawned upon her.

She turned and looked at the nestling hornbrows playing spiritedly behind her. Fourth was pushing Fifteenth over the edge of the nest, and down the slope. Others were pushing and shoving each other in the crowded confines of the bowl. Still others sat quietly, or tried to nap, complaining sleepily when someone poked them.

Then Second looked over at her mother, who sat motionless nearby, keeping track of the many activities of her many offspring. Second quite suddenly saw the great form of her mother in a different light. She wondered why it had never struck her before. Her mother was just a much larger version of herself. And her father, who she could see sleeping over in the shade of the oak trees, he also was a larger version of her and her siblings.

She returned her attention to the distant nest. The little creatures were bumping heads, or chasing each other, or chasing little lizards, or other joyful activity of the like. Yes, she was certain that she was right about the little four-legged creatures.

First came over and joined Second at the rim of their nest. He nuzzled her affectionately around her snout, and then lay down beside her to watch the nestling four-leggers. After awhile, Second turned to First with growing excitement on her face. First, sensing that Second was looking at him, turned from his scrutiny of the jostling and scampering four-legged creatures. He could tell from the expression on Second's face, that she had something important to convey to him. But since their vocabulary, both verbal, as well as through facial and body language, was still pretty limited, he suspected that she would have difficulty with it if it was too complex.

Second stared at her brother for a moment longer, frowned, and then looked back at the little creatures playing around Roundfrill's nest. She though about how to tell First of her discovery. Then it struck her. She turned again to First, and rumbled at him. Sensing that she wished to play, First rumbled back at her, and started to stand. No, First, she motioned to him. She pointed at the nest of four-leggers, and rumbled.

First smiled, pointed at Roundfrill and rumbled. Second tried to convey a more encompassing gesture, and rumbled again. She pointed directly at the little four-leggers, and made a sign that meant "small", and rumbled again.

First frowned. He looked at the charging, rearing, butting little four-leggers. He rumbled questioningly, more to himself than to Second. Second rumbled an affirmative. First pondered the meaning of what Second was trying to tell him. Roundfrill and all the mighty threehorns rumbled. Everyone knew that. Was she trying to tell him that the little creatures rumbled too? Was she trying to tell him that the big ones and the little ones were the same?

First looked over at Pippit. He had for some time harbored the feeling that his parents were more than just large alien creatures. He had begun to suspect that his parents were just larger versions of him and his siblings. Was there a relationship?

First jumped up in his dawning awareness, and rumbled loudly. There was a pause in the playing behind him, while his siblings rumbled in response. He turned to those in the nest, and rumbled happily. There was another answering chorus of rumbles. First turned back to Second, nuzzled her along the top of her neck, and rumbled. She rumbled back.

First and Second could hardly contain themselves now that they had this new found knowledge. Seventh, noticing the excitement emanating from the two virtual leaders of the brood, came over to them to see if he could learn what was going on. In short order, they passed on their discovery to him. He sat in wonder beside them, gazing out at the baby threehorns.

The more he thought about it, the more sense it made. Those strange little squeaking creatures that had been their neighbors for so long, were related to the gigantic, rumbling horned creatures that still came to visit them every once in a while. They were babies, just like Seventh and his siblings were babies. These were amazing concepts.

Then he jumped to another conclusion. Roundfrill must be their mother, like Pippit was his. He was very pleased with himself that he had figured this out. Then he frowned. Then where was their father? Why didn't they have a father, who slept all day, and who guarded them all night, and who helped their mother feed them? Maybe one of those really gigantic threehorns that patrolled near their nest, maybe one of them was their father. All these new and amazing thoughts made his head spin.

Seventh was interrupted in such philosophical deliberations by Second. She stood up on her wobbly hind legs, clambered over the rim of the nest, and slid down the slope to the ground. First was right behind her. Seventh realized that they were going to visit the baby threehorns. He didn't want to be left out of such an adventure. He pulled himself over the rim of the nest, and slid down the slope behind them.

Fifteenth was just climbing back into the nest when he saw, on the opposite side of the nest, first Second, then First, and then Seventh climb over the rim, all heading in the same direction. All three doing the same thing was too compelling, so Fifteenth pushed through the nest past his siblings, and went over the rim after the others.

Sixteenth also watched all this. His curiosity was too great for him to resist, so he too followed the others. Before long, three more of the nestlings were following the others on another delegation to the baby threehorns. In time, each of the remaining eight hornbrow nestlings also became aware of the little group heading towards the distant nest. One by one, they too eventually followed the leaders.

Roundfrill noticed the eight baby hornbrows first, wobbling and weaving on a journey that would soon bring them to her nest. Behind them, in groups of one or two, came eight more little hornbrows. One of her daughters, who seemed to always be watching every move that her mother made, next noticed the baby hornbrows that had attracted her mother's attention. She alerted her siblings, and soon the little herdlet of seven nestling threehorns was rushing forward to repulse the invaders.

Second saw them coming, and stopped to await their arrival. First and Seventh pulled up on each side of her, and also decided to wait. Soon all of the nestling hornbrows were crowding up behind them. Some were already contemplating a hasty retreat, as the truculent little threehorns came charging up. Second refused to yield her ground. Her two brothers stayed with her, although at least one of them thought that flight was the better option.

The threehorns slowed as they neared those awaiting them. When they were less than ten feet apart, the threehorns came to a complete halt, uncertain of the intentions of these brave invaders. Some of the threehorns themselves thought that retreat might be the wiser course of action. Yet the more belligerent of the young threehorns commenced some aggressive behavior, hoping to frighten the invaders away. The dominant female reared up on her hind legs. The dominant male made short charging motions, jerking his head upwards each time to add emphasis. Several others pawed the ground, and made little snorting sounds.

Second approached the threehorns very cautiously. Her sibs waited to see what would happen, ready to join her, or run for their lives, as the situation might merit. Some already were backing hesitantly away.

The dominant male threehorn snorted uncertainly, and took a few steps forward. Two of his siblings had turned around, and were inconspicuously trotting back towards the safety of their nest.

The male threehorn squeaked fiercely. Second was filled with doubt. She was herself on the verge of a hasty withdrawal. Wide-eyed, she stared at the aggressive little threehorn. She pulled together what courage remained to her, and rumbled a greeting to the threehorns. She made it the best imitation she could muster under the circumstances. It sounded a lot like "varoom," with the "r" rolled over and over again. Perhaps more like a "varrrroom".

The male threehorn immediately ceased his aggressive displays. He stood stock still, blinking several times in quick succession. His sibs behind him also quieted down, staring at Second.

Second rumbled the greeting again. "Varrroom." First chimed in with a rumble of his own. "Varrrroom." The dominant male nestling waved his head from side-to-side, and made a tiny little sighing squeak. Then he rumbled a response to the hornbrows. "Varrrroom."

Second rumbled back at him excitedly. First joined her. Seventh and several others belatedly added their own rumbles.

All five of the remaining threehorns rumbled happily at the visitors. Even the two that had been retreating came scampering back, rumbling excitedly. They all got an equally excited reply from the whole group of hornbrows.

"Varrroom. Varrrroom," they repeated over and over.

Each group advanced towards the other. They sniffed at each other cautiously. Second reached out and gently touched the male threehorn on the head. He looked up at her with large eyes. She rubbed him behind the frill, and patted him on the back. He trilled, and then rubbed his flank against hers, and wagged his little tail in excitement. Suddenly, all of the threehorns and hornbrows were mingling. They were patting and rubbing each other, rumbling, and squeaking, and bleating in happy disharmony.

Second looked into the eyes of the little dominant male. She said slowly and distinctly, "Sun warm you."

He examined her face, and rumbled eagerly, "Varrroom".

She repeated, "Sun warm you."

He hesitated, pawing the ground. He looked around at his own siblings. They watched him expectantly. He was the leader. Whatever he did was the right thing to do. He returned his attention to Second.

"Sun warm you," she said again.

He nodded his head at her several times. Then, falteringly, he said, "Thun varm du."

Some of the nestling hornbrows giggled.

"That's right," cried First, "Thun varm du, thun varm du."

"Thun varm du," repeated the little male happily.

"Thun varm du," cried Second and Fifteenth in unison.

Soon all of the nestling threehorns and hornbrows were exchanging the greeting. "Thun varm du... thun varm du."

Pippit and Roundfrill, each of whom had been following her own nestlings at a safe distance behind, looked at each other. Here was something that perhaps they might have anticipated under the circumstances, but hadn't. They had never seen nor heard before in their entire lives of anything like this. This was the unimaginable – for their children were now playing amicably together. Neither had ever heard of hornbrows and threehorns getting along much at all, let alone playing together. Each sat down to watch in wonder.

Other threehorn females were attracted by the scene. They approached more closely, and stood around conversing in low rumbles. In no one's memory had such a thing ever happened before.

Thundermaker came cantering over, always curious about anything out of the ordinary. Most things out of the ordinary were a threat to his herd. He came up close to the youngsters, who quieted down appreciably as he neared them. He looked over the scene sternly, and sniffed a couple of times with great authority. He swung his head in great arcs, surveying every one of the young participants. Then he rumbled softly at them, "Varrroom".

They all rumbled in response, threehorn nestlings and hornbrow nestlings alike, "Varrrroom".

He snorted a few more times, still gazing severely at the young ones. Suddenly the little male threehorn offered to Thundermaker: "Thun varm du."

Thundermaker stared at the young one. Then the whole group of nestlings broke out with, "Thun varm du."

Thundermaker glanced at Roundfrill. It was almost as if she shrugged in response to his unspoken question. Thundermaker next looked at Pippit. She nodded deferentially to him. He returned his attention to the nestlings, who sat there expectantly awaiting a response.

"Thun varm du," he said to the nestlings.

"Thun varm du, T'maker. Thun varm du," poured happily from the little nestlings.

Thundermaker looked over at the congregation of assembled females. He snorted authoritatively. Then, satisfied, he sauntered away, to continue his patrol.

* * * * *

In the early hours of the night, on the twenty-seventh day after First had cracked his shell, Pippit lay beside her nest, awake. The rain had stopped hours ago, but the world was dank and wet. Low clouds still blocked the light of the moon.

Although her day had been long, and full, she was not yet ready for sleep. So she conversed with Panthrar in low tones, telling him of the adventures that their nestlings and Roundfrill's had enjoyed together that day. Everyday now, the young hornbrows and threehorns shared their games, learning much from each other, and enriching their own lives in the process.

Panthrar listened with interest. He missed much of what happened during the day, since he spent much of it sleeping. It was better this way, though, since they had not lost a nestling in nine days. And that was not for lack of effort on the part of the redrunners and the razorteeth.

After a time of silence, Pippit began a new subject. "You know, my husband, I look forward to going home."

Panthrar knew that she was referring to his home, the one that she was soon to be a part of – the Green Water Roam. Panthrar thought about Grendaar and Tessah, and Rohraar and Trugahr, and Monah and Koowoo, and all the others. He missed them mightily. Maybe he missed Dandraar the most. He and Dandraar had done so much together as adolescents. Much had happened since he last saw Dandraar. He had become an adult. He had found a mate, and was raising a family. He and Pippit had been through many adventures together, and had done and seen things that many would find hard to understand, let alone believe. But he wanted to share all of these stories with Dandraar.

"I know, my wife, I too am looking forward to going home."

"I worry about getting our children home, my husband. It will be a long trek back. And without the herd, or the tribe, or even the roam ...", she trailed off.

She did not need to finish. Panthrar had been thinking of this a lot himself, now that the nestlings were almost large enough to leave the nest. It had been difficult enough for him and Pippit to cross the plateau. How were they going to do that safely with a brood of small, almost helpless nestlings to protect? And they would face much more exposure to predators, since nestlings traveled so slowly.

Maybe they could just stay here in the Valley of the Threehorns.

No, that wouldn't work. Once the threehorns left, as they surely would, it wouldn't be as safe here anymore. And by late summer, everything would turn brown, and food would start to get scarce.

"We will be just fine, my wife," he lied. After a pause, he lied again, "I have a plan."

She seemed mollified. They sat for a while in silence.

"I have been thinking, my husband," she began with some enthusiasm. Her mind had already put the possible dangers behind her. She thought of much more pleasant prospects. "When we get home, and have the Naming Ceremony, I think that I will name First, Tessaar, after your parents."

"That is a wonderful name, my wife."

"And I will call Second, Panthrit, after her parents."

"That is also a fine name, my wife."

"And we will remember Third by naming her Pippit, so that she won't be forgotten, and will have another chance at being conceived, and have another chance at life."

Panthrar was silent, because he could not trust his voice to remain steady.

Pippit went on as if no response from Panthrar was really necessary. "And I will call Fourth, Drassoom, after my parents. And I will call Fifth ...."

Panthrar didn't stop listening, but rather he was distracted by something imminently more urgent. He jerked his head upward and around, and tested the air.

Thundermaker had taken to sitting on the crown of the hill above their nest. It gave him a commanding view of the nesting area, and discouraged predators from sneaking up over the hill, as they had been doing of late with increasing frequency. At night, Thundermaker most often slept on the same crown, for similar reasons.

Thundermaker was there now. He had gone to sleep some time ago. Suddenly he had awakened. He snorted fiercely, and rose to his feet. He sensed trouble.

Panthrar interrupted Pippit, who had paused as soon as Panthrar's head had jerked up. "Excuse me, my wife, but I think I smell razorteeth."

Pippit was immediately alert. She looked into the nest, counting nestlings. They were all there, all asleep. They were sprawled all over the bowl, some hanging over the rim for more room and fresh air.

Panthrar rose to his feet and looked towards Thundermaker. Thundermaker was only a few hundred feet away. They exchanged glances. Panthrar tested the air again. It was unmistakable, the scent of razorteeth was heavy. They were nearby, and he smelled many bodies, a half dozen or more. He walked in Thundermaker's direction, signaling to him of the danger. Thundermaker nodded at him. Together they sounded the alert.

Quickcharger was patrolling along the north side of the nesting area. He signaled back his understanding. Hidepiercer, who was sleeping down by the stream, pushed himself to his feet, and shook the grogginess from his head. All the adult females lumbered to their feet, trying to shake the drowsiness out of their systems as quickly as possible.

A pack of razorteeth raced out of the woods that stood on the crown of the hill. They ran straight at Thundermaker. He squeal-roared, and lowered his horns at the on-rushing threat. Four of the razorteeth darted around to his left, and raced down the hill. They were headed right at Panthrar. Five more razorteeth sprang from the woods, and dashed around Thundermaker's right. He pivoted right, and chased after those five. The five scattered through the nesting area, with Thundermaker in pursuit. Female threehorns stood protecting their nests, stabbing at razortooth bodies as their flew by. Hidepiercer and Quickcharger converged on the threat, chasing after or blocking razorteeth as they bolted through the nesting ground, trying to snatch nestlings.

Panthrar hardly had time to think. The first four razorteeth were rushing straight for him. Four razorteeth could kill a hornbrow, if they got lucky. He pivoted hard on his left foot, swinging his tail counter-clockwise. The razorteeth jumped left and right, attempting to avoid the tail. Three did. He caught the fourth in the shins as it tried to jump over the tail. The impact sent it twirling head-over-heels off to the left, where it landed with a crunch. The other three razorteeth flew past Panthrar heading straight for Pippit and the nest.

Pippit could no longer effectively straddle the nest without stepping on nestlings. They were now too large, and there were too many of them to all fit within the hollow of the bowl. So Pippit stood between the nest and the razorteeth. As they closed with her, she pivoted and swung her tail in a sweeping arc. Two raced wide to the left, one to the right. The two to the left were farther away, so she turned on the one to her right.

The razortooth on Pippit's right dove at the nest and grabbed a nestling. It scooped up Thirteenth, and sprang to its feet.

Thirteenth screamed in terror.

Pippit dove at the razortooth. She tackled it at the knees, bringing it to the ground. It fell with its arms extended outward, Thirteenth was miraculously unhurt, but she was still held tightly in the razortooth's clawed hands.

Pippit managed to smash the razortooth with a clenched right fist. The razortooth lashed out at her with a partially freed right foot. It slashed Pippit across her right shoulder with its sickle-claw. Rich red blood spurted from the wound.

Pippit smashed the razortooth even harder a second time. It released Thirteenth so that it could defend itself better. Pippit hauled herself up closer to the razortooth, trapping its body between hers and the ground. She struck it again and again, with both clenched fists.

Panthrar ignored the razortooth that he had struck, and instead raced back to the nest. He saw Pippit's tail swing, and the razorteeth divide before her defense. While she dove at the one on her right, he dashed for the other two.

The two razorteeth that had dashed to Pippit's left, immediately converged upon the nest as Pippit fought the one on the ground. One sprinted up the slope of the nest, leaned into it, and grabbed Fourteenth. The other skirted the nest, and snatched up Thirteenth, who was panic-stricken and screaming on the ground.

Panthrar ran up the slope, and kicked the razortooth that held Fourteenth. The razortooth somersaulted over the nest, losing its grip on Fourteenth. The razortooth landed on top of Pippit.

Panthrar rushed towards the razortooth that now held Thirteenth. As Panthrar lunged at it, it ducked away from his outstretched arms and raced away into the darkness.

The razortooth that had landed on Pippit managed to avoid her as she rolled and reached behind herself to grab it.

Before Panthrar could pursue the razortooth with Thirteenth, the razortooth on Pippit's back jumped at him, both rear feet extended forward, razor-sharp sickle-claws aimed at Panthrar's side. Panthrar, his attention focused on the razortooth with Thirteenth, was struck on the left side. The razortooth gave him two foot long gashes as it landed on him. Panthrar roared in pain, as blood spurted from the wounds. He threw the razortooth from him with a sweep of his arm.

Before Panthrar could grapple with the razortooth that had wounded him, it sprang to its feet and ran towards the woods. It had a noticeable limp from Panthrar's kick, but it still ran well enough to get away.

Pippit pulled herself to her feet, and looked down at the motionless razortooth that she had continued to pummel until long after it had ceased to squirm underneath her. Panthrar looked around, but there were no more razorteeth in their vicinity. He listened for Thirteenth, hoping to follow her crying, but he was not rewarded by her call.

Panthrar went over and inspected the razortooth that Pippit had fought. It looked quite dead, but Panthrar stepped on it anyway.

While Pippit secured Fourteenth, and checked the nest and her other nestlings, Panthrar went looking for the razortooth that he had first struck. During the ensuing scuffle with the other razorteeth, it had regained consciousness, and had slipped away.

Panthrar returned to the nest. Fourteenth was bleating pitifully, but seemed to be none the worse for her close brush with death. Thirteenth was the only casualty. All the other nestlings were scrunched as far down into the nest as they could go. While Pippit cooed and trilled, trying to sooth their crying, Panthrar picked up the dead body of the razortooth that Pippit had killed, carried it through the woods, and threw it down the other side of the hill.

Then, as the nesting area was calming down, and returning to some semblance of order, Panthrar went looking for Thundermaker. Panthrar and the three male threehorns patrolled in every widening circles, hoping to find Thirteenth and the three missing threehorn babies. After an hour or so of fruitless searching, Panthrar returned to his nest, and the threehorns returned to their patrolling duties.

CHAPTER TWENTY-THREE
THE LONGEST JOURNEY

BY THE THIRTIETH DAY after First had broken out of his shell, the hornbrow nestlings were old enough, and large enough, to leave the nest. The females were about 23 inches long, and thirty-five pounds in weight. The males were 26 inches long, and almost fifty pounds in weight. Although the ends of their bones were still soft, the bones were hardening. The nestling hornbrows could move about with greater and greater proficiency with each passing day. They made many excursions from the nest to play, especially when they wanted to play with the threehorn nestlings.

Yet they always returned to the nest to eat. And of course to sleep. And they always headed for the nest whenever any danger, real or imagined, threatened them.

Old enough and large enough to leave the nest, though, didn't translate to willing enough. The nestlings couldn't yet conceive of a world that didn't include the security of their nest. It was the pool to which all things flowed: food, water, sleeping accommodations, protection from predators, not to mention the source of love, instruction, and frequent entertainment. No nestling in his or her right mind would want to leave such a bonanza willingly. Perhaps it is the same with all young, that the more secure and comfortable the nest, the less willing they are to leave it, even when time and nature demand that they must.

Early in the morning of the thirtieth day, Pippit and Panthrar walked away from their nest. They did not go far, and they did not leave the nest unprotected, but this was not evident to the nestlings. In fact, that they had left at all, was not immediately evident to the nestlings.

As the early morning sun climbed up from the embrace of the horizon, the more energetic of the young hornbrows spilled out of the nest and began playing in its near vicinity. But is was not long before the hungriest of the young hornbrows first noticed that there was no food piled up near the nest, as there usually was. Then they noticed that neither of their parents was sitting by the nest. This had never happened before. They complained, and soon all of their siblings knew that there was no food waiting for them to eat, and no parents standing guard over the nest.

Suddenly, they were all hungry, and many were frightened. They looked around in bewilderment. Some raced back to the safety of the bowl of the nest. Many began to cry and bleat pitifully.

Ninth, surveying the world about him, soon discovered their parents sitting up by the crown of the hill, near the edge of the woods, seemingly oblivious to the plight of their children. Ninth told the others, and they called to their parents to come feed them. Neither Pippit nor Panthrar seemed to hear the heart-breaking wailing.

Over an hour passed, and all of the nestlings were beginning to feel the legitimate pangs of hunger. Soon none of them were playing anymore. How could they, when it was becoming apparent that their parents might let them starve to death. They began to fuss amongst each other, as rumbling stomachs turned normally jubilant dispositions sour.

First, Second, and Seventh debated about what should be done. Some of the others chimed in with ideas. Seventh stood up on the rim of the nest, and said that it was his belief that their parents were not so far away that they couldn't hear them, since he had seen times when one or the other parent had heard them from further distances. He was certain that they could be heard, they were just being ignored.

First wasn't sure, since their parents had never ignored them before. He thought that maybe their parents were going deaf. He offered that they all call to their parents at the same time, and then maybe with the volume of their collective crying, they would be heard. They tried that, but all that happened was that their father, Panthrar, turned around, faced the woods, and lay down as if to go to sleep.

Eleventh wondered out loud if they had done something wrong, and that maybe their parents didn't love them anymore. She began to sob quietly. Her soul-mate, Twelfth, joined her. No wonder their siblings often referred to them as "the twins".

Second tried to comfort them. While she did so, she wondered out loud, although more to herself than to the group, if they could get help from the nestling threehorns. Seventeenth suggested that maybe if they called to Roundfrill, that she might come and feed them. They tried that for awhile, but Roundfrill seemed to no longer be able to hear them either.

The sun climbed still higher in the morning sky. The nestling hornbrows made a terrible racket, sometimes wrenchingly sad, sometimes piercingly obnoxious. Still their parents seemed unable to hear them. No adult threehorns came over to investigate, either.

First watched his parents studiously, and was convinced that on several occasions his mother did hear them, and on at least two occasions she almost started over to them. But each time, their father seemed to say something to her, and she ended by ignoring her nestlings. He conveyed these observations to his nest-mates. That their mother could hear them and yet not respond, and that their father might actually be encouraging her not to respond, was so alien and horrible that they all refused to believe it.

Second and Seventh began to develop a plan. Finally they decided that someone should risk the distant journey to where their parents lay in the shade of the conifer trees. That individual would get close enough to his parents that he was sure that they could hear him. Then he would tell them how hungry the nestlings were, and how desperately they needed food. Then they would all get fed.

After much discussion, the plan was agreed upon. First was selected to make the trip. He declined. But his little sister Fourteenth, whom he was especially partial to, pleaded with him so forlornly, that he finally acquiesced. Second and Fourteenth nuzzled First about the head and neck, wishing him well, and praising his bravery.

First was not ten feet from the nest, when he was already sorry that he had agreed to make the journey. The skygliders were astoundingly numerous and noisy this special morning. They screamed overhead, convincing him that one of them might swoop down and grab him, and fly away with him forever. Someone, one of the threehorn nestlings, had told him through some shared words and graphic and scary sounds, that a threehorn nestling had been taken thus.

He looked up into the sky. The skygliders were far overhead, winging and gliding, searching for food. Yet not one of them seemed the least bit interested in him. He looked over his shoulder at the nest. Fourteenth watched him with such big and trusting eyes, that he just couldn't let her down.

Onward he trudged.

When First was less than half way to where his parents lay, he startled a family of skinks from under a bush. They ran across his path, scaring him into instant paralysis. It took several minutes before he had recovered enough so that he could continue the journey. He looked back at the nest. No one seemed to realize how frightened he was. Second waved him on encouragingly. Tenth made silly gestures at him. Fourteenth's eyes seemed to have gotten even larger, if that was possible. The others just sat or lay there, around the rim of the nest, all sorrowfully dejected.

When First was about three-quarters of the way to where his parents were, he stopped to rest. "Mama, Papa," he cried in terror. His mother seemed to move uncomfortably, but she did not look at him. Neither of his parents answered him. He tried several more times, to no avail. He looked back at the nest. He would have liked to have fled back to the safety of it, but it was now too far away. A half dozen of his siblings waved at him. He waved back.

First pulled himself up, and continued his journey. He didn't stop until he was only ten or twelve feet from where his parents lay. He plopped himself down exhausted. "Mama, Papa," he said in a very small voice.

They both immediately turned in his direction, smiling warmly. "It is First, my wife," said Panthrar. "I told you that either First or Second would be the first to come."

"May the sun warm you, First, my fine young son," said Pippit. "You have made a long journey this day, longer than you can yet guess."

"Sun warm you, Mama. Sun warm you, Papa," replied First.

"May the sun warm you, First," said Panthrar. "I am proud of you, my son. Why have you made this long and difficult journey?"

"Me and Second, and Seventh, we decide. We hunger Papa. We hunger Mama. You so far away. Second say me come get you."

Pippit smiled at Panthrar, as if to say that she knew that Second had a hand in this. Panthrar asked, "Are you hungry, my son? Would you like something to eat?"

"Yes, Papa."

"See those berry bushes over there," said Panthrar, gesturing at some shrubs about fifty feet away. Although many of the berry bushes in the vicinity of the nesting ground had been stripped of their berries long ago, a small patch had been reserved for this special day.

"Yes, Papa."

"Come with me, my son, I will show you how to pick berries from a bush." With that, Panthrar arose, and walked very slowly towards the berry bushes. First stood up, and wobbled after his father.

*   *   *   *   *

Second could not understand it. She watched her brother successfully make the difficult journey to their parents. She saw him talking to them. She was certain that he would tell them how hungry he and his nest-mates were. But still they did not come. Instead, their father and First went over to some bushes. It looked like First might actually be eating the leaves on the bushes.

Second turned to Seventh and Fourth and Fourteenth, who were lying with her. She indicated that she was going to make the trip herself. Fourteenth whimpered. Seventh and Fourth nuzzled Second affectionately, proud of her bravery.

Second climbed over the rim, and slid down the slope. She ran as fast as her wobbly legs would let her, but she tired quickly. About a third of the distance to her parents, she had to stop and rest. She turned and looked back at the nest. Seventh tentatively climbed out of the nest, and slid down the slope to the ground. He sat there watching his sister. He signaled encouragement to her, but did not come any further himself.

After she was rested, Second stood up and again scampered as fast as her jelly legs would go. Again she stopped to rest. She could clearly see First eating berries directly from a bush. It didn't look that difficult to do. She could do that herself. Further in the distance, she could see Thundermaker coming along the top of the hill, on his patrol. He stopped when he saw the family of hornbrows, and turned around and walked back the way he had come.

Second got up and finished the last leg of her trip. She was starving, and intended to go directly to the berry bushes and satisfy her hunger. But when she passed close to her mother, something made her stop. Her mother was lying just within the edge of the shade, watching her.

"Sun warm you, Mama," she said to her mother.

"May the sun warm you, my brave little daughter," replied Pippit.

"We hunger, Mama."

"I know my dear child," said Pippit. Then she tried to explain, knowing the explanation was too complex for her little nestling, but feeling compelled to explain it anyway, perhaps for her own sake. "But each one of you must make this long journey by yourself. I cannot make it for you. Nor can your father make it for you. Each of you has to make this journey yourself. First has made the journey. You have made the journey. Soon the others will follow. See, even now brave Seventh is coming. So is Fourth and Eleventh. And look, here comes Twelfth and Sixth also."

Second turned to look back at the nest. She could see that what her mother said was true. Even the most timid of the nestlings were already over the rim, tagging along behind the more audacious. They were driven along not only by hunger, but by the fear of being left alone.

"Soon they will all be here," said her mother. "Go now to your father. He will show you something important."

"Yes, Mama," replied Second. She hesitated, and then she said tentatively, "Me love you, Mama."

"And I love you, my fine young daughter."

* * * * *

It was as Pippit had predicted. All the nestlings came to their parents, and learned to feed directly off of the bushes. Then their parents led them on an even longer journey down to the stream. It was a circuitous trip, and there were frequent rest stops. At each one Pippit or Panthrar would show them some interesting feature about the place that they lived, and explain it to them in simple words.

They heard about the evergreen woods at the top of the hill near where they had eaten, and about how redrunners and razorteeth used it to sneak into the nesting ground. They were cautioned to always be careful of the predators lurking in the depths of the woods.

They all gazed wide-eyed towards the woods. They would never go in there. They had a healthy fear of redrunners and razorteeth.

Then they moved on, stopping to visit with Roundfrill and her nestlings for awhile. The hornbrow nestlings excitedly told their friends of their great adventure, of eating directly from a berry bush. They did not realize that the threehorn nestlings had been making such trips for days now. But that didn't really matter anyway, and they all shared in the excitement of their first explorations of the world beyond the nest.

Next, Pippit lead the nestlings down the slope of the hill towards the stream. Behind her clustered fifteen tiny hornbrows, with very large eyes, and heads darting in all directions. They were trying to take in all the wondrous things that they had never seen from their nest. Panthrar followed discreetly in the rear, keeping an eye on his offspring. He was ever vigilant for anything that might endanger them.

They passed many other threehorn nests. Most had little herdlets of threehorn nestlings running around them, just like Roundfrill's had. The hornbrow nestlings were very excited over this discovery, and wanted to go meet each new brood. Pippit let them do this the first time, but then steered them away from the other nests, so that they could get to the stream before noon.

Panthrar and Pippit were amazed at the reception that their nestlings got at the nest they did visit. The threehorn mother, so familiar now with both the adult and the nestling hornbrows, behaved almost indifferently to their visit. Not so the youngsters.

Pippit and Panthrar hung back with the mother threehorn to watch the antics of the children. At first, the more dominant of the threehorn nestlings behaved very aggressively towards the hornbrow nestlings. They pawed the ground, snorting fiercely for such small creatures. They made charging and stabbing gestures, the intent of which Panthrar and Pippit were all too familiar with in the adult version.

Then several of the hornbrow nestlings rumbled to the threehorns. The threehorns rumbled back. Then they exchanged a series of squeaking and squealing and trilling, intermingling as if old friends. It seemed to Panthrar that their nestlings mimicked threehorns so convincingly, that the threehorns accepted them as their own.

After a while, the family of hornbrows continued on down the hillside towards the stream. Hidepiercer, who was lying near their path, got to his feet, and ambled slowly in their direction. The nestlings clustered even closer together, but otherwise did not react. Panthrar did, maneuvering to place himself between the threehorn and his brood.

Hidepiercer, noticing the caution of Panthrar, stopped. Hidepiercer then rumbled something friendly to Panthrar and Pippit. Panthrar was about to respond, when Fifteenth, with his perpetual little smile, rumbled and squeaked to Hidepiercer. Hidepiercer looked at Fifteenth, and rumbled in response. Fifteenth rumbled and trilled in return. Then the entire brood of nestlings rumbled and trilled at Hidepiercer. Hidepiercer sat down on his rear haunches, and watched the brood of hornbrows make their way down to the stream.

If Panthrar didn't know better, he would have been convinced that his offspring could communicate with the threehorns.

When the hornbrow nestlings got to the stream, they were amazed by it. All that they had ever seen of this substance before, was rain from the sky, and muddy puddles in and around their nest. Here was water in great abundance. There was so much of it, that it flowed over the rocks and pebbles, off and away down into the great valley. Yet more and more of it kept coming down from the hills. It just kept coming and coming, flowing by, in perpetual motion. The sun glinted off the water in sparkling patterns that delighted their eyes, partially blinding them at the same time. It was an incredible thing for them to behold.

Several of the young tested the water's edge. Eleventh leaned over and put a hand into a small side pool, watching tiny water bugs scurry away, some stroking with their many legs, others swimming or diving under rocks. Fourth experimentally placed a foot into the water, slipped on a stone, and splashed on his rump. Unhurt, he then watched curiously as the ripples circled away from him, bouncing off rocks in enchanting patterns.   .

Fish darted away as more and more of the young entered the water. Newts and salamanders wiggled to safety. The hornbrow nestlings tripped and stumbled into the shallows. A turtle, sunning himself on the other side of the stream, gave the interlopers one disdainful glance, and then plunged into the water and dove for the safety of an underwater ledge in a nearby embankment.

The nestling hornbrows splashed and played, and sometimes even drank from the stream. They were thusly employed for almost an hour. Their watchful parents hovered nearby, occasionally joining them in the water. Eventually, their parents herded them out of the water, and the nestlings napped in the shade of some nearby dogwood trees. Later that afternoon, they began the long journey back to the nest. It was an exhausted brood of nestling hornbrows that reached the nest, and again they napped for much of the afternoon.

When they awoke, the nestlings were anxious to go on another adventure. So their parents took them up the hillside to the edge of the conifer woods. Panthrar searched the woods diligently for potential dangers. He snooped under shrubs, and looked behind rock outcroppings, and patrolled deeper and deeper into the woods. Pippit, meanwhile, helped the nestlings to feed off of new evergreen seedlings, and low growing branches, and fallen limbs and cones.

That night, the nestling hornbrows slept in the security of their nest. They slept the sleep of the healthily exhausted, dreaming of long journeys and great adventures. Pippit slept soundly, only infrequently awaking to check her brood, and to look for the stalwart silhouette of her husband. Panthrar sat on his haunches near the crown of the hill, listening to a razortooth raid on a nesting area about a half of a mile away. Quickcharger lay beside him, chin on the ground, eyes open and alert.

*   *   *   *   *

Each new day was another day filled with adventure and wonder for the nestling hornbrows. They explored, under the watchful eyes of their parents, more and more of the nesting area and vicinity. They met more and more of the threehorn young. They went off on little quests with Roundfrill's brood, with Pippit and Roundfrill in attendance. Panthrar slept whenever he could, guarding the nest, and the nesting area, each night. Razorteeth still raided, and on the thirty-sixth night, they managed to take Fifth.

The hornbrow nestlings grew, and they learned about the world around them. By the fortieth day after First had hatched out of his egg, the females averaged 26 inches in length, and the males averaged 30. They gained weight at an accelerating rate. The females averaged 42 pounds in weight, and the males averaged 62. Their bones were hardening, and they found it easier and easier to move about. They hardly wobbled at all now. And although they still weren't as mobile as the threehorn nestlings, they no longer seemed handicapped. They played rough and tumble with each other. They played rougher than their mother thought was proper. Perhaps they had learned a little bit more about aggressive behavior from the threehorns than their mother thought was good for them.

Pippit used every opportunity available to teach her young something valuable. She taught them how to speak the hornbrow language of words, facial expressions, body language, and hand signals. She taught them about threehorns, and other green-eaters – which ones were harmless, and which ones to avoid. It was difficult convincing them that most hornbrows considered that threehorns were moody and temperamental, and given to unwarranted aggressiveness, and were creatures to generally be avoided.

Pippit taught her young about the predators. They learned of the opportunistic egg stealers, like eggsnatchers and swiftstealers and trailrunners. They were happy to steal an egg whenever they could. These large, gracile runners made it impossible to leave a nest unguarded for any length of time, but they wouldn't go near a guarded nest unless they were desperate.

Pippit described to them the dedicated nesting ground raiders, like redrunners and robrunners. They already had some knowledge of these, and were already developing the kind of ingrained antipathy to them that was common to all of their race. The nestlings also learned of the dangerous pack-hunting razorteeth, another predator that they had cause to hate. Their mother told them that these would be a threat to them until they were fully grown, and could still be one after that.

They learned of the perennial threat to both individuals and to the herd itself, the deadly large predators. She told them of dreadrunners, who although somewhat smaller than an adult hornbrow, were fast, strong, and extremely lethal to all but the largest and most courageous of the hornbrows. She told them that it was not wise to stay and fight a dreadrunner, you ran from one as fast as you could.

Pippit also told them about dreadchargers, the scourge of their world. Dreadchargers were larger and stockier than dreadrunners. Although not as fast as a dreadrunner, and possibly not as fast as a hornbrow in headlong flight, there were none-the-less quite swift. Dreadchargers were afraid of no other thing in their entire world, except perhaps a larger dreadcharger. Dreadchargers would eat anything, any green-eater, and even another predator. They could kill anything that they could catch. Even threehorns were afraid of dreadchargers. Only the long, sharp horns of a threehorn, backed by the might and weight and courage of an adult threehorn, would give a dreadcharger a reason to hesitate.

Pippit told her young of many things that would help them in life. She knew that they would not remember it all, certainly not from the first telling.

But she would repeat the lessons many times over the coming months, giving the nestlings the knowledge they would need to survive in what was often a hostile and very dangerous world. She had begun to teach them language, and the mores and rules of their culture, and of the sources of food and water, and of the seasons, and of the hunters and killers of their world. She taught them everything that she knew of, and could think of. But there were some dangers that even she did not know of.

CHAPTER TWENTY-FOUR
OLD SOLITARY

By the fiftieth day after First's hatching, Panthrar and Pippit deemed that their nestlings were old enough, large enough, and strong enough to travel. If they needed to. The females were between 28 and 29 inches in length, and around 55 to 60 pounds in weight. The males were an even more robust 33 to 34 inches in length, and some 80 to 85 pounds in weight.

Yet neither Panthrar nor Pippit wanted to travel this soon. They preferred to wait another ten days or so, when their young would traditionally be old enough to make the great trek. Then they would be better prepared to travel back to the coastal plain... to the place where the River of the Nine Tribes flowed into the Great Green Sea... to the home of the Red Dawn Tribe and the Green Water Roam... to the land of the People... to home.

The problem was that the herds of threehorns looked very much like they would be making their trek eastward and southward any day now. Some of the herds had already left, and more left every day. The herd that had occupied the next hill over from the nesting grounds of Thundermaker's herd had departed yesterday. It's departure left an appreciable gap in the defenses of the surrounding area. Now Thundermaker's herd was at the edge of the great congregation of threehorns, with no other threehorns between them and the empty hills to the south. Empty, that is, except for the ubiquitous predators.

It was just a matter of time before Thundermaker decided that it was time to move his herd. Panthrar and Pippit knew that they would have to leave with Thundermaker, whether they were ready or not. They couldn't stay in the Valley of the Threehorns by themselves. Nor could they hope to cross the upper plain by themselves. They needed the protection of the herd.

So they worried and fretted. Would their nestlings be able to travel as fast as the threehorn nestlings? And they thanked whatever fates that hornbrows thanked for each passing day that the trek did not begin. For each day would help their young grow stronger and better prepared for the ordeal ahead.

Pippit was engaged in such thoughts, as she stood on the bank of the stream, while her nestlings frolicked in the water. They had taken to chasing salamanders and newts in the water, and along the water's edge. They flipped over rocks on the shore, and watched the little creatures squirm and wiggle, trying to escape. They would catch them, and throw them into the water. Then the nestlings would pursue the little creatures, splashing about, making a lot of noise, but doing little damage. Fortunately for the little amphibians, being thrown in the water allowed most of them to swim away to safety, much to the chagrin of the little hornbrows.

Pippit had been thinking a lot about home lately. She dreamed of the time when she would be safe with her mate, and with her nestlings by her side, in her new home – the Green Water Roam. Lost in such thought, Pippit gazed up towards one of the nearby hills. She was suddenly startled back into the present by the sight of a hornbrow, standing at the very top of the next hill over. It was an adult male, and he was just standing there staring down at her and her young. Before she could react, the hornbrow turned, and sped back over the hilltop. Pippit blinked a couple of times. She stared long and hard, but the hornbrow had disappeared. Had she really seen a hornbrow, or had she been day-dreaming too much about the herd and home?

Pippit honked to Panthrar. Panthrar was sound asleep next to the nest. Yet he heard Pippit's warning, and was immediately awake and up. He hurried down to his wife and family, moving with amazing alacrity for someone who had been dead to the world only moments before. Thundermaker and Quickcharger, both on patrol at the moment, also came trotting over to Pippit.

When Panthrar arrived, shortly after the two threehorns, Pippit explained to him what she thought she had seen. He said he would go investigate. But before he left, he and Pippit tried to explain to the two threehorns what was amiss, and that Panthrar would go investigate. It was a complex message, but the threehorns understood enough to know that Panthrar was going to investigate, so they returned to their patrols. Still, as Panthrar climbed the adjacent hill, Thundermaker kept an eye on him, lest he need help.

Panthrar climbed the hill, not sure what to make of what Pippit thought she saw. Probably she was thinking of home again. Probably she saw some bipedal creature, possibly a predator, and had confused it with what she wanted to see.

He decided to be cautious, in case it was a predator. Hopefully she had been mistaken about the size too. A predator the size of a hornbrow was a dangerous, and likely a lethal opponent. That was just the right size for an adult dreadrunner. Even if it wasn't that large, he still needed to be careful. He was still nursing the wounds left by the razortooth that had helped steal Thirteenth. He looked forward to the opportunity to kill a razortooth, but didn't want one jumping him from behind. Or worse, a pack of them ambushing him.

Panthrar topped the hill, and searched the vista before him. Gently rolling hills spread out in unending undulations far towards the west. Eventually they turned into the immediate foothills and shoulders of the steeply ragged mountains that dominated the western horizon. Even now, the mighty tectonic forces were agitating the young and moody mountains, and an active volcano was spewing a scattering of smoke, ash, and hot gases into the sky. But that mighty force was over ten miles away, and of no immediate concern to Panthrar.

To Panthrar's left, the hills also continued in unending waves, to be broken only by the great river valleys much further to the south. On his right, the hills gently flattened towards the river that bisected the Valley of the Threehorns, before they again continued their march to the north.

Panthrar inspected the hill tops, and the hillsides, and the stream valleys, and the narrow creases and crevices and folds in the landscape. But he saw nothing. He spent a considerable amount of time scrutinizing every possible place that a creature could hide. Still he saw nothing of immediate concern.

There were swiftstealers and eggsnatchers grazing along a distant hillside. He even saw a few **bumpybacks**, something he hadn't seen in the valley before. But he saw no predators. And he saw no hornbrow. He decided that it was time to return to the nest, and sleep.

He explained to Pippit that he had seen nothing, but that it would be a good idea to be even more watchful for predators. If she had seen a predator as large as a hornbrow, the entire herd might be in jeopardy. As alert as they both remained, they saw nothing else of the apparition that day, or that night.

The next morning, while Panthrar was drinking at the stream after a night spent mostly in fighting sleep, he saw Pippit's apparition. It was indeed a male hornbrow. It was standing on the top of the adjacent hill, motionlessly watching him. He hand-signaled a hello to it, but it did not respond. He tooted a welcome to it, both to emphasize his good intentions, and to also indirectly alert Pippit. Still the creature did not respond. Then, quite suddenly, it turned around and sped out of sight.

Panthrar took off in pursuit of it. He splashed across the stream. Over his shoulder he communicated his intentions to Pippit, but he never broke stride as he charged up the adjoining hill. When he reached the top, he scanned the field for movement. There was nothing on the other side of this hill, nor anything in the narrow dale at the foot of the hill. There was nothing the size of a hornbrow in the little copse off to the right. Nor was there anything off to the left other than a few swiftstealers on the gentle slope running down to the river in the distance.

Then his attention was attracted by the movement of something nearing the hilltop on the next hill to the west. There were not many threehorns about, at least not in this direction. Thundermaker's herd now formed the outer defense for those herds that remained. So it was not hard spotting the creature that first Pippit and then he had seen.

Panthrar stood there silently, watching the hornbrow scrambling up the slope. His efforts eased, and his pace slackened, as he neared the moderate crest at the top of the hill. Panthrar wondered why the hornbrow was running away, rather than rushing boisterously and happily towards them, like almost any other hornbrow would have done in a similar situation. After all, there weren't any other hornbrows for tens of miles around, as far as Panthrar knew.

You would think that this one would crave the company of its own kind. The People were a sociable race, yearning for the company and protection of the group. This one must be a hard-core solitary, one who actually shunned the company of its kind.

Panthrar pondered whether to let him go in peace, or to call to him hoping to force him, out of inbred politeness, to respond back. Panthrar hadn't seen one of his kind, other than his mate and family, for so long, that he decided to try calling to the other again.

Panthrar honked a greeting. The solitary immediately stopped his climbing, and turned around to look at Panthrar. He was an old adult male, Panthrar could see that even from this distance. Panthrar honked again, and sent hand-signals of welcome to the stranger. The solitary finally signaled a greeting to Panthrar, and then commenced a slow trudge back towards Panthrar. He suddenly seemed in no hurry.

Panthrar waited for him, rather than going to meet him half way. He assumed that the solitary would want to join up with him and his family at least for a short while. He might even want to stay with them to cross the upper plain back towards home. If so, that might add some valuable protection for the young. Panthrar smiled to himself. The solitary was in for a shock when he learned of Panthrar's other traveling companions.

As the solitary approached him, Panthrar could begin to make out features, and see details. The solitary was a very old male, thin and rickety. He looked like he hadn't had a decent meal in weeks. But then, Panthrar thought, he too was a lot thinner than usual. Parenting took a lot out of you. But this one didn't look like he had been parenting, not lately anyway. As the solitary got really close, Panthrar thought that he looked familiar. He was much larger than Panthrar, perhaps 38 feet long, and over three tons in weight. Maybe he belonged to the Red Dawn Tribe. Certainly he was a member of the Great Eastern Herd, for Panthrar had seen that brittle and broken horn before. Still, he couldn't quite recall who he was.

As the solitary came within comfortable speaking distance, Panthrar made a gesture of welcome with his right hand, and said, "May the sun warm you, elder brother."

The solitary closed to within fifty feet, and then stopped and sat back on his haunches. He scrutinized Panthrar. He leaned forward, pulled a branch from a young spruce standing nearby, and munched upon it thoughtfully. Finally, he said, "May the sun warm you, younger brother."

There was another long pause, while the solitary continued to munch upon his spruce twig. Finally Panthrar broke the silence. "I am Panthrar the Swift, of the Green Water Roam of the Red Dawn Tribe. Presently I travel with the Roam of Thundermaker."

Panthrar waited patiently for the older hornbrow to tell him his name. It was just common etiquette among hornbrows to exchange their names, roams, and tribes. Sometimes they even gave their parents names, and their parents roams and tribes. And sometimes, if the occasion warranted, they gave even more of their lineage. But the old solitary did not offer his name, or anything else. He just sat there on his haunches, sucking on the needle-less spruce twig.

Finally Panthrar spoke again, "Do I not know you, elder brother?"

The solitary hummed for a moment, nodding his head in the affirmative. Then he said, "Yes you do, yes you do, younger brother. I believe that you do. And I know you. You are Panthrar the Swift, of the Green Water Roam of the Red Dawn Tribe. Who is Thundermaker?"

"Thundermaker is a threehorn, and my friend," replied Panthrar, noting that the old solitary did not react at all to the fact that he was friendly with a threehorn. Panthrar was beginning to believe that this old solitary had been standing out in the sun too long. To fill the growing vacuum of silence, Panthrar explained further, "After we became separated from the herd, my mate and I have been traveling with him and his herd. And you, elder brother, is your herd nearby?"

The old solitary did not answer. He just stood there, staring at Panthrar. Panthrar also stood, waiting for a response, trying to be as patient as possible. While they waited, the solitary reached over, and pulled another branch from the unfortunate spruce. He watched Panthrar almost blankly, chewing away on the spruce needles, stripping the twig completely clean, and then throwing it away.

Panthrar offered, "You are a solitary, elder brother? You have been traveling for some time away from your tribe and roam?"

The solitary scratched his head with his right hand. He gestured vaguely towards the south, "I am a solitary, younger brother. I have been traveling a long while. I have seen many strange and wonderful things. Wonderful things." He smiled at some pleasant recollection. Then he frowned. "I have seen many dark and horrible things. Horrible things." With that he shuddered violently. Then he turned and gazed off towards the south. He stood looking towards the south for a long, long while. So much time passed that Panthrar began to think that perhaps he had forgotten that Panthrar was there.

"Elder brother," Panthrar eventually said, "I am here with my mate and my nestlings. Would you like to come sit with us in comfort?"

The old solitary turned back towards Panthrar, but he did not answer. He just gazed vaguely in Panthrar's direction, with a bemused frown on his face. Panthrar wasn't sure what to do next, or what else he might do for the poor old hornbrow. So he turned around and headed back in the direction of his nest. After he had walked a few paces, he turned and gestured to the solitary for him to follow Panthrar. The solitary seemed uncertain, but stepped after Panthrar, none-the-less.

So this is how they came to the nesting area of Thundermaker, Panthrar leading the way, and the old solitary following. Little herdlets of threehorn young scattered out of their way, while threehorn females stood watching cautiously, with their young peeking out from behind their legs.

Hidepiercer trotted up from the left, while Thundermaker and Quickcharger came rushing up from the right. They approached very closely to the old solitary, sniffing and snorting at him. Thundermaker's smaller nose horn brushed the flank of the old hornbrow, but Thundermaker did not actually threaten him. That the old solitary was with Panthrar probably saved his life. That, and the fact that he did not react at all. He just stood there docilely, and let the threehorn males inspect him.

Thundermaker questioned Panthrar about this stranger. Panthrar tried to explain that it was all right, that this hornbrow was harmless. The threehorns eyed the solitary carefully, and circled him suspiciously. Females and young moved further away, giving the males plenty of room to maneuver, if they needed it.

Eventually, with some apparent reluctance, the threehorns accepted that this new hornbrow was probably not a danger to them or their young. Hidepiercer and Quickcharger soon sauntered away to resume their patrols. Thundermaker stayed in the vicinity of the old solitary for over an hour, drifting farther and farther away over time, until he also finally decided to accept him as harmless. Then he too went to the periphery to guard against predators.

Panthrar next lead the solitary to the vicinity of his nest, where his nestlings played, and his mate kept watch. Pippit came forward after the threehorns had finished their inspection. She stood about forty feet in front of her nest, and waited for Panthrar and the solitary to advance to her. She made a gesture with her right hand that meant hello and greetings. When Panthrar and the solitary had stopped before her, she nodded deferentially to both males, and said, "May the sun warm you, my husband."

Panthrar greeted her with the normal response, but he said it with true affection none-the-less, "May the sun warm you, my wife."

Pippit then turned to the solitary. "May the sun warm you, elder brother."

The solitary coughed, stared at the ground for a moment, looked into Pippit's face, and said, "May the sun keep you in its warmth, younger sister."

Pippit nodded again, and continued, "I am Pippit, once of the Flat Rock Roam of the White Moon Tribe... ." She paused, smiled at Panthrar, and went on, " ...now of the Green Water Roam of the Red Dawn Tribe."

The solitary looked down at the ground again. He mumbled to himself, and finally said, "I ..., I am ...." He paused a moment longer, then looked away.

Pippit and Panthrar waited, but that was all he said. Soon he seemed to lose interest in the conversation. He walked around Pippit and gazed into and around the nest. Nestlings had been playing everywhere, at least until their father had led the strange hornbrow up to their mother. Then they had all calmed down.

Pippit thought that perhaps the solitary was so old, or had been through so many tribulations recently, that he had forgotten his name, and where he had come from.

First and Second gazed up at the hulk standing over them, with their eyes opened widely, and chimed in together, "Sun warm you." Several of their nest-mates belatedly added their greetings also.

The old hornbrow leaned a little closer to the nestlings, smiled at them, and said, "May the sun warm you, little ones. Whom do I have the pleasure of addressing?" Panthrar and Pippit exchanged glances.

First stood up to his full height, and said proudly, "Me First." Then he sat down.

Second stood up, and said, "Me Second." She too sat back down.

Fourth stood up, but before he could speak, Seventh jumped up and said, "Me Seventh." Fourth shoved Seventh, who pushed him back. A scuffle was about to ensue, when the old hornbrow cleared his throat sternly. Seventh sat back down.

Fourth said, "Me Fourth." Then he quickly sat back down.

Sixth stood up, gave her name, and then sat back down.

Seventh jumped up again, but before he could speak, the old hornbrow said, not unkindly, "I know who you are, you are Seventh."

"Yes," said Seventh, who then also sat down quickly.

Ninth in turn stood up and identified himself, then Tenth identified herself. Eleventh and Twelfth stood up together. Eleventh identified herself, and Twelfth identified himself close upon her heels. Then came Fourteenth, Fifteenth, Sixteenth, Seventeenth, and finally Eighteenth.

When they were all done, the old hornbrow, whose attention hadn't strayed for a moment, said grandly, "And I am Old Solitary. That's what you may call me. Old Solitary." Panthrar and Pippit again exchanged glances.

Shortly thereafter, before the adults could initiate a conversation, the nestlings let it be known that it had been hours since they last ate. So an excursion down to the stream soon followed. Panthrar decided that he could wait until another time to learn who Old Solitary really was. He knew that he had seen him before, and it was only a matter of time before he would remember what his real name was.

The nestlings ranged here and there along the banks of the stream, eating tender shoots, or toying with the denizens of this wonderful place. Pippit stood quietly watching her offspring, periodically counting them to make sure that all were accounted for. Panthrar lay down beside the nest, hoping to catch up on much needed sleep. Old Solitary wandered off into the woods above the nesting area.

It seemed to Panthrar that he had just closed his eyes. But in fact, he had fallen into a sound sleep. Suddenly he was being shaken awake. He opened his eyes, and looked around. He was still shaking. He tried to get to his feet. He wobbled uncertainly, as if he were a hatchling, but still managed to stand up. The ground underneath his feet was heaving up and down. He looked for Pippit and the nestlings. Pippit was on her knees beside the stream, calling frantically to her nestlings. Nestling hornbrows were crying and bleating. Some tried to hop over to their mother, others lay clinging desperately to the ground. Some sloshed and splashed in the stream, rolling this way and that. Panthrar tried to run to his family, but fell flat on his face.

He got to his knees and looked around more carefully. Female threehorns lay on their bellies, four legs spread-eagle, or tried precariously to get to their feet. Most of their young had stopped where they stood, frozen in place, or were hugging the ground. The threehorn nestlings also were squealing in panic.

Just as suddenly as it had started, the shaking stopped. Panthrar sprang to his feet, and raced for the stream, dodging around panic-stricken threehorn mothers and their young. He heard Thundermaker squealing his rage at the unseen enemy. The male threehorn charged around in circles, stabbing upward with his horns, trying to chase away whatever it was that had attacked his herd.

When Panthrar got to the stream, Pippit was already on her feet, rounding up her brood. Panthrar breathed a sigh of relief. All were safe and accounted for. While he did another count just to be sure, Old Solitary quietly walked up and joined them.

Without preamble, Old Solitary said, "During my travels, I have been to the Smoking Mountain." Panthrar, finished with his counting, looked over at Old Solitary. The old male was staring towards the west. He continued, "I have talked to it, and it has talked to me." Old Solitary slowly pivoted around towards Panthrar, and delving deeply into his eyes, seemed to search his soul. "It is going to die. And I am going to die."

Panthrar gawked at Old Solitary. The old male hornbrow turned back towards the west. Panthrar followed his gaze. Smoking Mountain was belching huge volumes of smoke and gases, along with vapors and dust and ash. Great dark clouds were billowing upward into the distant sky. Panthrar stood in wonder. The pillar of spewn material was ascending ever upward, miles into the heavens.

Pippit noticed Panthrar, and then she too was staring westward. Soon their nestlings were doing likewise. So were the threehorns. All were staring at Smoking Mountain. In fact, so were the hundred thousand other creatures that happened to be within twenty or thirty miles of the erupting volcano.

CHAPTER TWENTY-FIVE

DAYS OF DARKNESS, NIGHTS OF LIGHT

Sмoking Mountain sent massive volumes of rolling clouds of smoke and ash into the sky. These were frequently accompanied by steam and gases, and such pyroclastic materials as cinders and slag and volcanic dust. These latter were often ejected at red-hot temperatures, giving the illusion that fire was belching from the mouth of the volcano.

Ultimately, the ash clouds would rise higher than ten miles into the atmosphere. Carried with the wind, the dark masses of particulates would block out the sun, turning day into night for those downwind of the mountain. Ash and dust would fall as far as one hundred miles away, but most of it would descend to the earth much closer to the mountain. The forces being unleashed by the mountain were so great, that particles would be ejected from the volcano's mouth at speeds of up to 2000 miles per hour. The dark swirling clouds of ash and gases and other materials propelled from the volcano's mouth would periodically be interlaced with flashes of lightning, caused by the positive electrical charges created by the vast forces at work.

Smoking Mountain, like most volcanos, would end up spewing forth many times more water vapor and other gases, by weight and volume, than all the solid materials combined that it would eject. The water vapor would burden the atmosphere, and mixed with the dense volumes of dust and ash also sweeping the turbulent skies, would fall as grimy rain.

About a half hour after the first ground shake, the earth shook again. It didn't last long, but it convinced the threehorns and hornbrows that their world was undergoing violent change. Shortly after the ground quit shaking, the sky filled with skygliders and skygiants, and all manner of little feathered birds. They were flying eastward, winging away from Smoking Mountain with all due haste.

Thundermaker took this as a sign. He collected his herd of dominant males, breeding females, and young, and headed down the stream valley towards the river to gather his juveniles. Panthrar and Pippit and their family followed behind. And Old Solitary trailed behind all of them.

It was slow going. The erstwhile nestlings, hastily graduated to **fledges**, struggled to make progress. But the rumbling of Smoking Mountain, and the world rapidly changing from a paradise to a hell, galvanized them onward. The charging little herdlets of threehorn young, now called **pups** since they had left the nest, soon tired, as they were not used to long trips. The longer, but less sure strides of the hornbrow fledges helped them to keep up, but just barely.

Thundermaker's herd reached the river, and rested. The herd of juveniles had already begun a retreat out of the valley. It could be seen about a half-mile ahead, rapidly making its way down the river valley towards the plain. Thundermaker sent Quickcharger ahead to find his juveniles, and to make sure that they did not scatter once they reached the plain.

Thundermaker's herd rested for about an hour, letting the pups and fledges regain enough strength for the next leg. Periodically the earth trembled, not as violently as before, but enough to continue to scare young and old alike. Each occurrence made the water in the river jump its banks, splashing most of the herd. It convinced both Panthrar and Thundermaker that they had best travel a little farther from the banks of the river, or risk being swept into it.

By early-afternoon, ash and volcanic dust had been falling for hours. A light sprinkling covered the ground, giving the world an eerily ghostlike appearance. Billowing clouds of ash and dust and water vapor rolled through the skies, obscuring the sunlight, and darkening the landscape worse than during the most torrential of rainstorms. The dark clouds reduced visibility considerably, and Smoking Mountain itself disappeared from view.

Occasionally, the suffocating stench of sulfur-dioxide reached the nostrils of the inhabitants of the Valley of the Threehorns.

Just before they began the next leg, it began to rain. It was unlike any rain they had ever experienced before. It was not a cleansing rain, like usual, but a muddy, grimy rain, mixed with ash and dust and bits of pumice. The rain combined with the ash and dust that had already fallen, creating a slippery mess.

The herd began its trip down the river valley, for the first time actually moving directly away from the active volcano. They traveled on an angle taking them away from the banks of the river. The adults tripped and stumbled in the slippery ash-mud. The pups and fledges slid and sloshed, somehow turning the ordeal into a game. That took their minds off of the hardships of the journey, and they probably traveled for twice as long as they might otherwise have. But it was slow going anyway.

Small mud-slides formed, and the herd stayed away from slopes. Grimy rain fell for most of the afternoon, broken only by intermittent periods when neither rain nor dust fell. At intervals, larger debris fell from the sky, battering the ground at random and scattered locations throughout the valley. Fortunately, none of this potentially dangerous material fell close to the herd.

Still they trudged on. Ahead of them and to their right, they could see other small herds of threehorns working their way towards the east. To their left, across the river, just barely visible in the overcast and raining environment, they could see other herds laboring through the mud and slime. Occasionally, they saw small herds of redrunners or hunting packs of razorteeth, making their way eastward also. The razorteeth seemed less concerned about stalking, and were more bent on putting distance between themselves and Smoking Mountain. At infrequent intervals, the herd ran across creatures, threehorns and others, confused by events, and traveling towards, rather than away from the volcano. The threehorns that they found going the wrong way, they tried to turn around. Because of this, their herd had soon swelled temporarily to over fifty adults, and many young.

All afternoon they traveled, and close to evening, they were only a mile and a half further down the valley than when they had started. Nightfall came, not as an easily perceptible change from light to dark, but only as a slowly and steadily darkening of the sky. The young, including the hornbrow fledges, were gathered into a large group. The adults were arranged around them in a loose circle. Panthrar, Pippit, and Old Solitary stayed together, forming part of the defensive circle around the young. They positioned themselves close to the young hornbrows, and also close to where Roundfrill and Hidepiercer lay. Thundermaker and his other females were nearby, although Thundermaker and the other primary males now gathered with him, still took turns patrolling the perimeter of the defensive circle.

At first Pippit fretted about her young, who were not close enough to her to satisfy her. She was afraid that some of the threehorn young, those that did not know the hornbrow fledges, might try to bully them. But Panthrar convinced her that the fledges had lived with threehorns long enough to be able to take care of themselves. Plus, and more importantly, they were much safer now. In the defensive circle, all of the young were safer than they had ever been in the nests. No razortooth could penetrate their present defenses. None would even think of trying.

Smoking Mountain rumbled throughout the night. Panthrar, who didn't sleep well that night, could see a pulsating glow in the sky, coming from the direction of the angry mountain. The fiery red bloom reflected off of the low-hanging clouds, partially illuminating the valley.

Pippit was also awake at times during the night. Besides the red glow reflecting low in the sky, she saw frequent flashes of lightning in the vicinity of the mountain. The ground shaking, the mountain thundering, mud falling from above, the sky on fire, lightning seemingly coming out of the mountain... All these natural phenomena, joined in affinal kinship with these other, to her, unnatural forces, combined to frighten her more than she had ever been in her life.

Thundermaker also kept a vigil that night. He was as confused as Pippit. In fact, most shared Pippit's bewilderment and anxiety. When he wasn't patrolling, Thundermaker lay between the mountain and his herd, grumbling regularly to himself.

Although it was wet and slippery, it wasn't raining when the herd took up its eastward journey the next morning. This was the fifty-second day since First had fought his way out of his shell. It was gray and overcast, and the hornbrows and threehorns were cold and miserable. They ate as they moved, eating leaves and needles that tasted of volcanic ash. They had to knock the slimy mud off of the plants to get at the leaves, or they pawed at the ground, pushing away the accumulating mess to find something edible.

The young complained less than expected. Although this wasn't like the world into which they had hatched, they really didn't know that this was extremely unusual. So they just took things in stride. The slipping and sliding of the adults, and the occasional crash to the earth of a five ton threehorn, caused them no end of merriment.

The adults didn't accept things quite as easily. They were miserable, and they were frightened. And within an hour after they had started their morning trip eastward, it began to rain again. It was a light, but continuous downpour of water mixed with ash and dust. The rotten egg smell of sulfur permeated the air.

The rumbling and eruptions of Smoking Mountain had chased a lot of creatures out of the hills bordering the main river valley. The razorteeth seemed ever-present. At least one pack of them was always visible to the herd as it traveled east. A lot of the fight seemed to have been taken out of them, temporarily, at least. And best of all, they spotted no ravagers. All the ravagers were probably out on the open plain.

They also saw a prodigious amount of redrunners. These fled the stream valleys in droves. The razorteeth seemed to be more interested in the redrunners as quarry, since they were much smaller than hornbrows, and more defenseless than threehorns. The redrunners were not unaware of this, and used their numbers and their speed to protect themselves from the razorteeth.

In addition to redrunners, there were a few robrunners. These just as frequently traveled with the redrunners as by themselves, as they were closely related. Panthrar had been surprised at first, when they had first arrived in the Valley of the Threehorns, to see so many more redrunners than robrunners. The latter were much more numerous in the Gathering Place than the former. The range of the redrunners must be further north than their cousins.

There were also a good many swiftstealers, and a few eggsnatchers and trailrunners, that had been flushed out of the hills. These agile and gracile creatures managed to keep out of the clutches of the razorteeth for the most part. They also avoided the larger threehorns and hornbrows. Now that there were no eggs to consider, the swiftstealers had no interest in the larger creatures at all, other than to keep out of their way. When they weren't a danger to your young, they were an elegant animal to behold. You could watch them racing across the valley, loping along at high speed, somehow managing to look graceful even when they slid in the mud.

The herd traveled two miles during the morning. Thundermaker accepted that as good progress, so he called a halt until the afternoon, to let the young rest. During the afternoon march, Pippit saw something that she rarely saw, a family of **rockbacks**. She quickly pointed them out to her fledges, and to the threehorn pups traveling with them. The group of rockbacks consisted of an adult male, an adult female, three juveniles, and a brood of ten or twelve recent nestlings. The rockbacks were just waddling out of the mist, traveling on a path that would cross that of Thundermaker's herd. They were on their way down to the river bank, perhaps looking for clean water to drink. They wouldn't find any there, but they wouldn't know that until they got there.

The fledges were really excited by the appearance of the rockbacks. They talked animatedly amongst themselves as the rockbacks drew closer. They noted that the rockbacks were four-footed like the threehorns, but lacked any horns or frills on their heads like the more familiar quadrupeds. They did have horns though. They had horns sticking out parallel to the ground, from the back of their longish necks, across their shoulders, and along their sides. Some of the knobs on their tails were also very horn-like.

The rockbacks had relatively small, narrow heads, with short, plump snouts. When they got closer, the young hornbrows could see that they had broad, horny beaks, like the threehorns, but when one of them yawned, they could see that it had no teeth. This fascinated them, so they discussed it. Threehorns had a sharp, horny beak, which was strong enough to use as a weapon, and they were well-equipped with teeth. Hornbrows also had a beak, and had teeth, many, many of them. Even the fledges had some teeth. Predators had sharp teeth – tearing, slicing, wicked teeth. But the rockbacks didn't seem to have any teeth at all. They did most of their chopping and slicing with their beaks.

The most interesting thing of all about the rockbacks, along with their side-protruding horns, and the thing that occupied the conversation of the fledges for the rest of the afternoon, was the hard stony backs of the rockbacks. Each rockback was armored with an array of bony plates and knobby studs that ran down their backs and flanks in alternating rows. The armor of the adults was most impressive, but even the youngsters were growing body armor.

The adults were large creatures. The adult male was slightly longer than their mother, perhaps 23 feet long. He was also over a ton heavier than their father. He was large, they agreed, as he waddled away on short, stubby legs. His family dutifully followed behind him. The hornbrows called to the young rockbacks, hoping to elicit a response, but they were ignored. The fledges conjectured what a ferocious creature the male rockback must be, and imagined him successfully fighting off the terrible dreadrunners. Dreadrunners – creatures that they had never met, but who they had heard a lot about from their parents. Especially from Pippit.

The herd of threehorns and hornbrows traveled another two miles that afternoon, slowly but steadily sloshing through sodden earth. That evening they browsed for a short while, finding food where they could, before again setting up a defensive circle. By now the herd had grown to almost a hundred adults, due to slower and wrong-way groups joining up with them on the trek out of the valley.

The next day was a repeat of the previous day. They slogged along through rain and mud, covering another four miles. Most of the predators, traveling much faster than they, were long gone – probably out of the Valley of the Threehorns, and working their way across the upper plain.

Still the herd trudged on, going only as fast as the slowest member. The threehorn young couldn't cover more ground than they presently were. And the hornbrow young were perhaps a little slower, always tagging along behind the main herd. But never without the company of the three adult hornbrows. And never without Thundermaker backtracking periodically to check on the status of these other "members" of his herd.

The earth shook intermittently, and stones fell from the sky at random. One adult threehorn female was struck in the head by a large stone falling from the sky. The stone knocked her to the ground, and blood trickled from the wound that the stone had made. Nothing anyone could do could wake her up or get her back on her feet again. After awhile the herd stopped trying to rouse her, and left her where she lay.

It took a lot of coercion to get her young to leave her. Most wouldn't. Foottangler and Rumblerunner, two adult females with small broods, stayed with the body, trying to get the young to leave the fallen body of their mother. Foottangler and Rumblerunner rejoined the herd later that day, when it was already so dark that it was difficult to find one's way. With them were all but two of the fallen female's young. The other two would not leave their mother. The last seen of them, they were lying in the mud before their mother, squeaking and trilling at her great face.

The next day was yet another copy of the last. In the late morning, the herd reached the mouth of the valley as it spilled out onto the upper plain. As they neared the edge of the plain, a large herd of threehorns slowly materialized before their eyes. It was what was left of the herd of juveniles and the herd of bachelors. Many juveniles and adult males had already departed, leaving either with other herds that had escaped the valley before Thundermaker's herd, or who had set out across the plain on their own in small groups. Quickcharger was with the herd, and had managed to collect and keep most of Thundermaker's juveniles and bachelors. These now joined up with Thundermaker's herd. The rest dispersed themselves amongst the other herds with Thundermaker, or with the other herds that escaped the valley that day. Few remained behind past this fifty-fourth day after First's hatching.

Thundermaker did not delay, but immediately set out across the plain, in a southeasterly direction. He was determined to put more distance between his herd and the angry mountain. Near his herd, traveled three other herds that had been traveling with him out of the valley. Two other herds that had been traveling with him out of the valley kept going directly east, more directly away from the Smoking Mountain. Sometime in the unknown future, they would turn south back towards their traditional migration route. But not now. They just wanted to get as far and as fast away from the mountain as they could.

The four herds that remained in proximity with each other, traveled along parallel paths. They didn't go much further before deciding to rest until the afternoon. While the young rested, and all fed as well as they could, Thundermaker took stock of the situation.

His "original" herd numbered roughly thirty adults, fifteen juveniles, and about eighty pups. It also included three adult hornbrows and fourteen fledges. Due to the confusion both in the escape from the valley, and the losses and gains from those that had remained behind in the juvenile and bachelor herds, his herd had actually grown. The "orphans" he had acquired exceeded those that had deserted. He now had over fifty adults, almost thirty juveniles, and well over a hundred pups. Plus the hornbrows. And no one of these disputed his absolute authority over the herd. Least of all the hornbrows.

The four herds traveled about two more miles that afternoon. In the evening, Thundermaker's herd formed a large defensive circle. The three other herds did the same thing nearby. The herds were close enough to communicate with each other, and their defensive patrols merged in some places.

Panthrar and Pippit and Old Solitary again stayed together, near where the fledges clustered in the defensive circle. Pippit made sure that her young were close enough for her to keep an eye on, and to speak to when necessary.

The herd was now over twenty miles from Smoking Mountain, twice the distance they had been when the mountain had first started its angry protestations. They felt somewhat safer. In addition, the ground hadn't shaken in over a day, and either the mountain was rumbling more faintly, or wasn't rumbling at all. Maybe Smoking Mountain had gone back to sleep.

The three adult hornbrows discussed the possibility of this among themselves. Actually, Panthrar and Pippit discussed it. Old Solitary didn't contribute much in the way of meaningful conversion. Then Panthrar changed the subject to something that he had been thinking about for days, during most of the flight out of the Valley of the Threehorns.

"I have been thinking, my wife," he said, as they snuggled together in anticipation of soon falling asleep. Old Solitary lay nearby.

"About what, my husband," prompted Pippit. She nuzzled him affectionately under his neck with the top of her snout.

"Normally the great trek home begins on the sixtieth day after the first egg hatches," said Panthrar.

"This is true," returned Pippit neutrally.

"Our eggs must have hatched soon after most of the eggs laid in the stream valleys near the Gathering Place," continued Panthrar.

Pippit thought about that for awhile. After she had calculated the passage of time, she finally agreed with Panthrar.

"Also," Panthrar went on, "the Gathering Place must be much farther away from the Smoking Mountain than is the Valley of the Threehorns."

"It could be, my husband," said Pippit encouragingly, beginning to suspect where Panthrar was going with his thought process.

Old Solitary finally acknowledged that he was listening to their conversation by interjecting, "No, I don't think so, younger brother. I think that the Gathering Place is the same distance away from Smoking Mountain."

"With all due respect, elder brother, I do not think that you are correct," said Panthrar. "The Gathering Place is many miles south of here."

Panthrar paused to think through the issue again. After a while, he offered, "It is possible that the People weren't frightened away from the Gathering Place by the roaring of the Smoking Mountain like we were."

"Do you think so?" Pippit said excitedly.

"I think they were frightened away," insisted Old Solitary.

"Yes," Panthrar answered Pippit, not quite ignoring Old Solitary. "And if they weren't, that means that they could be at the Gathering Place even now."

"Oh," exclaimed Pippit, "and that would mean that if we traveled due south, we might intercept them as they were leaving the Gathering Place..."

"Yes," nodded Panthrar.

"No," insisted Old Solitary.

"... and then we could travel with the Green Water Roam back across the upper plain," finished Pippit.

"That's what I have been thinking, my wife," confirmed Panthrar.

"I think that the Great Eastern Herd is gone, now," said Old Solitary. "They fled the Gathering Place at the same time, and for the same reasons, that we fled the Valley of the Threehorns."

The two younger hornbrows looked at the old male. Finally Panthrar said, "Elder brother could be right."

Pippit looked disappointed. She gazed southward for awhile, and sighed.

Panthrar added, "And even if elder brother were wrong, it probably wouldn't do us much good anyway. For how could we travel southward by ourselves, with these little fledges to protect? Surely there are many ravagers between here and there."

Old Solitary mumbled, "There must be many ravagers between here and there."

Pippit bowed her head, and stared at the ground before her. Panthrar was sorry he had brought up the whole subject, realizing how disappointed she really was. He silently berated himself for not realizing how this might affect Pippit.

Pippit looked up at Panthrar hopefully, and offered, "Maybe we could get Thundermaker to travel south with us. It would be safer traveling with his herd."

"You are right, my wife, it would be much safer traveling with Thundermaker," agreed Panthrar, "but how could we ever communicate such a complicated request to him, or convince him that it was a good thing to do?"

"It's too complicated for our limited friend," added Old Solitary. "Besides, younger sister, he will want to travel his old familiar path back to his old familiar stomping grounds, even if he wasn't worried about Smoking Mountain spitting fire and stones again."

"You are right, my husband. And you too are right, elder brother," said Pippit after a long sigh. "It is beyond our ability to convey such a complex request to him." She again stared forlornly at the ground before her. Old Solitary looked off in the direction of Smoking Mountain, mumbling quietly to himself.

Suddenly Panthrar felt an insistent poking against his right flank. He looked down to behold First and Second sitting patiently beside him, craning their necks upward to look at him. Several of their siblings were gathered behind them.

"Well, well, my little mud-wallowers," said Panthrar, "what have we here?"

Pippit looked up from her musings, and smiled at her brood. It seemed that all of them were crowding against First and Second, anxious to participate. Even Old Solitary got more alert, and smiled benignly at the little ones – he always seemed to respond most favorably to the children.

"Sun warm you, my fahder," said First and Second in unison, nodding in respect. The entire brood echoed their salutation.

"And may the sun warm you, my children," answered Panthrar.

"Sun warm you, my mudda," they said, nodding to Pippit.

"May the sun keep you all warm," responded their mother.

"Sun warm you, my Ode Sosstry," they said in turn to the older male, again nodding in respect.

"And may the sun keep you in its warm embrace," said Old Solitary with a flourish.

When the formal greetings were over, Panthrar asked, "What service may I perform for you, my little fledges?"

First said, "My fahder, we list'n to you." Then he paused for a moment, collecting his thoughts.

"Yes," said Panthrar encouragingly.

Second added, "You go sout'? You want go sout'?"

Seventh, the most articulate of the offspring, said, "You want to ask Tunnermaker to go south?" Apparently most, if not all, of the brood had been listening to their entire conversation.

"We would like to, my children," answered Panthrar. He spoke slowly and distinctly, so that his fledges would learn the proper pronunciation of the words. "But we do not know how to say the words to him to make him understand. Do you understand?"

"Yes, my fahder," nodded First. They all nodded along with their brother.

"You canna just ask him?" queried Fourth, as if to confirm the notion.

"No, my son, we cannot," answered Panthrar.

"But we do, my fahder" said Second.

"You understand, too?" asked Pippit of her daughter.

"No, my mudda," said Second, who then hastily corrected herself, "Yes, my mudda, we unnerstan. But we speak Roohraru."

"I'm sorry, my daughter, but I did not understand the last word you said," replied Pippit gently. "Could you repeat it?"

"Roohraru..." repeated Second tentatively.

"Roohraru," echoed First.

Old Solitary jumped to his feet in his excitement, startling the fledges, who suddenly cowered back. He approached the little hornbrows. "I am sorry, my children," he said apologetically. "Can it be that I understand you to mean that you speak Roohraru...?"

They all nodded emphatically.

"... And that Roohraru is the tongue of the great threehorns?"

They nodded emphatically again. Seventh said, "We speak Roohraru. It is the tong of the treehorns. Do you not speak it?"

The adult hornbrows exchanged glances. Finally Pippit said, almost in a daze, "No, my son, we cannot speak directly with the threehorns. We cannot speak to Thundermaker."

"But we do, my mudda," repeated Second excitedly.

Without waiting for another response from the adults, the young hornbrows trilled loudly at Thundermaker. The primary male threehorn was standing nearby. He turned his great horned and frilled head in the direction of the hornbrows. The fledges trilled again. Thundermaker sauntered casually over to where the hornbrows lay. He rumbled a friendly greeting to them. It sounded like, "Varoom."

Panthrar replied, "May the sun warm you, Thundermaker." Pippit and Old Solitary also greeted him formally. So did all the fledges, all together, blurting out a greeting in a jumbled and discordant babble of happy voices. "Varrroom," they had said to Thundermaker.

"Thun varm du," responded the great threehorn to the fledges.

"Thun varm du," they cried back happily.

Then First rumbled a long series of notes to Thundermaker. Thundermaker seemed to listen patiently. Then Second added some more rumbles and squeaks. Even Seventh added his squeaks and squeals to the chorus. When Thundermaker began to rumble and squeal back at the young hornbrows, the adult hornbrows stared in wonder, frequently exchanging glances.

Finally First turned to his parents, and said, "T'maker want go away from... from..."

"Smo King Mun Tin," said Seventh helpfully.

"Yes," confirmed First. "He tink Smo King Mun Tin bad."

"Yes," added Second. "But he tink 'bout it. He tell come mornin'."

Thundermaker looked at Panthrar and Pippit in turn. He rumbled a query at them. They just stared at him in shocked silence. Without waiting for an answer, Thundermaker squealed a good-bye, and turned and departed.

Panthrar looked at Pippit. Pippit shuddered slightly. They both looked down at their fledges. The young hornbrows were staring up at their parents jubilantly. Panthrar coughed to clear his throat, and said, "It is a wonderful thing, my children. You have done a wonderful thing."

CHAPTER TWENTY-SIX

OFF THE BEATEN TRACK

THE NEXT MORNING, THUNDERMAKER directed his herd southward. It was not an easy task. None of the other three herds wished to accompany his herd south. They preferred to follow the more traditional route southeastward, which also happened to take them more directly away from Smoking Mountain. The fact that the mountain was now quiescent did nothing to convince the primary males of those other herds that it would remain so. So Thundermaker's herd bid the others goodbye.

If that had been the only obstacle, Thundermaker's herd would have begun the trip southward relatively easily. But it wasn't. A number of dominant males within Thundermaker's own herd didn't agree with the decision to travel south rather than southeast. All of these were newly acquired members, who hadn't yet built up the respect and confidence in Thundermaker that his original herd members had.

When Thundermaker announced his intention to travel directly south to the River of the Nine Tribes, there was a lot of grumbling. A few members actually deserted the herd, and joined up with one or another of the three herds heading on the traditional route. Even so, when Thundermaker began to lead the herd to the south, he was immediately challenged by several males.

Thundermaker condoned no rebellion within his herd. The challengers had three choices: fall in line, leave the herd, or fight for the right to lead. The most dominant challenger, Hugehorns, opted for the latter.

When Thundermaker tried to lead the herd southward, Hugehorns blocked his path. Thundermaker attempted to casually divert around Hugehorns. Hugehorns moved in front of Thundermaker, again blocking his path. Hugehorns made it all too clear that he would not let the herd go south. Thundermaker threatened Hugehorns. Hugehorns returned the threat, and galloped ahead of Thundermaker. He again took up a blocking position. Thundermaker galloped towards Hugehorns to enforce his decision. The rest of the herd waited passively by to find out who would prevail.

Thundermaker and Hugehorns stood displaying at each other about two hundred feet to the south of the herd. They stood about sixty feet apart, swaying their heads from side-to-side. Thundermaker pawed viciously at the ground, snorting fiercely. Hugehorns did likewise. They pawed with their front feet, tearing furrows into the earth. Then they kicked up clods of soil with their hind feet. All the while, they snorted or squeal-roared, making upward thrusting motions with their heads, working themselves up to the excitement level necessary to actually attack each other. Slowly they approached each other. Neither had any intention of being intimidated by simple displays of strength. Both intended to put the other to the test.

As they got closer, they made short charges at each other. When they were only about ten feet from each other, they charged straight at each other, heads crashing, horns locking. Panthrar noted immediately that this was different from the pre-mating dominance fights. Then the males never actually risked hurting each other. At least not intentionally. They always approached each other cautiously, locking horns carefully. This was quite different. The other was simply a method of testing strength and determination, this was a battle for control of the herd. To loose a pre-mating dominance fight simply meant that you lost the opportunity to mate. Disappointing, definitely, but not life-threatening. To loose the present type of dominance fight meant that you lost your right to stay with the herd, and if you were really unlucky, your life as well.

The two dominant males struggled with each other, pushing harder and harder with their hind legs. They pushed against each other so forcefully that their front feet slowly rose up off of the ground. They twisted and turned their heads, trying to throw the other off balance. Their eyes blazed. Their breath came in short, ragged bursts.

Suddenly Hugehorns lost his traction and his left rear foot slipped. He stumbled, jerking his head away from Thundermaker. He quickly regained his feet, and waved his horns at the primary male to protect himself from being impaled in a vulnerable spot. Rather than trying to stab Hugehorns, Thundermaker just stood with four feet splayed, squeal-roaring deafeningly. He wanted to make his point quite clear, without actually harming the other.

Hugehorns backed away, turned and trotted in a wide circle. Eventually the circle culminated where it had begun. Hugehorns again stood facing Thundermaker. The displaying started all over again. Slowly they approached each other, snorting, roaring and squealing. Front and rear feet again tore up great chunks of earth. Heads jerked upward in clear displays of stabbing and ripping motions with their horns. Thundermaker had fire in his eyes. Hugehorns eyes blazed red.

When they were again about ten feet apart, they surged at each other like two great engines of destruction. There was a crashing thud as they struck each other, locking horns.

Thundermaker began to push Hugehorns backwards. Hugehorns tried to brace himself, locking all four legs. At first his position held. Both mighty threehorns strained against each other. Then, ever-so-slowly, Hugehorns began to slide backwards. His front feet began to lift off of the ground. Thundermaker pushed him slowly, but relentlessly backwards. Hugehorns churned his rear legs in a desperate attempt to stop Thundermaker's forward motion. It wasn't working.

Hugehorns lost his nerve. He pulled away from Thundermaker. He backed up rapidly, seeking a safer buffer between himself and Thundermaker. Thundermaker charged after him, causing him to back-peddle all the faster. Finally Hugehorns was able to turn and sprint away. Thundermaker pursued him only a short symbolic distance, and then let him go.

Hugehorns' sprint slowed to a gallop, then to a trot, and finally he stood stock still. He had retreated about five hundred feet. He turned and faced the herd, bellowing his defiance. Then he called to several of his companions who had also challenged Thundermaker. Two other males snorted their dissatisfaction with Thundermaker, and left to join the defeated male. These were quickly followed by two females, each with a small brood of pups in tow. A moment later, three juveniles also broke from the herd and chased after the retreating group, not wanting to be separated from their parents.

Thundermaker stood before his herd. He demanded that any other adult, male or female, who questioned his authority to lead the herd safely, should do so now. Either challenge me, go your own way, or follow me loyally, he demanded. No one else left the herd.

Thus the herd began its southward journey. With Thundermaker traveled forty-six adults, twenty-five juveniles, and almost a hundred pups. And with them, were three adult hornbrows and fourteen fledges. As time passed, each of the adult hornbrows would take turns either traveling with their young, or patrolling the outskirts of the herd with a dominant male, keeping an eye out for ravagers.

*   *   *   *   *

The herd moved slowly southward. It covered about two miles during the morning trek, and another two miles during the afternoon. It passed other valleys that broke the line of hills that bordered the western edge of the plain. From these valleys they beheld a constant exodus of creatures. These were leaving the hills, making for the open plain, putting as much distance as possible between themselves and the Smoking Mountain. They traveled on paths perpendicular to that of Thundermaker's herd. This made traveling a little difficult, since each group or herd had to avoid the other. Yet it was easier going for Thundermaker's herd than for the others. Few creatures wished to dispute the right-of-way with threehorns.

During the day they saw a sizable herd of swiftstealers and eggsnatchers traveling east. The herd passed across the front of Thundermaker's. It was so large that the rear half couldn't complete its passage before Thundermaker's herd reached it. It broke apart creating a wide path for the herd of threehorns to continue on its journey uninterrupted. The half to the east kept moving, while the half to the west stopped and waited for the herd of threehorns to pass. As the tail end of the herd of threehorns went by, the swiftstealers resumed their journey, spilling anxiously close to the threehorns as they hurried to catch up with the lead elements of their herd.

During the noon break, Pippit discerned a small herd of **headcrashers** filing out of a narrow glen and heading into the plain. Headcrashers rarely left the hills and mountains, and frequently kept to themselves, so they were an uncommon sight for everyone. They approached fairly closely, before detouring around to the rear of Thundermaker's herd.

Most of the herd watched their approach with unconcealed curiosity. Headcrashers were strange-looking bipedal vegetarians with short arms, strong hips and legs, and a stiffened tail. They ranged between fifteen and twenty-five feet in length, and up to two tons in weight.

Their strangest aspect was their head. Not their sharp little teeth, nor their small eyes and weak jaws, but their abnormally thickened skull plates with numerous little knobs and horn-like projections ringing the head like a weird crown. They were definitely not built for speed. Instead they butted anything that challenged them. Even so, they did not intimidate the herd of threehorns. Few creatures did. There was a momentary confrontation between the two groups over right-of-way. Then the headcrashers yielded, giving the threehorns a wide berth.

As the days of travel passed, Pippit and Panthrar used the opportunity of the long trek to continue to teach their fledges. They repeated, re-enforced, and elaborated upon lessons already begun, instructing their young in the rich and comprehensive history and culture of the People. The People had an extensive oral tradition that was passed on from generation to generation, often by rote. The fledges made this instruction easy, for they seemed to have an insatiable curiosity about everything. The free-form lessons, following a question-and-answer format, often seemed to twist and turn in all directions.

A short while after the headcrashers had passed, Pippit began the lessons anew. Sixteenth was bragging to Twelfth about their good fortune to be members of Thundermaker's roam. Twelfth insisted that they were not part of Thundermaker's roam. Pippit used that as a starting point.

"Sixteenth is correct, my little fledges," she began, "We are fortunate to be traveling with Thundermaker's roam. And while we are traveling with Thundermaker, we are part of his roam. Thundermaker is the roamleader, and we must do what he requests."

Sixteenth elbowed Twelfth, as if to say, see, I was right.

"But Twelfth is also correct. This is only our temporary home. Our permanent home is the Green Water Roam. You remember about the Green Water Roam, don't you?"

While Twelfth gave Sixteenth an elbow back, the other fledges chimed in, recalling past lessons about the roam.

"Who can tell me who the hornbrows are that are part of the Green Water Roam?" asked Pippit.

First said, "Grendaar is the r'mleader...."

"Yes," confirmed Pippit, "That is right. And what is Grendaar called?"

"Groundshaker!" most yelled, except Seventh, who after a pause, said, "The Ancient One."

Pippit looked at Seventh sternly, and he turned away, and stared at the ground. "That is what Old Solitary told me," he mumbled to himself.

Finally, Fifteenth, with his perpetual smile, said, "And Rohraar is the Second Male...."

Pippit nodded.

"... and Trugahr is the Third Male," added Fourth.

"... and Wubbar is the Fourth Male," said Tenth.

"... and Hew is the Fifth Male," noted Second.

"... and Tessah is the First Female," said Seventeenth proudly.

"... and Monah is the Second Female," said Eleventh, after a pause. And so it went, as the fledges listed all of the adults and adolescents in the roam, all by name, and all in order of hierarchy.

When they were done, First asked, "How did Grendaar become the r'mleader? Is he as brave an' as strong as Tunnermaker?"

Pippit looked over at Panthrar, who took his cue. "A long time ago," he began, "Long before I was hatched, my little fledges, there was another roamleader. His name was Nvraar. Nvraar was a very large, and a very strong roamleader. He was very wise, and he was loved by all the members of his roam. But he was getting very old."

"How ode, my fahder?" asked Fourteenth.

"Very old. Much older than I am now." Panthrar and Pippit smiled as the fledges oohed and aahed, for they thought that their parents were very old.

"How ode are you, my fahder?" queried Second.

"Well, let's see," responded Panthrar. "I have recently passed my fifth spring. I am working on six springs. But Nvraar was much, much older than that. They say he was almost thirty springs."

The fledges looked at each other in amazement. That was older than they could readily conceive of.

Old Solitary, who had been listening carefully, confirmed their amazement. "That is very old, my little fledges," he said. "How old do you think I am?"

"Very, very old," said Seventh.

"That's correct, Seventh, I am very old. I am over twenty-seven springs old."

The fledges oohed and aahed again.

Then Panthrar continued, "In those days, Grendaar was one of the dominant males of the roam, Second Male, in fact. He also happened to be Nvraar's nephew. Grendaar's mother was Nvraar's sister. When Nvraar could no longer lead the roam successfully, Grendaar took over as the roamleader."

"What happened, my fahder?" asked Sixth.

"Legend has it that Nvraar was fighting to protect the roam. They say that he was trying to frighten a dreadcharger away, and was pounding the ground so hard that the earth shook. They say that the dreadcharger was very worried, and that he was about to run away. Then the dreadcharger's mate showed up, and they both killed Nvraar. The roam became very frightened. It was in great disarray, and threatened to scatter. But Grendaar quickly took over, and lead the roam to safety. He held it together through those trying times."

"Is that what really happened, my fahder?" asked Fifteenth.

"It could have, my little fledge. But I think that Nvraar just got too old to guide the roam. You know what happens when a roamleader gets too old to guide the roam, don't you?" Panthrar asked.

He got a mixture of nods, shakes, and blank stares.

"Well, it's the same thing that happens to all old hornbrows. The old one leaves the roam and travels as far to the east as he can," explained Panthrar. "Then he comes to the Great Green Sea. Far out in the Great Green Sea lie the Desolate Islands. The old one walks into the water, and starts to swim. He must swim very far. He swims all of the way to the Desolate Islands. When he gets there, he waits for his turn to be re-hatched into the world again. That is what I think happened."

There was a long pause, while the fledges tried to digest what they had just heard. Finally Second asked, "My mudda, fahder is of the Green Water Roam. What roam do you belong to?"

"I now belong to the Green Water Roam," answered Pippit. "We all belong to the Green Water Roam, and to the Red Dawn Tribe. Before that, I was a packer. And before that, I belonged to the Flat Rock Roam of the White Moon Tribe. You remember, the White Moon Tribe is one of the Nine Tribes."

"Tell us of packers," suggested First.

"Okay, little ones," said Pippit. "As you know, you are all growing. First you were little, mottled eggs. Then you became hatchlings when you cracked the shell. Then you grew to nestlings. You stayed in the nest many days, and grew and grew. And finally, when you left the nest, you became fledges."

There were a lot of nods and smiles, as they were all proud of this accomplishment.

"As you keep growing, you will keep changing, and your needs will change. Six moons after your hatching, there will be the Naming Ceremony. You will receive your other names, and you will pass from fledges to yearlings. Well, there will come a time, many years from now, when you will have grown and changed to the point that some of you will not want to live in a roam any more...."

No, many of them shook their heads in disbelief. It was not a concept that they could quite accept yet, living beyond the protection of the roam.

"It is true. Some of you will want to leave the roam. Must leave the roam, in fact. Mostly young males leave the roam, but sometimes a young female does also. These adolescents then join packs. Packs are like a roam, but there are no yearlings or youngsters. And there are few females. Mostly there are males, adolescent males, and a few adult males. Packers live differently than roam-members. They live wilder, and freer. And during the great treks, they help the herd very much, for they guard it against ravagers."

"Is it good to be a packer, my mudda?" asked Ninth.

"That is something that each of you will have to decide for yourselves. When the right time comes."

"Tell us about solitaries," suggested Seventh.

And so the lesson went on. Sometimes they lasted for only a few minutes. Sometimes they lasted for hours.

* * * * *

On the next day of travel, the sun showed brightly through parting clouds. The dust and the ash had since fallen from the sky, and the water vapor had rained itself out. Smoking Mountain was quiet, and only a bit of smoke and some vapors now drifted from its peak. The peak seemed diminished. It could have been the distance, or the mountain might have blown part of its top off.

This was the fifty-sixth day after First hatched. The fauna that they passed got considerably more numerous and diverse during the day. They crossed the paths of hordes of trumpeters and cresttops and longsnouts. All of these were related to hornbrows, the first two somewhat distantly, the latter more closely.

Panthrar and Pippit talked about the wisdom of leaving Thundermaker's herd, and traveling with the longsnouts. These latter hadrosaurs were closely enough related to the People that they would likely share common words. The hornbrows would also blend in a lot better. But in the end, they decided to remain with Thundermaker. He was not a close relative, in fact his kind were considered extremely alien. But Thundermaker had become a friend. And he was virtually escorting them down to the River of the Nine Tribes to link up with their own kind. It was better to travel with such a friend.

The day progressed with the trumpeters and cresttops being heard for miles. The former could be recognized by their deep bassoon-pitched honks, and the latter by their flute-like toots. What an interesting harmony they made as the two herds traveled in near proximity to each other, signaling back and forth, almost as if each was trying to outdo the other.

Panthrar could not resist the urge to add a hornbrow mid-range honk to the melody, and honked until he was almost hoarse. Soon Old Solitary honked with him, gleefully playing counter-point. Pippit didn't know whether to be proud of Panthrar and Old Solitary, or embarrassed for all the attention they got from the threehorns. Many walked near them just to watch their honking. Some even tried to add their squeal-roars to the growing symphony.

The young ones, both fledges and pups, thought that these renditions were just about the most exciting thing that they had ever heard in their short lives. They imitated the adults, tooting and squeaking along with Panthrar, Old Solitary, and some of the threehorns. Hours passed thus delightfully distracted.

During the day they also saw a group of about fifteen **clubtails** fleeing the hills. These were distantly related to the rockbacks, except that in addition to all the body-armor, enhanced with spikes protruding out from the sides of the body, they also had a bony club at the end of their tails with which to defend themselves. They ranged from twenty to twenty-five feet in length, and two to three tons in weight, and thus were slightly larger and somewhat bulkier than the rockbacks. The fledges reveled over such creatures, and they imagined the clubtails accomplishing all kinds of feats of heroism and daring.

They became even more excited when their mother described to them the **giant clubtails**. These latter were much larger versions of the former, growing to thirty or thirty-five feet in length, and up to four tons in weight. That put them larger, although lighter, than threehorns. This prompted the fledges to imagine all kinds of contests between giant clubtails and threehorns. But in these flights of fantasy, the threehorns always seemed to prevail.

These thoughts and discussions filled the afternoon of the more cerebral of the brood. This was interrupted for only a short while when a herd of **twohorns** momentarily tried to challenge the right-of-way of Thundermaker. Thundermaker and Hidepiercer chased off the smaller horned quadrupeds without too much difficulty, the twohorns deciding that discretion was indeed the better part of valor.

By the end of the day the herd had covered almost five miles. The mountain remained quiescent, and offered little impediment to travel. In addition, the fledges and pups were getting stronger and more inured to daily travel.

They traveled another five miles the next day. That day they passed more trumpeters and longsnouts, as well as many ridgebrows. They also passed a large herd of onehorns. At first the onehorns also wanted to dispute the right-of-way, like the twohorns of the preceding day. Yet in the end, even their much greater numbers gave way to the larger bulk and greater ferocity of the threehorns.

One event marked the fifty-seventh day since First broke his shell as rather different from the preceding day. That event inspired excitement and awe in the pups and fledges, trepidity in the hornbrows, and skittishness in the threehorns.

When Thundermaker's herd first came upon the herd of over two thousand ridgebrows, his inclination was to plow right through it, forcing the ridgebrows to make a path for him, like so many other creatures had done before. Yet as he drew closer, he noticed that the ridgebrows showed no desire to make way for him. Instead they kept pushing forward, moving in a tight bunch, with those in the rear crowding up against those in front. It was only when Thundermaker had gotten very close, and some of the ridgebrows were actually threatened with impalement, that they reluctantly made a path for the threehorns. Even so, it was a tight path, with ridgebrows hurrying past the threehorns both in front of and behind Thundermaker's herd.

Panthrar and Pippit chattered incessantly with the ridgebrows. It was their first chance in a long while to actually speak with a herd of relatives. They were especially interested in knowing if the ridgebrows had seen or knew of the movements of the Great Eastern Herd. The ridgebrows could offer no information about the Herd, encouraging or otherwise. But they did pass on useful information.

As the ridgebrows passed before and around him, Thundermaker looked curiously at the anxiety clearly written on their faces. Somehow he suspected that their fear wasn't due to their passing so close to the deadly horns of him and his herd, although it should have been the reason. Finally the herd of ridgebrows cleared his herd, and moved onward to the east. For the first time, Thundermaker had an opportunity to see what lay behind the herd of ridgebrows. It was then that he learned what the hornbrows already knew. Stalking the herd of ridgebrows, at a distance of some half a mile away, were a number of dreadrunners. The dreadrunners were hunting the ridgebrows singly or in pairs, as dreadrunners were wont to hunt. Thundermaker stopped to look, while his herd continued its leisurely trek southward. Spread out in a wide arc to the west were six adult dreadrunners.

Thundermaker ambled casually to the west, accompanied by Hidepiercer. They moved at an unhurried pace, placing themselves between the dreadrunners and their herd. Quickcharger took the lead, guiding the rest of the herd to the south. Four of the new dominant males also joined Thundermaker and Hidepiercer, re-enforcing the defense. Thundermaker calculated the odds. They weren't good. He snorted nervously as he and his party of five dominant males traveled slowly towards the south, but well to the west of the main herd. They always kept themselves between it and the dreadrunners.

The dreadrunners stirred at the sight of the threehorns. Those farther to the north, one pair and a single hunter, skirted comfortably around the herd of threehorns, and continued their pursuit of the ridgebrows. The three dreadrunners closer to the herd stared in cold interest at the threehorns. They watched as Thundermaker and his compatriots gathered themselves as a buffer against the dreadrunners. Then first the pair, and next the other solitary hunter, cautiously approached the male threehorns.

Thundermaker was not ready to stand and fight. Instead he kept his group, which formed a kind of rear-guard, between the ravagers and the herd. The rear-guard slowly followed after the herd as it made its escape. Periodically he and his males would stop and face the ravagers, trying to discourage them from stalking the herd. They would paw the ground, making threatening gestures at the dreadrunners. Or they would make short charges at them. One favorite strategy was to turn sideways and let the dreadrunners see the silhouette of their mighty horns against the sky. They would stab their horns upward, showing the ravagers just what was in store for them if they came too close to the herd.

This kept the dreadrunners at bay, but they still returned displays of their own, showing that they were not intimidated. Rarely did they roar, but they frequently hissed mightily. The hisses were long, loud rushes that penetrated the balmy summer air. The hisses could be heard for miles, sending shudders through the frames of most who heard them.

Often one or another of the ravagers would open its jaws, displaying a fearsome array of lethal weaponry. When hunting smaller game, dreadrunners most often executed a proficient death-bite, killing their prey quickly and efficiently. When hunting threehorns, the dreadrunners most often used their teeth instead as slashing weapons, not risking the time necessary to execute the death-bite. If they could hurt a threehorn sufficiently with a sudden darting attack, they did not really need to kill it outright. They would just wait for it to bleed to death, or kill it later, when loss of blood had seriously weakened it.

The darting, slashing attack was how dreadrunners preferred to kill threehorns. And full-grown hadrosaurs. A smaller, younger hadrosaur, they might try to kill outright, riding it to the ground, and eventually delivering the death-bite in the back of the neck. A threehorn was a much more difficult opponent to overcome. Apparently Long-tail's killing of Eager-runner showed a proficiency that few dreadrunners had mastered, or would even attempt. But a slashing wound or two could ultimately vanquish even a threehorn. The threehorns knew this, and they knew what the dreadrunners were saying to them when they displayed the stabbing weapons so often.

The dreadrunners appeared unhurried, but once or twice they themselves made quick charges at the threehorns, either directly at Thundermaker, who was the obvious leader, or obliquely to the side as if to outmaneuver the guardians of the herd. Each time, the threehorns would spread out to block the ravagers.

The dreadrunners tracked the threehorns at a safe distance for about thirty minutes. By then they began to tire of the deadly game they were playing. The pair gave up first, and diverted back to the more serious pursuit of the ridgebrows. The ridgebrows were far easier prey than were the threehorns. A short while later the solitary hunter also gave up, and headed back towards the herd of ridgebrows.

On the next day, First's fifty-eighth day, Thundermaker's herd traveled almost six miles, reaching the banks of the River of the Nine Tribes that evening. During the early part of that day, they had passed yet more hadrosaurs. There were ten or twelve dreadrunners following a herd of over four thousand ridgebrows. The herd of ridgebrows also included several hundred cresttops, who stayed close to the others for mutual protection. Six or eight of the dreadrunners continued to stalk the ridgebrows, but four of the dreadrunners apparently felt that the much smaller herd of threehorns, mixed with a few hornbrows, made an easier target.

Thundermaker and his dominant males again formed a buffer between the ravagers and the herd. As the day progressed, Thundermaker and the others displayed more and more dramatically, trying to convince the ravagers to hunt elsewhere. It had no effect upon the hunters, who followed the herd at about a half mile distance throughout the day. By evening, it was a skittish group that reached the banks of the river. The dreadrunners were clearly visible only a short distance behind them.

Panthrar and Pippit knew even before they reached the river that a great body of hornbrows had passed by a day or two earlier. A mile wide path of churned up earth and cleanly stripped vegetation bordered each side of the river, testament to the passage of a very large body of the People. It could only be the Great Eastern Herd.

Pippit and Panthrar tried hard not to show their disappointment to their offspring. It was a bitter thing to realize that they had missed the Great Eastern Herd by only a day or two, and most of the fledges picked up on their parents' frustration anyway.

Meanwhile, Old Solitary seemed not the least bit concerned. There were times when Panthrar was convinced that the old male didn't even know where they were going, and just tagged along for the company. He loved to be with the fledges, and traveled beside them often. Panthrar was happy for that, for the prospects of one more adult being available to protect them if they needed it. Yet he was never sure if Old Solitary would really protect the fledges or not, if he was ever confronted with a life-threatening situation. Panthrar was equally unsure as to whether or not the old male would recognize a life-threatening situation if one bumped him on the head.

Then there was the issue of what Thundermaker would do next. That he had escorted them to the River of the Nine Tribes was nearly miraculous. It had only been accomplished because the fledges could speak directly with the threehorns. In fact, these days they were conversing with most of the herd on a continuing basis. But could they intervene on their own behalf again? And with four dreadrunners prowling the edges of the defensive circle at this very moment, would Thundermaker view such a request in his own herd's best interests? That was difficult to know. It was probably too much to hope for that he would now help them to catch up to the herd that lay only five or ten miles to the east.

Panthrar and Pippit discussed options late into the evening. The fledges listened quietly, and occasionally even offered opinions and advise to their patient and tolerant parents. The fledges were growing up fast. The males were now some 37 inches long and 130 pounds in weight, while the females were 31 inches long and 95 pounds in weight. In a month, the males would be 48 inches long and 255 pounds on the average, and the females would be 39 inches long and 190 pounds in weight. And they were getting stronger, if not yet sleeker. But they were growing up in other ways, too. They were learning more words, and pronouncing them better. Just as importantly, they were learning from direct experience a little more about the real world around them. First and Second promised to lead a contingent to Thundermaker in the morning to see if he would help them make their way the last remaining distance to the Great Eastern Herd.

With that issue resolved as well as it could be for the moment, Panthrar and Pippit snuggled closer to each other, and prepared to fall asleep. The herd was in a relatively tight defensive circle. Thundermaker or Hidepiercer, each with two or three other dominant males, took turns either patrolling the perimeter, or standing in place between the dreadrunners and the herd. The dreadrunners had made no attempt at stealth, and were congregated about a quarter of a mile upriver from the herd of threehorns. They made no overt moves against the herd, and seemed to be preparing to go to sleep. Perhaps they intended to attack the herd later, near daybreak.

Appearances notwithstanding, either Thundermaker or Hidepiercer, with their companions, stood between the dreadrunners and the herd, keeping watch. No one really believed that the night would be without its dangers, but until the dreadrunners tried stealth and disappeared from the threehorn's view, the superior detection capabilities of the hornbrows weren't needed.

This allowed Panthrar and Pippit, and Old Solitary to the extent that he was useful, to at least start the night by sleeping.

Panthrar was just dozing off when Old Solitary, who had been quiet all evening, spoke to him. "Are you awake, younger brother?" he asked.

"Just barely, elder brother," responded Panthrar groggily. "How may I be of service to you?" Pippit, who could fall asleep faster than Panthrar, stirred enough to assure herself that all was well, and then fell deeper into sleep.

"Do you think that the fledges can convince the threehorned one to take us to the Red Dawn Tribe?" queried Old Solitary.

Panthrar looked at the old male though half closed eyes. Old Solitary's eyes seemed brighter and more lucid than usual. Panthrar struggled to wake back up. "I hope so," he said.

"The Smoking Mountain is not asleep," said Old Solitary after another moment. It seemed like a change of subject.

"I wouldn't know, elder brother," yawned Panthrar, trying to remain polite and attentive to the older one, while wanting desperately to get some sleep before the dreadrunners made their move.

"I do know, younger brother. For I have talked to the mountain. It is just pretending to be asleep." Old Solitary looked at Panthrar meaningfully. "It does not want to die. But it will. And many others will die. I among them."

Panthrar was now awake. He stared at Old Solitary carefully. Was the old one ranting again? He seemed to be so lucid only a moment ago. "We will all die some day," he said, trying to placate the old fellow.

Old Solitary returned the stare unflinchingly, almost coldly. "Do you think I am crazy, younger brother?" he asked calmly, almost wearily.

Panthrar searched for an answer. He contemplated the old male's brittle, broken horn. Before he could reply, Old Solitary continued.

"Smoking Mountain will die. A violent death. And I will die. A violent death. You must get the fledges away from the mountain."

Panthrar was perplexed. He looked steadily at the old male. "But we are away from the Smoking Mountain, elder brother. Much further away than when it was throwing fire and stones into the sky."

Old Solitary shook his head, and said, "We are still too close. And the mountain cannot pretend forever to be asleep. It will awaken." Old Solitary could tell that Panthrar was not convinced. He paused, choosing his words, "I know you Panthrar the Swift, of the Green Water Roam, of the Red Dawn Tribe. I know you well."

Panthrar just nodded his head, not sure what to say. The old male didn't seem to mind. He went on. "I know you Panthrar the Swift," he repeated. "Son of Tessah of the Green Water Roam."

Panthrar was surprised. How could this old solitary know that Tessah was his mother. He had never told him that. Had Pippit?

"You have her eyes. And her coloring," mused Old Solitary.

"You know Tessah?" asked Panthrar.

"She is a beautiful female, your mother," said Old Solitary as if Panthrar hadn't spoken. "I have thought that she was the most beautiful female in the entire Great Eastern Herd ever since I first noticed her."

"Thank you, elder brother," said Panthrar falteringly, for the old male didn't even know that he was there.

"I think that I first saw her some fourteen years ago, when she was still just an adolescent." He gazed off into the distance, recalling the moment as if it had occurred only recently. He smiled. "Even then she was beautiful. Fresh, vibrant, special. I wanted her even then. But I had to wait until she had come of age."

Again he paused. Then he sighed. The old male struggled with his memories. "Yes, I loved Tessah even then. So I waited another year. It was not easy, for I always saw her face before me. I was young, too, although much older than she. And although I was not able to see her all that often, her face floated before me always. And the thought of her lifted me up. The year passed."

He frowned. "Others were becoming interested. But I waited the year, sure that I could win her. Then another came along. Another... " he trailed off, almost bitterly.

Panthrar lay there staring at Old Solitary, who suddenly seemed so much older, so much more frail, so much more vulnerable. He had felt the quiet passion in the old male's voice. Panthrar reflected. He had heard that his mother had inspired such passions. But he had never met someone, other than Grendaar, who actually spoke of her thus.

Old Solitary lay there, quietly, lost in his own thoughts. After a long while, when Panthrar had thought that perhaps he had fallen asleep, and when Panthrar himself was again dozing, Old Solitary mumbled, perhaps to himself, "We must save the fledges. Tessah would want that."

CHAPTER TWENTY-SEVEN
ON AND OFF THE TRAIL

THE DREADRUNNERS ATTACKED AT dawn. Panthrar was awakened by the warning squeal of a dominant male threehorn. Jumping to his feet, he directed Pippit to stay with the fledges, while he and Old Solitary rushed to help with the defense of the herd. Pippit called to her young. As they clustered about her, she counted, calling off names in order.

Panthrar and Old Solitary hurried towards the west, where male threehorns stood squeal-roaring. Six dreadrunners were advancing towards the defenders. All six of the dreadrunners seemed to be working in concert. They rushed at the four threehorns presently blocking their path, running low and horizontal, hissing as they came. The shrill hissing was intimidating, and Hidepiercer and his group backed before the ferocious onslaught of the six charging ravagers.

Thundermaker and his group, who had been napping on the periphery of the herd, rushed to the aid of Hidepiercer and his group. The dreadrunners rushed in amongst Hidepiercer's group before Thundermaker arrived, causing a momentary panic. The threehorns scattered, trying to avoid the slashing claws and ripping jaws of the ravagers. The padded feet of the threehorns thundered and dust swirled as they dodged about trying to avoid the lightning movements of the dreadrunners.

A dreadrunner ran beside Hidepiercer as he tried to escape. It leaned down and ripped at him savagely. Although he stutter-stepped and twisted, trying to avoid the jaws of the pursuing ravager, the dreadrunner followed every move. Its teeth found leather-hard hide, and softer underlying flesh. Hidepiercer jerked away in pain, not quite avoiding the slashing teeth. He received a ragged, foot long wound to his left flank.

Hidepiercer swung around, trying to impale his attacker with his horns. The dreadrunner braked hard, feet sliding. Then he jumped back, trying to avoid Hidepiercer's horns. The dreadrunner was not quite fast enough. Hidepiercer stabbed at him, his horns penetrating armored flesh. But the dreadrunner was quick, his reflexes were exceptional. He managed to jump back only a split second too late to avoid the horns altogether. He received a superficial nick on his thick-skinned belly. He roared at Hidepiercer angrily. Then he turned and bolted away. In the momentary lull, Hidepiercer tried to examine his wound. It wasn't debilitating. He would get a female to lick it clean later.

Thundermaker pounded past Hidepiercer, the ground shaking as he accelerated by. He chased Hidepiercer's erstwhile attacker, until he saw that Quickcharger was in distress. He abandoned the rapidly retreating ravager, and instead went rushing to Quickcharger's assistance.

Quickcharger was backing as rapidly as he could away from two dreadrunners that were trying to attack him from both sides at the same time. Quickcharger swung his horns desperately back and forth, trying to discourage the dreadrunners, while they closed in upon him relentlessly.

One of the attackers had skirted most of the defenders, and was making directly for the defensive circle. Panthrar and Old Solitary had been trying to provide what assistance they could, while staying out of the way of both the jaws of the attackers and the horns of the defenders. They stood in classic defensive stances, watching the dreadrunners, tooting warnings and directions to the threehorns. Suddenly, they found that they were the only ones between the dreadrunner and the herd of females and young.

Panthrar honked an alarm. He and Old Solitary had spread out so that they could each use their tail to better advantage, yet they were close enough to support each other. Their tails began to arc rapidly back and forth. Panthrar leaned forward. He could see the dawn sun glistening red off of the fearsome teeth of the charging dreadrunner. It was now close enough that he could see its eyes savage with deadly intent. Panthrar's breath was coming in quick, ragged gasps. He steeled himself for the ordeal ahead.

Old Solitary pawed the ground with his right foot. He reached down and filled both hands with dirt. He would throw the dirt into the eyes of the dreadrunner when he got close, hoping that would give him an advantage. The dreadrunner, jaws fully extended, ran straight for Old Solitary, the larger of the two hornbrows. Panthrar had a flashing thought that Old Solitary's prediction about his death was about to come true.

Panthrar angled himself so that he could attack the ravager as it attacked Old Solitary. The dreadrunner came swiftly. Old Solitary stood firm, knowing that the killer was coming for him. At the last moment, and only fifty feet from Old Solitary, the dreadrunner stopped short. He roared furiously, then sprang away to the left and towards the melee with the threehorns. Panthrar and Old Solitary exchanged glances. They had come that close to possible death.

Thundermaker bellowed mightily, and charged for the dreadrunner on Quickcharger's right. Hidepiercer, who was now right behind Thundermaker, charged for the dreadrunner on Quickcharger's left. On hearing Thundermaker's challenge, both dreadrunners looked around, startled. They sprang away to avoid the yearning horns of the defenders.

Thundermaker slowed to a stop. He swung his head about, snorting ferociously. He watched as all six dreadrunners loped away on an unhurried retreat. Satisfied that they were really retreating, Thundermaker turned back to the herd to assess the damages. It was only then that he saw that one of the other dominant males was down. He trotted briskly over to his fallen comrade to determine how badly he was wounded.

A hasty inspection told him that it was indeed serious. In the confusion right at the beginning of the attack, Headknocker had been assaulted the way the dreadrunners had also tried to attack Quickcharger. With Headknocker they had been more successful. The dominant male had been ripped on both flanks. One wound was only a minor cut, but the other was a three foot long gash from which blood was flowing profusely.

Almost as soon as Thundermaker arrived at his side, Headknocker struggled to his feet. Headknocker snorted and winced in pain, staring bright-eyed as his companions. They stood watching him as he weaved about, almost falling. He tried to walk, wobbling uncertainly as his head seemed to spin in circles.

Several females came over to support him, and to help attend to his wound. Among the females that came to help was Roundfrill, Foottangler, Rollypolly, and Raggedtail. Roundfrill attended to Hidepiercer. The other females attended to Headknocker. They soon learned that the wound on Headknocker's left flank was too deep. It wasn't going to be possible for the females to staunch the flow of blood.

Thundermaker eyed the dreadrunners, who themselves stood about a thousand feet away, curiously watching the threehorns. Thundermaker decided to not waste any time. He immediately roused his herd, placing Quickcharger in charge. The herd moved away from where the dreadrunners had retreated up river, marching directly into the rising sun. The yellow-orange orb was a bright, hot ball that promised a warm, sunny day. Quickcharger led the herd along the north bank, following the river downstream.

Meanwhile, Panthrar, who had been standing with the adult male threehorns surveying Headknocker, hurried back to his mate and their brood. Except for the knowledge of Headknocker's probably fatal wound, he would have been happy. He had survived his first real "contest" with a dreadrunner, and he hadn't run away. Neither had Old Solitary. Considering how frightening a dreadrunner could be, he realized that said a lot about himself, and about Old Solitary. What's more, he smiled to himself, Thundermaker's herd was traveling east, along the path of the Great Eastern Herd. At least for the moment.

Headknocker stumbled along behind the herd, supported on one side by Foottangler, and on the other side by Raggedtail. Rollypolly followed behind. Headknocker moved very slowly. His wound was painful, but he moved in stoic silence. If he was lucky, he might survive his wounds. More than likely though, he wouldn't. It didn't look good for him.

Behind him came Hidepiercer. Hidepiercer was escorted by Roundfrill, who periodically attended his wound by licking it clean. Eventually the saliva would help the blood congeal. Hidepiercer knew that his wound wasn't that serious, and if allowed a few days, he would be okay. He knew that his herd would make sure that he got those few days to recover.

Hidepiercer was anxious to re-join the herd. So, with Roundfrill in tow, he sped up and detoured around Headknocker's entourage. The extra activity caused his wound to start bleeding again, but he wouldn't stop to let Roundfrill clean it until he had reached the front of the herd to join up with Quickcharger.

Behind Headknocker and his attendant females, trailed Thundermaker and six other males. They intended to keep the dreadrunners at bay while the herd escaped. Thundermaker could see that Hidepiercer was well enough that he could run for his life, if need be. That was good. He could also see that Headknocker was in a poor way, and couldn't run at all. That was bad.

The dreadrunners followed at a leisurely pace. Once or twice they got threateningly close, but it was only to re-assure themselves that one of the threehorns was indeed seriously wounded. They knew a killing wound when it was delivered, and knew that it was now just a matter of time. They would not unnecessarily risk the horns again.

Towards mid-morning Headknocker stumbled and fell. The three females that attended him could barely get him to rise. He struggled to his feet, wincing from the pain of his wounds. He stood weaving back and forth for awhile, swinging his great head about, barely seeing his nearby companions. It was clear that he was nearing the end of his endurance.

Headknocker took up his final journey once more. He was able to take only a few more steps, when he stumbled and fell again. He lay where he had fallen, breathing in ragged gasps. The females pushed against him, trying to help him to his feet. They could not get him to rise again. Thundermaker and the other males talked with him at length, encouraging him, but he could not be made to get back to his feet.

Impatiently, the dreadrunners inched closer and closer, as Headknocker slowly bled to death.

Meanwhile, the rest of the herd continued to move eastward, pulling farther and farther away from the dreadrunners.

Thundermaker and his males refused to abandon Headknocker while he was still alive. Headknocker's eyes slowly closed, yet he continued to breath fitfully.

Both curious and impatient, the dreadrunners came perilously close to the fallen male and his protectors. When the dreadrunners got too close, the threehorns displayed aggressively against them. The dreadrunners hissed frightfully, trying to chase off the threehorns. The threehorns turned and charged at the ravagers. The dreadrunners backed away rapidly. They were still not willing to risk the horns of the quadrupeds unnecessarily. It would seem that this reversal of their behavior was astounding. But it was really quite sensible. When they were hungry, and needed to kill, they were extremely bold. Now that food was relatively certain, they were not willing to take any chances at all.

After another hour, Headknocker was fading quickly. Even so, the dreadrunners were loosing their patience. Finally they circled around the defending males and females, and it appeared as if they intended to follow the herd. Thundermaker knew that he could not risk the herd to stay by one dying comrade. If the dreadrunners ever penetrated the defenses and attacked the pups, the effect could be disastrous. The dreadrunners seemed to know this also, as they played brinkmanship with the threehorns.

Thundermaker made his final farewells to his unconscious friend, and bid the others do the same. Then he sent them back to the herd. Slowly Thundermaker walked away from his herd-mate, knowing that shortly the dreadrunners would return. Headknocker, in shock and unconscious, would soon be dead.

Thundermaker trotted back to the herd. The dreadrunners avoided him, and instead returned to the carcass of the fallen threehorn.

Thundermaker noticed two things as he finished the last bit of distance back to the herd by galloping. The first was that the vegetation was sparse this close to the river. After almost twenty thousand hornbrows and probably an equal number of fledges had passed by, that was not so surprising. He decided to cross the river as soon as he could, hoping that there were better foraging conditions on the other side.

The dearth of vegetation made him think. It was a great herd to be sure, this Great Eastern Herd of hornbrows. He had seen it many times in his travels, mostly in the spring or summer, sometimes in the fall. But he had never gotten very close to it. It was so large that he had never tried to penetrate it like he had done to so many other herds. He suspected that he could get lost on the inside of it if he did try to pass through it. He was sorry that he had missed it thus far this summer, but he might yet see it before the summer was out. For the sake of his hornbrow friends, he hoped that he would.

The other thing that Thundermaker noticed was that a band of about fifteen or twenty razorteeth was paralleling his herd, about a quarter of a mile to the north. He hadn't noticed them before. If they closed in, he knew that they would be looking for an opportunity to incapacitate a juvenile or a pup or fledge, more likely one of the latter. But they wouldn't attack during the day, unless they were presented with a target that they couldn't resist. He'd have to make sure that didn't happen.

In the middle of the afternoon, the herd found a place where the river could be crossed. Most of it was fordable, but the herd would have to swim for a short distance. They would have to be careful with the pups and fledges, but this would be a good learning experience for them. It took over an hour for the herd to cross, primarily because each mother took the time to show her brood the best places to step, and the best technique for swimming.

Being the smallest, the pups and fledges had the farthest to swim. They swam naturally, without appreciable fear of the water. This was a good time to learn something that would come in handy many times in their lives. Swimming was an effective technique for escaping from ravagers. For although ravagers were also good swimmers, four-footed swimmers could swim faster, and could maneuver much more quickly, than the tiny-fore-limbed ravagers.

Panthrar, Pippit, and Old Solitary actually swam back and forth several times each, following beside the fledges, coaxing and encouraging them to keep their heads up, and their four limbs churning water. It was probably more of an ordeal to the parents than to the fledges, as the latter thought it was a wonderful game. Once across, they wanted to do it again, going back in the other direction. The adults wouldn't let them do that, and the herd continued eastward along the southern bank of the river.

Shortly after the herd had finished crossing the river, the band of razorteeth also crossed at the same ford. As the last razortooth pulled herself out of the water and shook herself dry, Smoking Mountain began to rumble again. The razortooth looked back in the direction of the mountain. Large volumes of smoke and gas and ashes were once more spewing into the sky. She shuddered, and quickly followed after her band.

That night the razorteeth visited the defensive circle. They prowled just within the edge of vision, completely circumnavigating the herd several times. That both the hornbrows and the threehorns knew that they were there didn't seem to concern them. They could see that the circle could not be breached, so they made no attempt at stealth. Instead, after they were finished with their inspection, they went in search of easier prey.

The next day was First's sixtieth day. He and Second had talked to Thundermaker several times as the opportunities presented themselves. So it did not surprise them when, as Thundermaker's herd again took up the trek, it proceeded eastward along the south bank of the River of the Nine Tribes.

Smoking Mountain grew more active during the day. Twice it shook the ground so violently that it caused the herd to huddle together in fear. Once its vibrations were so violent, that it was felt even as far away as the escarpment, where great chunks of rock broke off and crashed down into the jungle at its feet. The columns of smoke and ash that had begun the day before, drifted over the plain, again obscuring the sun. A dark nimbus soon blanketed the sky. It got cooler, and shortly before noon, rain began to fall. The rain started as a messy drizzle, water vapor heavily laden with dust and ash. As the day progressed, the rain became more intense. By evening, it had become a steady downpour.

In the drizzle of early afternoon, dreadrunners appeared on the north side of the river. Panthrar first detected them. He thought that he could see dark bipedal forms moving swiftly in the hazy rain across the wide river. He alerted Pippit, who confirmed that they were indeed dreadrunners. It was possible that they were the same ones that had attacked the morning before, but now there were five of them. Old Solitary noted that they must have been starving to have consumed the carcass of a threehorn so quickly, and to again feel the need to hunt. He believed that they were another group, following the trail left by the Great Eastern Herd, searching for the weak and the stragglers.

Panthrar went to tell Thundermaker that ravagers were paralleling the north bank of the river. Thundermaker quickly turned his herd away from the river, hoping that they had not been spotted by the ravagers. Slowly the herd climbed a nearby ridge, slipping and sliding in the mud. Small mudslides shimmied and struggled their way down the sides of the ridge.

At length, the herd crested the promontory and disappeared behind it. Thundermaker kept traveling south for almost a mile, before he again turned east. It was hoped that between their evasive moves and the thickening rain, that even if the dreadrunners had seen them, they wouldn't be able to track them down.

The herd covered six miles that day, but it wasn't six miles of truly forward progress. Panthrar could only hope that the Red Dawn Tribe was traveling more slowly. The signs that the Great Eastern Herd had traveled this way were growing more evident with each passing day. Even the rain could not hide the trail. He could only hope that this meant that Thundermaker's herd was gaining on the Great Eastern Herd. He fidgeted when they had to deviate away from a direct path, but he too didn't want to run into ravagers again. So he kept his frustrations to himself. Pippit seemed to have her hands full as it was, watching after fourteen active fledges. And Old Solitary, whose mind seemed to wander more and more, often totally forgot that they were trying to catch up to the Herd.

Thundermaker's herd stayed in a defensive circle all that night. Some time after midnight, the band of razorteeth returned, and prowled the outskirts, looking for some advantage or opportunity to exploit. They stayed for hours, keeping away from the occasionally patrolling threehorn. Well before dawn, they disappeared.

For the next two days the herd continued eastward, paralleling the river, but about a mile to its south. Occasionally the ground would shake, but never enough to impede progress. Rain poured frequently – the messy, muddy rain of ash and grim.

Traipsing through mud seemed to be becoming a way of life. Gone were the halcyon days of late spring when Pippit and Panthrar tended their nest and raised their little nestlings, when the days were bright and cheery, the nights were warm and starlit, and the rain only lasted long enough to keep the vegetation green. Now the days were cool, dark, and wet; and the nights were cold, black and miserable. The unusual conditions had a darkening effect upon the spirits of the herd, as they trudged torpidly eastward. The rain and the mud made for slow going, but it helped keep them hidden from ravagers.

Each night, though, the razorteeth seemed to find them. And each night the razorteeth tried in vain to find a weakness in the defensive circle. They would prowl the periphery of the herd, sometimes for a few minutes, sometimes for a few hours, before going off to look for easier prey.

At dawn on the sixty-third day after First's hatching, the razorteeth were still circling the defensive circle, when suddenly they fled past the herd toward the east. Their hasty departure should have aroused the suspicions of the herd to possible danger, but it didn't. The razorteeth had been prowling in the vicinity of the herd for too long now, and their departures were often abrupt. This time it was for a reason.

Five dreadrunners came charging out of the gloaming darkness in the west. They ran low and fast, not quite at a full speed, right past the patrolling threehorn. The tardy sentry twirled around and without thinking to squeal a warning, charged after the dreadrunners.

The five represented a hunting pair, and three solitary hunters. They were not quite working together, for pack hunting was not a favored tactic of this kind of ravager. Yet even as they approached the defensive circle, they all roared, and the roars were almost in unison.

Threehorns and hornbrows sprang to their feet in startled confusion. Those closest to, and facing the attack, saw five dreadrunners, mouths agape, hissing voluminously, coming their way. Before any kind of an organized defense could be mustered, members of the circle panicked. Threehorns began to scatter away from the charging dreadrunners, and suddenly a stampede ensued.

Pippit and Panthrar, assisted by Old Solitary, tried to keep their fledges between them, as they too ran for their lives. Fledges and pups cried in fear, running between lumbering giants that were potentially just as deadly to the little ones as any ravager was. Juveniles squealed in panic, following any likely adult that looked like it knew what it was doing. Adults just ran for their lives, some seeking the protection of numbers, others feeling safer away from other tempting targets. Female threehorns, the maternal instinct stronger than that of self-preservation, herded pups before them, turning to face a charging dreadrunner only if necessary to deflect an imminent attack. Some dominant males tried short delaying tactics of a sort, but they were ineffective before five hungry and determined ravagers.

The hunting pair brought down an old, childless female, who had been running interference for a mother and her brood. They cut her out of the herd, and continued paralleling her, one on each side, as she sprinted in panic. In concert, they slashed her on both sides. One of the pair, the one with a gnarled paw, succeeding in hamstringing her. She crashed to the ground in a heap, plowing mud as she slid to a halt. Avoiding her horns, the other of the hunting pair of dreadrunners, the female with the longish tail, was able to mortally wound the old female threehorn behind the neck. The unfortunate old female died soon thereafter.

One of the solitary hunters mortally wounded a young juvenile. He managed to leap successfully onto the back of the fleeing threehorn, and rode it to the ground. A deft death-bite quickly ended the struggles of the youngster.

Then the herd was away and running, clear of immediate danger. Thundermaker and several of the other dominant males mustered a fighting retreat, which prevented the other dreadrunners from making additional kills. While the dreadrunners fought over the successful kills, the herd slipped into the hazy rain, and disappeared.

After a short sprint in the mud, the herd slowed dramatically. It coalesced. It finally drew to a halt, exhausted from its efforts to escape. Males swung their heads left and right, streams of condensation spraying from their nostrils as they snorted from fatigue and fear. They searched wide-eyed for possible pursuers, as females collected and counted their young. By some miracle, Pippit found all fourteen of her young, although not all had managed to stay with the adult hornbrows during the stampede. Some had joined up with pups and their mothers in the flight from the dreadrunners. Yet all had somehow gotten through the ordeal.

While he caught his breath, Thundermaker had time to wonder if perhaps the reason they were encountering so many ravagers was because they were traveling along the "green band" that bordered the river. The green band, which now was no longer very green, traditionally attracted hadrosaurs. The hadrosaurs moved in great herds. The great herds in turn attracted disproportionate numbers of ravagers. Great herds could protect themselves from so many predators, or at least the relative losses did not seem so great. Not so with a small herd of threehorns.

Certainly Thundermaker was not used to suffering so many ravagers out on the open plain, where he traditionally traveled. There was less food to browse out on the open plain, but there were also fewer ravagers. As the stragglers and lost of the herd slowly filtered back, answering the squeal-roars of the leaders, Thundermaker pondered the wisdom of continuing the eastward journey. Perhaps southward out onto the open plain was better.

While the herd coalesced, he weighed each alternative. In the end, he lead the herd first towards the river, and then east again, along the southern bank. It was not blind friendship that prompted his decision, although he did feel friendship, and a kind of kinship, for the stalwart hornbrows that had spent so many months and shared so many tribulations with him and his herd. Nor was it sympathy for the lost hornbrows, although he, like all herbivores, was keenly aware of the importance of the herd in protecting the individuals. He wanted to help his bipedal friends, but in the end he reached his decision based upon much more pragmatic grounds. With the sun and the stars blocked for hours, and sometimes for days at a time, and with the horizon and familiar landmarks often lost in the grimy rain, he was simply afraid of getting lost if he strayed too far from the one still clearly identifiable landmark – the river.

So a direction certain was preferable to traveling around in circles. Both were likely to be equally as dangerous in these unusual times. For even ravagers could get lost in these conditions. Maybe it was just as dangerous out on the open plain at the moment, as it seemed to be near the river. He couldn't be sure, but still he decided that is was best to stay close to the river. With that conclusion, he led his herd eastward, hoping to put as much distance as possible between the herd and the dreadrunners.

CHAPTER TWENTY-EIGHT
DREAD BEASTS

THE HERD MANAGED TO avoid being discovered by ravagers for another two days. They were days of cloudy mists and heavy rains, days when Smoking Mountain complained so loudly, that it could be heard even this far away. These days were followed by cold, wet nights. And the days and nights always seemed filled with the presence of the ubiquitous razorteeth. The little predators seemed to be getting bolder, as their food supply grew more scarce.

Then, in the early afternoon of First's sixty-fifth day, dreadrunners again appeared. There were four of them this time, and they stalked the herd relentlessly all afternoon. One of the dreadrunners had a large reddish patch on the back of his neck.

Panthrar trailed behind the main herd, along with Thundermaker and six other males. They knew that another attack was forthcoming, either at dusk, or the next dawn, for these seemed to be the times that dreadrunners most favored. Thundermaker was determined to not be taken by surprise again, as he had been the last time. And this time he hoped to escape without any casualties, if he could.

Towards evening the dreadrunners moved in closer to the herd. The herd coalesced into a tight phalanx, while Thundermaker, Panthrar, and seven of the males formed a separate rear-guard. The rear-guard prepared for an attack by the dreadrunners.

Suddenly, running on soft pads from down-wind of both the threehorns and the dreadrunners, a large biped came bolting out of the mists from the south. It was a large, male dreadcharger. He rushed amongst the dreadrunners, snapping and hissing. He attacked them with a vengeance, almost as if they were they prey. Only the greater agility and speed of the smaller ravagers saved them from the fangs of the dreadcharger.

With the sudden appearance of the dreadcharger, the situation immediately changed. The dreadrunners, who were intent upon a kill of their own, suddenly had to defend themselves from the larger ravager. They scattered out of his way, but then circled back hissing and roaring at him, trying to worry his flanks.

The dreadcharger stood regally while the dreadrunners ran about him. He quickly swung his mighty jaws left and right, threatening the dreadrunners with six and seven inch, serrated, stabbing teeth. He was almost twice their size, forty-five feet long, and more than twice their weight, over seven tons. He was imposing and magnificent, terrible and deadly. Singly, or even in pairs, they were no match for him. The four of them working together just might slay him, if they were careful. His head was more than four feet long, and his jaws made up most of that. He was slower and less agile than they, yet still he jumped and sprang at them with considerable agility. The dreadrunners ran furiously about the dreadcharger, looking for an opening to deliver stabbing slashes. They had to try to kill him, or chase him off, or they would have to retreat and leave the herd for him to prey upon.

The impact that the appearance of the dreadcharger had upon Thundermaker and his determined males was significant. While they were willing to fight off dreadrunners, they were not willing to take the offensive with a dreadcharger. Thundermaker and his males, with Panthrar in their midst, turned and rushed back towards their herd. Thundermaker signaled the herd to retreat with all haste. The herd accelerated to a trot, a speed that the pups and fledges could keep up with, at least for awhile, but only if they ran. The herd retreated as quickly as it could, while the dreadcharger and the dreadrunners fought for the privilege of preying upon Thundermaker's herd.

Panthrar turned to watch in fascination as the greatest living forces in his world waged their life-and-death contest with each other. He stood watching while the dreadrunners formed a circle around the dreadcharger, slowly closing in on him. The dreadcharger was called Savage. He was an old male, of twenty-four years. He had reached a length of forty-five feet, and a weight of 7.3 tons. He was a formidable creature.

Even so, the dreadrunners were giving him trouble. When he lunged at one, it would scamper away. But then the dreadrunner to his rear would dart forward to take advantage of his unprotected side. The dreadrunners had not yet dealt a mortal wound, but they had managed to deliver a few slashes. Savage bled from these, and from a half dozen minor cuts. It just seemed a matter of time before one or another of the dreadrunners would find a sufficient opening to deliver a potentially lethal bite or slash. They would not try to deliver a death bite. That would likely be fatal to the dreadrunner that tried to deliver it. Instead they would try to inflict a series of deadly slashes, that through loss of blood would eventually weaken or kill the dreadcharger.

Panthrar turned and looked at the retreating herd. Soon they would be lost in the mist. But their trail was still evident, and a ravager would be able to follow their spoor for days afterward. Unless the rain fell heavily enough to wash it all away. Panthrar looked up into the darkening sky. A light rain pelted him. Water ran around and into his eyes. He blinked. It collected in the tiny ridges and furrows, and ran down his face. The rain would be refreshing, if it wasn't so grimy. He looked again towards the retreating herd. Who knew if the rain would continue? A downpour could start any time now, or the rain could stop completely. Looking back at the ferocious contest going on, he shrugged.

Savage roared horrifically. He had managed to keep the dreadrunners at bay thus far. Now all five ravagers were standing almost motionlessly, trying to catch their breath. Red-patch stood before the dreadcharger, taunting him, daring the dreadcharger to attack him. Savage would not take the bait. As he panted, he swiveled his head this way and that, alert to any attempts to take him off guard. Even so, one of the dreadrunners on Savage's right-rear flank moved stealthily around towards his back.

Panthrar stood entranced as the dreadrunner tried to sneak up on the dreadcharger. It held itself extremely low to the ground, head pointed upward, jaws extended. It crept quickly and quietly, hoping to deliver a fierce bite and then retreat before the dreadcharger could retaliate.

Panthrar's attention was suddenly distracted by a faint pounding to the south. He tried to penetrate the mists, but he could not see far. He could detect no scents in the lightly pouring rain. Yet he knew that something was running in the direction of the five ravagers. Panthrar began to slowly back away. Out of the haze to the south, a large bipedal form was running towards the group. Panthrar could see it now. It was another dreadcharger. Panthrar turned and fled after Thundermaker's herd with all of the speed that he could muster.

The second dreadcharger roared a blood-curdling challenge as she hurtled towards the dreadrunner closest to her. The dreadrunner, startled by the attack from its rear, sprang almost fifteen feet into the air, and a good fifty feet to the side. The lunging dreadcharger missed him, and braked to a halt near Savage. It was Prancer, a young female of eight years of age. Prancer was thirty-seven feet long, and 6.7 tons in weight. Thus, although she was much smaller than Savage, she was considerably larger than the dreadrunners.

The two dreadchargers quickly took the offensive, darting at the dreadrunners. The dreadrunners, using their greater speed and agility to advantage, bolted away from the angry giants. The dreadrunners realized that they were pursuing a lost cause. Led by Red-patch, they collected together, and began a retreat of their own.

The two dreadchargers let them go. They watched as their smaller competitors melted away into the mists to the west. They then looked in anticipation at the trail of the threehorns that lay before them.

But they waited. They glanced to the south. Something was approaching on soft-padded, three-toed feet. Soon they were joined by a third dreadcharger. It was Seeker, a female of nine years of age. Seeker was slightly larger and heavier than Prancer.

The three dreadchargers touched nose to nose, sniffing in recognition and in greeting. But still they waited. Out of the mists another giant, bipedal form appeared. It was a fourth dreadcharger. His name was Terror. He was Savage's cohort, a much younger male of eleven years of age. He was also somewhat smaller than Savage, being only about forty-two feet long and 7.1 tons in weight. The three dreadchargers exchanged greetings with Terror. Still, the dreadchargers were apparently in no hurry. They began preening themselves.

After a short while, the ranking female of the troop strode out of the mists, with six young cubs trailing behind her. The five adult dreadchargers exchanged greetings, and began preening each other, nose touching and rubbing each other around the head and neck. They rumbled softly to the cubs, who hopped about at their feet. Then they preened the cubs.

The cubs looked expectantly at the adults. Some of the cubs sniffed at the ground where the dreadrunners had been, and growled. Others sniffed at the trail left by the threehorns, and whined with large gaping mouths. The mouths were filled with tiny needle-like teeth.

Although their stomachs were grumbling, the preening made the cubs more content. Soon all were mewing. Several licked their chops, others panted in expectation.

When the social grooming was finished, four of the adults of the troop strode off after the threehorns. Growler, the ranking female, moved off at a slower pace with the cubs. Growler was a mature fourteen year old. She was forty feet long, and almost seven tons in weight. She was the rock about which the troop gravitated. Only Savage, the leader of the troop, had a greater say in things that mattered to the troop.

As ranking female, Growler cared for all of the cubs of the troop. She was the one who protected them, taught them, and made sure that they got fed. They weren't even all her own cubs. In fact, of the six, she could claim only one as hers. All of her other cubs had already perished. The other five belonged to Seeker and Prancer. But that didn't matter to Growler. She treated them all equally well, and gave them all a fair share of her love and attention.

As the hunters, moving along at a more rapid rate pulled steadily away, Growler shepherded the cubs along the same trail. They were still young, only seven or eight feet in length, and still needed constant attention and protection. The cubs focused on the trail of threehorns, and rumbled their excitement.

Frequently, though, Growler's attention was elsewhere. Often she gazed behind her. Soon she had the cubs before her, while she took up the rear. She couldn't see or hear anything to which she could definitely ascribe her concerns, but she had a suspicion about the dreadrunners. They were a tenacious and unpredictable lot. Most likely their temporary alliance would now end, and they would break apart and go their separate ways. On the other hand, they might not.

Meanwhile, the herd of Thundermaker fled all afternoon. When the darkness of night finally descended – a gradual diminishing of visibility that characterized the passage from a heavily overcast day into a heavily overcast night – the herd was exhausted. They had run about as far as many of them could. Thundermaker could not afford to keep traveling in the darkness. He might end up with more casualties from mistakes and carelessness than from attacks by predators. The young were especially vulnerable to any panicky misjudgments by the adults. So the herd formed into a tight defensive circle, and spent a restless night fearful of an attack by dreadchargers.

Even the patrols of the dominant males were abbreviated versions of what they had been before. For dreadchargers were far worse than dreadrunners, and no one wanted to be too far away from the protection of the herd.

Dreadchargers were the most fearsome creatures in existence. They were large, courageous, and deadly. They were far larger and heavier than dreadrunners.

A dreadrunner was about the size of an adolescent hornbrow, and roughly one third of the weight of an adult threehorn. Dreadrunners were quick, agile and ferocious, but they were not indomitable. They were greatly intimidated by the horns of a threehorn. Even an adult hornbrow could occasionally fight off a dreadrunner. Dreadrunners could be dealt with. Even their hunting tactics helped the defenders, for dreadrunners generally hunted singly or in pairs. Pack-hunting was a thing of only temporary convenience to a dreadrunner, and even then, only exercised during the great treks, when the herds were exceptionally large.

Dreadchargers were different. They were far more awesome. They were larger than an adult male hornbrow, and heavier than an adult male threehorn. Their weaponry, the slashing and stabbing, sharp and serrated teeth contained in massive jaws, were more than twice as large as their smaller cousins. These teeth were truly impressive weapons, and highly efficient in meting out deadly wounds.

It was true that dreadchargers were slower and less agile than dreadrunners, but they were fast none-the-less. They could attain speeds of up to 35 miles per hour for short distances. That was more than fast enough to catch a running threehorn or hornbrow, if the hunting dreadcharger could get close enough before panicking the herd. Fortunately for their intended prey, they could maintain that rapid sprint for only a short distance, so they had to get close to a herd undetected, or the herd would likely run safely away.

Dreadchargers countered this potential disadvantage by hunting in well-organized packs, or troops. Their favorite method of attack was to single out an old or weak or young member, stampede the herd, quickly isolate the intended victim from the herd during the confusion of the chase, and kill it by a concerted effort of the troop. This was a very successful approach, and could only be thwarted by one of two approaches: by never letting the troop get too close to the herd in the first place, or by a well-organized defense.

When they had to, hornbrows fought in circles. And as long as the circle could be kept intact, the dreadchargers could be frustrated. It was risky with dreadchargers, but it could work.

Of course, hornbrows preferred to run from dreadchargers. That was the strategy of choice. And given enough of a head start, a fleeing hornbrow couldn't be caught by a pursuing dreadcharger. Getting that head start took the kind of keen senses of sight and smell and hearing that hornbrows were equipped with, and keeping away from dreadchargers took the kind of steady endurance that hornbrows had evolved with. So they would run rather than fight. This was a very effective defense. Except when the herd was slowed by fledges. Then it couldn't run away. Then it was forced to fight.

But that's what packers were for. They would stay and fight in circles, delaying the ravager while the herd escaped. Then they could run swiftly away, unhindered by fledges.

Threehorns, on the other hand, might flee if presented with the opportunity, but threehorns preferred a fighting defense. They had a hard time detecting the stealthy approach of ravagers anyway. But what they had lost in the form of an early-warning system, they had more than made up for by the development of serious defensive weaponry. And if the threehorns could get enough adult males and females chasing each dreadcharger, these terrible hunters could be foiled. For as large and as fearsome as the dreadchargers were, they still had considerable respect for the lethal horns of a stout-hearted threehorn.

All creatures in the world feared dreadchargers. And with good cause. You had to either successfully run away from them, or you had to convince them to run away. If you couldn't accomplish one or the other, they would follow a herd for weeks, killing a new victim every day or two. Day by day, they would pursue the herd relentlessly. They could decimate a herd that way. If the herd was small enough, and if it couldn't eventually evade the troop, the dreadchargers would virtually hunt the herd into extinction.

So it was that with the first lightening of the horizon on First's sixth-sixth day, Thundermaker roused up his herd and moved again eastward. The rain had stopped before daybreak, and the visibility had increased to about a quarter of a mile. Streaks of scarlet sunlight broke through a few spotty openings near the horizon of a still turbulent sky.

The wind whipped a froth on the swollen river to the herd's left. It was a river that could no longer stay within the confines of its banks. The river swirled up onto the edges of the plain, forming fingers of water where dry land had once stood, creating obstacles around which the herd had to detour.

A low ridge could be dimly seen to the herd's right. It formed a purplish line against a grey backdrop. And behind the herd, even as it had barely begun to move, four dreadchargers appeared.

The dreadchargers closed rapidly with the herd. There was no finesse involved. The dreadchargers were hungry, and they were going to make a quick kill. The herd immediately quickened its pace into a trot, while Thundermaker, Quickcharger, and most of the other males moved into a protecting pattern at the rear of the herd. Even Panthrar and Old Solitary joined with the rear-guard, although both hornbrows knew that death's cold hand would soon touch someone.

The dreadchargers came almost at a run. Savage wanted to make a quick kill. If he delayed too long, the herd would try to protract the chase for as long as it could, possibly all day. So on came the dreadchargers, as quickly as they could.

Savage led the assault in a line abreast. The four dreadchargers rushed straight for the defenders. The rear-guard of the threehorns turned to face the attackers, for it would be lethal if the dreadchargers were permitted to strike the unprotected rear flanks of the threehorns. The threehorns fanned out in an arc, facing the ravagers. Two hornbrows were interspersed within their ranks.

On came the dreadchargers. The hissing that they emitted stirred deep racial memories of fear and trepidation within threehorn and hornbrow alike. It was a genetically coded reaction that had evolved over ten thousand generations. Savage and Terror came to a sudden stop only a hundred feet in front of the threehorns. Seeker and Prancer broke to the sides, one to the left, the other to the right. The females were intent upon flanking the defenders, and attacking from the rear. The two male dreadchargers, meanwhile, displayed ferociously before the rear-guard. They growled and roared and hissed in turn, and snapped their massive jaws in the direction of the threehorns. They advanced slowly, worrying the front of the threehorn line, while the females raced in a flanking maneuver.

As the female dreadchargers tried to turn the flanks of the defenders, the threehorns at the ends of the line responded by pulling back and around, into a small defensive circle. All four dreadchargers snapped and hissed at the edges of the circle, trying to find an opening to strike a deadly blow.

The threehorns in turn made short charging motions whenever a ravager got too close, hoping to stab a careless dreadcharger. Yet the threehorns were unwilling to break the circle for fear that a slaughter might ensue. Thundermaker and his males were in a precarious position, surrounded as they were by four dreadchargers. And the hornbrows felt almost useless, and rather defenseless, as they had neither the room to swing their broad, heavy tails, nor the freedom to bolt out of harm's way.

Prancer turned and looked at the retreating herd. It was moving with as much haste as it could muster to escape to freedom. Suddenly Prancer dashed away in pursuit of the herd. A moment later, Seeker turned and followed her.

Thundermaker knew that it was time to act aggressively, or live to regret it. He could not let the two female dreadchargers reach the herd. He began rumbling instructions to his companions. Half would attack the two male dreadchargers head on, the other half would chase after the two female dreadchargers pursuing the herd.

Before Thundermaker had completed his instructions, Savage, who had been snapping at one of the male threehorns to Thundermaker's right, suddenly froze. Then he suddenly backed quickly away. He stood straight up, and cocked his head to the left. He turned and glared towards the west. Then he turned back, and gave a gruesome roar.

Terror stopped his worrying of a threehorn, and looked over at Savage. The two females stopped in their tracks, and also turned back to look at Savage. He gave another gruesome cry, and then turned and ran towards the west. Terror also pivoted, and raced after Savage. Seeker and Prancer charged back towards the defending male threehorns and hornbrows. They skirted the circle, and hurried after the two male dreadchargers.

None of the dreadchargers gave even a backwards glance to the surprised defenders. Thundermaker and his companions did not pause to question the cause for their deliverance, they just quickly collected themselves together, and hurried after the retreating herd. When he reached the herd, Thundermaker turned it first north towards the river, and then east again. He tried to follow the river's edge, what there was of it now, cutting across spill-overs, and splashing through shallows. He hoped to hide his trail.

Occasionally he glanced out from the shore at the muddy waters, swollen and turbulent, rushing to the east.

The four dreadchargers raced for all they were worth towards the west. Once or twice Savage roared a throaty challenge, but otherwise they sped silently back towards the direction from which they had come.

Soon they could see Growler, facing away from them. The cubs were clustered around and behind her. There were other bipedal forms there also, challenging Growler. As the dreadchargers appeared racing out of the mist, the three dreadrunners who were snapping at and worrying Growler, turned and dashed away. They were led by a male with a red patch on the back of his neck. They moved at lightning speed, running for their very lives.

The troop raced past Growler in pursuit of the dreadrunners. They set up a hideous hissing. It was a terrible sound that carried for miles. It was calculated to encourage the dreadrunners to run faster and farther than they might have otherwise done, and to not come back.

Knowing that they had run too far already, and would never catch up to the fleeing dreadrunners, the pursuing dreadchargers soon gave up the chase. When they returned to Growler, they inspected the scene that they had only caught so briefly before. They were angry, and roared out their wrath and their frustration to an indifferent world. Growler stood looking over the body of a dead cub. Periodically she would lean down and lick it, as if trying to revive it. It had been killed by one of the dreadrunners. Nearby lay the body of the killer. Growler had pounced upon him even as he was taking the life from her cub. She had made short work of the perpetrator, ripping him fearfully down the side.

The members of the troop examined the body of the cub, sniffing it carefully. They nudged it and licked it, but it did not move. They roared fearfully, looking about them as if to find the culprit who had done this horrible deed. They kicked up dirt with their hind legs. They noiselessly displayed mouths agape, and then snapped them closed, whining to each other. They roared at the horizons, but there were no answering roars.

All the while, the cubs whimpered in fear. Some stood stock still. Others raced about, agitated by the roaring of the adults. Several sniffed at the still form of their erstwhile companion.

After a while, Savage went over and inspected the body of the dead dreadrunner. He scrutinized the wound approvingly. Growler had expertly gutted the creature. The smell of the victim's fresh blood excited him. All-at-once, he leaned forward and took a large bite out of the carcass. He chewed it twice, tearing the ragged flesh with his killing teeth, and then swallowed the bite, virtually whole. He stooped over and took another bite.

Terror came over, and joined him. Terror ripped flesh off of the thigh, and cast it into the air with a jerk of his head. He then caught the falling flesh on its way back down, jaws clamping shut with a decisive snap. He swallowed the meat whole. As if on a signal, the three females rushed over to quench their gnawing hunger.

The cubs clustered about Growler, mewing and whining, begging for food. After swallowing her first bite, Growler began pulling off meat in small shreds, and feeding it to the cubs. They jostled and shoved each other, fighting for the scraps. Occasionally Growler would take a bite for herself. But most of the time, she occupied herself with feeding the young.

After Prancer had quenched her gnawing hunger pangs, she likewise began tearing off shreds for the cubs. So too did Seeker. This gave Growler more time to attend to her own hunger.

When the troop had finished with the carcass of the dreadrunner, there was very little left of it. Roughly cleaned and broken bones, and partially eaten body parts lay scattered about. But the troop had consumed most of what was worthwhile. When they finally departed, razorteeth and other scavengers would come and pick the bones clean.

Meanwhile, with fully distended stomachs, they moved off a short distance, and dozed in the warm morning breeze. The sun played in and out of the clouds for much of the day, while the satisfied dreadchargers dozed or slept. They totally ignored the body of their dead cub. Eventually they would just leave it where it lay, for whatever wished to scavenge it.

CHAPTER TWENTY-NINE
DRY RAIN AND WET FEAR

THUNDERMAKER AND PANTHRAR STOOD watching the low ridge-line to the south. With them were five other males, including Old Solitary. From time to time, one or another of them would bend down and graze some of the verdant ferns that grew in the area. Quickcharger, Hidepiercer, and a half dozen other males were clustered behind the herd, observing their trail leading out of the west. They were waiting to see if ravagers were still pursuing them. The herd proper was spread out between the two groups of guards, taking a short break in its journey to the east. They had found a sea of lush ferns that had somehow thrived in the cloudy, rainy weather induced by the intermittently erupting volcano. They were gorging themselves.

Far off to the northwest, Smoking Mountain was again active. They could no longer see the volcano, for they were too far away from it, but the eight mile high column of dense gray smoke and ash that it was emitting was clearly visible. The pillar of smoke rose up like an inverted cone, over 40,000 feet into the sky. The pillar billowed from the heat below. At 40,000 feet, a strong current of air sheared off the top, or base of the inverted cone, and blew a great cloud eastward.

It hadn't rained for four days. Sunshine had finally won its battle with the clouds two days earlier, and had mostly prevailed since. The herd had relished the warmth encouraged by the sun. But now, the new dark clouds rolling eastward seemed like harbingers of yet more foul weather.

Although they had somehow evaded ravagers for the past four days, razorteeth frequently stalked the herd. As the pups and fledges grew larger, the razorteeth were becoming less and less of a threat. The pups were now over three feet long, and weighed about 200 pounds. The fledges were also continuing to fill out. The female fledges averaged 34 inches long, and 125 pounds in weight; while the male fledges averaged 41 inches long and 170 pounds in weight.

The young ones were becoming quicker and more agile. They were better able to stay out of the clutches of an attacking razortooth long enough for an adult to come to the rescue. Even so, the razorteeth were never given much of an opportunity to attack the young. The pups and fledges traveled close to their mothers. They were further ensconced within the protective circles of additional adult females, the old childless ones, and the older juveniles who were not yet old enough to mate.

Occasionally the razorteeth would make an attempt at isolating a juvenile threehorn. This happened often when a juvenile wandered carelessly away from the herd, prompted by curiosity or an urge to explore. But the razorteeth were fooling themselves if they thought they could bring down a twelve foot long threehorn. They could only hope that the juvenile somehow got itself incapacitated. Then they would make short work of it. But unless the juvenile got itself in some dire trouble, such attacks always ended to the razorteeth's regret.

The herd hadn't seen a single ravager in four days. They had done their best to hide their tracks, consistently walking within muddy shallows for long periods of time. Such a strategy didn't often hide their scent or their tracks well enough, but it was worth trying. It seemed to be working this time. Something had protected them from ravagers for four days, in any event. It was hoped that perhaps the ravagers had lost their trail in the swirling shallows of the flood-swollen river. It turned out to be a fleeting hope.

Panthrar noticed movement to the south. He scrutinized the ridge-line carefully. In short order he pointed out a line of four bipedal shapes standing out along the top of the ridge-line. Thundermaker and his cohorts strained their eyes. They couldn't see the bipeds, even when Panthrar pointed right at them.

The shapes were traveling in single file along the summit of the low ridge. After awhile, Panthrar noticed, dimly in the distance, about a half mile behind the four, a fifth bipedal form following the other four. The fifth biped was too far away for Panthrar to see if it was accompanied by young. If Pippit were here on look-out, rather than down amongst the fledges browsing the rich ferns, she might possibly be able to see that far. She had exceptionally keen eyesight.

Thundermaker wheeled and grunted loudly to his herd. All heads were up, looking about for danger. Thundermaker moved quickly eastward, the herd following. A sense of urgency began to build up as the news of ravagers spread through the herd. Panthrar led the other five males to join up with Hidepiercer and Quickcharger's group. The dozen or so males formed a rear-guard to block the ravagers and assure the herd's escape.

Almost as if watching the drama from afar, Smoking Mountain rumbled loudly in distress. Perhaps the fated mountain was only trying to survive its own hubris. Its pangs sent shivers through the earth. As it cried out for all the world to hear, the threehorns broke into a trot.

* * * * *

Savage had lost the trail of the herd of threehorns days ago. But he had followed the river, knowing that during the dry season most green-eaters would prefer to be near the traditional source of water, and in the green band that bordered it. Yet this had been an extremely unusual dry season. It hadn't been dry at all. Berry bushes and flowering shrubs, which thrived only along the river during the dry season, were growing all over the plain at the moment.

Still, tradition was hard to break. He almost always hunted along the border of the river at this time of year, and hadrosaurs were always plentiful here. On the other hand, threehorns usually weren't. If he wanted to hunt threehorns, he normally had to follow the horned ones out onto the open plain. Normally he hunted the upper plain during the rest of the year, tracking herds of horned green-eaters.

The troop of dreadchargers had found themselves well behind the great herd of hornbrows that traveled this river at this time of the year. The great herd was their usual source of prey during this season. But they had missed the herd's early departure. Even so, there were always small groups of stragglers. And there were other prey available, horned ones, and armored ones, and crested hadrosaurs, and uncrested ones.

And where the prey was, there were always the predators: the larger ones and the smaller predators. Dreadchargers could, and would, eat almost anything: prey or predator. So Savage and his troop did not go hungry. They were very efficient hunters. Two days ago, they had eaten a longsnout.

Now Savage could hardly believe his luck. Below him, near the river, was a large band of threehorns. It might even be the one that had escaped him some days ago, when that foul dreadrunner had killed one of the cubs.

Seeker, ever anxious to track and pursue the prey, was already sliding down the slope of the ridge after them. Savage envied her, her impetuous youth, but he would have preferred a more indirect approach. That was no longer possible, for she was difficult to call back once her excitement level was up. Instead, he decided to follow her. Terror and Prancer were close on his heels. Growler and the cubs would follow soon.

The dreadchargers sauntered across the flats after the band of threehorns. They were not driven by hunger, so they were not in a hurry. They would stalk the herd, getting ever closer, and maybe attack it late in the afternoon, when the sun was at their backs. That would give them the advantage.

If the sun stayed out. That was difficult to predict, as that terrible mountain was again on fire. He could not see the mountain itself, but he noticed the glow of red in the lower layers of the column of dust and smoke.

Two hours later, the ravagers had closed considerably with the herd. The ravagers noted that a band of males was lagging behind the main herd. It looked like they were going to fight the dreadchargers. Savage shrugged to himself. A male threehorn tasted no different than a female threehorn, and its flesh was no more tough. If it came to that, they would just have to kill a male.

As Savage approached closer to the herd, he noticed a strange thing. There were a few hornbrows with the threehorns. That was unusual. Was this the herd he had seen days ago? Had the hornbrows been with the herd then? It didn't matter. But perhaps it was just lucky that hornbrows were with this herd of threehorns. For hornbrows were tastier than threehorns. Maybe they would kill a hornbrow instead.

Panthrar watched as the dreadchargers drew slowly closer. A sour, almost bitter taste developed in his mouth. The herd moved frustratingly slowly with pups and fledges amongst it. But it was always thus. For a few months out of the year, they were much more vulnerable to ravagers. And in a few more months, if they lived, they would be able to more easily flee ravagers. Then the ravagers would have to resort to clever deceptions and stealthy approaches. But not now. Now they just jogged along, for hours at a time, steadily closing the gap between themselves and their intended prey. When they were close enough, they would charge the herd in their dreadful way, roaring or hissing, and kill someone. Panthrar shuddered involuntarily.

Savage perceived that they were close enough now, and it was almost time. There was no sense waiting until late afternoon. He started a running approach. His companions did likewise, spreading out in their usual hunting pattern. Terror was to his right, Prancer and Seeker were on the wings.

Suddenly the ground shook so violently that Savage stumbled and almost fell. He stopped running. So did his companions. They looked around. Far away in the northwest, tremendous clouds of smoke were pouring into the sky. It was an incredible sight, far more spectacular than anything the mountain had done thus far. They could see a bright glow, as if of fire, burning on the horizon. It was lighting up the clouds of pumice and ash and dust from below. Even as they watched, though, the scene changed. The dark masses of clouds built up in the sky. The billowing clouds got more and more dense, and spilled further and further to the east, carried by an unseen jetstream.

The troop stood as if mesmerized by the gigantic and violent forces of nature. It seemed as if they had forgotten the herd of threehorns. While they delayed, Growler and the cubs caught up with the hunters.

The heavens become saturated, over-saturated. What had gone up, began to come back down. A furious rainstorm began to fall in the distant northwest. It fell so heavily, that it obscured the view of the pillar of smoke.

A dense, black curtain was forming, and in the process it blocked out the northwestern horizon. As they watched in awe, the rainstorm seemed to be sweeping closer. The blanket of darkness covering the sky moved ominously towards them, and with it came the curtain of storm.

The ground shook again. They could hear deep rumblings, and sharp cracks, as of thunder, coming from the northwest. The wind picked up, blowing first a little towards the mountain, and then away from it. The wind blowing from the northwest increased in velocity. Savage marveled at the power of the mountain, but then his revery ended. He mustn't forget the herd of threehorns. He did not want to lose the opportunity that he and the troop had just spent so much time and energy acquiring.

Reluctantly, he turned back in the direction of the herd. He growled. Terror turned first to Savage, and then to the herd. Prancer and Seeker, who also had been intrigued by the mountain and the storm, also swiveled around. The threehorns seemed less interested in the mountain and the storm than they. The herd was galloping as fast as its slowest member, away from the dreadchargers. Savage spit his disappointment, and hurried after the threehorns.

Again the ravagers rushed forward to close with the herd. It was getting to be hard work. This herd did not want to be caught.

The sky rapidly darkened as they pursued the herd. Then it started to rain. Or at least that is what he thought it was at first. That impression did not last long. This was not rain. It was not wet.

Savage could not help himself. He slowed as he watched the particles fall to the ground. They bounced as they hit the earth. He slowed to a walk. It was "raining" dust and pebbles everywhere he looked. Then he stopped completely, glancing about.

Grit and gravel were bouncing off of the top of his head. He didn't like that. He grumbled. His troop-members had also stopped. They also complained about the debris falling upon them. He could see in the distance ahead that the threehorns were also being rained upon. They too seemed confused by the dry rain.

Savage looked upwards. An object about the size of his clenched fist dropped from the sky, just missing his head. He jumped to the side. He stooped over and examined the object. It was a black, rough-edged, pock-marked stone. He sniffed at it. It was hot. The heat rising from it warmed his nose. A few more of these stones fell. Fortunately, none of them struck either him or his troop.

He looked back towards Growler. He could see her in the distance, struggling through the dry rain, still herding the dismayed cubs along after the hunting party. They seemed alright, if somewhat distraught, by these odd happenings.

Savage looked towards the herd of threehorns. They too had stopped running. They were huddled together, in a defensive circle, trying to protect themselves from the unseen enemy.

Savage and his troop moved cautiously towards the threehorns. Thundermaker saw them coming, and signaled his rear-guard to move against the dreadchargers. There was much confusion within the herd. None had ever seen dry rain before. Pebbles and dust struck everyone. Stones pelted some of them, but none were large enough to be incapacitating.

Seeker was clearly spooked. She did not know whether to advance upon the threehorns, retreat to Growler and the cubs, or run for her life. Savage noticed that she was getting skittish. He moved over to her to lend her his support.

Terror also was unhappy with events. He did not think that this was a good time to hunt. He thought that perhaps the world was ending. He bellowed out a roaring protest.

Only Prancer seemed totally unaffected by the strange things that were happening. Dry rain. Strange, but was it really hurting anyone? It was just one more weird thing in a whole series of strange events. It was the mountain. She was convinced of that. The mountain must be doing it. None of these things had happened until the mountain had started spitting fire.

Seeker also thought that it was the mountain to blame. She hated that mountain. Why was it doing these things? It was not behaving the way a mountain should behave. Had it gone mad?

Suddenly, Seeker lost her nerve. She started to run for her life. Away from the mountain. She ran straight at the rear-guard of threehorns. They bellowed and squeal-roared at her, trying to warn her away. She was not to be diverted. She roared thunderously at them, running straight at the waving horns.

Savage was startled by Seeker's charge. They were not yet ready to charge. He roared once, but she didn't hear him. So he followed Seeker's attack.

Prancer did not hesitate. She was anxious for the chase and the kill. She could almost taste blood now. She sprang after Savage and Seeker.

Terror shrugged to himself. Whether this was a good time to hunt or not, he must support his troop-mates. He noticed that neither Seeker nor Prancer was trying to outflank the threehorns. So he ran in a curving path that would take him around the south side of the herd.

Thundermaker could not believe his eyes. The dreadchargers were running right for the horns of the rear-guard. If they persisted with this strategy, he and his cohorts would be able to impale them quite easily. This directness had never happened before. It made him nervous. It must be a trick. The ravagers wouldn't throw themselves upon the deadly horns of his companions. They were up to no good. They were going to do something sneaky, something unexpected. But he didn't have time to figure out what that might be. All that he had time to decide, was that he just couldn't wait and let it happen.

He squealed at his companions. A dozen nervous male threehorns broke ranks, charging straight at the advancing dreadchargers. Most went for the three coming at them, but several veered off after the one trying to circle them.

Panthrar and Old Solitary were taken by surprise. They could not understand Thundermaker's command, so they were left standing there when the threehorns surged forward to meet the dreadchargers. They stood side-by-side in indecision. It was not in a hornbrow's make-up to go charging after a dreadcharger. To stand and fight was one thing, although running away was better. But to charge after one? That was an incredible concept. It also seemed like a stupid idea.

Savage suspected that Seeker must have panicked. For she tried none of the skillful maneuvering of which she was capable. She just ran straight for the threehorns. Worse, she was in jeopardy of getting seriously hurt, or even killed, if she didn't change her course soon. Savage and Prancer veered and jumped away from the charging horns, scampering this way and that as two or three threehorns each chased after them. As he zigged and zagged away from the horns of his pursuers, Savage looked over his shoulder to see what had become of Seeker.

Seeker saw the threehorns clearly. They were in her path, but she was not to be deterred. She must get away from this dry rain, and that terrible mountain. She gathered her strength as she closed with the three threehorns that were bearing down upon her. They were on a collision course, and impact was imminent.

At the last possible moment, Seeker jumped up and forward. It was the best jump that she had ever made in her life. Panic gave springs to her legs, and wings to her feet. It was the kind of jump that even a dreadrunner would have been proud of. She completely cleared the threehorn directly in front of her. The threehorn jerked his head up, trying to catch her on his horns, but she sailed over the pointed spikes with inches to spare. The threehorn, and the ones on either side of him, charged underneath her. They braked, looking up and back in wonder as she sailed over them.

If she could have, she would have smiled, she was so proud of that jump. It culminated in a fairly graceful landing. But there was no time to think about it. She must hurry. She wouldn't even stop to see what the threehorns behind her were doing.

Seeker sped forward, as fast as she could go. She saw two hornbrows blocking her path. They stood before her, swinging their broad tails in sweeping arcs. She knew what they intended, but she wouldn't give them the chance. She roared hideously, and charged straight for them. If they didn't move out of her way, they might regret it. She opened her gaping mouth, bearing her teeth to give them even more reason to get out of her way. To emphasize her determination, she hissed volubly.

Panthrar and Old Solitary saw the fearsome dreadcharger jump completely over the threehorns, and then come rushing for them. Death was coming to embrace one or the other of them. They felt certain of that. Even so, they could not run, the herd depended upon them. Without even thinking, they prepared for battle, swinging their tails in wide arcs.

As the dreadcharger closed to striking distance, Panthrar closed his eyes, and swung his tail with all the force and might that he could gather. Old Solitary also pivoted, swinging his tail. One or the other, or perhaps both tails, were calculated to strike the dreadcharger. If both tails struck true, they would knock the dreadcharger completely off her feet. Then maybe they could pierce her with their horns.

But Panthrar's tail struck nothing. He felt the rush of air as he pivoted almost completely around, almost losing his balance. He opened his eyes and looked about. Old Solitary had the same funny, perplexed look on his face that Panthrar was sure was on his own. They had both completely missed the dreadcharger. It was embarrassing. He would have to aim better next time. And probably keep his eyes open, too.

Just before the moment of impact, both of the hornbrows swung their tails as hard as they could, one pivoting to the left, the other to the right. It was a well-coordinated attack, but Seeker didn't intend to stay and fight. She jumped lightly between the two hornbrows, and over their broad, racing tails. It was an easier jump than the one she had performed to avoid the threehorns.

The two male hornbrows turned to watch her go. She ignored them. On she sped. Now the herd itself was in her way. She ran straight for it. To her, it was not a serious obstacle. She roared a challenge to the herd. As she sprang onward, propelled by powerful hind legs, she leaned forward, and again bared her deadly fangs.

Panthrar looked around, trying to determine where the dreadcharger had gone. He gulped noisily. The ravager was heading straight for the herd. Panthrar trumpeted shrilly, and charged off in pursuit of the ravager. Old Solitary was right behind him.

Panthrar looked for Pippit and the fledges. They were in the midst of the defensive circle. Panthrar sped for his mate, and his fledges. He must get to them before the ravager could do them any harm. That was all that he could think of. He did not stop to think that he might be doing a stupid thing – pursuing a dreadcharger.

The herd panicked, and split apart before Seeker could get to it. Females and pups and hornbrow fledges... hornbrow fledges? ...scattered in all directions. She ignored them. Onward she sped. Putting distance between herself and the ugly mountain.

The herd was running, fleeing in all directions. Panthrar tried to keep Pippit in his sight, chasing after her and the fledges. Old Solitary was still at his heels. Pippit and the fledges were running towards the river. Panthrar and Old Solitary intercepted them there. Pippit stood contemplating the swirling, rushing waters of the River of the Nine Tribes.

Savage dodged this way and that, trying to avoid impalement by the desperately charging threehorns. He now had four of them pursuing him. They seemed determined to puncture him if they could, and he was even more determined to make sure that didn't happen. Even so, he still tried to keep an eye on poor Seeker. He watched in amazement as she jumped over the threehorns; cheered her on as she rushed past the hornbrows; and felt pride when she scattered the herd. She was an incredible female, even when she was scared to death.

Savage tried to circle back around to Seeker, but the threehorns insisted on keeping him away from the herd if they could. He scrambled back and forth, feinting left and right, trying to get past them. He could fool one or two of them, but never all four at once. Still he kept trying.

Prancer was luckier. She managed to get past her two pursuers relatively easily. Then she bolted for the herd, with another male hot on her tail. She managed to avoid the male, and sprang into the midst of the herd. Seeker had already scattered it, and female threehorns were running helter-skelter, pups at their feet. It seemed a miracle that the pups managed to stay clear of those madly churning feet.

As Prancer rushed in amongst the herd, females and their young rushed away from her. She ran first this way, then that, trying to catch a female or juvenile, but she would then be distracted by another female almost running into her. She would stop chasing the first, swing around and chase the second, only to be distracted by a third. Doing this, she was wasting a lot of energy getting nowhere.

Prancer stopped and hissed. The reaction that her hissing created among the threehorns amused her. Every one of them seemed to stop in their tracks, look at her in wonder and consternation, and then turn and run in the opposite direction.

She looked about for a likely victim. Down at the river's edge, she saw a group of hornbrows. How they had managed to get caught up in this wild melee of stampeding threehorns, she couldn't imagine. But that didn't matter anyway. What mattered was that hornbrows were pretty tasty. Prancer rushed for the hornbrows, hoping to trap one of them against the river's edge.

Growler approached the wildly stampeding threehorns cautiously. They seemed to be running around and around in circles. She saw one large group of male threehorns chasing Savage, and another chasing Terror. It was taking all of the ability and attention of the two males to stay ahead of the horns of their pursuers. They could not get near the herd.

Growler also saw Prancer in the midst of the herd, rushing around, trying to make a kill. Seeker was nowhere to be seen.

Growler directed the cubs to hide in a swale that they had just passed. She watched as the five of them hurried to obey her. Then she surveyed the surroundings carefully one more time, to assure herself that no threat lurked nearby. When she was sure that the cubs were not in any immediate danger, she hurried towards the herd to help make a kill.

The hornbrows saw Prancer coming their way. Pippit's resolve seemed to harden. "Into the water, my little fledges. Into the water and swim. Swim for your lives. Swim to the other side."

Some of the fledges started jumping into the water. Others looked at the rushing, swirling river with some trepidation. Pippit nudged several into the water. Panthrar nudged other fledges into the water. Old Solitary jumped into the water, pulling fledges in with him, and shoved them in the direction they were supposed to swim.

"Swim little fledges, swim," he cried.

Pippit counted as the fledges started swimming for their lives towards the opposite bank. Twelve. She counted twelve. There were two missing. Pippit turned to face the oncoming dreadcharger. She started to swing her tail back and forth.

Panthrar saw what she intended. "Into the water, my wife," he said to her.

"No, my husband, you will need me here."

"The fledges will need you more, my wife," said Panthrar quickly, as the dreadcharger was rapidly drawing near. "Now into the water, and stay with your fledges, good mother."

He pushed her into the water for emphasis. She stumbled forward, splashing into the cold torrent. She glanced backwards at her mate, but he had already turned back to face the charging ravager. Pippit then turned, and swam rapidly towards her fledges. They were managing to keep their heads above water, but were swimming in disarray. They were heading in all directions.

Pippit swam amongst them, speaking encouragement. She got them to gather around her. Then she half-led, half-herded them toward the distant shore.

CHAPTER THIRTY
THE RIVER

Panthrar took a few steps forward, to meet the approaching dreadcharger on firmer ground. He leaned forward, as low and as menacing as he could make himself. The dreadcharger moved with deliberate, unhurried grace. Panthrar swung his tail in wide arcs, trying to time the swings with the approach of the ravager. He knew that he must keep his eyes open this time, for he would be allowed only one mistake. If he was permitted even one, that is. But he knew that even if he was allowed that one mistake, he would never make another.

The dreadcharger slowed as she approached him. She seemed secure in the knowledge that he could not get away. She leaned forward and low, advancing one steady step at a time. She did not hiss, she was not trying to frighten him. Her head swung from side-to-side, estimating distances, checking her flanks, trying to discover the unexpected. But she never quite took her eyes from him. She was determined that he would not escape her.

Panthrar wished that he could turn and look one more time at his beloved Pippit and their fledges, but he couldn't. He knew that he must not take his eyes off of the ravager. He was going to give the best account of himself that he could. He would buy Pippit and the fledges time to escape. Who knows, he thought to himself, I might even be able to defeat the ravager. But he knew that was really wishful thinking. It would have been nice to have had time to say goodbye to his mate and fledges.

All at once, he became aware of splashing behind him. Oh no, he thought to himself, Pippit has come back to help me. She was far too brave for her own good, he thought. He could not bear the thought of her being torn by this bloody killer. Mentally, he searched desperately for a way to protect Pippit from her own bravery. He thought that it would be best to rush forward to engage the ravager before Pippit could get out of the water. Then he heard, "Confound this slippery mud."

It was Old Solitary. The old male did not swim away with the fledges, as he had thought. He had stayed to help Panthrar.

Old Solitary came slipping and sliding out of the water. He muttered to himself as he again slipped in the mud. Once on shore, he ran around Panthrar's right. Panthrar looked at him in amazement. Old Solitary was trying to outflank the dreadcharger.

The dreadcharger paused, and hissed at Old Solitary. She was warning him away. She had her sights on the younger male. He would be easier to kill.

Old Solitary moved closer to her. She eyed the old male warily. Then she snapped at him for good measure. Maybe she needed to deal with the old male. She took a step towards Old Solitary.

Panthrar took his cue. He darted to the left. The ravager stopped, and jerked her head towards Panthrar. She growled, and looked back again at Old Solitary. The larger male was both a bigger meal, and possibly the greater threat. She took two quick steps toward Old Solitary, who was now facing her, with only twenty or thirty feet separating them. A dreadcharger could leap that distance in the blink of an eye. The old male's tail was swinging back and forth in rapidly accelerating strokes.

Panthrar knew that he must act soon, or the ravager would either jump for Old Solitary, or turn and pounce at him. He decided to risk it. He closed with the dreadcharger. The dreadcharger swiveled her head at Panthrar, and hissed, just as he pivoted. He swung his tail in a counter-clockwise arc with all of the force that he could muster. His head also pivoted, in a clockwise direction, as he turned to watch where the blow was expected to strike.

The ravager began to spin in Panthrar's direction, reaching for him with her small forelimbs. Her opened jaws darted forward to grab him. It was the wrong thing to do. She should have tried to jump over the tail, or to jump backwards, and then close with him.

The tail struck her hard across both knees. The ravager stumbled sideward. Her angry hiss increased in both volume and pitch. She was still trying to snap her jaws closed on Panthrar, even as she tried to regain her balance. She missed him, as he dashed forward and to the side, out of harm's way. She had almost regained her balance, when she was hit by the heavier tail of Old Solitary. She spun around and toppled to the ground.

"Quick, younger brother, to the river," Old Solitary yelled as he backed away from the ravager.

Panthrar stared at the ravager struggling to her feet. It wasn't easy for her, for her tiny forelimbs weren't much help, and the double blow had temporarily knocked the wind out of her. He exchanged glances with Old Solitary.

Quick, the old male gestured impatiently. Then he turned and raced to the water's edge. Panthrar was right beside him. The two male hornbrows took a few steps into the shallows, and then plunged into the cool river almost simultaneously. They began swimming with strong strokes towards the opposite shore.

They paddled with fore-legs and hind, and sculled with their tails. Panthrar turned and looked back at the ravager. She was still trying to struggle to her feet. He then looked along the surface of the water, searching for his mate. He could see Pippit and the fledges far out in the middle of the river. They were some distance downstream, making for the opposite bank. The powerful current was carrying them all downstream.

Prancer was angry. After she got enough of her wind back, she hissed frightfully. She struggled up onto her hind feet, and shook her head. She looked out into the river, at the escaping hornbrows, and roared angrily. She then glanced behind her. No one had seen her temporary setback. Good. Much of the herd of threehorns was moving rapidly downstream. The male threehorns were waging a fighting withdrawal. Savage, Terror, and Growler were in pursuit. As she watched the conflict, several of the female threehorns and their pups splashed into the water, and began swimming for the distant shore. They were already a quarter of a mile downstream from her, and the river was sweeping them further away.

Prancer turned back to the swimming hornbrows. Again she roared. She approached the edge of the river. She bent down and looked carefully into the swirling, muddy current. She snorted. Then she again looked towards the hornbrows, paddling rapidly away. She glared at them a moment longer. Then she jumped into the water, and began swimming as rapidly as she could after her intended prey.

Panthrar kept glancing over his shoulder to see if the dreadcharger would pursue them into the river. After a while, he was disheartened to see the dreadcharger do that very thing. He told Old Solitary that the ravager was coming after them.

Old Solitary turned around, treading water. "Younger brother," he said, "this may be the chance we are looking for."

"What do you mean, elder brother?" said Panthrar, spitting out water that he had accidently swallowed. "It would have been better if the ravager had stayed on the shore."

"What you say is true, younger brother," said the old male through heavy breathing. "But in the water, a four-footed creature swims much faster, and with greater stability, than a two-footed creature. See what I mean," said Old Solitary, as he gestured towards the laboring ravager. Then Old Solitary smiled, "Plus, there are two of us."

Hornbrows, with four good paddling limbs, and a broad, strong, flat tail, could easily outswim a biped. Added to this advantage, was the disadvantage that ravagers had, with their tiny fore-limbs, which added little to their motive power.

Old Solitary started swimming back towards the ravager. "Come, younger brother. Let's make this dreadcharger sorry that she ever met these two hornbrows."

"Okay, elder brother," responded Panthrar, also breathing heavily from his exertions. "But can we make her swim out here to us? She'll be more tired that way."

"An excellent idea, younger brother."

The two male hornbrows began swimming leisurely towards their original destination, the other side of the river, while trying to conserve their energy. They watched as Pippit and the fledges made it to the shore, and pulled themselves from the water.

Pippit helped her fledges climb out of the water and get safely onto the bank. Twelve, she counted to herself with some distress. She hadn't made a mistake. She looked into the water, hoping to see two more fledges endeavoring to cross the river. She looked all the way across to the other side. There were no fledges to be seen. She quickly looked at all the faces, to identify the missing ones by name. Eleventh and Twelfth were missing.

"Did any of you see Eleventh or Twelfth?" she asked her fledges. "Did anyone see where they might have gone?"

"I saw them, my mother," said Eighteenth, the youngest. "Eleventh almost got stepped on by old Raggedtail, as she ran away from the dreadcharger. So Eleventh had to dash out of her way."

"I saw too, my mother," said Sixth. "Eleventh then tried to run back to us, but Foottangler and Rollypolly rushed by with their pups, so she couldn't get back to us."

"That's right, my mother," said Fourteenth breathlessly. "So Eleventh went off with Foottangler and her pups. I saw them all running together, as fast as they could, away from that horrible dreadcharger."

"I hope she is safe," fretted Pippit. "Did anyone see Twelfth?"

They all thought for a moment. Then Fourteenth offered, "After Raggedtail rushed on by, I thought I saw him chase after Eleventh."

"What Fourteenth says is correct, my mother," confirmed Eighteenth. "I saw Twelfth trying to catch up to his twin. Do you think that he is with her now?"

"I hope so, my little fledges," said Pippit, although the worried frown did not leave her face. "I hope that they are together and safe, with Foottangler and her pups. Now wait while I look for Panthrar, your father."

Pippit looked anxiously back into the river. So did all of the fledges. Pippit saw Panthrar and Old Solitary swimming slowly towards her. She also saw the ravager swimming frantically towards them. So did the fledges. They began to hoot and trill warnings to their father. Pippit signaled to the two males, telling them that the ravager was gaining on them. They signaled their intentions back to her. Pippit's frown deepened in concern. Then she waved her understanding.

"Come my little fledges, we can not wait here. It is not safe." She collected her fledges about her, and slowly headed east, frequently looking back at her mate.

Then Pippit became distracted by the threehorns. In the misting rain, partially obscured by the distance, she saw three or four females with their pups swimming across the river. She moved rapidly along the bank then, heading down river. She made for the point where the threehorns would come ashore.

She and her fledges got there well ahead of the threehorns. They waved and tooted encouragement to their friends. While they waited, Pippit noticed two dreadchargers on the opposite shore. One, Terror, plunged into the water after the threehorns. The other, Savage, watched the first for a moment, then he hurried downstream, where the majority of the herd had retreated.

A third dreadcharger appeared. It looked first at Terror, swimming across the river, then at Savage, chasing after the herd. After a moment's hesitation, it turned around, and ran back up-river. It was Growler, going back for the cubs.

Panthrar and Old Solitary kept a constant eye on Prancer, as she struggled to catch up with them. They let her intercept them about two-thirds of the way across the river, where the water was still very deep, and where even a mighty dreadcharger could be drowned.

As Prancer drew close to them, they turned and swam around to either side of her. She tried to lurch at them, snapping her jaws ferociously, and hissing violently. They stayed just beyond her reach. Suddenly she moved towards Old Solitary, pushing hard with her front and rear limbs, and her tail, trying to close with him. The old male swam hard away from her, never letting her get too close. Meanwhile, Panthrar swam strongly after the ravager, and lunged at her back. He was able to climb partially upon her, forcing her underneath the water. She thrashed violently, and Panthrar was forced to jump away from her before she slashed him with her fearsome razor-sharp teeth.

Prancer came to the surface, spitting and gasping. She looked around, and saw Panthrar. She hissed horribly at him, and then choked. She coughed, spitting water from her lungs. Then she jerked her head around and saw Old Solitary, who was trying to sneak up behind her. She hissed and spit at him, too. Old Solitary started back-pedaling. Prancer had murder in her eyes. She began swimming as fast as she could after Panthrar.

The younger male turned and swam away, while the older male followed the same strategy as his comrade. He swam briskly, and caught up with the ravager. Taking a deep breath, he lunged onto her back, and held onto her for dear life. He wrapped both his arms and his legs around her torso. They both went under. The water churned and frothed.

Panthrar turned and swam cautiously back to near the point where the two had gone under. He didn't want to get too close, lest the ravager come up upon him from below. He stuck his head under water, trying to see into the muddy depths. He couldn't see more than two feet in front of his face. He raised his head, and looked along the surface of the water. Old Solitary surged to the surface about a hundred feet away from Panthrar. He breached the surface like an old **sea-ravager**.

"Swim," yelled the old male, as he began swimming for his life. "Swim, swim." Panthrar turned and swam as fast as he could.

About thirty feet behind him, the dreadcharger broke the surface. She was coughing and hacking and spitting up water. She pounded the water with her tiny fists. She groaned noisily, and shook her head.

The two hornbrows swam a safe distance away, and then stopped and turned to watch the ravager. She tread water for some time, frequently coughing, trying to completely clear her lungs. After awhile she became quiet. She looked over at the two treading hornbrows. If looks could kill, she would have slain them both on the spot. She then looked back at the shore from which she had come. It was many hundreds of yards away. She looked again at the hornbrows. They started to swim towards her. Prancer turned, and began swimming as fast as her spent strength could take her, away from the hornbrows, and towards the distant southern bank of the river.

Panthrar and Old Solitary exchanged glances. Old Solitary smiled. Panthrar hooted a loud victory cry. Then they turned and swam towards the north bank of the river.

When Panthrar and Old Solitary pulled themselves ashore, the first thing that they looked for was Prancer. She was about half of the way across the river, treading water, watching them.

Then they heard squealing and bellowing coming from somewhere to their left, from somewhere in the expanse of the river. Far down the river, they could just barely see threehorns working their way across to their side. Behind the threehorns, they could also see the mist-obscured form of a dreadcharger.

They looked back at Prancer. She was already swimming slowly back in their direction. It wasn't over yet. Panthrar grimaced at Old Solitary. Then they both hastened down-river, looking for Pippit and the fledges. As they ran along the bank of the river, it began to rain again. Panthrar hadn't even noticed until now, but sometime during the passage across the river, the dry rain had stopped. Now it was raining wet rain. But it was the same grimy, slippery mess that they had endured before.

Panthrar and Old Solitary found Pippit and the fledges on the bank near where the threehorns would come ashore. Panthrar and Pippit nuzzled affectionately. She said nothing of the cold knot of fear that she had felt each time he tried to fight a dreadcharger. His bravery thrilled her. He was courageous beyond the normal hornbrow. So was Old Solitary for that matter. But she couldn't bear to lose him. Nor Old Solitary. She was thankful that they both had come back relatively unharmed.

Panthrar trilled to his fledges. They trilled in response. Many of them came up to him and rubbed against his legs. He nuzzled each in turn. Some then went over to Old Solitary, and rubbed against his legs. He also nuzzled the fledges, speaking gently to each one.

Pippit, who had been examining the river, said, "There are three females with their pups coming our way. There is also a large dreadcharger chasing them." Panthrar looked up as Pippit concluded her report.

The hornbrows stood and watched as the threehorns swam toward them. They signaled encouragement to the pups, who began to swim faster when they saw the hornbrows. Panthrar and Old Solitary splashed into the shallows, and waded out to the pups. Pippit had to restrain her fledges from plunging back into the water to "assist" their father. She stood on the shore, keeping order among the fledges. The two males helped pull the tired little threehorns safely to the shore. Highstepper found firm footing, and waded past the two hornbrows, breathing heavily. Through gasps of breath, she said, "Thun varm du, thun varm du."

Without even thinking, the hornbrows returned, "Varoom, varoom."

Then Bluntnose came ashore, surrounded by her pups. "Thun varm du," they all said.

"Varroom," came the response.

A third female struggled ashore. She was an old, childless female who trailed the two mothers, helping to protect the pups.

Terror was coming close to shore. Old Solitary turned to Pippit, and said, "Younger sister, take the fledges and head east. Travel quickly. Take the threehorns with you. The Great Eastern Herd is somewhere close by. The signs are unmistakable. Go to them."

Pippit looked around. She had seen the clear indications of the recent passage of the vast herd, without really being conscious of how close they truly were. There was much evidence that the herd had passed this way only a short time before. She looked at Panthrar.

"Go my wife," he said to her. "We will be along shortly."

She hesitated. As if to add emphasis to the moment, Terror roared mightily. Pippit looked into Panthrar's eyes. She pleaded with him without saying a word, please do not fight the ravager. He returned her look of love. I must, his expression said. He could find no easy words. Finally he managed to say, "Take good care of our fledges."

Pippit held back tears that were gathering in her eyes, and gathered her young. She called to the threehorns, who had been slowly spreading out towards the north, and rushed eastward. She moved as fast as the slowest fledge could run, with pups and adult threehorns following close behind.

Old Solitary turned to Panthrar. "What do you think, younger brother? Shall we make this dreadcharger sorry he ever met these two hornbrows?"

Panthrar looked back up the river to Prancer. She was taking her time crossing the river. In fact, Terror was closer than she, and getting perilously close to shallow water. If he got to shallow water, he could fight them on his own terms. If he got past them, he could wreak havoc with the young. If he killed one of the adults, though, he would probably be satisfied, and wouldn't pursue the others.

"Let's go drown a dreadcharger," said Panthrar, with a bravado that he didn't feel. With that, the two males charged into the water, trying to get to the dreadcharger before he got to shallow water.

The ravager slowed, trying to assimilate the recondite behavior of the two hornbrows. It mystified him. Hornbrows coming forward to attack a dreadcharger? They must have lost their senses. So much the better for him, he thought, now he wouldn't have to chase after them. He tread water, watching as they swam vigorously to him.

Panthrar and Old Solitary split apart as they neared the ravager. Terror watched silently as they approached. He had already decided to deal with the larger one first. That would probably be enough to frighten off the smaller one. Terror made for Old Solitary.

It was a repeat of the scuffle with Prancer. Panthrar swam after Terror as Terror pursued Old Solitary. Old Solitary swam with renewed effort, as Terror swam surprisingly fast, much faster than Prancer.

Panthrar neared Terror, hoping that Old Solitary would keep him distracted. Old Solitary did his part. He stopped swimming altogether, treading water in front of the dreadcharger. He made a tempting offering.

Terror slowed, gathering himself for the final spurt.

Panthrar was almost beside Terror. He took a deep breath, and lunged onto Terror's back. Terror was forced under water. Panthrar tried to wrap his arms and legs around the large ravager. Terror thrashed about violently, trying to turn and sink his rapier teeth into Panthrar.

Panthrar hung onto Terror's back as if his life depended upon it. For one could rightly say that it did. Even so, he felt his grip slipping in the foaming water. Suddenly he was forced to let go. He pushed himself away from Terror, and turned and swam with the strength of every fiber in his body. Terror also turned, and slashed at Panthrar with a hind foot. Even in the dulling medium of the water, Panthrar could feel the ripping pain of three sharp claws tearing the flesh in his upper tail. He swam all the faster.

Terror tried to literally spring out of the water in pursuit. He would have caught Panthrar in the next herculean surge through the water, except that he found that Old Solitary was suddenly clinging to his back. The old male forced the ravager under the water. They both sank below the surface. Submerged and panicky, Terror jerked and twisted. He tried to dislodge the hornbrow, or to turn enough to rip at him, but Old Solitary clung tenaciously to his back.

Panthrar swam around in circles, trying to locate the pair. He swam through a trail of his own blood in the process. Old Solitary surged to the surface right in front of him. The old male didn't have to yell "swim" this time. Both hornbrows swam for the shore with all their might.

Terror broke the surface coughing and sputtering. He swam around in a confused circle, growling and coughing, trying to clear his lungs. Panthrar and Old Solitary heard him splashing about as they reached shallow water, and raced to the shore. Water cascaded with each footstep, rushing up to meet the rain falling from the skies.

When they reached the shore, Panthrar turned and stared at Terror. The ravager seemed totally pre-occupied with getting air into his lungs, and water out. Panthrar felt a stab of pain. He inspected his wound. Blood was oozing freely from it. He licked at it briefly. It would leave a scare, but it wasn't debilitating.

He looked at Old Solitary. The old male was trying to lick the deepest of a scattering of slashes and cuts he had received from the dreadcharger.

Panthrar glanced up river. Prancer had reached the shore. She was running towards the two male hornbrows. "Run, elder brother," warned Panthrar, "The female comes."

Old Solitary jerked his head quickly in the direction that Panthrar had indicated. The female dreadcharger was running low and horizontal. When she saw that the two hornbrows were looking her way, she hissed threateningly. She was still over five hundred yards away, but she was closing rapidly. The two males turned and sprinted toward the east.

CHAPTER THIRTY-ONE
A DISTANT HILL

PIPPIT GUIDED HER CHARGES for over an hour. The fledges and the pups were again tiring, after so much activity and so much stress. She and the threehorns first slowed to a fast walk, gently encouraging the young to keep up that pace. Finally the adults had to slow down to what was for them a slow walk, for that was all that the pups and fledges could maintain. Frequently, either Pippit, or one of the female threehorns, or even one of the young, would glance back from where they had come.

The rain was ending, but a heavy mist persisted. The mist reduced visibility considerably. Pippit could see little further than a quarter of a mile, at best. As it ended, the rain seemed cleaner than it had been in days. It was as if the sky had cleansed itself of all of the dirt and debris.

Pippit was worried. When they had first left Panthrar, they had heard a lot of roaring. Now they heard nothing. But they all imagined a silently stalking ravager behind them, trying to close the distance for a kill.

Pippit fretted over Panthrar. Where was he? Where was Old Solitary? Had they survived the confrontation with the dreadcharger? Or had they not? That was a thought that she could barely allow herself to ponder. It was too tragic for her to dwell upon. She wanted to go back and look for Panthrar, but she knew that she could not leave the fledges.

At the same time that Pippit was worrying about her mate, Panthrar and Old Solitary were still being pursued by Prancer. They were faster than the ravager, at least over a long chase, so they had kept ahead of her. But still she followed them, determined to make a kill. Long ago they had slowed to a fast walk, or a slow jog, knowing that the dreadcharger would also tire, and be forced to do the same. Still they kept alert, lest she spring out of the mists at them.

Time passed. Still onward pushed the two hornbrows. And on came Prancer, unwilling to give up the chase. They had long ago lost sight of her. But they could occasionally hear her, or scent her. They knew she was still behind them.

Far ahead, Panthrar could make out shapes. Moving in and out of the edge of his vision in the misting rain, he saw the hulking forms of threehorns. He and Old Solitary were catching up to Pippit and the threehorns.

Old Solitary, breathing heavily from the continuous exertions of the past hours, said, "I see your fledges ahead, younger brother."

"And I, elder brother." After a moment of thought, Panthrar added, "It looks like we must stay and fight again."

Old Solitary did not respond at first. He stared at the ground as he and Panthrar jogged along, moving at a pace that they could maintain for hours. It was a pace that was more rapid than the hunting jog of a ravager, and therefore one that could keep them ahead of a ravager forever. But it was a jog that was far faster than one that a fledge could maintain.

Suddenly the old male spoke, "Go to your fledges, younger brother, they need you. I must fight this ravager alone."

"I cannot let you fight the ravager alone, elder brother. It would be suicide if you did."

"I cannot permit you stay and fight with me, younger brother. I must fight this ravager alone. The mountain told me of this, long ago."

The mountain again, thought Panthrar. Poor Old Solitary was obsessed with that mountain. "And I cannot let you end it like this, elder brother."

They traveled for awhile in silence. Then Old Solitary stopped. He turned to look back in the direction from which the dreadcharger would come. Panthrar also stopped, and turned to face the old male. Old Solitary looked at the younger male, and said firmly, "Go to your fledges, son of Tessah."

Panthrar looked deeply into the old male's eyes. There was almost a hint of pleading there. Panthrar wavered. Finally he said, "I cannot, elder brother."

Old Solitary briefly glanced back towards the west, then he said, "Do not let my gesture be in vain, son of Grendaar. Go now, to your fledges, and to your mate."

Panthrar was perplexed. He was not sure what Old Solitary was talking about. But that wasn't all that unusual. Then he said with a finality that Old Solitary could hardly argue with, "We stay together, elder brother."

Old Solitary shrugged, and turned back toward the east. They traveled for awhile in the direction of Pippit and the threehorns. Then the older male said, "I think that you are right, younger brother. We should catch up with Pippit and the others. That way we can protect them better. Then if a ravager shows up, we will fight it."

That's more like it, thought Panthrar. He nodded his assent.

After awhile, they again saw the large, bulky forms of the threehorns moving in and out of the mist at the edge of visibility. Old Solitary turned to Panthrar and suggested, "You go ahead and tell younger sister that we are here. I will drop back for a moment and see if I can determine if the ravager is still following us."

With that, the old male turned abruptly around, and began jogging back towards the west. Panthrar just stood there, watching the old male depart, motionless in indecision. There was more here than he understood, he thought to himself. What was the old male doing? Why did the wretched old thing with his emaciated body and his broken horn, why did he think that he must make this sacrifice?

* * * * *

Old Solitary jogged back toward the west. The world was eerily silent. The fog seemed to blanket everything. He listened carefully, but he could hear no one, neither Panthrar who he had left standing back behind him, nor the ravager that he was sure was in front of him.

After awhile, Old Solitary saw the ravager appear out of the haze. She saw him at almost the same instant. The female quickened her pace. She moved silently. She neither hissed nor roared. To her surprise, the hornbrow didn't run away. Instead it continued to trot straight towards her.

Now what, she asked herself? These hornbrows behaved in the most peculiar ways. But why worry? What could it do to her?

On she came. Old Solitary stopped and waited for her. When she was close enough, he threw a mud-ball at her, and then bolted for the river. The mud-ball smashed right into the startled face of the ravager. She shook her head in quick jerking motions, flinging the grimy debris from her face. Prancer stifled the urge to roar. She displayed her sharp killing teeth, and emitted a low menacing hiss. She snapped her mouth shut savagely. Then she charged after the hornbrow.

Old Solitary ran straight towards the river. As the ravager gained upon him, he dodged right and left, trying to elude the jaws of the killer. The dreadcharger followed every move, trying to close with the him. Old Solitary got closer and closer to the river. But the sprinting dreadcharger was gaining faster.

Prancer made a determined leap at the scrambling hornbrow. He was almost at the river's edge. Old Solitary felt, rather than saw, her hurtling body arcing through the air at him. He dove to the left, sliding in the mud. He just managed to avoid the raking talons and serrated teeth of the ravager.

Prancer hit the ground, rather than the back of the hornbrow as she had planned, skidding in the slop. She tried to reverse direction, to again close with the hornbrow. Her body turned, but her feet lost their traction in the slippery mud. Head, shoulders and torso went one way, feet, legs and tail went another. She was again airborne, stretched out parallel to the ground, for one brief moment. Then she crashed to the earth.

Old Solitary scrambled in the mud, lurching towards the bank of the river. He moved as fast as he could toward the shallows, hoping to get into deep water before the dreadcharger caught up with him. He ran on all fours, white foam erupting all around him, as he tried to will his way into deeper water.

Prancer managed to get to her feet with amazing alacrity. She was very angry at this old hornbrow. She hissed at Old Solitary, and then bolted after him.

Old Solitary heard the dreadcharger's footsteps splashing in the water behind him. The moment had arrived. He had to turn and fight. If he tried to run any further, the ravager would be on his back, and it would all be over. He shrugged to himself. If he had only made it into the deeper water. He might then have had a chance.

Prancer knew that the hornbrow couldn't escape. She slowed as she stepped through the swirling shallows. Her two short forelimbs seemed to stretch in his direction. The two little fingers of each hand flexed in anticipation.

The old male continued to back into deeper water. He leaned well forward, swinging his broad, flat tail back and forth, keeping it just above the surface of the water. The young female slowed further, approaching the old male cautiously, but unfalteringly.

Prancer took two quick steps forward, opening her mouth, displaying deadly teeth. Then she snapped her jaws shut with an unnerving smack. Old Solitary wanted to keep back-pedaling, but he knew that if he backed into deeper water now, it would inhibit the swing of his tail. He was almost waist deep. If only he had had a few moments more. He might have gotten into deep enough water to equalize the battle, or he might have gotten away completely. But not now, they were almost face-to-face.

Prancer opened her large gaping mouth, and prepared for the final leap. Old Solitary stared fixedly at the rows of five and six inch teeth, the moist tongue, the cavernous throat. He smelled the fetid breath of the meat-eater. He felt the chill of the water rushing around his legs. There was a mortal quiet in the air. Time seemed to stand still.

"Haaarooooon." The loud hooting challenge of a male hornbrow broke the deadly stillness. It came from so close that it sounded like it had come from the ravager herself.

Prancer jerked her head around to the left towards the source of the sound. Old Solitary looked also. Panthrar came splashing through the shallow water, charging straight for the dreadcharger.

He was close, unbelievably close. Most of his approach had been as stealthy as a predator. He had avoided stepping into the water until he was as close as he could get. He had restrained himself from honking until he was almost upon the ravager. Even so, he had only honked because he could see that if he didn't distract the dreadcharger, she would be upon Old Solitary before he could get there.

It worked. He was darting forward at near to full speed. Before either Old Solitary or Prancer could react, Panthrar smashed into the side of the dreadcharger. It was not elegant, but it was effective. Prancer stumbled to the right, almost knocked off of her feet by the force of the blow. She roared horribly, jaws leaning, yearning, grasping at Panthrar.

Old Solitary recovered from his surprise. He swung his tail around as hard as he could. The blow struck the ravager on her belly. The impact forced Prancer to her knees. She hissed and snapped at the older male. Old Solitary sprang back, avoiding the massive jaws of his adversary.

Panthrar, on his knees in the water after the impact, scrambled on all fours away from the ravager. His heart pounded in his chest. He was certain that the ravager would sink her teeth into his back before he could rise. He sloshed in the muddy water all the faster, trying to get to his feet.

Panthrar got to his feet, and turned toward the ravager. She too was struggling to her feet. Old Solitary, recovering from the delivery of his first blow, struck the ravager again. It had less of a wind-up, and the ravager shrugged it off. She lunged at the old male. He fell backwards, just avoiding the deadly jaws.

Panthrar hopped in the shallow water towards the dreadcharger. He pivoted hard, just as she snapped again at Old Solitary. Old Solitary pushed backwards once more, into deeper water, desperately trying to stay out of the range of the death-dealing, razor-sharp teeth.

Prancer, still off-balance, missed the old male again. A split second later, she sensed Panthrar's presence, and jerked her head around. Panthrar's tail struck her hard in the hips. Prancer staggered sidewards, and tripped. She fell into the shallows with a mighty splash. The heavy blow likewise sent shivers up through Panthrar's frame. He lost his footing, and crashed into the muddy water.

Prancer scrambled in Panthrar's direction. He saw venomous anger in the flashing red eyes of the dreadcharger. He pushed himself away from her, toes slipping in the mud. Frantically he kicked in the shallow water, trying to propel himself to safety. His fingers reached for a handhold. Slimy mud oozed through his fingers,.as he searched in vain for anything to help him – something to pull himself away from her faster, something to throw at her, a weapon to help subdue her, anything.

* * * * *

Grendaar stood on the low hill, like he had done every day since the great trek back to the coastal plain had begun. He stood alone, staring into the west, hoping to see the son that he could never bring himself to believe was really lost forever. He kept hoping against hope, that the impossible would occur, and that Panthrar would materialize before his eyes, appearing out of the mists in the west.

Each time that he saw this in his mind's eye, he saw the swift adolescent male come rushing to him on winged feet. They would smile at each other, and nuzzle each other, and then Panthrar would offer him a branch of tender berries. Then they would travel together, and Grendaar would listen to all of the tales that he was certain Panthrar would have to tell him.

An hour or more ago, his reveries were broken by the distant roaring of a ravager. That reminded him that he was very vulnerable, out here so far from the herd. He would soon have to turn and travel back closer to it. But he had done this every day. Standing on a high piece of ground, staring towards the west. Every day he had risked his life to be out here, waiting. Often he had to elude a foraging ravager. Once he had even fought a dreadrunner, and chased it off. But then he had been lucky, and the dreadrunner not hungry enough to press the issue too strongly.

Grendaar turned and looked back towards the east. It had stopped raining, but the humidity was still high. There, far to the east, sitting on a hillock of his own, was the ever-faithful Dandraar, watching his father. Dandraar just sat there silently, unmoving, perhaps a quarter of a mile away, at the edge of visibility. No matter what Grendaar said or did, he could not make Dandraar go back to the safety of the herd. Dandraar kept the vigil with his father, in his own way.

By now, the herd must be at least a mile to the east. It was moving at a slow leisurely pace, unrushed by ravagers. The rear-guard was unusually strong, since there had been so many attempts upon the herd by ravagers of all sizes. But the packers kept them at bay. Out here away from the herd, it was a miracle that Grendaar and Dandraar had managed to avoid detection for so long.

Grendaar looked once again to the west. He tried to penetrate the dense mist. He heard the ravager again. This time much closer. He tried to see through the frustrating fog. Was that movement? He stared hard at the spot where he thought he had seen movement. If it was a ravager, he would have to retreat quickly. No, it was much smaller. A razortooth, perhaps, or some prey. Prey running away from the advancing ravager.

He continued to stare. Yes, it was a small form, not quite bipedal, coming his way. It was uniquely familiar, not a razortooth at all. But how could it be what it looked to be? For it seemed to be a fledge hornbrow, running in his direction. He stirred. A protective instinct surged through him.

A cloud of mist suddenly blocked his view. He strained to see the fledge, but couldn't. Had it just been his imagination? He turned back to assure himself that Dandraar was still there. It was a unnecessary gesture. Dandraar would always be there. Grendaar silently signaled to Dandraar to be alert. Something seemed to be coming out of the mists to the west. Dandraar vibrated with excitement.

Grendaar waited. But nothing re-appeared. Perhaps it had been his imagination after all. His imagination seemed to be getting much more active in his old age. Grendaar sighed. He picked up the staff that had been lying at his feet. It was time to go. He turned and signaled to Dandraar that it had been a false alarm. He would walk back away with Dandraar, before he selected another hill or ridge to stand upon and wait.

* * * * *

Pippit could clearly hear the ravager behind her. It was close. It was attacking something, of that she was certain. And it didn't take much imagination for her to realize who it would be that the dreadcharger was fighting. She was frantic. Panthrar was fighting a dreadcharger, so close to her that she could hear it. She could hardly bear it. She must go help him. Desperately she cast about for a solution. Maybe she should leave the fledges with the threehorns.

Second was running well ahead of the rest of Pippit's fledges. That little fledge always seemed to be taking unnecessary chances. Fortunately her brother, First, was always near her. They tended to look after each other.

"Look, my mother," Second called back to Pippit through the haze that separated them, "It is one of the People. It's a giant hornbrow."

Pippit tried to stare through the curtain of moisture-laden air. She continued to walk towards the east, trying to penetrate the fog. Then she saw it. Through the gently swirling mists to the east. On a distant hill. Barely distinguishable. It was a male hornbrow, standing like a sentinel.

Pippit cried out the recognition signal of the Red Dawn Tribe. The distant male hornbrow called back to her the correct response of a member of the tribe.

Pippit called to her fledges. "Quick, my little fledges. See the giant hornbrow on that distant hill? Run to the giant hornbrow. Run to him. Do not stop until you are under his protection."

They turned to her in seeming incomprehension. Many stared up into her face, questioningly. They did not want to leave her. Some stared at the distant hornbrow. Others looked, but couldn't quite see him in the heavy mist.

Pippit repeated her instructions. "Run to the giant hornbrow, my little fledges. Run to the top of the hill. Keep a watch in all directions as you run, but run to the hornbrow. If you see anything other than hornbrows, call to me, and I will come."

First asked, "Where will you be, my mother?"

Without hesitation Pippit responded, "I am going to help your father. I will bring him back to you."

First paused, looking towards the distant hill. Suddenly he understood what his mother was trying to do. Then he said, "Come, my little fledges, let us run to the giant hornbrow. Come, I will race you there. I bet I will be the first one there."

First began to run, but he looked back to see if his brothers and sisters would follow. Second also understood. She took a few steps forward. "Come, my little fledges," she said, "Let us race First. I will beat him."

"No, I will be there first," said Seventh. Then they were all running towards the lone hornbrow on the distant hill.

Pippit turned to the threehorn females, who couldn't see the giant hornbrow at all. They too looked at her questioningly. "Thun varm du," said Bluntnose politely. "Orphnig kontable rasmussen?" she asked.

"May the sun warm you, my sisters," said Pippit to the three females. "There is safety," she pointed. "Run to safety. Run to safety."

They looked quizzically in the direction she indicated. The little hornbrows were scampering along in that direction. Then they looked at her again. "Scruffty? Orphnig kontable rasmussen?" asked Highstepper.

Pippit looked impatiently back towards the west. Then she said, "Follow me."

Pippit ran towards the giant hornbrow. The threehorns followed at a gallop, pups charging ahead, enjoying the game, exhaustion temporarily forgotten.

Pippit honked that these threehorns were friends, and that they were not to be feared. The male tooted an acknowledgement. Pippit continued to run towards the hill until she was sure that the threehorns saw where they were going. Then she quietly let herself slip behind them. She watched a moment longer, as her fledges swarmed up the hill to the male hornbrow. The threehorns were also running to the hill. Then Pippit turned around, and sped as fast as she could go in the direction of Panthrar and the ravager.

In her anxiety over Panthrar's well-being, she failed to notice a small bipedal shape. It had been standing right beside her as she watched the fledges and the threehorns racing for the hill. As she ran towards where she thought she would find Panthrar, it raced along as well as it could, trying to keep up with her.

* * * * *

Grendaar turned quickly. He heard the recognition call of the tribe. The source of the call was quite close. He wasn't aware of anyone behind him. There couldn't be, since he had been trailing behind the herd for all of these days. These must be stragglers that he wasn't aware of.

He tried to penetrate the fog, but couldn't. He called back to whoever it was that had called him. Then he saw.... Well, he couldn't believe his eyes. He ran to the edge of the hill. Yes, it was a dozen or so little fledges running towards him.

He called encouragement to them. They seemed to be running almost merrily to him, zigging and zagging playfully. But he must have been mistaken, for then he saw what they were running from. A group of threehorns was chasing them.

He was just about to call the rear-guard of the Great Eastern Herd, when he saw an adult female hornbrow in the midst of the threehorns. Was she fighting them? No, it didn't look like it. She was running with them. What a confusing sight. The female signaled to him that these were their friends, and were not to be feared. Not quite believing what he heard, he signaled back that he had heard her. Then he saw threehorn pups running with the females, and felt a little reassured. As he watched the race to his hill, the female hornbrow suddenly turned around, and sped away.

The little fledges rushed up to the giant hornbrow, and then stopped in hushed awe. They had never seen such a large hornbrow before. First, the

390

eldest, felt that it was appropriate for him to speak for the brood. He executed his best bow, just as Pippit had taught him, and said, "May the sun warm you, oh great one." His brothers and sisters all bowed, and chimed in, in a ragged series of greetings.

"May the sun warm you, my little fledges," replied Grendaar. He pointed at the approaching threehorns, "Are these your friends, or your enemies, little ones?"

"They are our friends, oh great one," said First.

"They are our roam, oh great one," added Fourth.

"Your roam?" questioned Grendaar.

"Our temporary roam, oh great one," corrected Second.

"Yes, oh great one," explained Seventh, "We are of the roam of Thundermaker."

"The roam of Thundermaker?" mused Grendaar, frowning, trying to comprehend.

By now, the female threehorns and their pups were galloping up to the top of the hill. The closer they got to Grendaar, the more they slowed. Finally they came to a stop, uncertain of the reception they would get. They looked around for the rest of the hornbrows, expecting that they had finally found the great herd that they had been following for so long. They were surprised to find only one hornbrow.

Highstepper stepped forward. She said, "Thun varm du."

Grendaar looked at her in surprise. It seemed almost as if she was greeting him. He was slow to react.

"Thun varm du," she repeated.

"Thun varm du. Thun varm du," giggled the fledges. "She is greeting you, oh great one," they offered in unison.

"Thun varm du," said Bluntnose. Then to the fledges, "Ogtrossen gennep?"

Before the fledges could explain, Grendaar said, "And may the sun warm you, great horned ones...."

The fledges giggled and trilled. They squawked at the threehorns, who visibly relaxed.

"... may the sun warm you all. And your little pups, too," finished Grendaar. He was positive that the fledges were actually talking to the threehorns. He would have to follow up on this later.

With the greetings at least minimally dispensed with, Grendaar asked the fledges, "Was that your mother little ones? And where did she run off to?"

"That was our mother, Pippit" said the dark-striped Fourth.

Pippit, Grendaar repeated to himself. That is a familiar name. Where have I heard it before?

"She went off to help our father and Old Solitary fight off the dreadchargers," added First. Dreadchargers! Grendaar's concern heightened. He silently signaled to Dandraar to join him. Dandraar came at a run.

Then Grendaar said calmly to the fledges, "Do not be frightened little fledges, and tell your friends that all is well. But I must now make a loud noise to call for some help."

Grendaar paused only momentarily, barely leaving enough time for the fledges to explain to the threehorns. Then Grendaar turned to face the east, raised his head to the heavens, and wailed a long, loud, low-frequency honk, "Hooonnnooonnnoonnn."

To those standing near him, it was ear-splitting. Notwithstanding the warning, the fledges and pups flattened themselves to the ground. Slowly they backed away from Grendaar. Their widened eyes clearly signaled their fright and awe.

The adult female threehorns were somewhat less concerned, for they had seen this type of hornbrow behavior before. As twice more Grendaar signaled the warning, they looked about, expecting to see more hornbrows materialize.

Pups hovered between their mother's legs, ready to flee if need be, looking out in wonder at the giant hornbrow. The fledges quickly overcame their awe, and looked in admiration at the giant before them. Second was the first to recover enough to ask, "Who are you, oh great one?"

"Why..." Grendaar paused, just realizing that he had not yet given his name. It was embarrassing to be so impolite, even if the circumstances dictated that he get vital information as quickly as possible. "I am Grendaar, little ones," he said. "Grendaar of the Green Water Roam, of the Red Dawn Tribe."

"Grendaar," said the small voices in awe. It almost reverberated, as eleven little voices repeated it to themselves. They exchanged glances, hardly believing their ears.

"The Groundshaker," added several. "The Groundshaker," repeated several more.

Grendaar was startled. They couldn't have just come upon that name. "How do you know I am the Groundshaker?" he asked.

First swelled up proudly and said, "You are our grandfather, oh great one."

Grandfather? Others nodded while Grendaar stood in shocked silence. He stared first at the fledges, and then, slowly, in disbelief, he stared towards the west.

"Your mother is called Pippit?" he asked. They nodded, but he did not see them, for awareness was painfully overcoming him. "And your father? He is called...?"

"Panthrar," they responded in unison.

By now Dandraar had joined the group. Noting the presence of threehorns, he approached warily. He was leaning forward, his tail already flicking back and forth. Nodding politely to Grendaar, he asked, "How may I be of service to you, my father?"

Grendaar gave short shift to a lifetime of etiquette, as he quickly summarized: "This is Dandraar, little ones, he is my son. And these are the fledges of Pippit, my son. And of Panthrar. Pippit has gone to help Panthrar fight the dreadcharger. And these, my son," said Grendaar gesturing to the threehorns, "are the friends of these fledges."

Dandraar looked at Grendaar in amazement. He couldn't quite assimilate all that he had heard. The fledges of Panthrar? Friendly threehorns? A dreadcharger? Before he could say anything, Grendaar commanded, "Stay with Dandraar, little fledges, until I return. Dandraar, take care of your nieces and nephews." Grendaar sprang forward, running down the hill. He turned once to look over his shoulder. "And summon the rear-guard."

Grendaar accelerated down the slope of the hill, and ran as fast as he could towards the west. His staff lay forgotten on the hilltop.

CHAPTER THIRTY-TWO
TERROR

Pippit hurried in the direction she expected to find Panthrar and Old Solitary. She ran low and horizontal, with her broad tail extending straight back behind her. Although she ran on her two hind feet, she occasionally resorted to running on all fours. This allowed her to keep up her speed.

Fear gripped her heart. She strained to get there more quickly, wherever "there" was, to find Panthrar, before something awful happened to him. She knew that she was getting close, for she could hear the splashing of large bodies struggling in the water. She veered closer to the river's edge.

Suddenly she could see ghostly movement, dimly through the mist, in the shallows of the great river. As she came upon the scene of the fight, she beheld the terrible vision of Panthrar on his back, scrambling in the shallows, his hands and feet thrashing furiously, trying to get away from the dreadcharger. A female dreadcharger was struggling unsuccessfully to her feet, stumbling after Panthrar. The dreadcharger hissed and growled, stretching out to grab hold of the young male. Old Solitary was rapidly wading to shallower water behind the ravager.

A cold knot of fear gripped Pippit's heart. But she was no longer the frightened little adolescent that quaked at the slightest hint of a ravager. Her fear was for her mate. Without hesitation, she ran to Panthrar. She ran up beside him, and splashed past him to a stop. She stood between Panthrar and the ravager, staring determinedly at the dreadcharger. Panthrar, wet and muddy, did not need to look up to know who had intervened on his behalf. As Pippit began to swing her tail back and forth, Prancer finally got to her feet.

The dreadcharger seemed unaffected by the fact that she now faced three hornbrows. She too had finally gotten to her feet. She stood less than thirty feet away. It was a distance that the dreadcharger could cover in a heartbeat. Prancer drew her head back in a hiss, and then jerked it forward, snapping at Pippit.

Pippit was frightened almost out of her wits, but she stood her ground. More from fear than from bravado, she honked loudly at the ravager. She wanted to run away as fast as she could, but she wouldn't leave Panthrar. She could sense Panthrar rising to his feet beside her. It gave her courage. The male hornbrow quietly said, "Move more to the right, my wife, so that we have plenty of room to swing our tails."

Without thinking, Pippit moved to obey. As she moved to the side, Panthrar charged forward. Almost within the clutches of the dreadcharger, he pivoted, swinging his tail with all his might. The ravager jumped back to avoid the blow. As she did so, Old Solitary, who was standing behind her, swung his tail with all of the force he could muster.

Prancer, not knowing that it was coming, was struck totally unprepared. The force of Old Solitary's blow knocked her completely off of her feet. Limbs akimbo, she collapsed into the water, bruised, winded, and angry. As she struggled in confusion, the hornbrows rained repeated blows upon her with their broad, flat tails. Even Pippit joined in, trying to incapacitate the ravager long enough for them to get away. Prancer was knocked almost senseless by the desperate hornbrows.

Then they raced to the shore. It was only then that they beheld a little fledge, sitting near the bank, breathing heavily. She was watching her parents fight the dreadcharger. Her expression was a mixture of alarm, relief, pride, and confusion.

"Fourteenth," exclaimed Pippit, "What are you doing here?"

"I have come to help, my mother," came the innocent reply. "Shall I strike the vile dreadcharger?"

"No, my little fledge. You must stay away from the dreadcharger."

As the adults gathered around the fledge, she said, "Now we can bring father home to the little fledges."

The three adult hornbrows moved closer to the fledge. While Pippit nuzzled and inspected her fledge, Panthrar looked back at Prancer. The female dreadcharger was still dazed by the repeated blows. She could not quite pull herself up onto her hind feet.

*   *   *   *   *

Grendaar ran towards the noises of battle. He was getting close. Now he could hear voices. He ran through a small patch of fog, and saw three hornbrows, clustered around the small figure of a fledge. He changed his course slightly, moving directly toward them. As he ran, he inspected the scene. He could also see a dreadcharger laboring in the shallows of the river.

He examined the dreadcharger. She seemed befuddled, and was having difficulty getting to her feet.

He looked back at the hornbrows. His heart leapt with joy. One of the hornbrows was Panthrar. A second was the female he had seen so recently. Pippit. He recognized the third hornbrow, also, although he was surprised to see him. He was just about to call to them, when he saw something else.

Further up river, racing out of the mists along the bank, came a large, male dreadcharger. He moved fast, holding himself low. His red eyes blazed fire.

Grendaar hooted, "Danger!"

All four hornbrows jerked their heads towards Grendaar. Panthrar's eyes lighted in recognition. Old Solitary's eyes clouded slightly. Pippit's eyes held anxiety. Fourteenth's eyes held confusion. Then they all saw Grendaar signal: "Dreadcharger!"

All three heads of the adults swiveled around towards the west. Fourteenth, not correctly interpreting the message, looked at Prancer, who was still splashing around in the water, still not on her feet.

Terror, hugging the bank of the river, was charging down on them at a frightful speed. The three adults turned and bolted in panic. Fourteenth turned in dismay to watch them depart.

Pippit looked about her feet, expecting to see Fourteenth there, running along with her. She was not. As she ran, Pippit looked over her shoulder. Fourteenth was just rising to her feet, staring at her departing parents. The little fledge was still unaware that the fearsome giant was bearing down upon her, running almost silently on soft, padded, three-toed feet.

Pippit stopped and turned towards her fledge. "Run, Fourteenth," she screamed. "Runnn!"

At Pippit's cry, Panthrar and Old Solitary looked over their shoulders. So did Fourteenth. The little fledge saw the gruesome giant, mouth agape, teeth fully extended, bearing down upon her. Terror held himself low, seeming to stretch forward to grasp her all the sooner. To Fourteenth, the awful giant seemed to be looking right at her.

She screamed shrilly, and then dashed in the direction of her parents. Prompted by a well-formed instinct for self-preservation, her four little legs propelled her forward faster than she had ever moved before in her life.

Panthrar and Old Solitary were already moving at full speed back towards Fourteenth. They raced past Pippit, who was frozen in shock at the near-certainty of the imminent death of her fledge – and the unhappy circumstance that she was helpless to do anything at all about it.

The hornbrows racing past her snapped her into action. As she sprang forward to try and help her fledge, Grendaar, who had by now built up a considerable degree of speed himself, also raced past her.

All four of the hornbrows were running towards Terror. Panthrar and Old Solitary were in the lead, followed by Grendaar, who was followed by Pippit.

Panthrar and Old Solitary sped side-by-side. They both were judging speeds and distances. Fourteenth was getting closer to safety with every footstep. But the ravager was gaining much more rapidly. Panthrar could see that he would get to Fourteenth before the ravager did. But he could also see that before he could pick her up, turn, and race away, the dreadcharger would be upon him. He decided to race past Fourteenth, station himself between the fledge and the ravager, and let Pippit snatch the fledge to safety.

As he ran, Panthrar tried to convey this plan to Old Solitary. Together, they might hold off the dreadcharger until Grendaar got there. Then they all might escape to safety. Through ragged gasps of breath, the older male grunted concurrence.

"Run to your mother", Panthrar yelled to Fourteenth as he sped past her. He braked to a halt just past the fledge, and prepared to do battle.

Old Solitary joined him, standing on his right. Somehow Old Solitary managed to say, between heavy breaths, "Let's make this dreadcharger sorry he ever met these two hornbrows." They both pivoted, swinging their tails at Terror. The ravager braked, trying to avoid being struck by the tails.

Grendaar raced up, taking a position on the left side of Panthrar. He did so just as Terror dashed forward, trying to attack Panthrar while his back was turned, halfway through the pivot.

Grendaar swung his tail at the dreadcharger. Terror maneuvered backwards, again trying to avoid being struck full-force by an adult male hornbrow. Terror could see that here was a hornbrow almost as large as he. He would have to attack it carefully.

Panthrar and Old Solitary, finishing their turns, were again facing the ravager. They honked deafeningly, and made short charging gestures, trying to distract the ravager while Grendaar completed his turn.

Pippit hurried up to Fourteenth, got between her and the ravager, and herded her towards the east as fast as Fourteenth could run. In the distant east, she could hear a low rumbling. Packers were coming. She ran with her fledge towards the sound.

The three male hornbrows were spread in a small semi-circle in front of the ravager. Their tails swung in powerful arcs, looking for an opening to topple him. Terror snarled and spit at them. Hissing voluminously, he took a threatening step towards them.

They honked loudly back at the ravager, and took a tentative step backwards. Then they took another. And another. Slowly they retreated. And with each backward step, the dreadcharger took a threatening step after them.

Grendaar knew that time was on their side. If they could hold off the dreadcharger just a short while longer, the packers would arrive. Then a legitimate defense could be mounted. Protection of fledges seemed to inspire packers. It was at this time of the seasonal cycle that they were at their most aggressive. They just might be able to chase off the dreadcharger.

Terror could hear the packers also. They were hooting and honking as they came. Dandraar had told them that it was a dreadcharger that they were coming to repulse.

Terror seemed to hesitate. The gap between the ravager and the three male hornbrows widened. Maybe he didn't want to tangle with several dozen soldier hornbrows. Maybe he knew something that the hornbrows didn't. With the ravager's hesitation, the three hornbrows saw their opportunity to escape. As if on some hidden signal, all three turned around simultaneously, and bolted towards the east.

They might have escaped unharmed, for Terror still seemed to hesitate. But to the surprise of all three, Prancer stood blocking their retreat. She had regained her senses in the shallows of the river, and had painfully struggled to her feet. It was then that she saw the hornbrows who had been taunting her for so long, facing Terror. As quickly and as quietly as possible she had left the river, and sped for a position to block their retreat.

The hornbrows slowed almost to a complete stop. Oh what a delightful twist of fate, she thought, now these pests are trapped. It delighted her even more to see the looks of dismay on their faces when they saw that to escape, they must get by her. One surely wouldn't. Which one really didn't matter to her. She roared frightfully, and charged. Terror also roared from behind them, and then he too charged.

In an instant flash of clarity, Panthrar could see it more clearly than he had ever seen anything in his life. Grendaar should try to bolt around to the right of Prancer. If he kept moving fast, he might escape. Old Solitary should try to bolt around to the left. Then he too would escape. That would leave only Panthrar in the precarious position of being in the middle, with nowhere to go but forward towards Prancer, or backwards towards Terror. At least two of the hornbrows would likely escape. But one surely wouldn't.

Panthrar knew that it was just fate. If he hadn't been in the middle, then he could have been one of the ones to escape. But the two larger males had just been trying to protect him. So they had placed him in the middle. What had been a protected position only a moment before, had suddenly become an ill-fated one. Now it was his time.

Without hesitating, he ran straight for Prancer. If he struck her hard enough, he might bowl her over, and get by her before Terror was on his back. But Terror was too close. It was the futile hope of the hopeless.

But Grendaar and Old Solitary seemed to have different ideas. They also sprinted straight for Prancer. Old Solitary brushed Panthrar aside as he raced for the female dreadcharger. "Run for your life, son of Tessah," he cried. Then he and Grendaar sprang at Prancer. Terror was close behind all three.

Grendaar ran with his head up. He clearly intended to try to knock the ravager off of her feet, and to keep running, hoping that in that way, they all could escape.

Old Solitary had a different plan in mind. Old Solitary held his head low, horn pointed at the center of the dreadcharger's chest.

Prancer had plainly seen the threat coming. She focused her main attention on the horn, as she tried to ward off Old Solitary's impending blow. She gave the Groundshaker only cursory attention. She judged the threat of the other more serious.

Grendaar and Old Solitary struck Prancer at almost the same time. Grendaar hit her hard on the left shoulder. She tried to push him aside, but staggering, missed. She still kept her primary focus on the on-rushing horn. Grendaar brushed past her, and kept running. He looked over his shoulder as he ran, to make sure that the other two also got by the ravager.

Old Solitary didn't try to brush past the ravager. Prancer, tottering from Grendaar's blow, standing on only her right foot, left foot clawing at air, waved her tiny fore-limbs futilely at Old Solitary as, a split second later, he also made contact. With head lowered, he plunged his broken, ten inch horn into the chest of the dreadcharger.

Prancer screamed frightfully in pain and distress. The force of the impact caused her to stumble backwards. She tried to push Old Solitary away, but he held her tightly. She tried to bite him with her five and six inch killing teeth, but he was too close to her, and she couldn't maneuver her jaws to get a fast hold on him.

Panthrar darted around to the right of Prancer. He was free and clear, and could have gotten away, but he slowed as he saw that it looked like Old Solitary was not going to be quick enough to get away from the ravager. In fact, it looked like the old male was holding on to her tightly.

When Grendaar saw Panthrar slow, he too slowed. He was not going to lose his son after all this. Both males of the Green Water Roam stopped completely, hesitating, hoping that Old Solitary would push himself away from the struggling ravager, and break away to safety.

Then Terror struck. He hit Old Solitary with the force of an avalanche. He bowled both the hornbrow and the female dreadcharger over with the strength of his attack, ripping Old Solitary off of Prancer in the process. Prancer staggered and fell to the ground.

Terror wrapped himself around the old male, and quickly sank his massive jaws into the back of Old Solitary's neck. The old male cried out in distress. It happened so quickly, that neither Panthrar nor Grendaar had time to react. Then it was too late to do anything but watch.

Terror sank his teeth in deeper. Old Solitary staggered, and fell to the ground. Terror shook the old male hard, ripping, ripping. Old Solitary screamed in pain. He struggled, trying to break free from the fatal hold of Terror.

He could not get away. His struggles weakened. He could feel the earth tremble as the packers approached. Or was that his heartbeat, thundering in his head, slowing, slowing. But it didn't matter. He knew that the packers would arrive too late to save him. His lower body was already numb from the death-bite of the ravager. And the weight of the dreadcharger was crushing the air out of him.

He shifted his head, his chin sliding in the mud, so that he could see Panthrar and Grendaar. They stood immobile, frozen in time and place, staring into his eyes. Panthrar looked like he was in shock. Even Grendaar looked stricken. Old Solitary mouthed the words, "Thun varm du." Then he sighed, and gave up his life-force.

Panthrar stood stock still, like a stone. The world slowed around him. He felt numb. He felt dizzy. All he could see was Old Solitary lying there in the mud, with the giant dreadcharger clinging to his back. Panthrar felt a sudden chill gripping him. He shivered. He was nauseous.

Grendaar looked side-long at Panthrar. He could see how grief-stricken the younger male was. Panthrar took a step forward. Grendaar tried to get Panthrar's attention, but Panthrar was lost in a world of grief only of his own knowing.

Terror shook the old male again. Then he released Old Solitary. He looked straight at Grendaar and Panthrar, and roared mightily.

Panthrar took another step forward. He growled a deep-throated challenge.

Terror climbed off of Old Solitary. He stood watching the two hornbrows, especially the younger one. He seemed the more threatening. Grendaar pulled at Panthrar. "Come, my son, there is nothing we can do for him now."

For a moment, Panthrar seemed to come out of his reverie. He turned and looked at Grendaar with unseeing eyes. Why? He asked himself. Why had Old Solitary done that? Why did he not try to do what Grendaar had done? It might have worked. Then they all could have gotten away. But what his father said was true. There was nothing that he could do for the old male now. If he died fighting the dreadcharger, then Old Solitary's sacrifice would have been in vain.

Terror went over to Prancer's assistance. She lay on the ground, breathing heavily. She held both of her hands over her wound. That did little to stem the steady flow of blood. Never taking his eyes off of the two hornbrows, Terror began to lick Prancer's wound with compassionate determination.

The two hornbrows stood less than a hundred feet away. Old Solitary's body lay motionless. Panthrar was numb. He felt like he had lost one of his best friends. Beyond that, he felt nothing. He couldn't think at all.

"Come, my son," Grendaar said gently. Panthrar stirred. He looked at the unblinking eyes of his friend. "Thun varm du," he said. Then both he and Grendaar backed away.

Panthrar let himself be led away by Grendaar. Grendaar was anxious to put as much distance as he could between them and the dreadchargers. It was not safe here.

Terror looked up as they slowly moved away. He thought that Prancer's breathing organ might be punctured. He was not sure that she was going to make it. He growled at the hornbrows. They quickened their pace.

Terror had never encountered a more difficult group of hornbrows and threehorns in his life. He looked over at his kill. He half expected that even the flesh of this old male would be tough. He sighed, and began licking Prancer's wound again.

Grendaar led Panthrar in the direction of the packers. They were getting close now. The ground shook from their approach. Soon they would be swarming around these two sons of the Red Dawn Tribe. Then he and Panthrar would be completely safe once more.

Later, Grendaar told himself, he would have time to think about the heroism that he had just witnessed. It was something that he had not expected. Yet he knew, but for it, either he or Panthrar would be the one lying back there now. He guessed that there was a lot about Adeldraar that he didn't know.

EPILOGUE
THE NAMING
CEREMONY

Pᴀɴᴛʜʀᴀʀ ᴀɴᴅ Pɪᴘᴘɪᴛ sᴛᴏᴏᴅ in the cool, glowing darkness of the full moon. Above them, outside of the brilliant lunar envelope, a million stars graced the night. Several hundred feet, and almost a hundred hornbrows, separated them. Although they stood apart, they were together in spirit. Pippit gazed at Panthrar. He seemed lost in thought.

A soft breeze, dancing on the waves, blew off of the ocean. As the breeze lifted up off of the water, it blew foam from the breakers up onto the shore, and ruffled the fine-grained sand of the beach. The beach was a broad, level expanse, almost a thousand feet of white sand that stretched for miles in each direction.

Crustaceans scurried across the beach, earnestly engaged in their night feeding rituals, while trying to keep from under afoot of the congregation of hornbrows. A few nocturnal night-feeding birds pursued the crustaceans, indifferent to the assembly of the giant hadrosaurs.

The breeze crossed the beach, and then abruptly met the forest, where it whispered lazily through the fronds of the palms that stood like a line of green sentinels. Immediately past the beach, the forest became a dense, primitive jungle of tall trees, thick understorey, and rich, rotting compost. The narrow white ribbon of sand was a world apart. The immense verdant universe of jungle was a macrocosm teeming with life, that stretched a hundred miles to the distant escarpment.

Panthrar looked up at the moon. Its brightness almost hurt his eyes. It was the sixth full moon since the hatching of this year's fledges. The sixth full moon was an important event for the People. It was the traditional time when the newest crop of hornbrows passed from fledges to yearlings. All that they required to make the transition complete was to lose their hatchling names, and to be given the names that they would carry for the rest of their lives.

Panthrar had a difficult time suppressing the urge to engage in reverie. He smiled to himself. These occasions caused many to dwell upon the events of the past. One's own Naming. The Naming of one's friends. Other important events in one's life.

He forced himself to keep his mind on the present by looking around at those here with him. The entire roam had collected at this special spot, at the edge of their territory, to witness the ceremony. In fact, on this night of nights, all of the roams of all of the tribes that composed the Great Eastern Herd, were each in their special places, observing similar ceremonies.

Panthrar looked to his right. Grendaar sat upon a large flat rock. It was a short, wide boulder, that when Grendaar sat upon it, elevated his head a few feet above the others. The rock was located above the high water mark, in the broad expanse of beach. The sea water rarely splashed upon this special rock, except during heavy storms.

Around Grendaar stood all of the adult males of the roam. Rohraar stood to Grendaar's right. Trugahr stood on Grendaar's left. Wubbar stood beside Trugahr, and Panthrar stood beside him. Other males stood beside Rohraar, further to the right.

All the rest of the roam stood before the assembly of males. Each of the adult females stood with their fledges, forming seventeen separate pockets of excitement. Behind these stood a large ring of adolescents and youngsters.

Tessah was already leading her latest brood up to Grendaar, where she would announce each fledge's name. As the assembly of adult males accepted the name, each fledge would pass the threshold from fledgehood.

Many things would change by the end of the ceremony. For one, the fledges would enjoy a new status. It would be another beginning for them – one in which they were tied less to their mothers, and more to the roam.

Other things would also change. The new yearlings would no longer have one mother, but many. All adult females in the roam would be addressed as "mother". And they would no longer one father, but many. All the adult males of the roam would be addressed as "father". They would address all other hornbrows as either "elder brother" or "elder sister". All, except the other fledges going through the Naming Ceremony this night: these they would call either "brother" or "sister".

Panthrar reflected with regret that one other thing would change. He could no longer refer to Pippit as "my wife", nor she refer to him as "my husband". Instead, he must call her "my sister", and she call him "my brother". This was the way it must be, until they mated again next season. And they knew that they would, mate again next season, for they loved each other greatly.

So it was for all of the People. The People did not mate for life, unless of course the male prevailed in the dominance fights, and the female selected him at the appropriate time. And provided that they could do this every year. Then they could remain mated for life. Grendaar and Tessah had managed to do it. So would Panthrar and Pippit.

Panthrar and Pippit would always maintain a special relationship, but soon, in only a few more minutes, they would no longer officially be a mated pair. At least not until next spring. This was the way it had always been for the People, but the thought of it still made Panthrar sad.

Panthrar looked through the crowd of females and broods to Pippit and their brood. They were standing near the back of the assemblage. Pippit was at the bottom of the hierarchy of adult females within the roam, even below Mungu and Tuojah and Jasmaan, and therefore she would take her fledges through the ceremony last. Panthrar didn't mind this. They were home now, and that was all that really mattered. He could see that Pippit was both excited and proud. The fledges, soon to be yearlings, were fairly bursting with excitement. All nine of them.

Panthrar's mood turned even more melancholy. His mind wandered back to the dreadful crossing of the upper plain. It seemed like a lifetime ago now. It had been the most eventful, but most difficult crossing of his life.

He smiled at the memory of his escape from the ravine, and his journey to the foothills with Pippit. He recalled the meeting with Thundermaker, and their long and pleasant sojourn with him and his herd. But that crossing was not the dreadful memory. It was the return trip that so often stirred uneasy memories.

Between the eruption of Smoking Mountain, and the constant pursuit by ravagers, in retrospect, it seemed like a miracle that they had survived the crossing at all. If it hadn't been for Thundermaker and his herd, they never would have.

Yes, there were the pleasant memories. Of him and Pippit getting trapped in the ravine, of days of watching the antics of the dreadrunners, and nights of sneaking out of their little hideaway to forage. Memories of their crossing to the breeding grounds, of their unlikely alliance with Thundermaker, and of their long, happy stay with Thundermaker's herd.

And then there were the precious memories, ones he would remember for the rest of his life, nest-building, mating, hatching the young, and guarding them against a hostile world. And later, when they had finally rejoined the roam, the happy moments of introducing Pippit to Grendaar and the other males, and to Tessah and the other females. And the proud memories of him and Pippit introducing their fledges to the roam.

Somehow, in the excitement of those days of being re-united with the roam, the bitter memories of Old Solitary's death seemed less painful. But since then he had thought of Old Solitary many times. He had heard of the old male's hasty departure from the tribe. Not from Grendaar, of course. Ever since that fateful day when Grendaar, Panthrar, and Old Solitary had stood together fighting Terror, Grendaar refused to speak poorly of Old Solitary.

Trugahr had told Panthrar of the events in the Gathering Place. But to Panthrar, that story, and the others, seemed about someone else. They were not about the Old Solitary that he knew – absent-minded, but lovable. They were not about someone who loved his and Pippit's fledges almost as if they were his own, someone who would have given his life for the fledges. Sadly, he did give his life, saving not only one of the fledges, but possibly Panthrar and Grendaar as well.

Panthrar's mind re-joined the present. Tessah had already finished naming her fledges, and now Monah was naming hers. Soon Koowoo's fledges would be up before the males. Panthrar again gazed at Pippit and their fledges. Pippit caught his eye, and smiled at him. Then she attended to her charges, who were poking and elbowing each other. They were excited.

Panthrar reflected back. Twenty-four eggs. A remarkable feat for such a young female. And nineteen hatchlings. He knew that he would never forget, until the day he died, watching First fight his way out of the shell.

This was a special brood, his first brood. They were all special, and he was proud of all nine of them. He also thought back to the loss of each and every one of those who were not here to share in the happiness of the Naming. Five eggs lost, three stolen by redrunners, two probably lost to little lizards. Third and Fifth, both killed by razorteeth. Eighth, the first of the hatchlings to be lost, stolen by a redrunner. And Ninth, killed by a dreadrunner. And Thirteenth, by another razortooth. And Seventeenth and Eighteenth, both lost in the jungles of the home range of the Green Water Roam. And Nineteenth, another victim of the relentless razorteeth.

They had never found Eleventh and Twelfth. He refused to believe that they were dead. He was positive that they were safe and living with Thundermaker and his herd. He was sure they were. Maybe they were part of Foottangler's brood. Or better yet, maybe Roundfrill had adopted them.

Thundermaker's herd had never been able to join up with the Great Eastern Herd. Seventh had once confided to Panthrar that Thundermaker had always secretly wanted to mingle with the herd, at least once in his life. He had always wanted to roam unimpeded within the Great Eastern Herd, that spread for many miles in all directions. You could easily get lost in the midst of such a herd. Well, it wasn't meant to be. Savage and his troop had pursued Thundermaker's herd, driving them south and away from the great herd.

Highstepper and Bluntnose, and their pups, and the old childless female, Rumblerunner, had traveled with the Green Water Roam and the Red Dawn Tribe almost all the way to the ravine. Then some of the packers had spotted a herd of threehorns far to the south. Rather than travel with the hornbrows down the ravine to the coastal plain, the female threehorns had elicited to join up with the distant herd of their own kind. Some of the packers escorted them to the herd of threehorns, or at least far enough so that the females could actually see the herd that they were trying to join up with.

Panthrar couldn't help but chuckle, and hoped that no one realized that his mind was a hundred miles away. The separation of the fledges and the pups was a wonderful and heart-warming thing to remember, although it was a very sad occasion for the young ones. He hoped that they would indeed be able to keep their promises to re-unite on the upper plain next spring.

Suddenly Panthrar's mind again returned to the present. Wubbar was looking at him. He must have commented to Panthrar, but Panthrar had no idea what he had said. Panthrar coughed self-consciously. Pippit and the fledges were filing up through the crowd, to stand before Grendaar and the males. Panthrar held his breath.

Pippit and the fledges executed perfect bows to Grendaar and the males. Then Pippit went through a series of formal greetings. When they were over, and the responses returned, she began.

"This is First," she introduced. The handsome, seven foot long, eight hundred pound male, who had once been only fifteen inches long and a pound and a half in weight, stepped forward and bowed before the males. "With the permission of the males of the roam," Pippit intoned ritually, "I name him Tessaar, after the parents of his father."

"Welcome, Tessaar," beamed Grendaar.

Tessah, near the front of the roam, smiled. Many of the adult females glanced at her, nodding their approval.

"Thank you, my father," Tessaar said. He then turned and bowed to the assembled roam. There were murmurs of approval and acceptance. Then he stepped aside.

"This is Second," Pippit continued. Second stepped forward. She was five and a quarter feet long, and 650 pounds in weight. After Second bowed, Pippit said, "With the permission of the males of the roam, I name her Panthrit, after her parents."

"Welcome, Panthrit," said Grendaar.

Panthrit turned and bowed amid murmurs of congratulations and acceptance. Pippit stole a look at Panthrar, and they exchanged smiles.

And so the ceremony continued.

"This is Fourth." The young male with the dark stripes stepped forward. "With the permission of the males of the roam, I name him Drassoom, after the parents of his mother."

"This is Sixth." The young female with the dark tail stepped before the males. "With the permission of the males of the roam, I name her Grendet, after our honorable Staffholder."

"This is Seventh." The philosophical young male took his place before the adults. "With the permission of the males of the roam, I name him Thundaar, after a true friend and a valiant guardian."

The males of the roam, who had listened in awe and disbelief to so many of Panthrar's stories, nodded their agreement.

"This is Tenth." The smallest female of the brood walked up with a lightness in her step. She was less than five feet long. "With the permission of the males of the roam, I name her Frillah, after the mother of her brood's friends and neighbors in the hatching grounds."

"This is Fourteenth." First's, no, Tessaar's breathless "little sister" stepped forward. "With the permission of the males of the roam, I name her Adel, after the brave one who saved her life."

Grendaar paused and looked first to the left, directly at Panthrar. His eyes held very little surprise. Then he looked to the right. Finally he smiled. "Welcome Adel," he said.

"This is Fifteenth." The young male with the strange twist to his mouth, the one that made him look like he had a perpetual smile, stepped forward. "With the permission of the males of the roam, I name him Draar, after the old male who was a true and trusted friend of his brood."

The males of the roam rumbled agreement.

"And this is Sixteenth." The rambunctious male with the insatiable curiosity moved up before the males. "With the permission of the males of the roam, I name him Olsosstry, after the one who his parents and his brothers and sisters will never forget."

Pippit glanced at Panthrar. He was beaming. She sent him a sign of affection. Then she proudly led her brood back to their places.

The ceremony was drawing to a conclusion. Grendaar took some time to speak of family and friends, of roam and tribe and tradition. He spoke of loved ones now gone, but always remembered. He spoke of aspirations made, of plans foiled, and of dreams fulfilled. He spoke of the long past of the People, and of the long future to come. He spoke of the unrelenting difficulties of life, and of the unbounded joys. He concluded with the most important, of the enduring values of family and of roam, and the hope and expectations of a new generation of hornbrows.

Then it was over. Wubbar slapped Panthrar on the back, and said something congratulatory. Panthrar murmured some thanks, but his thoughts were elsewhere. His mind's eye beheld his first sight of Pippit, in the great ravine. Of their trek across the upper plain. Of their time in the Valley of the Threehorns. Of the incredible joy of their first nestlings. Of the fear and trepidation of the return journey. Of all of the love and adventures they had already had together, and the promise of more to come.

Slowly he moved towards Pippit and their brood. She smiled a comely smile at him. He smiled back, and then gazed upon his rambunctious yearlings. He was content, and all was well with the world.

THE END

APPENDIX ONE

THE SETTING
LATE CRETACEOUS
NORTH AMERICA

Today we have come to learn that the earth's crust floats upon a liquid mantle of super-hot rock. We also know that for hundreds of millions of years at least, and perhaps since the earth first cooled and formed a crust, the crust has been moving upon that mantle. The crust is not one solid piece, but instead is a jig-saw puzzle of many pieces. Each piece is moving at a different speed and in a different direction from its neighbors. The pieces are moving like bumper cars, crashing into and careening off of each other, but in an excruciatingly slow drama that is imperceptible to those that live on the surface of the crust. Due to this, the continents during the time of this story were not in the same locations that they are today. If, seventy million years ago, we were to soar above the planet and view it from space, we would have great difficulty recognizing the continent upon which this story takes place.

None-the-less, a great continent existed then, as it does now, in the northern part of the planet. It lay on the side of the world that would one day be called the western hemisphere. In those most ancient of times, the majestic western mountains of this continent were just forming, pushing their way up as the plate upon which the continent sat, shoved against its neighboring plate to the west.

Seventy million years ago, an immense inland sea divided the eastern and western parts of the continent from each other. This sea advanced and receded a number of times over the course of many millions of years. At times the vast sea stretched from the giant gulf that was the southern border of the continent, to the cold northern sea at the top of the world. At other times it was only a giant gulf, and the northern parts of the continent rejoined each other. In our day the sea is sometimes referred to as the Colorado Sea, or the Niobrara Sea, or by other exotic names. But not then. Then, at the time of this story, it was simply called the Great Green Sea.

Along the thousand miles of the western shores of the Great Green Sea, a lush coastal plain existed. It varied in width, but where this story takes place, it stretched a hundred miles between the sea and a low escarpment. Large, wide rivers meandered across the coastal plain, on an eastward journey that began in the young mountains to the west. From many of these rivers, deltas jutted out into the sea, offering rich habitats for a variety of flora and fauna. And along the edge of the sea, marshes and sandy beaches helped join the land to the water.

Further inland, swamps formed along the coastal plain's rivers. Along these grew giant sequoias, swamp cypresses, china firs and araucaria. Vast forests of tall evergreens, giant cycads and small flowering hardwoods covered great expanses. There were pines and spruces, giant redwoods and cypresses and firs. There were also oaks and hickories and magnolias. It was a warm, rich world full of life. On the coastal plain, and in its rivers and ponds and marshes and deltas, a vast array of both plant-life and animal-life abounded.

Not so on the upper plain, beyond the escarpment to the west. Here the land was drier. For almost fifty miles the upper plain stretched, from the low escarpment that separated it from the coastal plain, to the rolling foothills in the west. Beyond the foothills, further to the west, lay the newly forming mountain range. On the upper plain, except in the spring, little rain seemed to fall. What rain did fall rushed away in the rivers to the lush coastal plain below.

Plant life was somewhat more limited on the upper plain. Large evergreens formed in clumps or small forests. Dogwoods and other small flowering trees formed the understoreys of the diminutive forests, and grew along the narrow, winding rivers. Giant palm-like cycads also grew along the rivers, and around the shallow lakes. These lakes would rapidly refill each spring, after a winter of dry hardpan. By autumn, the shallow lakes were barely more than mud-flats.

Grass did not cover the great upper plain, as grass had not yet evolved. Instead, moss and ferns formed the carpeting under the small forests. These and berry bushes. Berry bushes grew everywhere. Berry bushes covered the expansive open areas of the upper plain. Berry bushes were like the grass for the large denizens that roamed the upper and lower plains in that ancient time.

In some distant period even further in the past, the pent up forces of plate tectonics, the same forces that were forming the already mighty mountain range to the west, had forced the upper plain to rise upward, leaving a low escarpment between the upper plain and coastal plain. The escarpment was only 600 or 800 feet in height for most of its hundreds of miles of length. Yet even this low wall would have served as an impassable barrier for most of the land animals of the day.

Fortunately, for time unmeasured, the rain and the seasons had worked their will upon the escarpment. Rivers that crossed the upper plain became waterfalls at the escarpment. In many locations, the waterfalls cut deep gorges into the cliffs. The gorges eroded into large gullies in the upper plain, and the gullies into deep ravines. Eventually, some of those ravines eroded to the point that the ravine floors met the floor of the coastal plain. Now, in addition to the escarpment rising above the coastal plain, numerous ravines cut through the plateau of the upper plain like ax cuts on a table edge. These ravines offered pathways up from the floor of the coastal plain to the top of the plateau.

The world of seventy million years ago was filled with life. The predominant land-animal was the dinosaur, and dinosaurs were a rich and varied species. They included small bipedal omnivores like *Ornithomimus* and *Troodon*, and large bipedal carnivores like *Albertosaurus* and *Tyrannosaurus*. They also included a variety of large herbivorous crestless duckbills like *Edmontosaurus*, *Kritosaurus*, and *Maiasaurus*; and their crested relatives like *Corythosaurus*, *Lambeosaurus*, and *Parasaurolophus*.

Then there were more exotic dinosaurs like the headrammers, the spiked and clubbed tanks, and the horned and frilled chargers. The headrammers included *Pachycephalosaurus* and *Stegoceras*. The side-spiked, tank-like herbivores included *Nodosaurus* and *Panoplosaurus*; while the armored club-tailed dinosaurs included *Ankylosaurus* and *Euoplocephalus*. The horned and frilled herbivores included dinosaurs like *Triceratops*, *Monoclonius*, and *Chasmosaurus*.

In the seas were giant marine reptiles, not really dinosaurs at all, like the thirty foot long *Mosasaurs*, and the forty foot long *Elasmosaurs*. And in the air, was a multitude of pterosaurs of all sizes and shapes, including *Pteranodon*, a large, tail-less pterosaur, and *Quetzalcoatlus*, with a wingspan approaching fifty feet. *Quetzalcoatlus* was the largest pterosaur, and indeed the largest winged creature to have ever soared above the earth.

There were more familiar creatures that inhabited this world. There were snakes and frogs and lizards and salamanders in a profusion of sizes and shapes and colors. There were crocodiles in many sizes, including *Deinosuchus*, which grew to fifty feet in length. There were duck-like birds, and early herons or egrets. There were also mammals, small opossum-like creatures like *Alphadon* and *Eodelphis*, that tried to keep out of the way of almost all the other creatures that lived in that world.

The duckbilled dinosaurs, or hadrosaurs, are of particular interest to this story. They were a group of dinosaurs that were medium to large, heavily built bipedal/quadrupedal herbivores. The two families of hadrosaurs include the hadrosaurids and the lambeosaurids. The former were generally crestless, while the latter had a variety of crests ranging from small to rather large. All hadrosaurs had powerful jaws and self-sharpening cheek teeth for chewing leaves and twigs in roomy cheeks. Hadrosaurids had a flat skull, or one with small crests or bumps of solid bone, and had relatively longer, lower jaws, and slimmer, longer limbs than the lambeosaurids. Both browsed largely on all-fours, relying on keen senses of sight, smell and hearing to warn of danger. Lacking powerful defensive adaptations like the horned dinosaurs, frightened hadrosaurs ran off on their powerful hind legs, body held low, and with the tail held out horizontally behind them for balance. They were among the last and largest of the bird-footed, bird-hipped dinosaurs. Full grown, they ranged in size from 12 to 50 feet. Hadrosaurs lived in the Late Cretaceous, in North and South America, Europe, and Asia.

Although hadrosaurs are called the duckbilled dinosaurs, this is for the most part an inaccurate description. Hadrosaurs, rather than having a broad, flat beak like a duck, had a strong, rather rigid beak with a sharp, notched margin, more like a tortoise or a turtle. It could produce a hard, sharp bite. Further back in the jaw, hadrosaurs had hundreds of small, diamond-shaped grinding teeth. Each tooth was locked against its neighbors by a bony cement to form what has been referred to as a "battery" or "magazine" of teeth. The teeth wore down from the top to form a broad, rough surface, like a millstone, for grinding the toughest of plants. Combined with strong jaw muscles, this apparatus provided hadrosaurs with one of the most efficient and powerful plant crushing and grinding machines that ever evolved.

The brain case of the hadrosaurs was fairly large. This has been interpreted to mean that they not only had a substantial intelligence, but also had well-developed senses. They had large eyes, which probably meant that they had excellent vision. The ears and accompanying equipment were also well-developed, probably meaning a good sense of hearing. Perhaps most striking of all, it is also likely that hadrosaurs had an extremely well-developed sense of smell. Their olfactory membranes and related passages and equipment were large and highly developed.

All-in-all, hadrosaurs were fairly interesting creatures. They were among the last of the dinosaurs. They were intelligent, and they had well-developed senses of sight, smell, and hearing. They were also social creatures. Evidence shows that they moved about in vast herds, sometimes in the order of tens of thousands of hadrosaurs. There is also evidence that they nested in colonies, and fed and protected their young after they hatched.

APPENDIX TWO
LATE CRETACEOUS INHABITANTS OF WESTERN NORTH AMERICA

Greek or Latin Name (Other Names) "English translation", how the name was derived or developed; [Family] [Period] [Geographic dispersion, alphabetical]: *Storyname*; description of the animal.

Albertosaurus (Gorgosaurus) "Alberta reptile", referring to place where found; [Tyrannosaurid] [Late Cretaceous] [western North America]: *Dreadrunner*, a ravager; a bipedal meat-eater with a hugh skull (lower and longer-snouted than Tyrannosaurus), vast jaws held sharp, serrated, saborlike teeth that were sharp on both sides (smaller and point more backward than Tyrannosaurus), teeth were ideal for killing and for tearing apart flesh; semi-forward facing eyes with good binocular vision; a thick, short, muscular neck, and a short, deep broad-chested and narrow hipped body, with a relatively short and slim tail; the great legs bore three forward-pointing toes with relatively short, rounded claws; the fore-arms were strong but tiny (smaller than in Tyrannosaurus) and ended in two-fingered hands; probably a fast runner, at full speed, the body was held nearly horizontal, with the stiff tail helping keep balance; 26 to 27 (29?) feet long; weighed 1.5 to 2.5 tons. (See also Daspletosaurus and Tyrannosaurus).

Ankylosaurus "stiffened (or fused) reptile", because of stiffened dermal armor; [Ankylosaurid] [Late Cretaceous] [Alberta, Montana]: *Giant Clubtail*; a four-footed vegetarian well covered by thick bony scales, nodules, and spikes; ate vegetation by clipping with its beaklike mouth; defended itself by swinging its long, agile tail tipped with a bony club (club composed of a single round bone); although bulky, it could move with surprising speed on sturdy limbs; 30 to 35 feet long, 4.0 plus tons. (See also Euoplocephalus).

Cerasphoros "horn bearer", because of short horn on brow; [Hadrosaurid] [Late Cretaceous] [Alberta, Montana]: *Hornbrow*; a large, bipedal/quadrupedal, duck-billed herbivore with a toothless beak, batteries of grinding cheek teeth, cheek pouches, and strong jaws; four fingers on each hand, three toes on each foot, a minor frill running along the back, and a short horn on the forehead; 40 feet long, 4.0 tons. (See also Edmontosaurus, Hadrosaurus, Kritosaurus, Maiasaurus, Prosaurolophus, and Saurolophus).

Chasmosaurus "opening (or cleft) reptile", referring to openings in its frill; [Ceratopsid] [Late Cretaceous] [Alberta]: *Twohorn*; a four-legged vegetarian with a long frill and two long brow horns and a small nose horn; it could run fast as well as fight, it could also rear up on its hind legs to face an opponent or predator, displaying its frill to the fullest; frills may have been brightly colored to aid in courtship or threat displays; 17 feet long, 2.5 tons. (See also Anchiceratops, Arrhinoceratops, and Torosaurus). (See also Eucentrosaurus, Monoclonius, Pachyrhinosaurus, Styracosaurus, and Triceratops).

Corythosaurus "helmet reptile", referring to the shape of its crest; [Lambeosaurid] [Late Cretaceous] [Alberta]: *Cresttop*; a large, bipedal/ quadrupedal, duck-billed vegetarian with a toothless beak, batteries of grinding cheek teeth, and with a large bulbous expansion on the top of the skull made from the nasal bones (a hollow "cocked hat" head crest flattened from side to side), a "crested helmet"; females and young had smaller crests; 35 feet long. (See also Hypacrosaurus, Lambeosaurus and Parasaurolophus).

Dromiceiomimus "emu mimic", referring to its bird-like qualities; [Ornithomimid] [Late Cretaceous] [Alberta]: *Trailrunner*; a small bipedal herbivore, possibly omnivore, with a small skull (but with a proportionally large brain) with no teeth but with a horny bill and very large eyes; a long, slim, curved, mobile neck; three large curved claws on relatively long forelimbs (probably not used for locomotion, but with hands capable of grasping); hind legs are long and strong and capable of running at high speed, shins are longer than the thighs (and likely longer than other Ornithomimids), long feet are each armed with three claw-tipped toes; long tapered tail being more than half its length, held level with the back helped keep balance when running; 11 to 12 feet long. Dromiceiomimus is most easily distinguished from other ornithomimids by its relatively shorter back, and its comparatively longer and more slender forearm and hand. (See also Ornithomimus and Struthiomimus).

Edmontosaurus (Anatosaurus) "Edmonton reptile", referring to where it was found; [Hadrosaurid] [Late Cretaceous] [Alberta, Montana]: *Longsnout*, sometimes called *Longnose*; a large, bipedal/ quadrupedal, duck-billed vegetarian with a flatish head, batteries of cheekteeth in shallow jaws, and very elongate nose openings, and no bumps on the head; 35 to 42.5 feet long, 3.5 or more tons. (See also Cerasphoros, Hadrosaurus, Kritosaurus, Maiasaurus, Prosaurolophus, and Saurolophus).

Eodelphis "early opossum" [Late Cretaceous] [Alberta, Montana]: a small marsupial mammal, about two-thirds the size of its modern equivalent; one of the largest of the mammals of its time, and the largest known marsupial from the Late Cretaceous.

Euoplocephalus "well armored head", referring to the armor on its head; [Ankylosaurid] [Late Cretaceous] [Alberta]: *Clubtail*; a four-footed vegetarian, somewhat smaller than Ankylosaurus, well covered by thick bony scales, nodules, and spikes; ate vegetation by clipping with its beaklike mouth, had tiny teeth; defended itself by swinging its long, agile tail tipped with a bony club (club composed of multiple round bones); although bulky, it could move with surprising speed on sturdy limbs; 20 to 25 feet long, 2.0 to 3.0 tons. (See also Ankylosaurus).

Hadrosaurus "big reptile", referring to its size; [Hadrosaurid] [Late Cretaceous] [Montana, New Jersey, New Mexico, South Dakota]: a large, bipedal/quadrupedal, duck-billed herbivore with a toothless beak, batteries of grinding cheek teeth, cheek pouches, and strong jaws; four fingers on each hand, three toes on each foot; 26 to 32 feet long, 3.0 tons. (The first dinosaur discovered in the US)(See also Cerasphoros, Edmontosaurus, Kritosaurus, Maiasaurus, Prosaurolophus, and Saurolophus).

Ichthyornis "fish-eating bird" [Ichthyornithiformid] [Late Cretaceous] [Kansas, Texas]: *Featheredflyer*; a long-winged, strong-flying, tern or seagull-like bird with a fully-toothed, flat bill; 8 inches to 1 foot long.

Kritosaurus "noble reptile", because of its "Roman nose"; [Hadrosaurid] [Late Cretaceous] [Alberta]: *Humpsnout*; a large, bipedal/quadrupedal, duck-billed vegetarian with a toothless beak, batteries of grinding cheek teeth, flat-headed with large nasal openings extending upward and ending in a prominent bump; 30 feet long, 3.0 tons. (See also Cerasphoros, Edmontosaurus, Hadrosaurus, Maiasaurus, Prosaurolophus, and Saurolophus).

Lambeosaurus "Lambe's reptile", in honor of paleontologist L. Lambe; [Lambeosaurid] [Late Cretaceous] [Alberta, Montana]: *Hatchetcrest*; a bipedal/quadrupedal vegetarian with pebbly skin; toothless beak, batteries of cheek teeth; a hollow, hatchet-shaped crest with a backward pointing bony spike that perhaps anchored a neck frill; 40 to 50 feet long. (See also Corythosaurus, Hypacrosaurus, and Parasaurolophus).

Maiasaurus "good mother reptile", because it was found near a nest of its young; [Hadrosaurid] [Late Cretaceous] [Montana]: *Ridgebrow*; a bipedal/quadrupedal, duck-billed vegetarian with a broad, short toothless beak, batteries of cheekteeth in shallow jaws, and with a short, boney crest extending forward between the eyes; generally about 30 feet long, and 3.0 tons. (See also Cerasphoros, Edmontosaurus, Hadrosaurus, Kritosaurus, Prosaurolophus, and Saurolophus).

Monoclonius "single stem (or horn)", referring to the single horn on its nose; [Ceratopsid] [Late Cretaceous] [Alberta, Montana]: *Onehorn*; a short-frilled vegetarian with a large nose horn, very small brow horns, and bony knobs sticking downward from the top of the frill; short tail and bulky body; could run fast as well as fight; 18 to 20 feet long; weighed 2.5 tons. (See also Eucentrosaurus, Pachyrhinosaurus, Styracosaurus, and Triceratops). (See also Anchiceratops, Arrhinoceratops, Chasmosaurus, and Torosaurus).

Nodosaurus "knobby reptile", because of its knobby skin; [Nodosaurid] [early Late Cretaceous] [Kansas, Wyoming]: *Old Rockback*; a quadrupedal herbivore with a fairly narrow head with a relatively narrow snout, a skull hole behind the eye, massive jaws with small leaf-shaped teeth and a horny, toothless beak; large and small plates ran down its back and flanks in alternating rows, and the skin bore large knobby plates between the ribs;

short, sturdy limbs, and the heavy tail lacked a club; 18 feet long, 2.0 to 2.5 tons. (See also Panoplosaurus).

Ornithomimus "bird mimic", because it resembles a bird; [Ornithomimid] [Late Cretaceous] [North America]: *Swiftstealer*; a small bipedal herbivore, possibly omnivore, with a small skull (but with a proportionally large brain) with no teeth but with a horny bill and very large eyes; a long, slim, curved, mobile neck; three large curved claws on relatively long forelimbs (longer than Struthiomimus) that were probably not used for locomotion, but with hands capable of grasping; hind legs are long and strong and capable of running at high speed (but are shorter than both Dromiceiomimus and Struthiomimus), shins are longer than the thighs, long feet are each armed with three claw-tipped toes; long tapered tail being more than half its length, held level with the back helped keep balance when running; 10 to 14 feet long. (See also Dromiceiomimus and Struthiomimus).

Orodromeus "mountain runner", because it was found in the mountains, and was a swift runner; [Hypsilophodontid] [Late Cretaceous] [Montana]: *Robrunner*; a small bipedal herbivore (omnivore) with a small head, large eyes, a horny cropping beak with upper teeth, self-sharpening cheek teeth that were replaced by new ones as the old ones wore out, cheek pouches, and strong jaws; short arms, with five-fingered hands, tipped with claws; long, agile shins and feet that imply an ability to sprint, four-toed feet tipped with claws; a long tendon-stiffened tail for balance; 8 feet long. (See also Parksosaurus).

Pachycephalosaurus "thick-headed reptile", because of its thick skull; [Pachycephalosaurid] [Late Cretaceous] [western North America]: *Headcrasher*; a bipedal vegetarian, sharp teeth, small eyes and weak jaw muscles, with a skull with thick bone and knobs on the back, but not dome-headed, probably butted heads for defense or in mating contests; short arms, strong hips and legs, and a stiffened tail; walked with a level back, and were not designed for running fast; 15 to 26(?) feet long (14 feet high?), 2 tons. (See also Stegoceras).

Panoplosaurus "fully armored reptile", referring to the plates on its back; [Nodosaurid] [Late Cretaceous] [Alberta to Texas]: *Rockback*; a quadrupedal herbivore with a fairly narrow head with a relatively short, plump snout, a skull hole behind the eye, massive jaws with small leaf-shaped teeth and a broad, horny, toothless beak; large and small plates ran down its back and flanks in alternating rows, and the skin bore large knobby plates between the ribs; short, sturdy limbs, and the heavy tail lacked a club; 23 feet long, 3.5 to 4.0 tons. (See also Nodosaurus).

Parasaurolophus "like Saurolophus" or "similar crested reptile", because this dinosaur also had a crest; [Lambeosaurid] [Late Cretaceous] [Alberta, Utah]: *Trumpeter*; a bipedal/quadrupedal vegetarian; toothless beak, batteries of cheek teeth; a hollow, five or six foot crest protruded from the back of the skull, possibly used for tooting, perhaps the crest anchored a neck frill that extended to the back; 30 to 35 feet long. (See also Corythosaurus, Hypacrosaurus, and Lambeosaurus).

Parksosaurus "Parks' reptile", named after dinosaur collector and researcher, W. A. Parks; [Hypsilophodontid] [Late Cretaceous] [Montana]: *Redrunner*; a small bipedal herbivore with a small head, large eyes, a horny cropping beak with upper teeth, self-sharpening ridged cheek teeth that were replaced by new ones as the old ones wore out, cheek pouches, and strong jaws; short arms, with five-fingered hands, tipped with claws; long, agile shins and feet that imply an ability to sprint, four-toed feet tipped with claws; a long tendon-stiffened tail for balance; 7 to 8 feet long, 150 pounds in weight. (See also Orodromeus).

Pteranodon "winged and toothless", because it could fly, and was toothless; [Pterosaurid] [Late Cretaceous] [Kansas]: *Skyglider*; a large, advanced pterosaur with no tail; it had a strange hammer-shaped head (6 feet long from tip to tip) with a toothless beak sticking out the front, and a long bony crest sticking out the back; it may have lived by the seas and other bodies of water, fishing in flight; 26 foot wingspan, 33 pounds in weight, could possibly glide to speeds of 25 MPH. (See also Quetzalcoatlus).

Quetzalcoatlus "quetzalcoatl", named after the Aztec god, the feathered-serpent; [Pterosaurid] [Cretaceous] [Texas]: *Skygiant*; the largest pterosaur; with no tail and no head-crest, but with a long neck (head and neck combined were 8 feet long); flew over inland plains, and possibly was a scavenger; 36 to 50 foot wingspan, about 180 pounds in weight. (See also Pteranodon).

Struthiomimus "ostrich mimic", because it resembled an ostrich; [Ornithomimid] [Late Cretaceous] [Alberta]: *Eggsnatcher*; a small bipedal herbivore, possibly omnivore very similar to Ornithomimus, with a small skull, perhaps a little smaller than Ornithomimus, with no teeth but with a horny bill and large eyes; a long, slim, curved, mobile neck; three large curved claws on relatively long forelimbs (but shorter forelimbs than Ornithomimus), probably not used for locomotion, but with hands capable of grasping; hind legs are long and strong and capable of running at high speed (hindlegs are longer than Ornithomimus), shins are longer than the thighs, long feet are each armed with three claw-tipped toes; long tapered tail being more than half its length, held level with the back helped keep balance when running; 7 feet tall, 10 to 12 feet long, its tail was 3 feet longer than its very short body. (See also Dromiceiomimus and Ornithomimus).

Thescelosaurus "wonderful reptile", referring to the excellant condition of the first specimen found; [Thescelosaurid] [Late Cretaceous] [Alberta, Montana, Saskatchewan, Wyoming]: *Bumpyback*; a long, low bipedal/quadrupedal herbivore with a small head, teeth in the front of the jaws, and cheek teeth; a plump body, perhaps with rows of bony studs down the back; five-fingered hands; thighs longer than shins, four-toed feet with hooflike claws, a stiffened long tail; 11 feet long.

Triceratops "three-horned face", because of the three horns on its face; [Ceratopsid] [Very Late Cretaceous] [Wyoming, Montana]: *Threehorn*; a three-horned vegetarian with a small nose horn, prominent brow horns (up to 3 feet long), and a short solid frill; short tail and bulky body; it could run fast as well as fight; inhabited forests of redwoods and other tall trees; cropped food with beaklike mouth; 25 to 30 feet long (6 feet at the shoulder; 9.5 feet at the top of the frill), 5.0 to 6.0 tons. (See also Eucentrosaurus, Monoclonius, Pachyrhinosaurus, and Styracosaurus). (See also Anchiceratops, Arrhinoceratops, Chasmosaurus, and Torosaurus).

Troodon (Stenonychosaurus) "wounding tooth", referring to its serrated teeth; [Troodontid] [Late Cretaceous] [Alberta, Montana, Wyoming]: *Razortooth*; a small bipedal meat-eater, with slim jaws bristling with pointed saw-edged teeth (teeth are numerous, short, small, semitriangular, with small number of large serrations); with long arms, grasping fingers tipped with large claws; swift and slender on bird-like legs and feet, with a sickle-shaped toe claw that swung back and forth, and a stiffened tail; had a very large brain and prominent eyes with overlapping fields of vision (better developed than in any other dinosaur); probably lacked a fully-developed sense of smell; may have been a night-hunter; 6.5 feet long.

Tyrannosaurus "tyrant reptile", because of its great size, and its terrible teeth and claws; [Tyrannosaurid] [Late Cretaceous] [western North America]: *Dreadcharger*, a ravager; a bipedal meat-eater with a hugh skull (larger and fuller than Albertosaurus), vast jaws, 7 inch, razor-sharp teeth (more forward pointing than Albertosaurus), semi-forward facing eyes with good binocular vision; a thick, short, muscular neck, and a short, deep broad-chested and narrow hipped body, with a relatively short and slim tail (not as graceful as Albertosaurus; relatively shorter and stockier than a similar sized Albertosaurus); the long and powerful legs bore three forward-pointing toes with relatively short, rounded claws; the fore-arms were strong but tiny (larger than in Albertosaurus) and ended in two-fingered hands; probably a fast runner, at full speed, the body was held nearly horizontal, with the stiff tail helping keep balance; 39 to 45 feet long (the skull alone was over 4 feet long), almost 20 feet tall (perhaps taller), 7.0 to 7.5 tons (perhaps heavier). (See also Albertosaurus and Daspletosaurus).

APPENDIX THREE
GLOSSARY OF TERMS

Adolescent

A term used by the People to describe a *Cerasphoros* that is older than a youngster, but younger than an adult. Adolescents range from 3 to 5 or 6 years old. The transition from adolescence to adulthood occurs when the individual first becomes ready to breed. At that time males start to engage in dominance fights, though generally with other young males; and females begin to show a willingness to mate. Adolescents range in size from 18.5 to 25 feet at 4 years, and from 20.5 to 27 feet at 5 years of age. They range in weight from 1.8 to 2.4 tons at 4 years, and from 2.0 to 2.8 tons at 5 years of age. The major reason for the ranges is the difference between males and females. Horns on males range from 8 inches at 4 years, to 10 inches long at 5 years of age. Horns on females range from 2.5 inches at 4 years, to 4.5 inches long at 5 years of age. (See also: Cerasphoros, Progression Through Life.)

Black Valley Tribe

One of the tribes of the Great Eastern Herd. One of its roams is the Purple Sand Roam.

Cerasphoros

Cerasphoros, meaning "horn bearer", it is the scientific name of the group of hadrosaurids that refer to themselves as hornbrows, or The People. For a detailed description of this form of hadrosaurid, see People, The. For more infromation on hadrosaurs, see Hadrosaurs. (See also *Cerasphoros* in Appendix Two.)

Cerasphoros, Progression Through Life:

* **Hatchlings**, roughly 20 to 30 to a nest, are 15 inches long and 1.5 pounds when they break the shell.

* **Nestlings** range from hatchlings (15 inches long, 1.5 pounds) to those that are 2 months old (31 to 37 inches long, and 95 to 130 pounds). For every 100 hatchlings, 60 survive through the nesting period to become fledges.

* **Fledges** are older than nestlings, but younger than yearlings (2 to 6 months old: at 3 months old: 39 to 48 inches long, and 190 to 255 pounds; at 4 months old: 47 to 60 inches long, and 340 to 425 pounds; and at 5 months old: 55 to 72 inches long, and 500 to 625 pounds. Fledges are able to make the great treks, but in their first summer, the going is slow. For every 60 2 month old fledges, 30 survive to become 6 month old yearlings.

* **Yearlings** are older than fledges, but younger than youngsters (6 to 12 months old: at 6 months: 5 to 7 feet long and 650 to 800 pounds; at 9 months: 7 to 10 feet long and 1000 to 1400 pounds; and at 12 months: 9 to 13 feet long and 1200 to 1800 pounds). For every 30 6 month old yearlings, 20 reach the age of 9 months, and 15 survive to become a youngster.

* **Youngsters** range between 1 and 3 years old.

* **Adolescents** are older than youngsters, and range from 3 to less than 6 years old.

* **Adulthood** comes to a *Cerasphoros* sometime between 5 and 6 years of age. At that time males start to engage in dominance fights, though generally with other young males; and females begin to show a willingness to mate.

Clubtail
An armored quadrupedal herbivore, 20 to 25 feet long and 2 to 3 tons in weight; see *Euoplocephalus* in Appendix Two.

Cousin

Any of several types of hadrosaurids closely related to the *Cerasphoros*; see *Edmontosaurus* and *Maiasaurus* in Appendix Two.

Cretaceous Period

One of the three periods of the Mesozoic Era, the age of dinosaurs. The Cretaceous was the last of the three periods, from roughly 144 to 66 million years ago. During the Cretaceous, dinosaurs became increasingly varied and sophisticated, until their relatively sudden extinction 66 million years ago. The super-large plant eaters of the Jurassic gave way to smaller, more agile types of dinosaurs. Toothless birdlike dinosaurs, large flesh-eating tyrannosaurids, armored ankylosaurs and horned ceratopsians, and duck-billed dinosaurs with and without crests dominated the land. Pterasaurs still filled the skys, but birds also came on the scene. The flippered mosasaurs and the long-necked pleisiosaurs were the chief sea-going lizards. There were also frogs, salamanders, turtles, snakes, crocodiles, and small mammals.

Although the early Cretaceous was as balmy as the Jurassic, by the middle of the Cretaceous, a gradual but accelerating worldwide cooling took place. Also, beginning in the late Jurassic, and continuing into the early Cretaceous, a progressive drying took place. The more equatorial regions appear to have been less heavily forested, and may have developed an almost treeless savannah environment, with the ground covered with ferns and horsetails. In the higher latitudes, the forests were dominated by conifers, cycads, and ginkos. At the time of the People, the first flowering plants were appearing, although they looked more like shrubby weeds. Smaller broadleaf trees filled in beneath a canopy of conifers. Towards the close of the Cretaceous, broadleafed trees were actually forming the canopy themselves.

Examples of vegetation include mixed conifer forests, with an understorey of broadleafs; also ferns, mosses, horsetails, cycad fronds, swamp cypresses and araucaria. By the Late Cretaceous, hickories, oaks and magnolias thrived in North America.

Cub

A term used by many of the carnivores to describe their young, after they have progressed through the hatchling and nestling stages, and before they mature into yearlings. The term is most often applied between the ages of two and twelve months.

Desolate Islands, The

A mythical place where old hornbrows journey to when they are about to die of old age.

Dreadcharger

A bipedal carnivore, with a hugh head (larger and fuller than a Dreadrunner), vast jaws, 7 inch, razor-sharp teeth, and semi-forward facing eyes with good binocular vision. It has a thick, short, muscular neck, and a short, deep broad-chested and narrow hipped body, with a relatively short and slim tail (not as graceful as a Dreadrunner, and relatively shorter and stockier than a similar sized Dreadrunner). It also has long and powerful legs bearing three forward-pointing toes with relatively short, rounded claws. The fore-arms are strong but tiny (larger than in a Dreadrunner) and ending in two-fingered hands.

The Dreadcharger is a fast runner. At full speed, the body is held nearly horizontal, with the stiff tail helping to keep balance. Dreadchargers are around 39 to 45 feet long (the head alone can be over 4 feet long), and almost 20 feet tall. It weighs 7.0 to 7.5 tons.

The body is colored a raw umber, with a broad, burnt umber or dark brown stripe running from the top of the head, down the back, and all the way to the tip of the tail. Narrow burnt umber stripes run parallel to the back stripe, down the neck, body, upper leg, and tail. Portions of the front of the neck, belly, underside of the tail, and heel and foot-bottom are a sand color. There are red patterns on the face, around the horns, and down the snout.

See also *Tyrannosaurus* in Appendix Two.

Dreadrunner

A bipedal carnivore, with a hugh skull (lower and longer-snouted than a Dreadcharger), with vast jaws having sharp, serrated, saborlike teeth that are sharp on both sides (smaller and pointing more backward than a Dreadcharger), teeth that are ideal for killing and tearing apart flesh. The head also has semi-forward facing eyes with good binocular vision. The Dreadrunner also has a thick, short, muscular neck, and a short, deep broad-chested and narrow hipped body, with a relatively short and slim tail. The great legs bear three forward-pointing toes with relatively short, rounded claws. The fore-arms are strong but tiny (smaller than in a Dreadcharger) and ending in two-fingered hands.

The Dreadrunner is a very fast runner. At full speed, the body is held nearly horizontal, with the stiff tail helping to keep balance. The Dreadrunner is 26 to 27 feet long, and weighs 1.5 to 2.5 tons.

The body is colored a yellow-orange. Narrow multi-colored stripes (terra cotta, dark brown and vermilleon red) run parallel to the body length, down the neck, body, upper leg, and tail. Portions of the front of the neck, belly, underside of the tail, and heel and foot-bottom are a cream color. There are also terra cotta, dark brown and vermilleon red patterns on the face and snout.

See also *Albertosaurus* in Appendix Two.

Eggsnatcher

A small bipedal herbivore, possibly an omnivore, very similar to Swiftstealers and Trailrunners. The Eggsnatcher has a small skull, perhaps a little smaller than a Swiftstealer, with no teeth but with a horny bill and large eyes. It has a long, slim, curved, mobile neck. The Eggsnatcher also has three large, curved claws on relatively long forelimbs (but which are shorter than Swiftstealers), which are not used for locomotion, but which have hands capable of grasping. The hind legs that are long and strong and capable of running at high speed (the hindlegs are longer than Swiftstealers). The shins are longer than the thighs, and the long feet are each armed with three claw-tipped toes. The Eggsnatcher has a long tapered tail more than half its length, which is held level with the back when running, and which helps keep them balanced when maneuvering at high speeds. The Eggsnatcher is 7 feet tall, 10 to 12 feet long (its tail is 3 feet longer than its very short body). The basic body color is a light warm-gray. This is accented with sepia brown patches along the back of the neck, and down the back of the body and tail. There are also sepia brown stripes along the front of the arms and legs. See also *Struthiomimus* in Appendix Two.

Fledge

A term used by the People to describe a *Cerasphoros* that is older than a nestling, but younger than a yearling, that is, 2 to 6 months of age. At 3 months old: range from 39 to 48 inches long, and 190 to 255 pounds; at 4 months old: range from 47 to 60 inches long, and 340 to 425 pounds; and at 5 months old: range from 55 to 72 inches long, and 500 to 625 pounds. Fledges are able to make the great treks, but in their first summer, the going is slow. For every 60 2 month old fledges, 30 survive to become 6 month old yearlings. (See also: Cerasphoros, Progression Through Life.)

Giant Clubtail
An armored, quadrupedal herbivore, 30 to 35 feet long and 4 tons in weight; see *Ankylosaurus* in Appendix Two

Great Eastern Herd, The:
The Great Eastern Herd is one of the four great herds of the People (see also Great Herds, The; and Herds). It has some 17,500 individuals, and is comprised of nine tribes, also refered to as The Nine Tribes. The tribes are:

* the Black Valley Tribe

* the Golden Rim Tribe

* the Green Hills Tribe

* the Red Dawn Tribe

* the Silver River Tribe

* the Turquoise Sea Tribe

* the Umber Earth Tribe

* the Verdant Delta Tribe

* the White Moon Tribe

Great Herds, The:
There are four Great Herds among the People. These are the Great Northern Herd, with about 30,000 *Cerasphoros*; the Great Eastern Herd, with about 17,500 *Cerasphoros*; the Great Western Herd, with about 15,000 *Cerasphoros*; and the Great Southern Herd, with about 20,000 *Cerasphoros*.

Green Hills Tribe, The
One of the tribes of the Great Eastern Herd. Some of its roams include

the Lush Wallow Roam and the Sparkling Water Roam.

Great Horned Rock, The

A great monolith located in the western range of the Black Valley Tribe, a day's journey east of the escarpment, with two horn-like projections jutting out from its top; held as sacred by the tribes living in its vicinity.

Green Water Roam, The

The Green Water Roam is one of 20 roams that make up the Red Dawn Tribe (see Red Dawn Tribe, The). Grendaar is the dominant male of the Green Water Roam (see Grendaar). The Green Water Roam is composed of 75 individuals, comprised of 5 adult males, 13 adult females, 2 adolescent males, 8 adolescent females, 26 youngsters, and 21 yearlings (see also Appendix Two).

Group Names

The various families, super-families, and clans of denizens had different names for the groups within which they traveled. Some examples follow:

*   band: of razorteeth;

*   herd: of onehorns, of threehorns, of twohorns;

*   pack: of redrunners, of robrunners, occasionally of dreadrunners, occasionally of razorteeth;

*   pack (sometimes herd): of eggsnatchers, of swiftstealers, of trailrunners;

*   roam: of cresttops, of hornbrows, of longsnouts, of ridgebrows, of trumpeters;

*   troop: of dreadchargers.

Hadrosaurs

These are a part of the group of dinosaurs known as the ornithischians, or "bird-hipped" dinosaurs. Hadrosaurs are a sub-division of ornithischians known as ornithopods, or "bird-footed" dinosaurs. Ornithischians did not evolve into birds, certain theropods did, and ornithopods do not have particularly bird-like feet. None-the-less, hadrosaurs are part of this group.

Hadrosaurs evolved rather late, sometime in the middle Cretaceous, but the short thirty million years or so that they existed, they evolved into an amazing variety of types. They are a group of dinosaurs that were medium to huge, heavily built bipedal/quadrupedal herbivores. The two families of hadrosaurs include the hadrosaurids and the lambeosaurids. The latter were generally crestless, while the former had a variety of crests ranging from small to rather large, and coming in a variety of shapes. Both families had powerful jaws and self-sharping cheek teeth for chewing leaves and twigs in roomy cheeks. Hadrosaurids had a flat skull, or one with small crests or bumps of solid bone, and had relatively longer, lower jaws, and slimmer, longer limbs than the lambeosaurids. Both browsed largely on all-fours, relying on keen senses of sight, smell and hearing to warn of danger. Lacking powerful defensive adaptations like the horned dinosaurs, scared hadrosaurs ran off on their powerful hind legs, body held low, and with the tail held out horizontally behind them for balance. They were among the last and largest of the bird-footed, bird-hipped dinosaurs. They ranged in size from 12 to 50 feet. They lived in the Late Cretaceous, in North and South America, Europe, and Asia.

Although called the duck-billed dinosaurs, this was for the most part an inaccurate description. Hadrosaurs, rather than having a broad, flat beak like a duck, had a strong, rather rigid beak with a sharp, notched margin, more like a tortoise or a turtle. It could produce a hard, sharp bite. Further back in the jaw, hadrosaurs had hundreds of small, diamond-shaped grinding teeth. Each tooth was locked against its neighbors by a bony cement to form what has been referred to as a "battery" or "magazine" of teeth. The teeth wore down from the top to form a broad, rough surface, like a millstone, for grinding the toughest of plants. Combined with strong jaw muscles, this apparatus provided hadrosaurs with one of the most efficient and powerful plant crushing and grinding machines that ever evolved.

The brain case of the hadrosaurs was fairly large, certainly large for a reptile. This has been interpreted to mean that they not only had a substantial intelligence, but also well-developed senses. They had large eyes, which probably meant that they had excellant vision. The ears and accompanying equipment were also well-developed, probably meaning a good sense of hearing. Perhaps most striking of all, it is also likely that hadrosaurs had an extremely well-developed sense of smell. Their olfactory membranes and related passages and equipment were large and highly developed. (See also: Cerasphoros; and Appendix Two: Late Cretaceous Inhabitants of Western North America.)

Hatchling

A term used by the People to describe the very young while they are still in the nest, just after they have hatched. There are roughly 20 to 30 eggs laid in a nest. Upon breaking the shell, each hatchling is about 15 inches long and 1.5 pounds in weight. (See also: Cerasphoros, Progression Through Life.)

Headcrasher

A thick-skulled bipedal herbivore, 15 to 26 feet long and 2 tons in weight; see *Pachycephalosaurus* in Appendix Two.

Herds

Among the People, there are many herds that assemble each spring to make the annual trek to the western foothills for the purposes of mating, breeding, and raising hatchlings. There are four Great Herds (see also: Great Herds, The), and a number of Lesser Herds (see also: Lesser Herds, The). The Lesser Herds are further broken down into the Minor Herds and the Micro Herds.

Hornbrow

A large bipedal/quadrupedal duck-billed herbivore, with a toothless beak, batteries of grinding cheek teeth, cheek pouches, and strong jaws. It has four fingers on each hand, three toes on each foot, and a minor frill running along the back. It also has a short horn on the forehead. Hornbrows grow from 34 to 40 feet long, and weigh from 3.0 to 4.0 tons.

The coloration of a hornbrow is much the same throughout its life. As a new hatchling, the basic body color is a deep yellow. It was a dark yellow, like aged lemon. There is also a broad stripe running down the back, not only covering the barely formed frill, but along both sides of it as well. This stripe runs from the upper jaw, across the top of the head, down the back, and all the way to the tip of the tail. The stripe is a mixture somewhere between a brownish orange and burnt sienna. Secondary stripes of this same color run perpendicular from the back stripe across the flanks of the body, and across the broader base of the tail. These secondary stripes lighten and narrow as they run across the body, turning closer to a dark orange. The underside is a very pale yellow, mixed with an off-white. As the hornbrow grows older, it loses much of the secondary stripes. In addition, the yellow darkens into a yellow ocher, and the brownish orange into a deep golden brown. As an adult, the frill darkens considerably, especially during the breeding season.

(See Cerasphoros; Horns; and, People, The.) (See *Cerasphoros* in Appendix Two.)

Lesser Herds, The:
There are a number of Minor Herds among the People, ranging in size from about 4,000 *Cerasphoros* (2 tribes) to about 12,000 *Cerasphoros* (5 or 6 tribes). There are also Micro Herds, which are single tribes that have struck out on their own, and range in size from about 1500 to 3000 *Cerasphoros*.

Longnose
See Longsnout.

Longsnout
A large bipedal/quadrupedal duck-billed herbivore, 35 to 42.5 feet long and 3.5 or more tons in weight; see *Edmontosaurus* in Appendix Two.

Mesozoic Era
Meaning "middle life", it is often called the "Age of Reptiles". It lasted between roughly 248 and 66 million years ago. By the preceding era, the Paleozoic, invertebrates, fish, amphibians, and reptiles had already appeared. During the Mesozoic, mammals and birds appeared. But during the Mesozoic, reptiles, and the reptile-like dinosaurs, were dominant. This era included not only a wide variety of dinosaurs, but also giant sea-going reptiles like pleisosaurs and mosasaurs, and giant flying reptiles known as the pterosaurs. There are three periods in the Mesozoic Era: the Triassic, the Jurassic, and the Cretaceous. (See Cretaceous.)

Nestling
A term used by the People to describe the very young while still in the nest. Nestlings range from hatchlings (15 inches long, 1.5 pounds) to *Cerasphoros* that are 2 months old (31 to 37 inches long, and 95 to 130 pounds). For every 100 hatchlings that break the shell, 60 survive through the nesting period to become fledges. (See also: Cerasphoros, Progression Through Life.)

Night-scrounger
A small opossum-like mammal; see *Eodelphis* in Appendix Two.

Nine Tribes, The
A name given to the collection of nine tribes that make up the Great

Eastern Herd; a synonym for the Great Eastern Tribe (see also: Great Eastern Herd, The).

Onehorn
A horned quadrupedal herbivore, 18 to 20 feet long and 2.5 tons in weight; see *Monoclonius* in Appendix Two.

Packs
Packs are groups of the People, and serve as an alternate to membership in a roam. They are loosely organized, ever changing groups made up primarily of adolescents, with a few adults who generally serve as leaders. Packs are primarily made up of males, although there are some adolescent females, and occasionally an adult female (adult females are extremely rare in packs). Packs do not rear young. Their fast-moving, loosely-organized, somewhat independent approach to life is not conducive to nuturing youngsters. During the spring, when the tribes and herds assemble, packs tend to operate on the periphery of the herd, and they function well as the outer ring of defenders. Most of the risk takers belong to packs, and they generally perform well as the first line of defense of the herd (and consequently of the young of the herd), but there is also a fairly high mortality rate amongst those that protect the periphery. A single pack generally contains 15 to 30 individuals. Its composition is generally 4 to 8 adult males, 10 to 20 adolescent males, and 0 to 3 adolescent females.

People, The
A species of hadrosaurid, more specifically *Cerasphoros*, that are bipedal/quadrupedal herbivores (see also: Cerasphoros; and Hadrosaurs). Although bipedal/quadrupedal, and although they move equally comfortably on all-fours or on their hind legs, they are by preference bipedal. Adults range in length from 20 to 40 feet (males from 28 to 40 feet, and females from 20 to 35.5 feet). Adults range in weight from 2.3 tons to over 4.0 tons (males from 2.8 to over 4.0 tons, females from 2.3 to 3.3 tons). They have three toes on each hind foot, and four fingers on each hand. Unique to hadrosaurs, they are equipped with a small horn on their foreheads. Horns begin to show in adolescence. Horns on adult males range from 11 to 16 inches in length, and on adult females from 5.5 to 11.5 inches in length. They also have a prominent frill along their backbones for display. Frills are more pronounced on males than on females or the young.

Pup

A term used by many of the ceratopsians (horned dinosaurs) to describe their young. It is especially used for young threehorns, or *Triceratops*, after they have progressed through the hatchling and nestling stages, and before they mature into yearlings. The term is most often applied between the ages of two and twelve months.

Razortooth

A small bipedal carnivore, with slim jaws bristling with pointed saw-edged teeth (the teeth are numerous, short, small, semitriangular, and with a small number of large serrations). Razorteeth have long arms, and grasping fingers tipped with large claws. They are swift and slender on bird-like legs and feet, with a sickle-shaped toe claw that swings back and forth. Razorteeth have a stiffened tail, which helps them keep their balance when running at high speed. They have a very large brain and prominent eyes with overlapping fields of vision (better developed than in any other dinosaur). They often hunted at night, but they lacked a fully-developed sense of smell. Razorteeth are about 6.5 feet long.

The basic body color is a medium warm-gray. This is accented with red markings on the top of the snout, around the eyes, along the upper lip, and at the base of the skull. There is also a narrow red stripe running along the back for the entire body length, starting at the base of the skull, running down the back of the neck, the back of the body, and down the back of the tail to the tip. Short triangular red stripes jut perpendicularly out from the back stripe, out into the neck, body, and tail. The hands are also red, as are the underside of the forearms, and the back of the shins.

See also *Troodon* in Appendix Two.

Ravager

A term used generically to mean any of a variety of the larger carnivores. Thus, this term can be applied to either *Albertosaurs* or *Tyrannosaurs* (see Dreadrunner and Dreadcharger) (see also: Appendix Two: Late Cretaceous Inhabitants of Western North America).

Red Dawn Tribe, The:

The Red Dawn Tribe is one of 9 tribes, called The Nine Tribes, that compose the Great Eastern Herd, a herd of about 17,500 *Cerasphoros*. There are 20 roams, or clans, in the Red Dawn Tribe. Some of these roams of the tribe include: the Black Sand Roam, the Crescent Beach Roam, the Crooked Tree Roam, the Dragonfly Roam, the Falling Waters Roam, the Green Water Roam, the Horn Rock Roam, the Three Pebbles Roam, the Two Rivers Roam, the Two Trees Roam, the White Fern Roam, the Winding River Roam, and the Yellow Mud Roam.

Redrunner

A small bipedal herbivore (omnivore), and occasional eggsnatcher and nestlingnapper, with a small head, large eyes, a horny cropping beak with upper teeth, and self-sharpening ridged cheek teeth that are replaced by new ones as the old ones wear out. They also have cheek pouches, and strong jaws. Redrunners are equipped with short arms, with five-fingered hands, tipped with claws. They also have long, agile shins and feet that imply an ability to sprint, four-toed feet tipped with claws, and a long tendon-stiffened tail for balance. Redrunners are 7 to 8 feet long, and about 150 pounds in weight.

The basic body color is a red-brown, although the face is a medium warm-gray. This is accented with a dark red on the lips and lower jaw, and along the top of the snout, which turns into a narrow stripe that flows along the back of the neck, down the back of the body, and along the back of the tail to the tip. Another dark red stripe begins at the back of the throat, down the neck and chest, along the underside across the belly, and down the underside of the tail almost to the tip. There are also five dark red stripes that completely encircle the neck, from just behind the skull, to just above the shoulders. Dark red also accents the undersides of both the arms and legs.

See also *Parksosaurus* in Appendix Two.

Ridgebrow

A large bipedal/quadrupedal duck-billed herbivore, 30 feet long and 3 tons in weight; see *Maiasaurus* in Appendix Two.

Roam

A word used by the People to mean a family grouping or clan of *Cerasphoros*. They are organized primarily both for the safety of the individual members, and for the raising and protection of the young. Roams range in size from 50 to 100 individuals. They are generally composed of 4 to 6 adult males, 10 to 15 adult females, 2 to 4 adolescent males, 5 to 10 adolescent females, 20 to 40 youngsters, and 0 to 50 yearlings.

Robrunner

A small bipedal herbivore (omnivore), and occasional eggsnatcher and nestlingnapper, with a small head, large eyes, a horny cropping beak with upper teeth, and self-sharpening cheek teeth that are replaced by new ones as the old ones wear out. Robrunners also have cheek pouches, and strong jaws. They are equipped with short arms, with five-fingered hands, tipped with claws. They also have long, agile shins and feet that imply an ability to sprint, and four-toed feet tipped with claws. There is a long tendon-stiffened tail which helps with balance when running at full speed. Robrunners are about 8 feet long, and weigh about 150 pounds.

The basic body color is a light yellow-green, or apple green. This is accented with a light yellow on the lips and lower jaw, and along the top of the snout, which turns into a narrow stripe that flows along the back of the neck, down the back of the body, and along the back of the tail, ending about two-thirds of the way down to the tip. Another light yellow stripe begins at the back of the throat, down the neck and chest, along the underside across the belly, and down the underside of the tail almost to the tip. There is also a narrow light yellow stripe running down each side of the body, beginning at the base of the skull, and ending near the tip of the tail. There are also single light yellow stripes running down each arm and leg.

See also *Orodromeus* in Appendix Two.

Rockback

An armored quadrupedal herbivore, 23 feet long and 3.5 to 4 tons in weight; see *Panoplosaurus* in Appendix Two.

Roohraru

The language of the threehorns.

Sea-ravager

A sharp-toothed predatory marine reptile with a long neck and tail that swam with flippers, 35 to 47 feet long; see *Elasmosaurus* in Appendix Two.

Silver River Tribe

One of the tribes of the Great Eastern Herd. One of its roams is the Quiet Tributary Roam.

Skygiant

A very large pterosaur, with a wingspan of 36 to 50 feet; see *Quetzalcoatlus* in Appendix Two.

Skyglider

A large pterosaur with no tail, 26 foot wingspan; see *Pteranodon* in Appendix Two.

Solitary

A term used by the People to describe an adult male (and on rare occasions, an adult female) that leaves the tribe after reaching adulthood; some forty percent of adult males do this; a solitary prefers to live by himself, or in companionship with another solitary male or two, and only rejoins the tribe (herd) each year during the time of the great trek to the ancient breeding grounds.

Swiftstealer

A small bipedal herbivore, possibly an omnivore, similar to both Eggsnatchers and Trailrunners, with a small head, and with no teeth, but with a horny bill. Swiftstealers have a proportionally large brain for their size, and very large eyes. They have a long, slim, curved, mobile neck. They also have three large, curved claws on relatively long forelimbs (not used for locomotion, but their hands are capable of grasping). Their forelimbs are longer than Eggsnatchers. They have hind legs that are long and strong and capable of running at high speed, with shins that are longer than the thighs, and with long feet that are each armed with three claw-tipped toes. Their hindlimbs are shorter than both Eggsnatchers and Trailrunners. They also have a long tapered tail more than half their length, which is held level with the back when running, and which helps them keep their balance during high-speed maneuvers. Swiftstealers are about 10 to 14 feet long.

The basic body color is a medium green. This is accented with ultramarine patches along the back of the neck, and down the back of the body and tail. There are also ultramarine stripes along the front of the arms and legs. The underside of the belly, and the backs of the legs tend towards a cream color.

See also *Ornithomimus* in Appendix Two.

Threehorn

A three-horned quadrupedal herbivore, with a small nose horn, prominent

brow horns (up to 3 feet long), and a short solid frill. Threehorns have a short
tail and a bulky body. They can run fast as well as fight, and seem to have a
propensity for impulsive charging, sometimes at anything that moves. They
tend to inhabit forests of redwoods and other tall trees, as well as the vast
upper plains. They crop their food with a strong, beaklike mouth. Threehorns
grow to 25 to 30 feet long (6 feet at the shoulder, and sometimes as high as
9.5 feet at the top of the frill). They weigh 5.0 to 6.0 tons.

The basic body color is a burnt ochre, with undertones of burnt umber,
and with the underside tending towards a light sand color. The three horns
range from a red-brown (terra cotta) to a carmine red. There are also carmine
red accents on the face and frill, on the upper beak, along the top of the snout,
around the base of the horns and eyes, and along the ridges and the edge of
the frill. In between the ridges of the frill, there are ovals of burnt umber,
encircled in rings of red-brown.

See also *Triceratops* in Appendix Two.

Trailrunner
A small bipedal herbivore, possibly an omnivore, similar to both
Eggsnatchers and Swiftstealers, with a small head (but with a proportionally
large brain). Trailrunners have a beak with no teeth, but with a horny bill. They
have very large eyes. They also have a long, slim, curved, mobile neck. They
are equipped with three large, curved claws on relatively long forelimbs (which
are not used for locomotion, but their hands are quite capable of grasping).
They also have hind legs that are long and strong and capable of running at
high speed, with shins that are longer than the thighs (and likely longer than
either Eggsnatchers or Swiftstealers). Their long feet are each armed with three
claw-tipped toes. They also have a long tapered tail more than half their length,
which is held level with the back when running, and which helps them to keep
their balance during high-speed maneuvers. Trailrunners are about 11 to 12
feet long. Trailrunners are most easily distinguished from both Eggsnatchers
and Swiftstealers by their relatively shorter backs, and by their comparatively
longer and more slender forearms and hands.

The basic body color is a yellow-orange, with sepia brown markings.
The whole upper portion of the snout is sepia brown, as is a small skull-cap.
A long stripe of sepia brown runs along both sides of the body from the skull-
cap, narrow along the neck, widening along the body, and narrowing again
along the tail, before broadening out high on the tail, thus covering much of

the last two-thirds of the tail. There are also sepia brown highlights along the front of both the arms and the legs.

See *Dromiceiomimus* in Appendix Two.

Trumpeter
A large bipedal/quadrupedal crested duck-billed herbivore, 30 to 35 feet long; see *Parasaurolophus* in Appendix Two.

Turquoise Sea Tribe
One of the tribes of the Great Eastern Herd. One of its roams is the Pinnacle Island Roam.

Twohorn
A two-horned quadrupedal herbivore, 17 feet long and 2.5 tons in weight; see *Chasmosaurus* in Appendix Two.

White Moon Tribe:
One of the tribes of the Great Eastern Herd. Some of its roams include the Crooked Rock Roam and the Flat Rock Roam.

Yearling
A term used by the People to describe a *Cerasphoros* that is older than a fledge, but younger than a youngster. Yearlings range from 6 to 12 months in age. At 6 months: range from 5 to 7 feet long and 650 to 800 pounds; at 9 months: range from 7 to 10 feet long and 1000 to 1400 pounds; and at 12 months: range from 9 to 13 feet long and 1200 to 1800 pounds. For every 30 6 month old yearlings, 20 reach the age of 9 months, and 15 survive to become a youngster. (See also: Cerasphoros, Progression Through Life.)

Youngster
A term used by the People to describe a *Cerasphoros* that is older than a yearling, but younger than an adoescent. Youngsters range in age from 1 to 3 years old. Youngsters range in size from 13.5 to 19.5 feet at 2 years, and from 16.5 to 22.5 feet at 3 years of age. They range in weight from 1.1 to 1.6 tons at 2 years, and from 1.5 to 2.1 tons at 3 years of age. The major reason for the ranges is the difference between males and females. Horns on males range from 2.5 inches at 2 years, to 4 inches long at 3 years of age. Horns on females range from hornbuds at 2 years, to 1.5 inches long at 3 years of age. (See also: Cerasphoros, Progression Through Life.)

APPENDIX FOUR
LIST OF CHARACTERS

Note: All characters described in this appendix are *Cerasphoros*, or hornbrows, except as otherwise noted.

Adeldraar: an adult male, roamleader of the Winding River Roam of the Red Dawn Tribe, also subchief of the Red Dawn Tribe, keeper of the sacred staff of the Red Dawn Tribe, and holder of the title Staffholder; 27 years old, but very old and dignified looking, 3.3 tons, 38 feet long, 10 inch horn that once was 15 inches, but is now broken, it still appears thin and brittle.

Ahbrell: an adult female of the Green Water Roam of the Red Dawn Tribe; 6 years old, 2.3 tons, 21.5 feet long, 5.5 inch horn.

Bebann: an adult male of the Winding River Roam of the Red Dawn Tribe; 18 years old, 4.0 tons, 37 feet long, 15 inch horn.

Binboh: an adult female of the Green Water Roam of the Red Dawn Tribe; 9 years old, 3.0 tons, 26.5 feet long, 7.5 inch horn.

Bluntnose: a female *Triceratops*, or threehorn; 27 feet long, 5.0 tons in weight.

Dandraar: an adolescent male of the Green Water Roam of the Red Dawn Tribe; 4 years old, 2.4 tons. 25 feet long, 8 inch horn.

Davgot: an adolescent male packer, once of the Green Water Roam of the Red Dawn Tribe; a nestmate of Dandraar's; 4 years old, 2.4 tons, 25 feet long, 8 inch horn.

Draggot: an adult male, a pack-leader, once of the Two Trees Roam of the Red Dawn Tribe.

Duffnott: an adolescent male packer of the White Moon Tribe.

Eaceh: an adult female of the Green Water Roam of the Red Dawn Tribe; 7 years old, 2.6 tons, 23.5 feet long, 6.5 inch horn.

Eager-runner: a male *Triceratops*, or threehorn; 27 feet long, 5 tons in weight.

Eldooran: an adult male, roamleader of the White Fern Roam of the Red Dawn Tribe, also tribemaster of the Red Dawn Tribe, ceremonial titles of Herdmaster and Protector of the Vast Plains; 25 years old, 4+ tons, 38.5 feet long, 16 inch long, and unusually thick horn.

Fanfahron: an adult solitary male, once of the Sparkling Water Roam of the Green Hills Tribe; 15 years old, 3.9 tons, 37 feet long, 15 inch horn.

Foottangler: a female *Triceratops*, or threehorn; 27 feet long, 5.1 tons in weight.

Fordah: an adult female, first female of the Yellow Mud Roam of the Red Dawn Tribe; 14 years old, 3.3 tons, 32 feet long, 10 inch horn.

Gaffstar: an adult solitary male, once of the Three Pebbles Roam of the Red Dawn Tribe.

Gathraar: an adult male, second male of the Yellow Mud Roam of the Red Dawn Tribe; 12 years old, 3.8 tons, 34.5 feet long, 14 inch horn.

Gemuth: an adolescent male of the Dragonfly Roam of the Red Dawn Tribe; 5 years old, 2.8 tons, 27 feet long, 10 inch horn.

Ghirarah: an adult female of the Green Water Roam of the Red Dawn Tribe; 6 years old, 2.5 tons, 22 feet long, 6 inch horn.

Gnarled-paw: a young male *Albertosaurus*, or dreadrunner, 23 feet long and 1.7 tons in weight.

Grendaar: an adult male, roamleader of the Green Water Roam of the Red Dawn Tribe; 31 years old, 4.0 tons, 39 feet long, 16 inch horn.

Groundstomper: a male *Triceratops*, or threehorn; 28 feet long, 5.4 tons in weight.

Growler: a female *Tyrannosaurus*, or dreadcharger; 14 years old, 40 feet long, 7.0 tons in weight.

Gumboo: an adult female of the Green Water Roam of the Red Dawn Tribe; 8 years old, 2.8 tons, 25 feet long, 7 inch horn.

Headknocker: a dominant male *Triceratops*, or threehorn; 29 feet long, 5.8 tons in weight.

Heddar: an adult solitary male, once of the Falling Waters Roam of the Red Dawn Tribe; 9 years old, 3.6 tons, 32 feet long, 13 inch horn.

Hew: an adult male, fifth male of the Green Water Roam of the Red Dawn Tribe; 6 years old, 3.0 tons, 28.5 feet long, 11 inch horn.

Hidepiercer: a dominant male *Triceratops*, or threehorn; second male of his herd; 29 feet long, 5.7 tons in weight.

Highstepper: a female *Triceratops*, or threehorn; 26 feet long, 4.9 tons in weight.

Hugehorns: a dominant male *Triceratops*, or threehorn; 30 feet long, 5.9 tons.

Jasmaan: an adult female, formerly a packer, once of the Crescent Beach Roam of the Red Dawn Tribe, then of the Green Water Roam of the Red Dawn Tribe; 6 years old, 2.3 tons, 21.5 feet long, 5.5 inch horn.

Jedraar: an adult male, third male of the Yellow Mud Roam of the Red Dawn Tribe; 9 yrs old, 32 feet long, 3.5 tons, 13 inch horn.

Kinput: a adult solitary male, once of the Green Water Roam of the Red Dawn Tribe; 13 years old, 3.8 tons, 35.5 feet long, 14 inch horn.

Koowoo: an adult female, third female of the Green Water Roam of the Red Dawn Tribe; 10 years old, 3.1 tons, 28 feet long, 8 inch horn; slow and lethargic; breeds every other year, with very large clutches.

Long-tail: a young female *Albertosaurus*, or dreadrunner, 22 feet long and 1.6 tons in weight.

Monah: an adult female, second female of the Green Water Roam of the Red Dawn Tribe; 12 years old, 3.3 tons, 30 feet long, 9 inch horn; a good breeder and mother, breeds every year; somewhat independent.

Nvraar: an adult male, former roamleader of the Green Water Roam of the Red Dawn Tribe; Grendaar's uncle, the brother of Grendaar's mother.

Ograar: an adult solitary male, once of the Quiet Tributary Roam of the Silver River Tribe; 14 years old, 4.0 tons, 38 feet long, 15 inch horn.

Panehh: an adult female of the Yellow Mud Roam of the Red Dawn Tribe; 9 years old, 2.9 tons, 26.5 feet long, 7.5 inch horn.

Panthrar: an adolescent male of the Green Water Roam of the Red Dawn Tribe; 5 years old, 2.8 tons, 27 feet long, 10 inch horn.

Pippit: an adolescent female packer, once of the Flat Rock Roam of the White Moon Tribe; 5 years old, 2.2 tons, 20.5 feet long, 4 inch horn.

Prancer: a female *Tyrannosaurus*, or dreadcharger; 8 years old, 37 feet long, 6.7 tons in weight.

Quickcharger: a dominant male *Triceratops*, or threehorn; third male of his herd; 28 feet long, 5.2 tons in weight.

Raggedtail: a female *Triceratops*, or threehorn; 28 feet long, 5.2 tons in weight.

Rattan: an adult male, roamleader of the Purple Sand Roam of the Black Valley Tribe.

Red-patch: a male *Albertosaurus*, or dreadrunner, 24 feet long, and 1.8 tons in weight.

Renthot: an adult male, roamleader of the Yellow Mud Roam of the Red Dawn Tribe; 17 years old, 3.9 tons, 37 feet long, 15 inch horn.

Rohraar: an adult male, second male of the Green Water Roam of the Red Dawn Tribe; 10 years old, 3.7 tons, 33 feet long, 13.5 inch horn; younger, stronger and perhaps more agile than Grendaar, although still not as seasoned and as canny; could probably beat Grendaar in a dominance fight, but fiercely loyal to the older male.

Rollypolly: a female *Triceratops*, or threehorn; 28 feet long, 5.4 tons in weight.

Rosarah: an adolescent female packer, once of the Horn Rock Roam of the Red Dawn Tribe; 4 years old, 1.9 tons, 18.5 feet long, 2.5 inch horn.

Roundfrill: an old female *Triceratops*, or threehorn, 25 feet long, and 5.0 tons in weight.

Rumblerunner: an old, barren female *Triceratops*, or threehorn, 26 feet long, and 5.1 tons in weight.

Rumpoo: an adult female of the Green Water Roam of the Red Dawn Tribe; 6 years old, 2.3 tons, 21.5 feet long, 5.5 inch horn.

Savage: a male *Tyrannosaurus*, or dreadcharger; 24 years old, 45 feet long, 7.3 tons in weight.

Seeker: a female *Tyrannosaurus*, or dreadcharger; 9 years old, 38 feet long, 6.8 tons in weight.

Sevren: a adult solitary male, once of the Black Sand Roam of the Red Dawn Tribe.

Stripes: a female *Albertosaurus*, or dreadrunner, 27 feet long, and 2.2 tons in weight.

Stripes' son: a cub male *Albertosaurus*, or dreadrunner, 10 feet long, and 0.6 tons in weight.

Sungu: an adult female of the Green Water Roam of the Red Dawn Tribe; 7 years old, 2.7 tons, 24 feet long, 6.5 inch horn.

Tandah: an adult female of the Green Water Roam of the Red Dawn Tribe; 8 years old, 2.8 tons, 25 feet long, 7 inch horn.

Tanmont: a adult solitary male, once of the Crooked Tree Roam of the Red Dawn Tribe; 15 years old, 3.9 tons, 37 feet long, 15 inch horn.

Terror: a male *Tyrannosaurus*, or dreadcharger; 11 years old, 42 feet long, 7.1 tons in weight.

Thallaar: an adolescent male of the Yellow Mud Roam of the Red Dawn Tribe; 4 years old, 2.4 tons, 25 feet long, 8 inch horn.

Thundermaker: a dominant male *Triceratops*, or threehorn; primary male of his herd; 30 feet long, 5.9 tons in weight.

Tessah: an adult female, primary female of the Green Water Roam of the Red Dawn Tribe; 19 years old, 3.1 tons, 33 feet long, 10 inch horn; slightly past her prime; slightly smaller than average; a good breeder and mother, breeds every year with large clutches; considered wise and fiercely protective of the roam.

Treah: an adult female of the Green Water Roam of the Red Dawn Tribe; 6 years old, 2.4 tons, 22 feet long, 6 inch horn.

Trimellon: an adolescent male packer, once of the Crooked Rock Roam of the White Moon Tribe; 6 years old, 3.0 tons, 28.5 feet long, 11 inch horn.

Trugahr: an adult male, third male of the Green Water Roam of the Red Dawn Tribe; 8 years old, 3.4 tons, 31 feet long, 12.5 inch horn; young, scrappy, but still not old enough or large enough to fight with the most dominant males.

Trumpaar: an adult solitary male, once of the Lush Wallow Roam of the Green Hills Tribe; 12 years old, 3.8 tons, 34.5 feet long, 14 inch horn.

Vectur: an adult solitary male, once of the Pinnacle Island Roam of the Turquoise Sea Tribe; 17 years old, 3.9 tons, 37 feet long, 15 inch horn.

Wubbar: an adult male, fourth male of the Green Water Roam of the Red Dawn Tribe; 7 years old, 3.2 tons, 29.5 feet long, 12 inch horn.

Zannah: an adult female of the Green Water Roam of the Red Dawn Tribe; 7 years old, 2.7 tons, 23.5 feet long, 6.5 inch horn.

Zurgott: an adult male, roamleader of the Dragonfly Roam of the Red Dawn Tribe, also subchief of the Red Dawn Tribe, keeper of the sacred blue stone of the Red Dawn Tribe, and holder of the title Stonekeeper; 19 years old, 3.7 tons, 37.5 feet long, 15 inch horn.

APPENDIX FIVE
BIBLIOGRAPHY

Digging Dinosaurs, John R. Horner and James Gorman (New York: Workman Publishing, 1988).

The Dinosaur Data Book, The Diagram Group (New York: Avon Books, 1990).

The Dinosaur Heresies, Robert T. Bakker (New York: Zebra Books, Kensington Publishing Corp., 1986).

Dinosaurs, Eugene S. Gaffney (New York: Golden Press, Western Publishing Co., 1990).

Dinosaurs, A Global View, Sylvia J. Czerkas and Stephen A. Czerkas (New York: Mallard Press, 1991).

Dinosaurs and Prehistoric Animals, Dougal Dixon, Barry Cox, R.J.G. Savage, Brian Gardiner (New York: Macmillan Publishing Co., 1988).

Dinosaur!, David Norman (New York: Prentice Hall, 1991).

A Field Guide to Dinosaurs, The Diagram Group (New York: Avon Books, 1983).

Find Out About Dinosaurs, Dougal Dixon (New York: Gallery Books, 1986).

The Illustrated Dinosaur Encyclopedia, Dougal Dixon (New York: Gallery Books, 1988).

The Illustrated Encyclopedia of Dinosaurs, David Norman (New York: Crescent Books, 1954, 1985).

Maia, A Dinosaur Grows Up, John R. Horner and James Gorman (Philadelphia: Courage Books, an imprint of Running Books, 1985, 1987).

The New Illustrated Dinosaur Dictionary, Helen Roney Sattler (New York: Lothrop, Lee & Shepard, 1983, 1990).

Peterson First Guides – Dinosaurs, John C. Kricher (Boston: Houghton Mifflin Co., 1990).

Predatory Dinosaurs of the World, A Complete Illustrated Guide, Gregory S. Paul (New York: Simon & Schuster, 1988).

The Rise and Fall of the Dinosaur, Joseph Wallace (New York: Gallery Books, 1987).

ISBN 142511254-4